HOLD IT 'TIL IT HURTS

HOLD IT 'TIL IT HURTS

A NOVEL

T. GERONIMO JOHNSON

COFFEE HOUSE PRESS
MINNEAPOLIS
2012

COPYRIGHT © 2012 T. Geronimo Johnson
COVER & BOOK DESIGN Linda S. Koutsky
AUTHOR PHOTO © Elizabeth Cowan

Coffee House Press books are available to the trade through our primary distributor, Consortium Book Sales & Distribution, cbsd.com or (800) 283-3572. For personal orders, catalogs, or other information, write to: info@coffeehousepress.org.

Coffee House Press is a nonprofit literary publishing house. Support from private foundations, corporate giving programs, government programs, and generous individuals helps make the publication of our books possible. We gratefully acknowledge their support in detail in the back of this book.

Good books are brewing at coffeehousepress.org

LIBRARY OF CONGRESS CATALOGING-IN-PUBLICATION DATA
Johnson, T. Geronimo (Tyrone Geronimo)
Hold it till it hurts : a novel / by T. Geronimo Johnson.
p. cm.
ISBN 978-1-56689-309-1 (alk. paper)
I. Title.
PS3610.O38339H65 2012
813'.6—DC23
2012023190

PRINTED IN THE UNITED STATES
1 3 5 7 9 8 6 4 2
FIRST EDITION | FIRST PRINTING

For my grandparents
Richard Walter English
Loretta Thomas English
Octavia Tenette English
William Lee Johnson
Queen Esther Johnson

And my older sister Loretta Marie Johnson

Peace be with you.

PART 1

MID-FALL 2004

CHAPTER 1

THAT EVENING AFTER HIS FATHER'S FUNERAL, ONCE THE LAST MOURNER BID solemn farewell and vanished into the foggy grove separating his childhood home from the nearest neighbor, Achilles's mother summoned him into the kitchen, the only room free of streamers and balloons, and handed him a big blue envelope that bore no return address or postmark, only his name spelled out in his father's heavy-footed block print. They sat opposite each other at the small oak table, bare save for the mail stacked in the shadow of an empty chair, far beyond reach of the day's last rays sneaking through the vertical blinds and fanning across the tabletop in fat sandy bands the color of his father's coffin. He handed it back. She pursed her lips and drew her shoulders out as she often did before a big announcement, but said nothing, for which he was grateful because he didn't want to have this conversation again. He'd always insisted that he had no use for his adoption paperwork. She'd always insisted that he would regret never meeting his black blood relatives.

"None of us is here forever," she said, as if that statement alone explained everything. Her tone had been equally matter-of-fact when relating the circumstances surrounding his father's death: killed instantly in a head-on collision while giving an employee a ride home. Even in moments such as these, his mother was steely as a sergeant, beyond surprise, never even commenting on why his father had been halfway across the state, driving an employee home at midnight on a Saturday. She'd scowled during the eulogy, and now looked again on the verge of anger. When Achilles didn't respond, she continued, "I don't want you to regret leaving this undone."

He didn't like the idea of being undone, but didn't see how crawling back to someone would make him done. Regret? He didn't think so. Having been to DC and seen how *they* lived, he couldn't care less about his birth parents. Even if tracking them down wasn't treasonous, what good could come of crisscrossing the country to confirm that his biological mother was a junkie whore and his sperm-donor dad an ex-con? And other than the occasional elementary school joke because he'd been short, black, and chubby while his parents were tall, white, and thin, race had never been an issue in his neighborhood or his school. "Burn it."

He'd hoped she would finally accept his decision, feel cheered by his fidelity, but instead she cringed. Her lips pulled tight, her head dropped a notch, and her expression passed from reserved and proud to stricken and mournful, and then, for the first time since he'd arrived home, to pained. Achilles moved his seat closer and clasped her hands in apology, though he didn't know what for. Why should he track down people who obviously didn't want him? Achilles didn't grovel.

"I just don't want it, or need it," he said. Accepting that paperwork was like pulling the pin out of a grenade.

"Think about it . . ."

Achilles excused himself, turning on the light as he left. He passed his brother in the hall and warned him away from the kitchen. Troy shrugged, offering his usual response to the topic: "Fuck it!"

Yet barely fifteen minutes later, Troy strode into their bedroom holding a blue envelope. Their parents' house was a two-bedroom ranch, so the brothers had shared the same room since Achilles's eighth birthday, when his parents first brought Troy—then six years old—home. Refusing to budge, Achilles sat on the edge of his bed as Troy stepped over him and ducked into the closet, tucking the envelope away behind the loose baseboard where they'd secreted their prized Matchbox cars, the shiniest samples of mica and quartz, and the porn magazines traded for pilfered cigarettes.

Troy avoided Achilles's eyes as he stepped over him to get back to his bed, which was so close to Achilles's that they couldn't sit facing each other without their knees touching. Troy flopped down and the mattress sank to the floor with a thump. In that room, they were like Gulliver in their favorite bedtime story. After reading to them, their mom had coaxed them to sleep by promising that dreams were real and that in them they could do anything, even fly, and they could be anyone, princes or kings or warriors or magicians, or ghostbusters as Troy had demanded one night. They could make up imaginary villages, design spaceships and castles, construct entire cities—tiny towns, she called them—secret places they would always carry with them. With him and Troy and the blue envelope in the room, it felt literally like a tiny town.

"Ass."

"She wants us to have them," said Troy.

"You believe that?"

Troy busied himself shuffling the DD214s—discharge papers—and other forms scattered on his desk, which only came up to his knees. He was a giant in a funhouse, his arms thicker than the desk legs. "It's like money. Just because you don't need it right now doesn't mean you shouldn't take it. Did you ever turn down your biscuit in Goddamnistan because you didn't need the money?"

Achilles shook his head. That was typical Troy, defending bullshit decisions with bullshit excuses. Couldn't he wait another week, a day even? It was a breach, a leak, inviting a ghost into the family. And *biscuit*? Troy sounded stupid using slang. "We have direct deposit."

"What? You don't know everything," said Troy. "Just because you take it doesn't mean you'll spend it. You never know when you might need it. You wouldn't dump all your rations just because you're full. Besides, give her a break. Be responsible for your own shit." He was fidgeting now, picking at the calluses on his palm as he did whenever someone demanded to see his aces. Troy pointed around the room, his arm long enough to reach most of his possessions from where he sat: the children's books, action figures, Black Sabbath and Public Enemy posters, roller skates; the rucksack, desert boots, flak jacket. "This is my home. Biops? Fuck 'em eight ways!"

But the next morning, only two days after they returned from active duty, and only one day after their father's funeral, Troy was gone.

He should have stopped him. Achilles had heard his brother get up and thought he was going for a jog. Alone, they jogged. Together, they ran and usually ended racing, as had happened the first day back as they neared home, Achilles's shorter strides almost doubled to keep pace with Troy's long legs, kicking the air, their noses pushing into the wind, chest to chest and neck to neck until Troy stole a strong lead by nodding toward a leggy brunette and puffing, "Janice," sending Achilles ducking behind a car until he could confirm there were no dolphins tattooed on the ankles or hearts behind the knees, by which time Troy was so far ahead that Achilles didn't catch up until he was already crunching up the gravel drive. Achilles wasn't trying to avoid Janice in particular, he just didn't want to see any-one else he knew until the funeral, where circumstances would demand brief condolences and he wouldn't be expected to endure stories about a father whom everyone suddenly seemed to know better than he, or to suf-fer such pity he would have thought himself the dead one.

All the while they were growing up, their father's motto was "be the ones to beat." So they had been competitive, especially with each other. But when Troy distracted him on that run, Achilles sensed something new was at stake, something he didn't want to win, but he couldn't run with-out trying to win. So as Troy dressed the morning after the funeral, Achilles remained motionless, holding his breath for the long moment when the room grew still and he felt Troy standing above him deciding whether to call Achilles's bluff of slumber and kick the bed, the floor squeaking as he shifted his weight from leg to leg, grinding the grit under-foot, before at last creeping out.

There wasn't a single store within walking distance of the subdivisions that had sprung up around his parents' house, so when he heard Troy's old Beetle coasting down the gravel drive, Achilles thought he was going for cigarettes. When he wasn't back at noon, Achilles assumed he was out sniffing around, or maybe up in Chambersburg, where Mrs. Bowler lived. Troy thought that was still secret, but word spread when someone slept with his high school algebra teacher.

Later that afternoon, Achilles discovered that Troy's blue envelope was gone, as were his watch, locket, and pistols. He searched behind the closet baseboard, and in another cubbyhole where Troy hid candy as a child, pot as a teenager, money as an adult, and, most recently, the photos from their tour. Empty. On a whim he checked the Teddy Ruxpin cassette player, where Troy used to leave notes in which he'd written what he couldn't say. Empty.

Achilles wasn't surprised by the desertion. When they were kids, Troy, who had lighter skin than Achilles, would cut pictures of celebrities out of magazines, hold them next to his face, and say, "Doesn't this look like me?" within earshot of their mother. Sometimes Troy was just an ass, and selfish too. As a child, he frequently squirreled food away in that closet cubbyhole. He ran away twice in middle school and once in high school, always returning before anyone noticed his absence, which had really jerked his chain. So Achilles didn't bother to call him now. It was his father's funeral too.

Nonetheless, Achilles couldn't help but feel a burn in his chest, an unspeakable fear that threatened to shake his bowels loose every time he stumbled over what Troy left behind: his boots, folded BDUS, and the helmet with CONROY written in permanent marker, all coated in the fine layer of dust that had followed them home. He knew it was irrational, but the sight of that equipment gave him the shakes, so he packed it all away in a trash bag, double-bagged it, and stuffed the bundle into the back of the closet under the cover of two blankets. Back in rotation, when someone died his gear remained hanging up as a memorial. The last three weeks of active duty, he'd used only the back flap of their tent to avoid passing Jackson's bunk and seeing his uniform laid out on the bed, the helmet set neatly on top.

He considered making a dental appointment, solely for that moment after the cleaning when the hygienist flossed his teeth. Routine, sure, but it felt so damn good, almost self-indulgent, so indescribably delicious that he'd never admitted to anyone how much he enjoyed the sensation. They would surely think him mad, but he'd missed it all—the sound of unseen cars on wet roads, burning leaves in the fall, sleeping late, his own bed, familiar faces at every corner, silverware in a drawer instead of a bin. Before his eyes though, every image he'd recalled in detail over the last few weeks—those shimmering fantasies he'd counted in place of sheep— faded like apparitions, none being as he remembered. *Seinfeld* reruns, Marvel comics, his rock collection, *Penthouse* Letters, James Bond novels, *Austin Powers* 1 and 2, butter pecan ice cream, *Schoolhouse Rock:* he flitted from activity to activity like a starving mosquito. Being home alone felt cowardly, like he was one of those FOBBITS who never left the Forward Operating Base. George was always whining about dilemmas of his own design. Comics were for kids—who else believed in superpowers? Austin's accent grated now that he'd met real Brits. Sugar had faded out of his diet. "Conjunction Junction" sounded like Army slang for FUBAR or gangbanging.

The only pleasures that retained a spark were *Penthouse* Letters, of course, and the Midnight Special: egg, mayonnaise, mustard, relish, and onion on a Pennsylvania Dutch roll. Also known as the Bedeviled Egg Sandwich, according to his mother. It was the Devil's Egg Sandwich according to his father, who'd invented it and therefore insisted that naming was his domain, as were all things egg. Wearing his plaid wool hunter's cap and a pencil behind his ear, their father helmed the stove every Sunday morning, crisping potatoes that Achilles and Troy had grated in a cast-iron skillet, frying thick slabs of bacon and scrapple, scrambling eggs in the bacon grease. Occasionally he fried apples or bananas as a treat. Though he never referred to it, the Betty Crocker cookbook always lay on the table open to hash browns, like a map kept nearby in anticipation of a detour. Nearly six foot four, his father's wingspan allowed him to shake the Jiffy Pop on the stove and grab a beer at the same time. But confining as it was, he always had his sons at his side in the kitchen.

After he discovered what Troy had taken with him, Achilles made a sandwich, but found he wasn't hungry. There was a limit to the number of times he could masturbate in one day, diminishing the pleasure even of *Penthouse*, so he spent several hours using the weight bench in the barn, working out until his arms were numb. Still he couldn't sleep.

Neither could his mother. At two a.m., he found her in the kitchen filling trash bags with food. The refrigerator, which that morning had been laden with the neighbors' Tupperware, was empty. His mother grew up on a farm and insisted that a woman who couldn't grow her own tomatoes wasn't worth her weight in lipstick. He shouldn't have been surprised that she threw the food away: she had long been suspicious of the neighbors she called beltway bimbos, the smug professional women who considered themselves more modern and feminist than housewives because they commuted to DC, made-up like two-dollar hookers. They filled their shopping carts with frozen organic vegetables and relied on landscapers to nurture their lawns. They used microwaves and pizza delivery services. "Think about that," his mother always said. "Someone else brings food to your house for you to eat. When I was coming up, that only happened when someone died." She also said, "A woman can do what a man does, but a man can't do what a woman does, so if the wife works outside the house, the house won't work," even though she'd held a job for thirty years.

After the food, they took down the decorations, the only sound that of the balloons being popped one by one, until birdsong announced sunrise. When the decorations were all bagged, she brought out a backpack, thrusting it into his hands. She asked if he liked it, if it was sturdy, reliable, dependable. The clerk had assured her it was the next best thing to military issue. Achilles didn't tell her that even though the tag listing all the features was the size of a greeting card, "near military specs" was no reasonable assurance of quality. If anything, it was cause for concern. Humvees that splinter on impact and sever limbs, mounted guns that stovepipe and blind the operator, defective body armor: no big deal as long as it wasn't a class-A accident, meaning costing over a million dollars. There's so much the recruiter doesn't tell you, and you can't even blame him, because if he did . . .

"Is it everything he said?" asked his mom, tugging at the zippers. She put on a black poncho. "It has matching rain protection."

"Sure. What's it for?" he asked, trying not to laugh. With the backpack on, she looked like a turtle.

"Training," she said, as if the answer were obvious. Made of black ballistic nylon, with red tags on each silver zipper, the modern design would have been out of place in their house, even if it weren't for the fact that she started wearing it all day, every day.

After a few days without hearing from Troy, a few days of not mentioning him while playing cards with his mom—especially blackjack, which he always won—of fighting the urge to search his gear for clues, of keeping the phone on and ready even when showering, Achilles left him a few messages ranging from "How's the ten-gallon?" to "I'm just checking in" to, finally, a long voice mail advising Troy against being such a dick at such a time, ending with the reluctant admission that even though Achilles had no desire to meet his own birth parents, he would gladly have gone along to meet Troy's. He so badly wanted his brother to answer, and not just to ensure that he was okay. He needed his brother to ask about their mom, to give Achilles an excuse to mention the backpack. Troy would know what to tell her. She spoke often of this trip she and their father had planned, a trip she'd wanted to take all her life, but the details were fuzzy. She made vague references to the East, which he'd initially taken to mean New York or Philadelphia. Sometimes she said Nepal, sometimes India. If asked for more details, she'd only say, "It's up in the air." It was puzzling because, as far as Achilles knew, she'd never been on an airplane.

One night, Achilles made a promise to himself. He would write his return address on his blue envelope and stick it in the mailbox without any postage. If it came back to the house, he could open it. He had only one question: Were he and Troy brothers? They'd asked this several times over the years, and the answer was always no. They looked nothing alike. Troy looked more like Wexler, one of their squadmates, who was light-skinned and resembled Prince. Still, what if they were? What if their parents didn't know? He tossed the envelope on Troy's bed before falling into a fitful rest, struggling to drown out the damned thrumming and the faint pulsations emanating from the closet, disturbances that faded only when he moved Troy's equipment to the storage shed farthest from the house.

At dawn he tiptoed down the hall, skulking like a thief returning to the scene of the crime as he put the envelope back on the table. His mother was already up having coffee and cinnamon toast, the pack on the floor next to her chair like a faithful dog awaiting a treat. At her insistence, *You're too thin,* he joined her. The warm bread was sweet and crunchy, the hot and gooey raisins nearly liquid. Pointing to the butter, she said, "Don't eat your bread dry." He took another bite. She pushed the butter at him until he accepted. She added, "You need to get out."

Her travel ensemble now included a tawny hunting vest with white piping around the armholes and flannel edges on the pockets, which were plentiful. It had more pouches and compartments than a photographer's vest. It resembled the overpriced travel gear virgin reporters wore to Afghanistan, equipment they ditched when the leather piping snagged on a door or a fancy buckle wouldn't close. It was a special breed of merchandise designed for people whose lives didn't depend on their equipment but who wanted to believe that it did. The more they paid, the safer they felt. She looked exactly like one of those women she called beltway bimbos when they dressed for a weekend camping trip, but he wouldn't be the one to tell her.

"I know you aren't ready, but I'm here whenever you want to talk," she said between bites of toast.

The truth was that he was and he did. He had a lot to say, starting with that day in Goddamnistan when Troy said, "I should have come alone," but how to begin? He attributed his cloudy head to the funeral but the truth was he'd felt the same way for quite some time. In fact, he couldn't remember feeling otherwise. He had the constant feeling that he had forgotten to do something important, and it kept him up at night when what he most wanted, and what he'd obsessed over for months, was to come home and sleep and fuck and fuck and sleep and sleep.

Janice was the only person he'd ever talked to about these feelings. Achilles had never told anyone in his unit, or anyone he didn't grow up with, that he and Troy were adopted. He wasn't ashamed, not at all. No. But after being told he talked white, it was unthinkable to provide the firing squad yet another clip.

One afternoon, a week after his brother left, Achilles went out to the Rockville quarry with Janice. They'd been sleeping together off and on since tenth grade, even during her married spells, which she was presently between. Janice was an average girl, the kind Merriweather would've said was a keeper because she wasn't so hot that everyone was after her, but she wasn't ugly, and best of all, she knew exactly where she fit into the scheme of things, so she appreciated any positive attention and didn't expect to be wined and dined. As Merriweather put it, a busted ride knew not to expect high octane. Before meeting Merriweather, Achilles had never thought of her like that, but in retrospect, maybe Merri was right. He'd heard of other guys slapping Janice around, but she'd never mentioned anything to Achilles and he never saw any bruises. Considering that she was full of vit-riol for all three ex-husbands, it was a minor miracle that he'd managed to stay friendly with her. He attributed it to honesty—he'd always been clear about not wanting a relationship, so they'd developed one. Though he didn't ask her to, she'd written while he was away. And though he'd never thanked her, he appreciated it very much.

The quarry was their safe place. Awe-inspiring. The sheer, staggered walls a giant's coliseum and, at the same time, evidence of what man could do. As teenagers, they'd watched the rock being toted out; now they watched the procession of trucks bringing dirt in, filling the quarry so it could be built on. A billboard at the entrance advertised more of the expensive subdivisions that had been built over the last several years, hem-ming them in.

"You know they were going to have a parade for you? The marching band, fire trucks, everything. A real hero's welcome."

A parade for Troy was what it would have been, another award for stu-pidity. Achilles sighed, but nothing could dampen his excitement about seeing Janice again.

High school was four years past, but she looked better than ever. Her brown hair, once stringy, was cut into a bouncy bob with gold highlights. Her lips were fuller, and her face permanently flushed, like she'd just fin-ished running or fucking. They sat at the edge of the quarry, opposite the truck entrance, Achilles stealing glances at her profile and taking in all the details: the thick eyelashes and red nails, the hearts and dolphins, the straight teeth and slender toes. When had he last studied a woman at such leisure? Occasionally she leaned forward to toss a pebble or a crab apple over the edge, and her hair would slip down, revealing her ear, or he'd catch a whiff of her perfume. She moved freely, her tattoos iridescent in the sunlight, like she was trying to draw attention to herself. Meanwhile, Achilles sat still for long stretches; being shot at taught self-control.

"So it's on you again," said Janice. She was talking about Troy.

Achilles nodded. Janice was also the only person he'd told about Troy's reckless behavior in Afghanistan, the only one who knew that some nights he had to stop himself from looking at Troy's bed to make sure his uniform and helmet weren't neatly stacked on top. "It's doubly fucked up because now that he's gone, I can't leave."

"She can take care of herself."

"It wouldn't be right for her to be alone. She's never been alone."

Janice frowned briefly, as if she knew something he didn't, while she rubbed his forearm with the back of her hand, eventually moving up to his bicep. She'd always liked his arms. He buttoned his sweater up to the neck. Seventy-eight degrees was now chilly.

They sat listening to the quarry trucks: the gasping brakes, the hissing pneumatics, the growl of the engines and gnashing of transmissions alternating as if engaged in conversation. Dump trucks streaming in and out like ants, each bearing a perfect mountain of dirt. Beeping echoed across the quarry as they backed up to the ledge and tilted their beds, offering their cargo to the sky. A stone or two would trickle off the dirt mound, next a minor cascade, then a slice would slip right off and rain down, and then, for a long moment, nothing happened. The mountain of dirt was suspended there in the tilted bed, defying gravity, like it was waiting for the Road Runner to pass and the Coyote to show up and without warning, the whole hogpile would give way, the dirt fanning out like a waterfall returning home. When the bed was loaded high enough, for a split second, one long lick of earth stretched all the way from the truck to the ground some three stories below.

It was a moment that made him yearn for childhood, for a time when he thought he had a choice between being the Road Runner or the Coyote, a time when he believed life was chock full of opportunities to start over. Not for his father, who swam in this same quarry as a child, who later came to this same quarry with the girlfriend who would become Achilles's mother. Had they sat under this tree, on the rocky ground, occasionally shifting their weight to brush away pebbles? At twenty-two, Achilles's age, his father had proposed to his mother. She had been the same age when she accepted.

Unexpected pockets of silence bubbled up through the clamoring waves below them, moments the whole convoy shifted gears at once, and they could momentarily hear the bees, or the wind leaning on the crab apple tree behind them, or Janice snapping her toes or, for Achilles, his own breathing and his heart, thumping away like a chopper.

"Hear that?" asked Janice in the sudden silence. She blushed, laughing awkwardly like someone who had just realized her slip was caught in her underwear.

Achilles nodded, and on the next silence he was ready, reaching for her hair with one hand while slipping the other behind her knee. She turned to face him, and delivered his first kiss in almost twelve months, her lips soft and silky, the chalky taste of lipstick making him inhale as sharply as he had at fifteen. He was just as nervous. In the past year he'd had sex only twice, and each time through a sheet, or it might as well have been because the women would either raise or lower their dresses, but never both. He'd regressed in Goddamnistan; even a shadow of cleavage had sparked conversation—symmetrical mountain peaks or two potatoes at the bottom of cotton sack or a pillow with a crease in the middle provoked a giggle fit.

He rolled on top of Janice as they wrestled out of their clothes. After the cool grass her breasts were hot, nipples rising to meet his fingers. He fished a condom out of his pocket, tore the edge of the packet off with his teeth, and handed it to her. She usually put the condom on, which was a source of much laughter and embarrassment in tenth grade. She tossed it aside. "Don't need that anymore."

Achilles didn't understand.

"I'm pregnant. Dale."

"How do you mean?" asked Achilles. Janice and Dale had married in eleventh grade and divorced the month after graduation. Dale kissing her hearts! Dale had a fucking stutter.

"No, this is good. I can't get pregnant again."

Achilles rolled onto his side.

"Come on Keelies. Don't be mad. Are you mad?" Janice tried to turn his face toward her, but he shrugged her off. "I didn't know if you were ever coming back. Don't be mad."

"I'm not . . . mad." He wasn't, not really. It was just that pregnancy was so permanent. Now she'd always have a connection to Dale that would be stronger than her connection to him. Everything would be different, even her pussy.

"C'mon." Her breasts swayed gently as she leaned over and grabbed his cock. "Moping isn't sexy in a man."

It was his first time without a condom, a new experience, like they'd somehow been joined beyond the body. Afterwards Achilles turned away, a knot tightening in his stomach when he realized Dale had done this first. "Did the condom break?"

She straddled him, her bemused expression melting as the implication dawned on her. "Oh Keelies."

When Janice reached for his hand, he pushed her away, and she settled down behind him, spooning. The clouds were clumped together in the east, like someone had swept them into the corner. Above him, against the bright sky, the silhouette of a hundred little crab apples, small as cherries. His mother used to put peanut butter on celery and dot it with raisins. They'd pretend it was a flute, unless their father was around. It then became a knife or a sword. He thought of the strange, spicy foods his mother was cooking now. She said she wanted to eat what her sons had eaten, so he didn't see the point in telling her they'd often eaten standard fare like spaghetti and beans-n-franks. He thought of the mail stacked on the table, the boxes in her bedroom, Troy's envelope, the surprising appearance of a preacher at the funeral service, and the church programs piling up in his mother's car. "Bingo!" she said whenever he asked about them. Whether that meant she was only going to church for the game, he didn't know, didn't want to ask, and felt embarrassed by his reluctance to push the topic. Did she think she was connecting to his father through prayer? She'd always seemed too lively for church and they'd never gone to services, so the idea spooked him. He thought of Teddy Ruxpin, his brother's now-silent emissary, and of Stuttering Dale. Good for Dale. Achilles didn't want a kid anyway, especially not with Janice. Every guy in town would tell it, "I could've been your daddy."

But none of that would have really mattered, because Achilles and his son would have known the truth: they belonged to each other, permanently, undeniably. The quarry fell silent and Janice reached for his hand again. He let her take it.

Several days later, Achilles answered an out-of-area call on his cell phone hoping it would be his brother. Instead he heard Kyle Wages say, "I just saw Troy."

"Where is he?" asked Achilles.

"I was on the bus, and he was gone by the time I got off and ran back." Wages paused. "Where are you now?"

"Where'd you see him?"

"A church," said Wages.

"A church?"

"They were handing out food."

Achilles was puzzled but exhilarated, and started packing before he hung up. He accepted the sighting as gospel. He, Troy, Merriweather, Jackson, and Wages had spent two tours together in deserts and mountains, parting only to piss, and often not even then. After some hesitation he decided to bring the blue envelope, a vial his mother had filled with his father's ashes, and the small swatch of Jackson's uniform that had come off in his hand that day. Everything clicked into place as he packed his rucksack. Obviously Troy was looking for his birth parents. Why else would he be in New Orleans in a food line?

His mother insisted on walking him out to his car, where she gave him a small box the size of an eyeglass case and told him to wait to open it. She offered her usual advice and extracted the usual promises, lingering at the car instead of walking back to the house and waving from the porch. He remembered that his father would usually walk her back.

"It's not like I'm shipping out."

"I know. That's not what I'm thinking about. I'm remembering the first day you went to school, and how you were ready to go even then. Not Troy. When his time came, he cried like . . . well, like Troy. He always whined a lot, not like you. You were always ready to go."

"I'll leave the envelope here."

She shook her hands emphatically, waving the suggestion off. "No! No! No! That's not it. It's your right to take that. You have to live for the future, not for the past. And so you need to know that your father hadn't lived here for almost a year. He moved out last May, two days before my birthday." She paused as if to let that sink in. "Oh, you better believe we argued about it. But I finally won. He packed up his old duffle. I asked him to think of it as a gift to me. But none of it had anything to do with you or your brother."

"You were getting divorced?"

"We hadn't decided," she said. "We were going to take this trip, then see."

"Why tell me now?"

"So that you know no one's perfect, and you know that nothing that happened is your fault."

"Like what?"

"None of it. I just want you to be you. Not your father, not your brother, not worrying about taking care of anyone but yourself."

Achilles was stunned. They'd called together, and even sent a photo of themselves gardening together, and when he'd last been home less than a year before, his father had been painting the house. The thought that they'd put on a show for him stung.

One hand on her arm and the other on her backpack, he walked his mother back to the porch, still cluttered with trash bags stuffed with decorations, and gave her another hug, slipping his hands under the ever-present burden. He respected her determination, but something still bothered him. Later he realized that she was doing some kind of penance. In the army, they ran with packs for conditioning and punishment, but unlike his mother, they unsaddled themselves at every available opportunity.

He patted the pack. She squeezed his hand one last time. "You don't have to do this."

But oh how he wanted to do it, to get out of that bedroom, that house, that town, to have a mission again. The route out of town scaled the eastern hills, offering a view of the valley and the endless identical carport subdivisions built during his early childhood, and outside of that, the ring of two-car garage developments from his teens, and outside of that, the mini-mansions that appeared while he was on active duty. From most angles, the roads resembled a random sprinkling of commas and parentheses. His favorite view was from the zenith, where he could see how the highway carved a semicircle, and that highway, taken together with all the looping and whirling roads inside that half-moon, resembled a sketch of the brain. When he was a kid he told himself the design was intentional, and he took comfort in a grand designer.

He'd promised his mother that he'd be careful, drive no more than nine miles over the speed limit, stop when tired (and let her know where), avoid sleeping in deserted rest areas, wouldn't eat much fast food, and was doing this because he wanted to. He'd sworn that he was. He did want to. What other choice did he have? On his eighth birthday he'd been promised a big surprise, expected a golden Labrador retriever, and received a brother. His mother said, "You'll never be alone." His father said, "Don't need blood to be brothers."

CHAPTER 2

THE WINDOWS WERE UP, UNLIKE ALL THOSE HOURS WITH GUN BARRELS resting on the doorframes. Troy had grown increasingly sullen the closer they came to home, his face set in the scowl he usually only wore after losing—a game, a bet, a race, a woman. He perked up when a dump truck with DC plates cut them off, snapping, "Rock'em sock'em, two-o-clock!" laying on the horn and swerving across three lanes onto the rough while Achilles barked, "Got it!" as he planted both feet on the floorboard, pressing his back into the seat to steady his aim while reaching for the weapon he didn't have. Achilles had expected that sooner or later they'd get zulu-foxtrot. It was the kind of shit they saw in old movies, salty vets tensing up if someone so much as snapped. They'd laughed off their *Deer Hunter* moment, each claiming the other would play Christopher Walken's character, and Troy went right back to sulking as if drunk, his head lolling back and his words garbled like he was forcing them out to keep from choking on them.

For the last few months everybody had talked about nothing but home, until the final weeks, when no one mentioned home at all, but Achilles knew they thought about it. Everyone wore a faraway look—not the kind that settled over them like a shroud after the first firefight, not the triumphant glare that was a shield, not the inward gaze they wore after Jackson died, when they avoided each others' eyes for the ride home, as Troy now seemed to be doing. It was another look, like quiet embarrassment, like they were each watching a film no one else could see, some romantic comedy they were forced to endure but ended up secretly enjoying. It was then that they redoubled the promise to stay in touch, start a Myspace page, have an annual reunion. Achilles knew the desperate promises wouldn't hold, not with everyone already retreating into the past.

Merriweather stopped playing rap, opting again for the gospel that had shaken their tent the first few weeks. Wages started writing Bethany more, scribbling every night by the glow of his flashlight, or clicking away on his laptop, depending on how the day had gone. "Some shit's just easier to type." Troy had found a battered Kama Sutra in a raid and immediately loaned it out, because it was "too much like window-shopping." He reclaimed the book not long before they left, openly studying it at dusk and dawn, reading and rereading like it was a newspaper and he had to catch up with the rest of the world.

Achilles's short list: food, sleep, Janice, a run through the creek behind his house. He knew the land inside and out, the shady grove that separated his house from Happy Garden, the trailer park where Janice lived. On hot nights, he'd often dreamed of those sweet-smelling woods, and the cool, clear creek that ran through them swashing about his ankles. He hadn't seen a frog in almost a year. He thought he might even go hunting with his father, which he hadn't done since high school. He still wouldn't shoot anything, but he now understood his father's pleasure at being in the woods away from the concrete and congestion. Hunting had never been about the animal, only the single-minded stalking of worthy prey. He didn't know what he'd tell Janice, but they could go to the quarry, walk through the woods like they used to. Maybe they'd get serious.

Troy's list: the PBR on tap at the VFW, a giant roller coaster, and women, "Anyone would do right now." The roller coaster surprised Achilles. His brother had explained, "I want to know if they still scare me." When they passed the amusement park, Achilles jokingly jerked the wheel toward the exit. Troy shrugged. "Does it matter? We have nothing but time now. Nothing fucking else."

"Whatever." Achilles couldn't remember being so excited. From the DC townhouses to suburban track homes, from scattered subdivisions to the rolling hills and farms: every familiar sight made him giddy as his birthday. The license plates, in English, all thrilled him, but he really felt at home once they were far enough west on I-270 that DC's *Taxation Without Representation* gave way to Pennsylvania and Maryland plates.

Achilles always paid close attention to plates because his father said they indicated who was a real Pennsylvanian and who was one of the capitol-city carpetbaggers who moved for the cheap farmland or to live in one of the subdivisions he called human kennels. Most importantly, he warned his sons, beware lady drivers with old DC plates or new

Pennsylvania tags. When he was in high school, Achilles pointed out that everyone who bought a new car received new plates regardless of where they were from. Smiling, his father said, "Son, I only give the advice. Whether or not you take it is up to you." Achilles grew less certain about how serious his father was but he remained vigilant about reading plates.

They switched places near Monocacy and Achilles drove the last leg to the outskirts of Hagerstown, from the evergreen-lined interstate to the two-lane highways banked by mounds of red and yellow leaves, to the crisp black roads that fed the new developments and the last few original freestanding five-acre plots, one of which their parents lived on, stopping at last where the arteries of commerce died out at the foot of the unpaved drive that wound through the wooded lot and ended at a cement stoop. The house sat atop a slow rise, commanding a view of the surrounding area, but the lot was so heavily wooded that not even the chimney could be seen from the road below. Achilles had felt isolated in high school, but now he appreciated the seclusion.

The old Private Property sign at the edge of the lot had been repainted, and next to it three more signs planted: Private Drive! Keep Out! Not for Sale! When the building boom started, barely a weekend passed that someone didn't tool a fancy sedan up the drive to make an offer on the land. Their father refused to sell because, first, they couldn't afford to move anyplace better, and second, he wasn't going to help any big-city scam artist cram twenty-five houses onto land meant for one— "People aren't meant to be that close together."

They crept up the driveway, stopping when they could see the house and the six cars parked around it, which they recognized as belonging to family members. They agreed that the re-up bonus was tempting, but neither could see volunteering to eat any more shit; however, Troy, fingering his Bronze Star, now looked uncertain. Achilles punched his brother on the shoulder, urging him out of the car.

The sun had set and a strong southern wind hummed through the trees. The sky was shot through with stars and the moon was so bright that when it passed between the clouds, the windows twinkled and the fresh white paint sparkled. They had helped their father repaint the house when they were home on leave only a few months before. Troy had worked on the walls, painting in hurried, broad strokes. Achilles, as always, was assigned to the trim because, his father said, only he had patience for it. It was short work. They only had to cover four walls holding together five rooms: two bedrooms, a kitchen, a living room, and a bathroom. The front door was in the center of the house and opened into the living room. To the left of the living room was the kitchen and then a short hallway leading to the bedroom the brothers shared as well as the only bathroom. To the right of the living room was their parents' bedroom. The one-story ranch looked larger than Achilles remembered it. They stood for a moment, taking it in. The living room was dim. Troy pointed to their parent's bedroom, which was well lit. "That must be where they're hiding."

"They sure aren't hidden too well," said Achilles.

"Probably don't want us to be too surprised."

"Right," said Achilles. He smelled food and hoped his aunt Rose had made baked spaghetti with hot dogs. He scanned the cars again. As far as he could tell, Janice's wasn't there.

Before going in they slammed the trunk and doors, kicked dirt and gravel, stomped on the porch. Just before he opened the door, Troy said, "Remember, act surprised."

Achilles nodded, standing tall. They wore desert BDUs and all their medals—peacocked, they called it—Infantry badges, Airborne wings, the whole bit. Achilles felt a sense of relief, like he had come up for air. Troy was bringing home a Bronze Star for saving Wexler's snatch, but Achilles was bringing home Troy.

Aunt Betsy, their father's only sibling, and her husband sat on the love seat, their two sons on the couch. Red, white, and blue streamers were strung from corner to corner. ACHILLES and TROY were spelled out in winking, glittering, purple-and-gold letters. The ceiling was literally covered with balloons, each one individually taped up, and a large American flag covered one wall.

"Wow," said Troy, throwing his hands in the air. "This is nice."

"Yeah," said Achilles, putting on his biggest smile. "We didn't expect this."

Aunt Betsy's face moved from concern to alarm as they peered around the room. "You don't know, do you? Oh God! You don't know."

They didn't know. Discharge papers in hand, the brothers had made several last-minutes adjustments to their final itinerary: spending a morning in Heidelberg; stopping off to see Merriweather, who was en route to Walter Reed; flying through Okinawa to see a friend from jump school. They didn't know their erratic agenda kept them one day ahead of the news that had shadowed them since Kabul. They didn't know—they couldn't—that two hours after they flew out of Bagram AFB, word reached the XO, who sent it on to the chaplain; or that the evening after they flew out of Turkmenistan, a messenger arrived in the barracks where they had billeted the previous night and scared the holy-living-Motor-City-shit, yes, all one word, out of poor Lance Corporal Jason *Conrad,* who didn't believe it was a mistake and couldn't be consoled until he had called his mom in Brewster-Douglass; or that the next morning, while they were dressing for the funeral, a green sedan with government plates would park in the driveway and two E5s in class AS would regretfully inform them that their father had died in an unforeseeable accident.

Aunt Betsy was correct: they knew nothing. Balloons and streamers, flags and flowers—at that moment all they knew was that the house was decorated for a party, but everyone was dressed for a wake. Aunt Betsy shepherded them across the living room to their parents' room, the three long steps feeling like three thousand with her all the way muttering, "Oh dear." Between the overhead lights and the lamps from which the shades had been removed, their parents' room, usually dim, was as bright as a crime scene. Their mother knelt in the middle of the floor, surrounded by boxes and piles of papers and old photographs, the stack closest to her topped by two large blue envelopes. Her eyes dull as stones, before she even spoke, Achilles knew their luck had run aground and silently cursed Troy for squandering it.

Their mother stood and wiped her hands on her pant legs as if shedding dust that only she could see. One deep breath in. And out. Another. "Your father was involved in a head-on collision. With a rig. He was giving a coworker a ride home. Laura Goman." She said the name as if they would recognize it. "They died instantly."

Their friends from the squad maintained a series of complex and contradictory unspoken agreements: today is better than tomorrow, so do it tomorrow; honor the past but don't live in it, and listen without interruption whenever it's mentioned, but don't encourage it as a topic of conversation; and firstly, never ask permission or apologize; then, most importantly—Be there. So Achilles didn't feel guilty about showing up at his friend's door at four a.m. Surely Wages expected this after they talked.

Wages lived in New Orleans's Mid-City neighborhood, at the corner of Carrollton and Banks, in a sagging rust-colored duplex across the street from a Catholic school surrounded by enough barbed-wire fencing to pass for a jail. "Look for the house with the scowl," he'd instructed, and indeed the black metal awnings tilted toward each other like the furrowed eyebrows of someone who didn't want to be disturbed.

The house had two front doors but one long front porch with a single set of stairs in the middle. On the neighbor's side of the porch: a clear plastic bag stuffed with balled-up diapers, a broken skateboard, a food can filled with cigarette butts. The wood around the windows was pitted and chipped, the paint on the siding peeling badly, which, given the color—shades of red, burgundy, and garnet, the colors of corrosion—created the impression that the entire house was a ship abandoned at sea, and now surrendering to the waters. When he'd helped his father repaint their house—or was it now his mother's?—his father had even hired someone to repoint the chimney. Compared to Wages's home, their house sparkled like a palace. Achilles felt awkward about seeing his friend's house in this condition.

The screen door was pitted with rusted metal and had pebbled glass slats that pivoted like Venetian blinds. Achilles rapped gently on the door frame, pressing his palm against the nearby slats so they wouldn't rattle. He heard music coming from within the house, but it could have been the neighbors. He didn't want to wake anyone unnecessarily. He knew Wages's wife Bethany, a nurse, worked odd hours. Wages, on the other hand, like most of them, barely slept.

Achilles had liked Wages from the moment they met. Wages was a skinny six feet, but unnaturally strong. He was the guy who never complained or wilted under the hundred-pound pack, the guy who never dropped it, but slid out of the straps and set it in the sand as smoothly as slipping off a sweater. Carrying that pack was like carrying a man on your back *all fucking day,* and Achilles soon discovered he wasn't up to the task. He could do it but he didn't like it. He didn't like how the tight straps felt like walking around in a full nelson. He didn't like how the deep ruts it wore into his shoulders always itched or how his feet calcified as his arches fell under the extra weight, so that even now they hurt all the time, especially when it rained and his legs stiffened like pencils glued to rocks and he walked like he was wading through water. Most importantly, he hadn't liked becoming so used to an unnatural burden that he felt naked without it. Not Wages. He did push-ups with that pack on and one-armed pull-ups without it, even though he was thin as the wind.

The Wages who answered the door, though, had filled out a lot. The bright blue walleyes, avian nose, and squat, broad forehead were all there, but closer together. His face was puffy, and his cheeks bowled out like he was holding his breath. He looked bigger all around, like the adult version of himself. Christ, he was even wearing a black suit and had his red hair in a ponytail. It was like seeing someone who had rehabbed or recently returned from the hospital. They might not be any happier, but they were always heavier, the cheeks filled out, the stomach softened by rich food and a sedentary lifestyle. He looked sickly, pallid. Wages was the first one he'd seen since they'd returned, and it took a moment for Achilles to realize that Wages was simply rehydrated and he wasn't sickly pale; he'd just lost the Afghani-tan.

All anxiety faded, and Achilles wheezed as his friend lifted him off his feet in a bone-crushing bear hug and spun him into the house, which smelled of garlic and fresh-baked bread. The Delfonics wafted out of the speakers.

Achilles fingered Wages's lapels.

"Who died, right? I know," said Wages, quickly adding, "Shit, sorry man."

"It's cool," said Achilles twice, wanting to let it pass. "You do look like you're going to a funeral."

"You're looking at the new head of security. I got the poker pit at Carousel Casino. Now I chill out in the monitor room and tell the other losers who to scope." He checked his watch. "Can't be late my first day as boss. I was about to leave a note for you." He handed Achilles a big manila envelope the same size as the blue one in the bottom of Achilles's bag. "Here're the keys and a map." He looked at his watch and bit his lip, which meant he was counting. Pushing Achilles toward the door, Wages said, "All right, I've got just enough time to give you the bird's-eye."

When they turned to leave, Achilles pointed at two sabers in the umbrella stand next to the door. "What's up with that?"

"She's not allowed to answer the door without a weapon in arm's reach. This is New Orleans," said Wages. "I want her to use a gun, but you know how women get about that. This is just as good because there's hella chance anyone can take a sword away from her. I hardly can."

Achilles had forgotten Bethany was a fencer. A photo of Wages and Bethany at a beach hung on the wall next to the door. She had round eyes and pert lips, and her face was prettier than he remembered. He'd only seen her in wallet-sized photos, and the one thing he recalled was that she had chocolate nipples even though she was also redheaded. The beach photo was flanked by pictures of Wages and Bethany with their parents. Wages had entered a land where Achilles would never follow. He couldn't see himself living like this, with a woman, let alone with his motley family on display: two black kids adopted and raised by white parents, charity cases like those bobble-head African orphans on late-night television. Both the fact of it and the withholding shamed him.

Wages tapped the photo of them standing in the surf. "She keeps this up to remind her of what she's working for."

Wages was stepping into the road before Achilles remembered that they didn't need to maintain strategic distance. He jogged to catch up. They crossed the street toward the school, slipped through a gap in the barbed-wire fence, and climbed up the permanent fire escape to the roof, which offered an unobstructed view of downtown and the surrounding one- and two-story houses, a spotter's wet dream. By the time they reached the third set of stairs, Achilles's shirt was stuck to his back. Troy wouldn't want to be here long.

Wages, whose temples barely glistened, ran two fingers along his forehead and slung off the sweat. "Can you feel it? We're right in the center of all this water." He pointed toward the tall buildings downtown. "The river's in front. The lake's behind. Water above and below. Don't it feel great? The air's alive."

Achilles felt it and didn't like it. When he'd opened the door at his last refueling point, the thick air had poured into the car like waves over a breaker and ridden shotgun the rest of the way to New Orleans. The air-conditioning in his father's old truck wasn't strong enough for the South, the only place he'd been that gave literal meaning to the phrase "in the soup." The sun had been down for hours, but the tar roof was still sticky underfoot.

It made sense that Wages liked it. Achilles had hated the desert, the air so dry it grated, gnawed at you like an animal sniffing out blood. He said it was proof there was no Mother Nature, only motherfucking nature, and none of it gave a damn about man. Achilles had liked the valley where they spent their last months and thought the spartan simplicity beautiful. He'd been loath to leave the drifting dunes and ragged rocky brows. True, it was unforgiving, but that was what he liked about it. No guardrails, no seat belts, and no airbags. If the whole world were like that, he and his friends would be kings.

Wages unfolded a tourist map across the top of an air conditioner, pointing as he talked. "This X is the church. That's downtown straight ahead where you see the cell towers and the JAX sign. That's the French Quarter, the center of the city, and also known as the Vieux Carré. The church is to the left, Uptown is to the right. None of it is more than a few clicks from here." He gestured toward downtown. "A little more to the left, where it gets dark, that's the church where I saw Troy. It's called St. Augustine. It's in the Tremé district."

Downtown, straight ahead of them, cell towers blinked their silent warning like fireworks in slow motion—pop . . . pop . . . pop. A sign winked JAX. Uptown looked like a continuation of Wages's neighborhood, just another stop upstream on the same river of streetlights. But where the X supposedly was, the Tremé, there was no light to be seen, save for one neon cross that shone cobalt blue. First their father's funeral and now this: Troy vanished into the night, as if finding his birth mother were more important than his duty to the woman who had raised them.

The clickity-clack of unsteady heels sounded below. A woman in a tight red dress staggered down the street, her hips pistoning up and down as if she was riding a bike uphill. Two teenage boys swimming in baggy jeans sniffed ten feet behind her, giggling and elbowing each other. The woman turned to face them. "I told you that's all you gon' get, unless you little fuckers pay. Everyone knows you pay me, don't play me. So give it up or stop snorting after me, you little Vienna Sausage motherfuckers."

"I got your banana fucker right here, bee-yitch!" the taller one yelled. "We don't need your prune ass anyway!"

"Yeah, that's right, bee-yatch," said the other.

Wages quietly chuckled, like he didn't want to be heard. "Not much milk left in those bags, but Lorenzo would still like them. Remember how Merri called him Manual Dingo? Remember Merri and Jacki always arguing like a married couple?"

Merri was Merriweather and Jacki was Jackson, and Achilles remembered. Twice the squad stopped at a brothel on the edge of Jalalabad, once on the way into town and once on the way out. At the first visit, Jackson was pissed to learn that none of the women would give him a blowjob. He had promised his girlfriend he would remain a virgin, and a BJ was only foreplay, as the former president had proven. During the second visit, Merriweather suggested anal, which Jackson found repulsive, even after Merriweather explained, "Like the dirty virgins say, anal ain't really fucking. Think of it like a blowjob. Think of it sideways, like the ass is a little mouth with big lips."

31

Jackson thought otherwise and waited outside. Both times they'd arrived in the early morning hours, like this, right before sunrise when it was the darkest, when those winking mesmerists, the stars, dazzled like fires in the night, like looking at the sun through a coffee can with holes poked in the bottom. The sky was silver at the far rim, like someone was peeling back the top to take a peek inside this bowl of stew.

A Hummer drove by, bumping a rap song he didn't recognize. They'd fought to protect that driver's right to buy that car and pump it full of big lizard. His right was his right. Another car rolled by, windows vibrating, the radio surprisingly loud given the hour; Wages's neighbor stood on the porch and lit three matches before his cigarette flared; the paperboy cycled by, each delivery a flashing white arc; the woman in the red dress staggered around the corner; the two teens crossed the street in the opposite direction: all unaware of being watched. People in peaceful countries so infrequently looked up. Didn't that mean he and his buddies had done a good job? Didn't they deserve to be proud? Didn't that make it okay that he missed it, that standing beside Wages made him yearn to be back in rotation with Troy, stacked up outside the door of some bad guy or providing cover fire in Korengal, where he knew what to expect, even if he didn't know where it was coming from?

But that was all foolishness, wasn't it? The land was hungry, insatiably so, and if they went back, who was to say the return trip would be a round trip? He was here now, he'd see Troy today, and after that he could worry about tomorrow. But he couldn't stop thinking that out of all the hours he and his brother had spent together, those last few days on the way home—from the morning they packed their duffels to boarding the c-130J at the Bagram Airfield to the night they set their bags down outside their mother's bedroom—the only thing that made any sense was when that dump truck had cut them off and he braced himself for the impact.

"If you wait, I'll go with you this afternoon," said Wages.

"I got it," said Achilles. Wages looked disappointed, as if Achilles had turned down his offer to take point. But Achilles needed to do this alone.

He had often wondered if his parents would have asked him to look out for his brother if they'd known how reckless Troy would become. Troy believed his adoption was a mistake, that his own real family was wealthy, and he regarded everyone who had more money with suspicion, as if they had profited at his expense. In eighth grade, he vowed to get famous, then rich, then expose his birth parents, seeding them with shame and regret.

During their last weeks in Goddamnistan, while everyone was afraid of catching the breakup baby, Troy volunteered for missions, declaring himself immune from harm until reunited with his real family, after which he would achieve his true destiny. Achilles volunteered as well, telling himself that fidelity could be worn like an amulet, but after the convoy to Baraki, when a bullet struck the window besides Achilles's head and he thought it was his vision splintering and fracturing, he swore he would never volunteer again. What Troy took as proof of divine intervention, Achilles took as evidence of unnecessary risk. Yet two days after Baraki, Troy volunteered for Faizabad and Achilles followed, against his better judgment, his father's voice echoing in his ears.

Before they shipped out, his father had pulled them both aside. "Don't come back without him," he told Achilles, and then louder, "Don't one of you come back alone."

His mother gasped.

"They know what I mean," said their father.

Achilles knew. The first weeks, possessed by cavalier notions of bravery and sacrifice, transfixed by the image of a cinematic slow-motion dive as he caught a nonlethal bullet to protect Troy, Achilles believed it would be better to die than to go home without his younger brother. After seeing what it really looked like, he was afraid to die, but he still wanted to believe he could be the hero, the one to beat, the other Achilles.

As soon as the sun was up, Achilles took Wages's map and headed to the center of New Orleans, which to him wasn't the Vieux Carré but the Tremé district, specifically St. Augustine Church at the intersection of Governor Nicholls Street and St. Claude Avenue, where Troy was last seen in the soup kitchen line. Even older than the church were the surrounding houses, duplexes so narrow they didn't have hallways, each room opening directly into the next.

Wages, whose house was built in the same style, called them shotgun houses, because a shotgun slug fired through the front door would strut straight out the back. "They're historic." Achilles called them hovels, "Historic my ass." Homes with cardboard taped over broken windows. Homes with no front yards, warped screen doors scraping cracked concrete stoops spilling directly onto the sidewalk. Homes too close together to ride a bicycle between. Homes with second floors only half the size of the first, the upper levels covering the back half of the house like sodden humps, tacked on as if there hadn't been enough money to finish building.

What Achilles thought most pathetic were the coffee can planters, ashen window boxes with bright silk flowers, and herb gardens planted in old rubber tires. Above it all, water-rotted cornices splintered off and gables sunk into obtuse angles pulling apart at the ridges, pressing down on the walls, bowing them out like water balloons, as if the houses were bursting at the seams. Rent pavement, overgrown lots, gaping streetlights. Old ladies squatting on stoops. Men driving shopping carts crammed with clattering beer cans, teens posting up on the corners passing fire and spirits. DC was the same. Why didn't they just move?

In Afghanistan, O'Ree, a career soldier, told Achilles, "People aren't none too different, but some is smarter, and you always assume the other guy is smarter. So when we come to the edge of a town, ask where you would hide if you were the other guy." A dormer window, the occasional large attic vent, the church bell tower? Clearly the bell tower was best. Achilles could see where a sniper would hide, but not his brother. Troy didn't fit in here. Achilles had once complained to his mom about being the only black kid in school. She'd said, "Don't exaggerate, honey. What about your brother?" She was right. What had he wanted her to do? Drive him to a neighborhood like this and enroll him in school? The anger he hadn't realized he felt toward his brother for running off collapsed as he imagined Troy meeting his biops.

On foot and unarmed, he walked quickly, passing homes with fitted sheets for curtains, the elastic edges curled up at the corners. Others had no blinds at all. A mother and two sons sat on a black couch watching TV, each eating from a to-go container. In the next house, a teenage girl and two young boys sat with their heads bowed in prayer, holding hands around a small dining table piled high with magazines. In another, a young boy with braided hair teased a Rottweiler puppy with a black baby doll. Meanwhile, the praying girl looked up and caught one of the boys putting on sunglasses and a wrestling match ensued. Overall, they appeared content despite the circumstances. Still, he couldn't imagine Troy or himself eating in front of the TV, playing with the dog, or praying at the table. *It's not called an eating room; dogs don't belong in the house no more than the truck do;* and *I got a good book right here, it's called* The Shining. Their parents had run an orderly, decent home. Three teens stood on the corner, or maybe they were men. He couldn't tell because of the hoods and low caps, but he felt them watching his every move, so he jaywalked, hurriedly crossing the street to avoid them, entering the church grounds from the rear.

St. Augustine was a white two-story church with a brick belfry capped in copper. The church capstone read 1834. The chancellery was behind the church, and in the courtyard between the two buildings sat a large anchor made of welded chains, dedicated, according to the plaque, to the Unknown Slave. Achilles stopped only briefly to examine it, anxious to get out of the heat and into the chancellery. The office was crowded with folding chairs and tables along one wall, and along the other sat a row of desks with handwritten name tents, according to which the desk closest to the door belonged to Levreau, a gaunt-faced man who, even when seated, appeared to be quite tall. He was on the phone but greeted Achilles with a smile, covering the mouthpiece with his hand and motioning for Achilles to sit while whispering, "Good afternoon, be right with you."

Achilles remained standing, reluctant to move because he was directly under the air-conditioner vent. Over the rush of air he heard gospel music. The office had two bookshelves, one lined with different books, the other stacked with identical copies of the same Bible; a sign on the office door read "Breaking the Twin Shackles of Sin and Oppression"; African prints lined the walls. Did Merriweather's church look like this? Achilles struggled not to laugh at a life-sized painting of Jesus with an Afro and a Village People beard, a Harlem Globetrotter in a bathrobe. A woman at the far desk typed on a computer, nodding her head to the music. An older woman stuffed envelopes. Levreau placed the handset carefully in the cradle, like it was fragile when it was only an old plastic dumbbell-shaped receiver. He seemed to be a man who focused intently on everything he did. "Yes sir. How may I help you?"

"I'm looking for my brother, Troy Conroy. He was here two days ago." Achilles handed him the most recent photo of Troy, taken a few days before the funeral at the hospital with Merriweather.

Levreau shook his head, then went around the room and showed the photo to everybody. Achilles held his breath at each exchange. Levreau returned to his desk looking disappointed. "Sorry. And I make a point to meet all the new parishioners. Is he new? How long has he been attending?"

"I don't think he's attending. He was here on Wednesday."

"Oh," Levreau gave him a knowing look. "We only feed people once a week, on Wednesdays. Have you tried the shelters?"

"No."

While Levreau rattled off a few names, Achilles pictured parks with gazebos, until the meaning of *shelters* sunk in. "It's not like that. He's looking for someone else who might be around here." Achilles stopped short. "He's not homeless. He's looking for somebody who might be homeless, but he's not homeless."

"Yes sir. Okay. I'll tell you what. I'll copy this, and put it on our bulletin board in the vestibule. Right up front. Everyone will see it when they come in. If he's been here, someone's seen him." Levreau vanished into a back room and returned a moment later with a hazy enlargement. Achilles wrote his number on the bottom of the copy.

"Do you know his name?" asked Levreau.

"Troy Conroy."

"I meant the person Troy's looking for."

"No." It felt funny to hear Levreau say Troy in that baritone.

"Well, try looking at St. Jude."

"Where's that?"

"Where is St. Jude again?" Levreau asked over his shoulder. No one knew. "It's brand new and might not be open yet. But it's supposed to be the biggest shelter in the city. Have you filed a missing person report?"

"No." Achilles was put off by the suggestion. Even trying a shelter seemed a waste of time. If St. Augustine didn't serve food every day, he'd just come back the following Wednesday. Troy wouldn't be staying at a shelter.

"Try filing a missing person report."

"I don't know the name of the people, or person, he's looking for." He'd have to ask his mom about that, again.

"I meant for your brother. That way, if he gets a traffic ticket, for example, praise Jesus, you found him. Car accident, praise Jesus, you found him. There's a substation nearby. I'll draw you a map."

Levreau sketched out a map and wished him luck. Achilles thought he could go to the police station and file that report, just in case. But it would be more helpful if he knew who Troy was looking for before he did. It was the time she'd usually be taking a nap, but he called his mother anyway, halfway hoping she wouldn't answer. To his surprise, she did, and hearing his voice asked, "Already?"

"Maybe not for a week," said Achilles.

"Where is he?"

"I'm not sure."

"Then how do you know he's gone for a week?" she asked.

Her question ticked the hairs on the back of his neck. It had been her idea to hand out envelopes. "It looks like the people he's looking for might be gone for a week."

She exhaled sharply. "At least we know he's okay. That's good enough. If you want to come back you can, or go somewhere else. I just mean you don't have to stay down in New Orleans all week waiting for Troy."

He could tell she was straining to sound upbeat. "It's okay. I don't mind. It's a chance to see Wages."

She was always more talkative on the phone, and for a few minutes droned on about seeing Janice at the store, and what the neighbors were doing (those she did talk to), and why Maryland had better highways than Pennsylvania. He heard her shifting and moving between breaths. Even after they'd been on the phone a few minutes, she was still breathing heavily, which worried him until he remembered the backpack. In the middle of telling him about a new pothole in town, she paused and said, "You're a good son, and a better brother."

She'd never said anything like that before, and Achilles didn't know how to respond. He mumbled his thanks and ended the call before he remembered to ask her the name of Troy's family. He was so taken aback by the compliment that he didn't want to call her back.

The police station was a converted gas station wedged between the Bluebird Diner and a liquor store. The offices were where the auto bays used to be, the front desk where the cashier would have sat. The remodelers had saved the night-service window, a little Plexiglas revolving door in the wall behind the front counter, and now a small TV was wedged into it, holding the attention of a heavyset officer. Achilles stood at the counter, his hands behind his back in parade rest, and waited to be acknowledged. The cop held up a finger until a laugh track died down, then finally looked up at him. "Help you?"

"Yes sir. Where do I file a missing person's report?" asked Achilles.

"Here. You got a name and address?" asked the officer, pushing a form at him.

"Yes sir. But, he doesn't live here."

"Does he have a local address?"

"No sir. All I know is he was last seen here."

"You could try posting flyers, unless he's the type that doesn't want to be found." Hearing a laugh track, the cop glanced back at the television. "Where was he last seen?"

"St. Augustine."

"In the Tremé? The Tremé. Huh!" His tone became weary and officious, as if he had explained this to Achilles one thousand times. "You file the report in the city where the person lives." He turned the TV up.

Achilles had known it was a stupid idea, one of those plans desperately followed just to keep busy, even though it was clearly pointless. *What if he has a car accident, praise Jesus, or gets a speeding ticket, praise Jesus!* Achilles wanted to yell as he left the station.

"Hey," said the desk sergeant. He wrote a number on the back of a card, tapping it twice. Leaning forward, he whispered sympathetically, as if sharing a secret, "Try the coroner." He motioned to the phone at the end of the counter. "You can use this one here. Go on. Guy sounds like he could be half the poor saps in there. It's worth a shot. In the cooler no one can lie about his name."

CHAPTER 3

"**T**HAT SUPPOSED TO BE SOME CLEVER SHIT LIKE 'DEAD MEN TELL NO tales?' Wasn't that in *Peter Pan*?" Wages was livid, redder than Achilles had ever seen him, pacing back and forth, breathing heavy. "'The cooler'? What the fuck? They store people like six-packs now? Fucking cops. They get fifty-plus GS to cruise around in their vests shooting unarmed people, and go home at night and talk about how fucking dangerous their jobs are. We got a few GS a month to be target practice for a bunch of fucking unappreciative, sorry-assed Dirka-Dirkas." He pounded the wall. "There's no justice without a bullet."

This was Wages—always protecting his men, no matter what. He'd been equally angry when the chin-scratchers suggested a report might be required about the alleged civilian casualties after Jackson died. Wages had yelled, "What casualties? What casualties? Right now? Right now? Not now! *Not now!*" And when their leave was denied because of a paperwork fuck-up, a conjunction-junction, he walked it through, foaming at the mouth the whole way. His men could never be wrong. If one of them fucked up, he took them aside to ream them. But in front of anyone else, his soldiers were always golden.

They were in Wages's living room. The furniture was what Janice would have called chocolate box, assorted like in her mother's trailer: everything matched because nothing matched. Wages slumped into a sparkling strawberry settee, about which he'd said, "I know, dude. Somewhere a seventies van is missing a bench seat." With a grin, he'd added, "Don't come a-knockin' . . ."

Achilles sat on a leopard-print chair shaped like a giant high-heeled shoe. The only normal piece of furniture was a cream-colored sofa that Bethany forbade Wages to sit on for fear he'd spill beer on it, staining it like he'd stained the carpet and the shoe chair. Wages was twenty-five, only three years older than Achilles, yet the house felt very adult and smelled homey. Bethany was cooking lunch, but the aroma of food was ever present. And it was orderly, the way your parents' house could be both clean and cluttered, bursting with collective memories.

It was only a few hours since Achilles had been turned away at the police station. In the daylight, he could see all the details he'd missed the night before. Instead of sheetrock, the walls were plaster, of the same texture as the sides of the quarry, equally cool to the touch, cracked and chipped in several places—with Wages's help no doubt—giving each room the appearance of having been hand hewn from chalky stone. The fixtures were ancient: the porcelain kitchen sink a long white slab with a built-in drain board; the bathroom sink a pedestal shaped like a thick-stemmed ivory flower gleaming under the vanity lights; the stove an old iron contraption that looked like it should be on train tracks; the refrigerator an antique icebox with a locking handle.

Photos everywhere—the hallway, the bathroom wall, the mantel. One picture of the squad: Merriweather, Troy, Achilles, Wages, Jackson, Wexler, and Lorenzo all huddled around a recaptured M2, a .50-cal machine gun that spit over five hundred rounds per minute. Wages called it the Generous Machine. The rest of the pictures were of Bethany and Wages. Frames lined the deep windowsills, the refrigerator, and the top of the window air conditioner. And in each one they were smiling brightly, Bethany toothy, chin up, always leaning into Wages. Wages always grinning, almost daring the camera. Achilles recognized a few pictures he had seen before, though smaller, as creased wallet-sized photos. In the more recent photos, Bethany looked chunkier, but a lot of ladies blew up while their men were away, which was desirable because weight gain was taken as a sign of fidelity. Weight loss, exercise, and new haircuts were cause for alarm, like the whistle before the rocket hit.

"Are y'all hungry?" Bethany called from the kitchen.

"Maybe," said Wages.

"I'm making enough just in case. You can bring it for lunch tomorrow."

Wages whispered to Achilles, "She knows I don't like bringing leftovers for lunch unless it's pasta. I like to bring pasta. It's okay cold. I don't put my shit in the microwave. It fucks food up. Makes it mushy." To Bethany he called, "What are you making?"

After a pause, Bethany answered, "Chicken."

Wages shook his head. "That's the problem with women. You tell them what you want and they nod and give you the rice-eye smile." Wages pulled his eyes into slants and nodded vigorously. "'Yeah, yeah, yeah' and then do whatever the fuck they want anyway. Hard to get along with."

The photos and the parenting magazines piled on the coffee table said otherwise. Wages and Bethany had a real connection. A card with a dried starfish glued to it stood on the end table. He couldn't see the handwriting inside, but the cover text was *I'd give an arm and a leg for you*. It didn't matter that a starfish's arms and legs were indistinguishable. Bethany was saying she'd give it all. She'd gained about fifteen pounds. She wasn't going anywhere.

Wages slapped the table. "Why didn't you give the cops this address?"

Wages always had a solution. Achilles hadn't thought of that. He'd been rattled by the suggestion that he visit the morgue. Or maybe he was just tired from driving. "I'll try that tomorrow."

"Then today we can go out."

All afternoon, Wages had wanted to take Achilles to the French Quarter for some daiquiris. He mentioned it again. "At least let me drive you through Uptown. You can see the streetcar and the river. Come on, man. It'll be fun. It's touristy. This whole town's a tourist trap. Let's get oscar-mike."

Achilles didn't like the idea of partying before finding Troy. It was like being on a convoy where you couldn't sleep until back at base. Sometimes you got so tired you horse-slept, but you never really rested until mission accomplished.

"What are you going to do, put him on a milk carton? Moping ain't gonna make him appear."

Achilles shot Wages the bird. He wasn't fucking moping! Was he?

"Whaddya all worried about? It's only been a couple of weeks. Y'all were knotted at the nuts for three years. Maybe he just wanted some time, with your father and all."

Wanted some time? What kind of time did Troy need? His mom was worried, even though she wouldn't admit it. Achilles, though, wasn't really worried, at least not like Wages thought, it was just that when Achilles brought Troy home, he would be free. It would make it all worthwhile. When he got into trouble as a kid, he used to imagine that he would die suddenly or get hurt or kidnapped, and then his parents would be sorry they hadn't treated him better. He imagined the doctor would be able to look at his brain and see how wrong they were about him, how much potential he had, how much fight and determination, how much he would have accomplished had he not died so young. But he lived, so he had to prove it.

"It just doesn't feel right," said Achilles. Wages raised his eyebrows and nodded, accepting that answer. Achilles almost mentioned the adoption paperwork but caught himself. That wouldn't change anything.

"You went to St. Aug. You tried to file that MPR. Go back tomorrow and use this address. Not that anything's going to happen anyway. Troy's indestructible. He can walk through a fucking minefield. He's fine. You should just wait and see if he comes back to the church next Wednesday. What else do you want to do? Tell me. We'll do it. Whatever it is, we'll do it right fucking now. Then we can go downtown for some drinks."

Achilles didn't have an answer.

Wages stood. "Let's go. I'll grab some beers for the road."

Bethany called them to the table. She pronounced Achilles "A-Sheel."

"That kills that." Wages yelled back, "Okay Nee-Nee, we're coming! And it's Ah-kill-ease." To Achilles he said, "She's heard me say it a thousand-and-one times."

While Wages walked into the kitchen, Achilles hung back and peeked inside the card, drawn again by the embossed gold lettering: *I'd give an arm and a leg for you.* The starfish was rough and smelled salty, and the tan parchment, thick and fibrous, closer to cloth than paper. Inside Wages had written a personal EKG in the same pointy handwriting that signed orders and described kill zones: *Even if I couldn't grow them back. Happy Anniversary. You're my biggest and best adventure! Love, Kyle.*

An adventure? Like his parents, trying new foods?

In the kitchen, Bethany had already set the table and was dishing out ravioli. Wages kissed Bethany on the top of the head.

Achilles admired Wages for sticking it out with Bethany. Before shipping out, Achilles had asked Janice not to write. He didn't think he'd want to be reminded of her, or home, or anything that he couldn't shoot. Those memories had pained him even in basic—the heat of Janice's skin, the broken gnome in the garden, his father's chipped tooth that he refused to have repaired until all the workers had dental insurance. The first week was okay. He'd be jogging in formation, pass a fir tree, and think of the hammock behind the house, or he'd be doing sit-ups and the jet passing overhead would carry him back to how his mom took him, and sometimes only him, to sit at the end of the runway to watch the planes land and take off. But none of that was a big deal. Those memories made sense, and besides, Troy was there with him.

The Army called it OSUT, One Station One Unit training, because they would work with the same squad and same instructors in the same location for fourteen weeks, first in basic training and then in infantry training. During the second week, Troy fractured his ankle, and was held back. Achilles was secretly glad to be ahead of him at something, but he was miserably lonely. Jerry without Tom, they'd called him. He tried not to think about home, but while Troy was being recycled, more random memories came unbidden. He'd pitch a tent and see his father at a T-ball game, polish his boots and remember his mom making a *Predator* costume out of leftover fabric and used inner tubes, fire his rifle and see the tiny scar on Janice's ear where her stepmother had pulled her earring out in a wrestling match. All those thoughts coming for no reason he could fathom, like a string of commercials on a television he couldn't turn off. So when he was shipped overseas, Janice promised to write him, and he made her promise not to.

But she did.

A week in-country, he regretted his decision but couldn't bring himself to tell her. He didn't have to. At the end of the month, a very apologetic letter arrived. She swore this was the only promise she'd ever break, but she couldn't stand the thought of him being over there without knowing that a woman other than his mom carried him close to her heart. She said that even if he had another girl, that was okay, and he didn't need to tell her. Of course he didn't have anyone else, but still he never wrote her back. He ignored that first letter for a few weeks, using it—unopened— as a bookmark, proud of his self-control. Every time he looked up a Persian word, he felt an additional measure of power over her, and thereby, the world. But after almost a month of active duty, he broke down, carefully peeling back the flap like it was a flower petal to reveal five sheets of pink paper covered front and back with blue ink. Her letters were more organized then he would have expected, a cross between the dictionary and a diary. She listed everyone they knew and told him what they were all doing, but instead of noun, verb, article, after each name she wrote one word summing up their behavior that week: *angel, asshole, prick, confused, stubborn, alien* (his favorite). Every name reminded him of her. Running his dry fingers over her round, heavy, and heaving cursive, he caught a whiff of her perfume, her lotion, her smooth neck; he masturbated with the letter pressed against his nose.

Achilles couldn't concentrate for the rest of the week. At home, he never thought seriously about Janice. She was easy to be with and listened without judging, but her family was crazy. Her brothers made all their money fighting pit bulls. In high school they went to jail for six months, came out muscled and tattooed, and suddenly hated Achilles. He never understood why. Fortunately her mother didn't share the sentiment. Janice had never known her father but lived with both her mother and step-mother, who became friends after her dad died. Seeing the mother and stepmother twittering like teenagers, walking down Main Street in daisy dukes and flip-flops, tank tops and movie-star shades, slivers of bleached white pockets bouncing against tanned legs, their shorts cutting hot pink creases high into the backs of their thighs, their breasts gliding side to side like they were on a boat, Achilles's father would point and say *white trash.* But they were always nice to Achilles, welcoming him into their trailer to drink beer while he waited for Janice, traipsing back and forth in jeans cut so high bikinis had more cloth in the crotch, and by the time Janice was ready, Achilles's engine would be so warmed up he'd drive straight to the quarry.

The letter brought those days back. (*Cunt* she had written for her mom. *Hippo* for her stepmother. *Fags* for her brothers.) With her language, she would have fit right into the army. He started composing letters to her in his head, assigning nicknames to people he didn't like. He thought about Janice at all hours. What was she doing? Who was she with? Was she cooking for that bastard husband of hers? Were the rumors that he beat her true? Was that why she often wore long sleeves in the summer? Achilles would kill Dale when he got back. If she wanted Achilles so much, why had she married Dale in the first place? For the first time, he wondered if he was better in bed than the others. Did she put their condoms on too? Should he have claimed her? Made her pregnant? Left his mark behind? He didn't open any more letters. His heart was a locked kennel. Had he a real girlfriend, he would have broken up with her long before shipping out so that he wouldn't have to worry and she wouldn't have to lie.

Achilles returned to the substation the next morning. The TV was gone, replaced by a small fan. An older, heavyset officer was working the desk.

His gut rested on the counter, his blue shirt puckered between the buttons. Without waiting to be acknowledged, Achilles said, "I need to file a missing person's report."

The officer pointed to the auto bay, that part of the building where they would have fixed cars when the police station was still a service station. "First door on the left. Look for the sign that says Community Affairs."

The auto bay was one open room with desks clustered in twos and threes. The glass garage doors were obscured by a row of cubical partitions, the equivalent of window offices, but the only view they offered was of the parking lot. With the neon fixtures suspended over each cluster of desks, the office looked like a bar, except instead of advertising beer, signs like Vice, Homicide, and Property floated in the air, the glowing letters casting a cool blue light. Under Community Affairs, a gray-haired suit in bifocals—Morse, according to his nametag—sat hunched over a crossword. Everything was scattered about his desk—stacks of paper, folders, candy bars—except for several miniature grandfather clocks all arranged in a neat line. Achilles waited to be acknowledged. He shouldn't have been so assertive at the front desk. Bucking authority ran counter to his military training.

Morse acknowledged him with a sigh. "Do you know a five-letter word for a pagan endeavor?"

"No sir."

"That's too bad." Morse pushed the crossword aside. "Me neither. How can I help you?"

"I need to file a missing person report for a resident."

"That's too bad," he said in the same tone he had used for the crossword. Morse pushed his bifocals farther up his nose. He breathed through his mouth, but had a round, friendly face. "A resident, you say?"

"Yes sir," said Achilles.

"Of what? A resident of what? A hospital? A nursing home?"

"New Orleans, sir."

"Right, but that's not necessary to file the report. Neither a New Orleans address nor residency status is necessary to file the report. Technically, aren't you here because he's not at home?"

"Right sir."

Except for the night Troy had been arrested over the goats, Achilles had never spent much time in police stations, but he felt at ease. Under Morse's supervision, Achilles filled out a form full of checks and boxes, describing

Troy: 6'–1", 185 pounds, light brown skin, brown hair, green eyes. It was an accurate description, but he couldn't quite see Troy in it. Those stats didn't catch his devious grin, or his saunter, or how he laughed at any joke, funny or not. Achilles was handed an Identifying Marks sheet with the outlines of a full face as well as right and left profiles, and on the reverse, the outline of a body. He made an X on the chin where Troy had accidentally shot himself by firing a pellet gun at a rock. Of course, Achilles was blamed. He put another X where that bullet had nicked his right shoulder in the Khyber Pass, taking his Airborne patch right off. He drew a line where his palm was cut on his birthday. He sketched hatch marks where Troy had burned himself pulling Jackson out of that fire, and two dots to represent the two moles under Troy's left eye, but the more he tried to correct the alignment, the larger the moles became until they looked like tears, and Achilles had to ask for a new sheet. He was more careful the second time.

Finished, the two sheets sat before him like an odd blueprint. Achilles had tried to include everything he remembered, even the long scar on his left side that Troy never explained, the one that was stitched up like a ladder to his chest, but it wasn't enough. Those numbers and dots and dashes weren't his brother. Were he to show this sheet to someone who knew Troy, they'd have no idea who this was, this vacant-eyed cartoon. *Morse,* he wanted to say, *you don't need this, you'll know him if you see him. You'll feel his intensity, like a dog that fights to the death. You'll know my brother by his heart, fearless and light, like a rock that floats.*

Morse read the completed forms to himself, mumbling as he went, and ending with "ABM."

Achilles felt a sense of relief—he'd filed the report, even though it probably wouldn't do any good. As Morse sorted through the paper on his desk, Achilles asked about the miniature clocks on his desk.

"Big Ben," he said. "You know London, England."

"Right," said Achilles.

"Apparently there's some old British show with a detective named Morse who also likes crosswords."

"Apparently? Haven't you seen it?"

"Have you?"

"I never heard of it," said Achilles.

"So why should I? Do doctors watch *General Hospital*? Does the President watch *West Wing*?" he snapped. Before Achilles could answer, he asked, "Do you mind if I record this interview?"

"Interview?" asked Achilles. "No sir."

"Sign here." He handed Achilles another form, saying, to no one in particular, "Mr. Conroy has given his written and oral permission for the interview to be recorded. Mr. Conroy, is your brother mentally ill?"

"Where's the camera?" asked Achilles.

"Everywhere." Morse turned his palms up, exasperated. "Are you ready?"

Achilles nodded, noticing for the first time the smoky glass globes mounted on the ceiling.

"Is he mentally ill?" he repeated.

"No sir."

"Emotionally unstable?"

"No sir."

"Given to unpredictable behavior?"

"No sir."

"In dire need of medication?"

"No sir."

"Using any mood-altering prescription drugs?"

"No sir."

"Does he have a history of illegal drug use?"

"No sir."

"Do you have any reason to suspect he has been a victim of foul play?"

"No sir."

"Has he ever run away or vanished before?"

"No sir." Those three times when Troy was a teenager didn't count.

"Why'd he come to New Orleans?"

"To see friends, sir."

"Did he see them?"

"I don't know, sir."

"Where do they live?"

Exasperated by the unending questions and the fact that the officers who walked by all nodded at Morse as if Achilles didn't even exist, he shrugged.

"Verbal please."

"I don't know, sir," said Achilles,

Morse leaned back in his chair. "Under what circumstances did you last see him?"

"The night of my father's funeral, sir."

"How'd your father die?"

"Car accident."

"Sudden and unexpected?" asked Morse.

Achilles nodded.

"Verbal please."

"Yes. It was a sudden and unexpected death," said Achilles. Most of what he had seen in the last two years had been. "Yes. Very sudden. Completely unexpected."

Morse leaned forward and scribbled on a notepad. "Did you argue at the funeral?"

"No sir."

"Was there an argument about the will?"

"No sir. No will was discussed."

"Was there any discussion of an inheritance?"

"No sir."

"Is there an inheritance?"

"No sir, not that I know of. My mother still lives in the house."

Morse wrote something else on the notepad. "Is he a habitual drug user?"

"No sir. We just spent two tours in Afghanistan. We were barely able to drink, sir."

"Afghanistan. Understood." He stopped writing and his demeanor shifted. "Anything else you remember?"

"No sir."

"Any known aliases or nicknames?"

"No sir." In fifth grade, a lot of people thought Troy was Hispanic. When they found out he was black, a few kids accused him of changing his name from Tyrone. In high school, his girlfriend called him T, and the varsity squad called him TC. When they were little, Achilles called him Tick, in recognition of his tenacious grip and because he followed Achilles everywhere. The squad called Troy "the Duke," because he was cocky and gun for anything. But Achilles didn't think any of that information was helpful. And to explain why the platoon called him the Duke would make him sound foolish, when he was only reckless.

"That's it. Interview number 786x2 with Achilles Conroy completed," Morse said, and pressed the return key with a dramatic flourish. "Got a photo to go with the file? You can keep the original. We just scan it in."

After scanning the photo, Morse said, "Sorry about the verbal thing—it's policy. And those questions. Half the time the person filing the report is the one who did them in. But don't worry. If anything comes up—hospital, moving violation, anything—you'll be the third to know. So you were in Afghanistan?"

Achilles nodded, then said, "Yes sir."

Morse looked sheepish for a moment, then said, "My son is in the 130th."

"They were right up the road from us, at the ANA," said Achilles.

Morse fiddled with his pencil. "His letters say everything is okay over there. But that's what they're supposed to say, isn't it?"

"It's relatively stable," said Achilles.

"Relatively?" asked Morse.

"It's stable. It's nothing like being outside the Green Zone in Baghdad."

"Are you just saying that?"

He was, but he said, "No sir."

"You want to know what I think?"

"Yes sir."

"Well, I'm not going to tell you. I bet you don't hear that too often. I got a son over there, just like you were, and I have too much pride—in my country, in my son, in all soldiers—to trash talk." Sergeant Morse nodded vigorously as if immensely satisfied with himself. "Do you know why your brother came to New Orleans to see these friends?"

"No sir."

"You don't have to call me 'sir.' You know, sometimes people inherit money and take off to start a new life. How long has he been missing?"

"A couple of weeks. About as long as we've been back."

"And your father on top of that. That's too bad."

"Thank you, sir."

"This must be awful hard on your mom. Her boys get back safely, then her husband dies, and a son goes missing." He shook his head.

"Yes sir." He hadn't really thought about that.

"Been to the bus stations and shelters?"

"Not yet."

"There's a big new one you should try out, St. Jude." Morse looked at the Identifying Marks sheet and frowned. He waved the paper in the air and pointed at the moles. "What's this? Is this what I think it is?"

"Two moles, sir."

"Oh! Well, we better make it clear these are moles and not tattoos." He nodded and printed *MOLES!* next to the moles. His handwriting was squarish and sharp, and he pressed down so hard he tore through the paper. "Does he have diabetes or hypoglycemia or any other condition that might cause him to act in a manner that could be misconstrued as intoxicated or violent?"

"No sir."

"You look like a good kid. You know what I mean. I've been at this for thirty years. Everyone's a kid to me, even the captain there." He pointed across the room to a younger man in a suit.

Achilles wasn't offended. He understood that at twenty-two, he was a kid compared to this man.

"You're not from around here. You seem like you're from a good home. And it's noble and all, trying to find your brother and all. But missing two weeks and with no history of running away or drug use, frankly, if I can be honest, and I know a soldier wouldn't want anything less, that's a bad sign. Ominous, you might say. Around here, it's too easy for someone to walk into the shit. This city has teeth." He slowly shook his head. "The Crescent City isn't all smiles. I hate to be the crotchety old asshole to say it, but have you tried the morgue?"

Achilles left the police station huffed by hearing the same suggestion twice, the *Wanted!* photos and FBI lists catching his eye, the explicit detail of the police sketches a contrast to the Identifying Marks sheet, which he realized with a shudder was only for identifying corpses. What had Wages said? Not now. *Not now!*

When Achilles talked to his mom a couple of days later, she was upbeat, and insisted that Achilles didn't need to stay in New Orleans, that Troy would return home on his own time. Her chipper tone made it hard for Achilles to believe her. He tried sounding optimistic in response, but it felt like an unspeakable gulf was growing between them and he didn't know how to stop it. It was one thing to be quiet, but when had they agreed to pretend? Or was he only now recognizing a chasm that was always there?

He called Janice and asked her, "Does she think I'm choosing him over her? Could that be it? It's not that kind of a choice, or a choice at all. What was she choosing when she gave us those fucking envelopes? It was like throwing gas on us and handing us a cigarette. What did she think we'd do? I put mine in Wages's attic, in his trunk. I don't want any fucking thing to do with it. It's almost like saying here's your ticket, you're free to go, have fun. So weird at the funeral. You saw her. And why a preacher? I don't get it, but I can do this and be done, I can do this and be done, I can do this . . ." at that point the voice mail beeped, offering him the option of pressing one to send the message with urgent delivery, two to send it with regular delivery, or three to erase and rerecord. He pressed three and hung up.

CHAPTER 4

ACHILLES FELT HOPEFUL WHEN WEDNESDAY FINALLY ARRIVED. WAGES HAD convinced him to relax, sit tight, and enjoy himself. "Treat it like a furlough," he'd said. "The war will always be waiting." They'd mainlined, played cards, and shot pool, but it felt strange without Troy there to gloat when Achilles scratched and say "Go fuck a pumpkin" when he dropped the eight. Wages tried, pushing Achilles like a drill sergeant, insisting "Sleep is for fags!" and "The liver is a muscle and you've got to use it!" Wages was filling in for everyone else—slapping the table like Merriweather after drawing an ace; screwing up his face, pursing his lips, and pinching his eyes like Wexler after downing a shot; running his fingers through his hair like Lorenzo did when bluffing; muttering threats like Jackson, who'd almost hummed them as if he didn't really want to be heard; and, sometimes, his favorite impression: Wages himself, gargling his tequila because he loved the taste so much, just like the sick fuck he referred to as Wages, the Sick Fuck, the Generous Machine, the White Chocolate Grenade.

It was fun, but Wages was hard to keep up with. He had stamina. Achilles was relieved whenever Wages went to work and he could finally steal a few hours of sleep. He didn't bother setting an alarm, knowing Wages would wake him upon returning. On top of this, Achilles jogged daily. The poster in camp said, "Today your enemy trained to kill you. What did you do?" Everyone knew most of those goat fuckers didn't actually train. They got by because they knew the environment and they blended. But the point was well taken. So each morning, he put in five miles; a short trip, but better than nothing. His route was always the same, a run to St. Augustine to see if anyone had taken his number from the poster Levreau had placed on the bulletin board in the vestibule. That

Wednesday morning he ran hard, racing like he had wagered. When he arrived at St. Augustine, in the late afternoon a few hours before the kitchen opened, the flyer was gone. He heard someone clear his throat and turned to see Levreau, dressed as a priest.

"I took that down," said Levreau. With the black band and the bright-red chasuble flowing like a cape, he looked like a superhero towering over Achilles. But while Achilles was solid muscle, the pastor was lean, his face thin and drawn as if from worry, so much so that Achilles wasn't surprised to discover that he was a pastor. He draped his chasuble over one arm like a matador, offering, "Vespers."

Levreau sat on a nearby bench, and motioned for Achilles to sit beside him. Achilles's shoulders knotted up. He told himself to relax. Levreau again patted the bench.

"I've been praying for you and Troy," said Levreau, his voice even.

It angered him to hear Troy's name spoken with such intimacy, like Levreau and Troy were friends, like Troy had a secret life in which Achilles wasn't included, which would have to be the case for Troy to befriend a black preacher.

Levreau withdrew a flyer from a box under the bench and handed it to Achilles. It was the size of a regular sheet of paper folded in half. The front had a picture of the church. The inside listed church activities. In no mood for a sermon, Achilles stood. Levreau turned it over in his hand. Troy's photo was on the back, staring right at Achilles.

"I had that picture added to our program for tomorrow's service, so everyone will see it tomorrow. After the sermon, I'm going to tell—excuse me—ask the congregation to keep their hearts, eyes, and ears opened. We're going to pray, to implore the Lord to grant you and your brother a speedy journey home. Let us pray."

The pastor took Achilles's hand in his own and bowed his head. His hands were warm and dry, scratchy. His voice dropped, becoming barely audible, "Lord, aid this young man in his quest. Guide him on his journey to find his brother. Shower them both in your divine grace. Restore their faith in your name, as you restored Noah's. Send them their dove, Lord, the white light of hope to drive out this darkest night. Return his brother, as you returned Joseph. Bless him as you did Jacob. Protect him as you protected Job . . ."

Achilles listened. Before some missions, Jackson had gathered them into a circle and recited passages from the Bible. While everyone else hung their heads low, Achilles looked at his buddies, heard the sand crawl under their shifting feet, and wondered if they would be holding hands again in twenty-four hours. Wages furrowed his brow like he was really praying. Wexler, always sleepy, hung his head lowest of all. Merriweather, quiet only during those moments, assumed a look of concentration and shook his blockhead gently from side to side, as if listening to music. Sometimes Achilles and Troy made eye contact and struggled to contain their laughter.

Achilles certainly didn't feel like smiling now. As the pastor spoke, Achilles noticed a mole under his right eye, the shiny pate, that there was no ring on his finger. Save for a small cross, the pastor wore no jewelry at all, which Achilles found surprising. He had expected the flamboyance and dramatic sermonizing so popular on television.

Achilles felt he should say something, that he owed it to Troy to generate positive energy. What emotion should he summon? Was prayer love, submission, or begging? He felt only frustration. He tried again to focus on his brother, and he kept seeing Troy, instead of Jackson, on the side of the road, or Troy, instead of Merriweather, in the hospital bed, the sheet flat where his foot should be and a shoe with a bolt screwed into the heel sitting atop his nightstand. Opening his eyes made no improvement.

The chapel doors were ajar, and he found the color of sunlight through stained glass garish and lurid. The emaciated black Jesus looked gut-shot and glassy-eyed, closer to a corpse than a god. Levreau's voice had risen not one decibel but now seemed to come from everywhere and nowhere at once, flooding the vestibule in a river of sound. With every mention of an unknown prophet, Achilles grew more uncomfortable, fighting the urge to fidget, certain that the pastor felt in his hands the lack of faith, or would soon look up and see Achilles's empty eyes.

He pressed his lids together tightly but saw only afterimages of the church. St. Augustine resembled nothing so little as the ostentatious megachurches he'd seen on TV. The vestibule was humble, the exterior wall merely painted cinder block. The wooden bench upon which they sat was worn and weathered, as if it had only recently been brought inside, and the battered and chipped holy water font was made of formed concrete. It too appeared to have been only recently rescued from the elements, the top tarnished with a greenish ring and the base the same dingy gray as the concrete playground pad at his elementary school. The school had had a blue rocking hippopotamus screwed deep into the concrete. He and Troy would take turns sitting on the hippo while the other pulled it back as far as possible, hoping to launch the rider into the sandbox a few feet away. When they weren't doing that, they were trying to toss each other from the merry-go-round or bounce one another off the seesaw. Back then, when he was eight and Troy only six, he could win at everything and made a point of letting Troy occasionally win. Troy's handicap steadily decreased, until by ninth grade, he was nearly as tall as some seniors. Troy was tall like their father, but Achilles was short like . . . who?

A tap on his shoulder brought him back.

The pastor smiled. "Nothing refreshes like prayer." The kitchen would soon be open, and Levreau offered to let Achilles wait inside, but Achilles declined, preferring to wait across the street at Seaton's Diner, which was air-conditioned. Levreau again took Achilles's hands in his own and said, "The Lord protects all who come to him. Remember, sometimes the Lord works behind the scenes." Achilles murmured his thanks as he inched toward the door. He couldn't wait to get out of St. Augustine, back under the sun, into the buzz and babble of the street, and away from that hall, where even the acoustics spooked him; away from those high ceilings that he would have expected to swallow even a rifle report but instead made every whisper a cry.

Outside he stood on the corner, on his X, his center of the city. Across the street, two young boys in frayed cut-offs belly-crawled under the houses from one property to the next, pointing their sticks at each other and making shooting sounds. They disappeared into the yawning crawl spaces, reemerged in the narrow strip of dirt between houses, then pressed their backs to the clapboard walls and made a show of dramatically peeking around corners. One of the kids pointed his stick at Achilles. "Bang!" Achilles made a fist and extended his index finger, but he found himself unable to shoot back, his hand hanging listlessly at his side. The kid raised the stick again, this time cocking the would-be rifle butt into his shoulder, taking careful aim, and even recoiling as he said, "Bang!" Achilles raised his hand to his heart. "You got me." The kid laughed gleefully, catching a mouthful of sunlight, and ran off, bare feet slapping sizzling pavement.

Seaton's was an old diner with a greasy laminated counter overlooking the grill. Most of the crowd seemed to be regulars. They talked to each other, ignoring Achilles, except for one old man seated at the counter gumming a snow cone. From his perch he had a clear view of Achilles's window booth, and continually snuck glances at the church program. After twenty minutes of peek-a-boo, the old man slid into the booth across from Achilles. He looked to be nearly sixty. His polished walnut skin hung loosely at his neck, which was partially obscured by a long lower jaw that jutted out like a shelf. Around his eyes, his burnished skin was much darker, a dusky coal the same color as his flat pupils and sparse hair. Deep fissures branched up and across his cheeks, like the roots of an upturned tree. His leather medallion cut in the shape of Africa bounced as he moved. "Where you from?"

Achilles recoiled from the smell of sour beer, leaning as far back as possible.

The man said, "Say 'New Orleans' and I'll tell you."

"Say New Orleans?"

"It's *Nawlins*, son, *Nawlins*. You ain't from 'round here. You want to fit in here, say *Nawlins*. This is the Tremé district—famous." He pointed across the street at St. Augustine. "That church over there, famous. This diner, famous. Me? Almost famous." He extended his hand. "I'm Bud."

Achilles winced inwardly as they shook. "Achilles."

"I knew an Achilles, pronounced 'A-sheel,'" he said, gnawing at his snow cone. Red syrup dripped onto the table, cherry from the smell of it.

Achilles pushed his newspaper and the church programs to the side, placing his pencil on top of them.

"You're the young fellow looking for the young fellow on the wall over there?"

Achilles nodded. "Yes sir. My brother. You've seen him?"

"No. I just do a bit of volunteer work at some shelters and get around a bit, so I might. There a reward?"

Achilles hadn't thought about it. Did it matter what he said? A few people were already milling around on the church lawn. Troy would arrive soon. "Sure."

"How much?"

Achilles didn't have much money on him, maybe two hundred dollars. He took in Bud's torn and faded T-shirt, the dingy towel bunched around his neck like an ascot, the shoestring holding the African medallion around his neck. He recalled the barefoot kids in the cut-off jeans and the families he'd seen. "A hundred?"

Bud smiled. "What's his name?"

"Troy."

"Nice pen," said Bud.

"Pencil. It's a mechanical pencil." His father had given it to him as a high school graduation gift. "It was my father's."

"A mechanical pencil. How about that. A pencil that is mechanical." Bud rubbed his long jaw. "How old are you, son?"

"Twenty-two."

Nodding as if it all made sense now, his gaze focused on the pencil, Bud asked, "Can I keep that flyer with the picture?"

"Sure." Achilles slid him the program.

Bud pointed to the number on the bottom. "This number good?"

Achilles tapped his cell phone, "I'm always here."

"I'm Bud. I'll get back with you."

He gave Achilles one last look and limped off. He didn't bend his left leg at all, and he bobbed to the side with each step as if the right leg was significantly longer. Merriweather had had a similar walk in the hospital. Even though his prosthetic was customized so that his legs were even, he stepped gingerly on his left leg, as if he didn't trust it to hold his weight, as if steel weren't so much terribly stronger than bone. Bud was about the right age for a Vietnam or Korea vet. Watching him hobble off, Achilles decided that maybe he wasn't so bad after all.

Wages had promised to stop by St. Augustine to keep Achilles company during the wait. The bus he took home every day passed right by the church, which was how he'd seen Troy in the first place. When Wages got off the bus that evening, everyone looked at the white guy in the black suit like he was lost. A couple of young guys Achilles hadn't noticed before immediately materialized, emerging from the cubbies between cars and trees, and spoke to Wages using a series of brief head gestures and hand signs that flashed too fast for Achilles to understand. Wages answered in kind. One kid in an oversized white T-shirt and denim shorts that came down to his ankles was particularly insistent. He gestured violently toward Wages, waving his hand like he'd burned his fingers, stepping closer with each wave of the hand, backing off only when it became clear Wages wouldn't. Achilles realized he was gripping the table and went outside to meet Wages.

"What was that about?" Achilles asked.

"You know. Ain't no window-shopping here." Wages laughed. "Dude just wants to know what I'm doing in the store if I ain't buying. The usual, you know."

"Yeah," said Achilles. With the fancy suit and nice shoes, Achilles would have assumed Wages was there to help the church. The only thing missing from that nice, clean jacket was a crucifix pinned to the lapel. He would never have thought Wages was interested in anything they sold here. Just look at them and look at him.

Of the hundred or so people who were now lined up around the block an hour before the kitchen even opened, only a dozen or so were white. White or black, they all wore scruffy, ill-fitting clothes, but the groups were distinctly different. One white man wore a funny suit that upon closer inspection proved to be a jumpsuit cut into two separate pieces, the top cropped so short he resembled a crazed mariachi player. That was the difference: the blacks looked poor, but the whites looked poor and crazy. Some of the icy aggravation Achilles felt about his brother's selfish decision melted into a sympathy that tingled, the way his fingers did while thawing out from a deep cold. His throat constricted at the thought of Troy in this line learning that one of these men was his real father. He tried to imagine a resemblance between Troy and some of the men but couldn't see it. For the first time it occurred to him that his brother might need him.

Achilles and Wages walked up and down the line to kill time. Some men wore authentic GI, but most pieces looked to have come from flea markets or army surplus stores, as they were too old or too new for the people wearing them. Wages counted the number of men dressed in fake camouflage, pointing out camo T-shirts, camo head wraps, camo sneakers, and even camo baseball caps. Though he understood and appreciated Wages's attempts to distract him, it wasn't too long before Achilles lost count as he silently, involuntarily, compared every face to Troy's.

Two older men wearing ragged army coats that could have been their own straightened when Wages and Achilles approached, their tones hushed and heads straight ahead, as if for inspection. He couldn't understand how so many of them wore jackets and coats in the heat. As they passed an old man in a jungle jacket, Achilles wondered, *Where are his friends?* How did someone become so separated from his tribe? If he had any friends, surely he wouldn't be in those worn boots and frayed jacket, in that line, in this neighborhood. The older men in the ragged army coats laughed, a few others chimed in. They had nothing to worry about, just show up and eat.

The block transformed during the twilight hours. The guard changed at the corners as the old surrendered their spots to the young, who were armed with more than beer cans and branches. Mothers called their children, who ducked conspicuously behind their friends. Volleys of catcalls were met with coos and curled fingers. Sullen figures darted into alleys, sauntering out minutes later with blazing smiles. Foreign cars big as boats docked long enough to exchange currency with skulking teens swimming in oversized black hoodies. Wages mumbled, "Who says you can't buy happiness?"

The sun had set by the time the last person was fed. The copper dome on the church's bell tower, verdigris by day, had turned crimson, then magenta, and finally black. The neon sign at the café across the street popped on. SEATON's flashed a red-letter warning. One of the few working streetlights buzzed overhead, spotlighting Achilles, who didn't know what to do next. He'd stared at people as if looking at them hard enough could transform them into someone they weren't. He had hoped, even believed, that Troy would show up. He had believed. He had. It was only a week since Wages had seen Troy, so it was natural for him to be hopeful, right? It was only fair; it wasn't weak or naïve, *Was it?* A silhouette turned the corner at the far end of the block, running toward them at a rapid pace. Achilles recalled the buoyant mood that had possessed him earlier on his own jog to the church, and felt foolish to have let hope get the best of him. As he watched the jogger approach, his loping stride not unlike Troy's, Achilles refused to believe it might be his brother, and turned away. He heard the footsteps slow to a walk as the man neared, holding his breath as he monitored Wages's eyes for a spark of recognition.

Wages looked down and said, "There's a fight on tonight."

Achilles sucked air.

The latecomer yanked at the church door. "Hope it's not too late."

Wages snapped his fingers in the air in front of Achilles. "Quarter? Better yet, I have all the southern comforts at home. I have Jim."

Drinking the night down would only depress him. Achilles wanted to be alone, to be anywhere except on that couch with a hundred pictures of Wages and Bethany smiling down on him, witnessing his private grief. Prayer hadn't helped. What was he doing wrong?

The latecomer charged out, his stride victorious, holding a foam container aloft. "God is good." He sat on the thin lawn at the edge of the circle of light, his back resting against the church, feet splayed out, sockless. Opening the container, he sniffed the mound of spaghetti and slice of white bread and smiled, nodding happily. The smile faded as he patted his pockets and poked at the food. He shrugged, and with two fingers began hurriedly scooping the pasta into his mouth, hunched over, holding the container close to his gut, one arm defensively curled around the food.

Wages poked Achilles in the arm and said, "I have Jack. Think about that." He spun on his heels and went into the church.

Achilles thought about asking the man if he knew Troy, but changed his mind as he watched him dig his chin into his chest to slurp at a spot of sauce on his shirt. He was looking in the wrong place. What was he going to tell his mother? He'd said today was the day. For a moment he was transfixed by the image of her eyes, the thought of her alone in the house, most of the neighbors she once knew gone, all having sold out to the young DC commuters who thought Mrs. Conroy quaint with her slight Southern accent and vegetable garden.

Wages returned with a plastic fork. Before accepting it, the man regarded the utensil with suspicion, then surprise, then gratefulness, holding Wages's eyes with his own, which were as deep with gratitude as if Wages had pulled him out of a raging river. He licked the fingers he had been eating with and wiped them on his pants. He shifted nearer to them, into the light. Scooting back so his butt was against the wall, he sat up straight with his arms at his sides and chest up, then crossed himself, brushed at his lap and, fork in hand, began to eat again, this time slowly savoring each bite. Humming, the man looked up and noticed Achilles watching. Licking his fork like a lollipop, he extended the container, making a motion to share. Achilles shook his head and turned to Wages. This was Wages the starfish. Achilles almost felt as if his friend had performed a miracle, but he didn't understand why he felt that way. He was confused, but as proud and as full of admiration as he had been when Wages scurried out to the middle of Bi'hah Road to drag Merriweather back to safety, ignoring the sharp, hot whistles in the air and the small craters trailing him. He was equally afraid that, once again, he could not have seen fit to do the same thing, that if it had been up to him, Merriweather would have lost more than a foot. Achilles was not valiant.

But Wages wasn't perfect either, he reminded himself. It was always Wages nipping at the bottle and keeping Achilles up, and complaining about Bethany but never confronting her.

Wages grinned and said, "I have Mark tucked away in the attic, in the trunk with your shit. You know I can't let Nee-Nee see the pricey shit."

Achilles's mouth watered at the thought of the soothing burn of the murky, caramel liquor. He could feel the searing that started in his gut and worked its way out through his body until he felt light as a balloon. He was on the verge of agreeing to swallow the night when someone in a yellow do-rag and orange safety vest started yelling and waving at them from across the street. Achilles recognized the bouncing Africa medallion as Bud flung himself into the street, hobbling and hopping through the traffic, ignoring the horns. The rims of his eyes were red, the whites yellow.

Sweating, panting, heaving as though the mere act of crossing the street had exhausted him, he spoke in sharp bursts, "You said . . . you . . . was always there! Waited . . . for you . . . three hours! You said . . . always there!"

"I meant here," Achilles tapped his cell phone.

Bud frowned. "Man it's . . . too hot for games. Too hot for games." He motioned for Achilles to step a few feet away, and, eyeing Wages suspiciously, whispered, "Who's he?"

"What's up with the vest?" asked Wages.

"Safety first at my age," said Bud, then to Achilles again, "Who's he?"

Achilles made a noncommittal gesture with his hand. "You've seen Troy?"

"You think I'm Stevie Wonder? I just called to say I love you?" When Achilles didn't return the smile, Bud said, "I wouldn't come if I didn't know some-some. One hundred fifty bucks. Can you do it or not?"

"That's not what I said," said Achilles.

"Yes or no?" asked Bud.

"Of course. But, you've seen him?" Achilles voice was shaking. "How long ago?"

"Yes or no?" asked Bud.

"Yes," Achilles said, almost yelling.

Wages stepped closer.

"Just a few hours ago." Bud looked down, but cut his eyes in Wages's direction. "He can't come where we're going."

Achilles nodded. "Okay."

"And I can't go in with you. They'll think I'm telling on people. So you go in alone. Alone, you hear? We drive by. I point it out. You drop me off 'round the corner. You go back and handle your business. And don't mention my name. Roger?"

"Okay," said Achilles.

"Okay then. Ten-four, like those truckers say. I used to be one."

"Let's do it," said Wages.

Bud shook his head. "No way. Can't do that. He'll be snow in August. I'll just come back." Bud backed away.

"Wait!" said Achilles. He turned to Wages. "It's cool. I know this guy from the church. This'll be just a few minutes, then we'll all meet back at your place."

Wages studied Bud. The Africa medallion bounced off his chest as Bud hopped from foot to foot. "I don't like it," he said.

"I don't like it," said Bud.

They each spoke as if the other wasn't there.

"He's from the church. It'll be cool," said Achilles, adding under his breath, "I can handle this. Look at him."

Wages relented.

"We'll be there in no time. I know this city like a pair of titties," said Bud as soon as he was in Achilles's car. If it was possible, Bud's breath was even worse than it had been in the diner. A humid mixture of onion and tooth decay flooded the car with every word. Achilles, who thought himself immune to smells, rolled down all the windows, which meant no AC. He floored it from corner to corner, red lights becoming stop signs, to force fresh air through the car, but he couldn't expel the odor of stale beer and sweat, like an old bar, an odor that intensified with every wave of Bud's arm. His funk was a larger body, a suit that pressed against Achilles, but what angered him was that it was unnecessary. This was America, land of running water and toothbrushes. Oblivious, Bud talked constantly, either giving directions or playing the part of the tour guide. He talked about Tremé and Storyville, the old red-light district, and Algiers, carnivals and krewes, ending each story with, "That's right. I know this city like a pair of titties."

Achilles nodded, not really listening.

"And I knows titties; snake charmers I call them. You better believe my snake's done a lot of charming, too. I been here since the Mississippi was born, know that? I seen it all. Lived through the big one, Betsy. That was a hell of a hurricane, old Betsy, biggest we ever had. Pray they'll never be another, but that was water off a duck's back. Now, I knew a *woman* named Betsy—three in fact—but this one in particular damned near killed me. Damn sure nearly did." His head drifted up in thought. "She was a looker, she was. Crazy, though, straight crazy. I wrote a song about her. You know John Lee Hooker? Took it. Sure did. "Whiskey and Wimmen." That was it. I was singing that damn song—turn left here—in a truck stop in Florida. His thieving ass heard me. Took my idea. When he come out with 'Serves Me Right to Suffer,' I said, 'Hell yeah it do!' But, I don't hold a grudge. Nope. Don't hold no grudges. That's one thing I like about me. Oh yeah, you know how it goes don't ya?" Bud hummed a few bars, then broke into song. *"Whiskey and women, almost wrecked my life, almost wrecked my life. Wasn't for whiskey and women, I'd have money today. Nightlife, nightlife ain't no good, ain't no good for me. I made a good start, but women and whiskey tore it down."*

By that point they had traveled beyond the neighborhood Achilles knew. "How much farther?"

Bud pointed straight ahead. "You ain't got long now."

Achilles focused on breathing. He imagined what he would say to Troy. First they would eat, then go to Wages's and hang out with Mark, Jack, and Jim. Wages said he'd have a third mug in the freezer. They'd call their mom. Maybe they'd go home for a few weeks. He imagines it clearly.

When he sees his brother, he is shocked. Troy is thin, thinner than the end of infantry school, during which, some days, it seemed they lived off naps and gnats. But he's still strong, and his embrace, as always, is suffocating and before tears can rise to Achilles's eyes, Troy does what Troy always does, takes advantage of his height by digging his chin into Achilles's shoulder. In retaliation, Achilles digs his fingers into Troy's biceps, and for a moment they grapple as they have since childhood. He wasn't too late. He feels the rush that comes from being shot at—and missed. Nervous energy animates his limbs, his fingers twitch, but he is conscious of being lucky to be alive, appreciative the way he couldn't be the day he first met Troy. They promised to look out for each other, and he was doing it.

He couldn't wait, nodding absentmindedly as Bud broke into song again. "Oh yeah, that was mine." He hit an air guitar. "That was it," said Bud. "The sweet spot."

"Nice song." It was. Bud's voice was rough, but perfect for the blues. He had a timbre similar to Father Levreau. They inspired trust. They couldn't be more different from each other or anyone else Achilles knew. Who would have thought that two strangers like these men would have such a major role in his life? Until this week, Achilles had never been close to a homeless person. There were the Afghan refugees, some by his own doing, of course, but they didn't count. Refugees had been removed from homes or displaced. Refugees would prefer to have homes. He shot a glance at Bud, his long chin wobbling and knobby fingers playing an invisible piano. Grinning, he had sung all the way. Bud turned and their eyes met, and he blinked once, slowly, like he understood the connection too.

"No." Bud threw his thumb over his shoulder. "That was it. We just passed the sweet spot. You give me the money. I tell you which house it is."

Achilles scanned the block. He had been distracted and lost track of where he was. Bud tapped his palm as Achilles counted out eight twenties. Achilles put two of the bills in Bud's palm and held the others, as if weighing them. Bud tapped his palm again. "Don't stop now."

Achilles shifted to look behind him. He had that feeling like water was in his ear. His breath came in short, shallow puffs, his heart thumped, his limbs throbbed with each flood of blood, his entire body expanding and contracting with every inhalation. *Focus.* "How do I know it's the right house?"

"I don't know you either," said Bud.

"Half now, half later."

Bud handed the money back to Achilles. "You come get me when you're ready to do business."

"I want to, but . . . He better be here." He removed the keys from the ignition in case Bud tried to run, balling his hands into fists, only somewhat reassured by Bud's steady, confident demeanor. Bud was now staring directly at him, as if this was the most important conversation he'd ever had.

"He here, hand to God." Bud touched the roof of the cab. "But, that's not the question. The question is, is you a man of your word or not?"

"Of course. My father always said a man's word is his only honor."

"You keep your promises?" asked Bud.

The question wasn't, *What if he's lying?* It was, *What if he's not?* Achilles handed him the money.

"Your father would be proud," said Bud. "Who is it anyway? Owe you money? Stole something?"

"My brother."

Bud folded the money into his pocket and opened the door. "Brother, huh? Ain't we all?"

"No!"

Bud shrank back like Achilles was spitting venom. "You must want to find him bad. Turn around, go back two blocks, look at the green camel-back on the left."

"Camelback?"

"A house with a half top floor, like a hump in the back, like a camel. Don't you know a camel, son?" With that he shut the door and gimped across the street, saying over his shoulder, "Another few years that truck will be a classic."

As Achilles made a u-turn, Bud gave him a thumbs-up and mouthed, "Good luck." Achilles considered giving the old man a love tap with the bumper and taking the money back.

CHAPTER 5

ACHILLES CIRCLED THE BLOCK A FEW TIMES BEFORE HE SAW A CAMELBACK that looked nearly green. He parked two streets away, flipped off the overhead light so it wouldn't come on when he opened the door, and walked to the house. The homes on either side of it were boarded up. Like Wages's home it was a duplex, so he knocked on both doors. No one answered. He knocked again. Still no response. Cursing his naiveté, he walked through the narrow passage between the houses, his shoulders nearly grazing the walls, glass crackling underfoot. The backyard was a concrete pad littered with fifty-gallon barrels. Achilles picked his way around the barrels, knocked on the back door, and, out of habit, stepped aside. A voice called, "What?"

Achilles identified himself.

A sleepy-eyed teen with a squat neck and a boxhead opened the door a crack. He wore a fake camouflage shirt under a black hoodie, and the edge of his cigarette was blackened as if lit by an unsteady hand. "Who you?"

"I'm here for my brother, Troy," Achilles held up a church program.

"St. Augustine?"

Achilles flipped the brochure over so the kid could see Troy's face.

The teen said, "Hold on."

Achilles put his foot against the door.

"Hey man, move your foot." Another voice asked who it was. The teen's face vanished inside the door as he said, "Some guy looking for his brother."

The other voice said, "Let him in."

"Lex say okay." The teen opened the door, regarding Achilles's foot like an uninvited animal.

A stratus of smoke floated between the bare bulb in the ceiling and the kitchen table, which was cluttered with forty-ounce bottles and half-full take-out containers. Lex, seated at the table, looked to be about thirty. His wide-set eyes were perfectly round, like egg whites in a cast-iron skillet, and he had stars cut into the side of his fade. His most prominent feature was his nose, almost as broad as his lips, larger even than Merri's nose, about which Merri himself always said, "I can smell what they're cooking for dinner tomorrow." Lex had cleared an area of the table upon which his bare feet were propped. He looked at Achilles just long enough to assure himself Achilles wasn't a threat, then returned his attention to a callous on his big toe.

Achilles nodded to him, relieved. For a moment he thought he'd been suckered. "Thanks."

The clipper clicked. Lex carefully folded it up and placed it on the table. Rubbing his hands together, he said, "Gimme that paper cut."

"What?" asked Achilles.

"Pay me, zigga." Lex wiped his finger across the table, then inspected it, like he was checking for dust.

"What?" Achilles bristled. He'd never been called zigga before except by Merriweather, and he seldom used it, sensing that Achilles didn't wear it well.

"The mint," said Lex.

"The mint," echoed the teen.

"The mint?" asked Achilles.

"Don't give me that Schlitz. You from Nebraska? You know! Mint, seed, scratch, pocket pussy," said Lex. "The ghetto passport. *Monay!*"

"I already paid." Achilles motioned with his thumb as if Bud was behind him.

"What, zigga? You already gave at the office or some shit? You think this a charity? You think Sally Struthers gonna stroll in here with some bobble-headed African negro on her tit and just hand the little mother-fucker over to you? Nothing here is free. This is a commercial enterprise."

"Like the spaceship," added the teen.

"What do you want?"

"What you got?"

"Maybe forty." He had given the rest of his cash to Bud, whom he'd promised not to mention.

"Forty." Lex laughed. "That won't pay cable. How I'm supposed to get my C-SPAN and ESPN off forty? What else you got? What's that you keep touching at your neck? That or that watch." He ran his fingers across the table again.

Achilles cursed himself for touching his throat like a little girl. He could get another watch, but his mother gave him the locket the morning he shipped out. The teen stepped closer, pausing when Achilles reached into his pocket. He pulled out his mechanical pencil. "This is antique. It's worth over a hundred dollars."

Lex and the kid laughed.

"It look like this shit pertain to written correspondence?" Lex said, "Clark Kent—looking zigga tried to give me a pencil. Like I'm gonna write somebody. Take that shit to the Jew. Someone's gotta pay."

Achilles felt claustrophobic. The kitchen was barely five feet across, and the door swung in, so he couldn't open it without moving closer to the teen in the hoodie. The table was directly in front of him, so he couldn't go deeper into the house without going around Lex. He handed Lex his watch and forty dollars.

"Took you long enough. Through the next room, stairs are on the right. Blow, show him."

"Thank you. We'll be out of here immediately," said Achilles.

"Whatever." Lex had returned his attention to his manicure. A nail clipping pinged off a beer bottle.

Blow cocked his head for Achilles to follow. The teen stomped more than walked, slapping his feet as if he wanted to sound larger than he was. Achilles followed him through the next room, which was cluttered with debris and candy boxes, to the bottom of the stairs. Blow called, "Yo, Black! Yo, Big Man! He here."

Big Man. Slim. Shorty. Son. Boo. Black people had so much slang, so many terms of endearment for people they didn't know. They addressed strangers as if they'd been friends forever. Jackson, from New York, had called everybody Son, and it made people smile. Wexler called everybody Chief, and it had the same reaction. And everybody meant every-single-thing. The convoy delayed by a herd of sheep at the gate: Merri said, *Check out these ziggas.* Jackson had leaned out the window to advise a straggler, *Alright, son, you gonna hit that spit if you don't speed it up.* Wexler, hitting the horn, added, *You heard him, Chief.*

"Might be sleep," said Blow with a shrug. He tried again, calling louder, "Yo Tony, your man is here."

"Troy, his name is Troy."

"Right. Big Man! Yo!" When there was no answer, Blow shrugged and flipped the switch, but the light didn't come on. "You can go up." He gestured for Achilles to go upstairs, leaning against the wall like a ferryman who wanted to dock for the night, shrugging as if he'd already made the trip too many times that day. "Yo, Tony!"

Achilles looked back at Blow, who was already turning away, and spoke into the darkness, "Troy!"

It felt like a river was bearing his body downstream to a raging waterfall, and Achilles could do nothing to stop it. Was it because Blow said Tony? Was it because the top light was conveniently out, so the staircase faded into darkness? Was it because the entire time he'd been in the house, he hadn't heard any noise upstairs? Was it because Bud had refused to come? Was it because Blow walked like he was warning someone he was coming? For some reason Achilles had that familiar feeling like being underwater, like someone had pressed the mute button. Blow speaks, but nothing comes out, as if he's talking into the wind. Achilles's body is backing up the stairs, turning away from Blow even as his mind says, *Leave! Now!* Retrace your steps and leave before you go over the edge. But Achilles climbs on. He's caught in the current.

A thud. The first blow surprises him. It always does, setting off a reaction he can see but can't stop, like being drunk and driven to do something foolish that even as you begin you know will end badly. The base of his skull and jaw rattle and he crouches and waits for the gravel and debris to stop raining down on his helmet, because that's what you do. You wait. You hesitate. You hesitate to open your eyes in case there's another blast. Like now. You hesitate to open your eyes in case there's something you don't want to see. So you wait. Wait for the rocks to stop rolling, for your helmet to stop clattering. You paw your face. All there. You wiggle your fingers and toes. All there. You run your tongue across your teeth. All there. Then when it's quiet, all you hear is the throb in your own head, the blood siphoning in your temples, and the distant yelling like now, *Give it up motherfucker*, you call them. You scream their names when it settles down. But the blows keep coming, the helmet keeps rattling. It isn't settling down, and Achilles has to know, he has to, so he calls out, even though they might not hear, he calls out, *Troy, Wages, Wexler, Merriweather, Jackson!* No answer. Again, *Troy, Wages, Wexler, Merri, Jackie!* No answer. Then just *Troy!* The only answer a laugh and another strike to the side of the face, and another, and another, and a kick, the way his father kicked. His father's kicks were precise and snappy, like his foot was the brick at the end of a long chain aimed at Achilles's mouth. But this is different, this is "nothing personal," as Blow is saying at the moment Achilles loses his hearing.

It lasts less than a minute but feels like a marathon. Achilles instinctively tucks his chin into his chest and pulls his elbows in like wings to protect his ribs. Blow leans against the wall, balancing on one foot and the other kicks and kicks. Straight leg kicks. From a distance, it probably looked like he was warming up for a soccer match or carving a rut in soft earth. The kicks land on Achilles's back and legs and the side of his head. One finds his stomach, and his breath rushes out in a whistle.

Just as Achilles manages to grab Blow's leg, Lex puts Achilles in a chokehold and jerks him up to a standing position. "Just relax."

Achilles turns his head just slightly to the side, nuzzling his chin into the crook of Lex's arm until he can breath, relaxing to save oxygen. Lex says, "That's right. Don't fight it."

Frantically, spastically, like a scorned woman, Blow slaps and claws at Achilles's neck until the locket breaks off, the loose chain snaking down to Achilles's waistband, the cool metal locket skipping down his chest. Achilles kicks him away and Blow comes back jabbing and kicking, swinging in wild arcs like he's swatting bees. The sound, like slapping a steak on cement, is more shocking then the actual impact of the punches landing on Achilles's face and neck. Achilles kicks Blow in the groin and when Blow bows to the pain, Achilles boots him in the face.

"Hush now. Shhhhh," croons Lex, digging his chin into Achilles's neck, snug as a lover. "It's just like going to sleep. It's faster if you don't fight it. It's only a little nap."

Knowing the occipital lobe is much harder than the nose, Achilles slams the back of his head into Lex's face.

The choke holds.

Achilles rears his head back again and again, his own teeth rattling each time he connects with Lex's chin. In his peripheral vision, Achilles sees blood sprinkle the flowered wallpaper as Lex swings his head from side to side to protect his face. It's a pretty pattern, red roses and gold thorns. The paper is thick, like felt, and the blood sits on the top like little orbs, like Red Hots. Achilles keeps trying. Finally he hears a crunch as he catches Lex's nose just right.

The choke holds, but Lex curses, his voice nasal, "Motherfucker!"

They fall onto the stairs, onto Blow, who bites Achilles's thigh. All three of them now pile at the bottom of the stairway. Lex shakes Achilles, and the locket slips to the floor.

Blow slips the locket into his pocket, and staggers triumphantly to his feet, standing with hands on hips, panting, leaning forward with each exhalation like he's breathing fire. He stomps on Achilles's stomach. Achilles swallows hard against the vomit bubbling up his throat. Blow makes a cutting motion in the air, like he's feeling his way through heavy curtains on a dark stage. Is that a knife in Blow's hand? Sweat, or blood, stings Achilles's eyes. Blow's face hovers there, and before grabbing the hand with the knife, Achilles sees that Blow has near-perfect teeth, like his parents always got him to the dentist, a slightly oily forehead splotchy with acne, that faint teenage mustache, a left eye slightly larger than the right, a ring that says Washington High. Achilles grabs the hand with the knife, finds the pinkie, and bends it back until it snaps, then the ring finger. Snap. Then the middle. Snap. Blow drops the knife and cries, "Shit!" backing into the corner, clutching his injured hand to his chest, cradling it like a bird.

Lex pushes with his legs, pulling Achilles up the stairs as he twists Achilles's head sharply to the side. Achilles claws weakly overhead at Lex's face. He was never good at getting out of headlocks; Sgt. Click always teased him about that in basic training. He could see the drill sergeant now, pacing back and forth in his t-shirt and creased BDUs, taunting Achilles. "Don't be a sissy, Connie. Don't panic. It feels like forever, but it's only been thirty seconds, and you can hold your breath for sixty. Don't panic. Release a little air to let out carbon dioxide so your body doesn't panic."

There's movement above him. He's sure of it this time. *Troy?* At the top of the stairs the darkness unfolds as shadow ripples over shadow like an undercurrent. He pushes upstairs, toward that movement, even as Lex squeezes tighter.

The pinch in Achilles's neck is sharp as a pin through the eardrum, hot enough to make him emit one high cry, "Troy!"

He sees his mom in her backpack, in his room, surrounded by boxes, stacks of paper, and those old *Playboys* he never threw away.

Pain gallops down his spine, running in spikes, leaving a trail of fire that's doused by the sensation of cold oil rising up his back the way it climbs a wick, the dark tide fingering his limbs until they're heavy, as if he's wading through a marsh. His legs twitch, his arms jerk involuntarily, his fists and feet knocking holes in the sheetrock. A cloud of white dust settles on his face and his body convulses, wanting to sneeze. With each beat of his heart, he feels he'll explode, his lungs grating, his skin straining like it's two sizes too small, his entire body growing taut as if overinflated, his head heavy, filled with water. The tingling in his limbs passes to burning then blistering then warm. They are almost to the top of the stairs. His eyes adjust. On the landing, wearing a Saints cap, leaning casually in the corner like a referee, a coat rack watches over them. Relaxed, Achilles pisses himself.

"Shit!" Lex shifts. Achilles finds air.

Come on, Connie. God hates a coward. Achilles reaches overhead, grabs one of Lex's ears with one hand, pulls out his mechanical pencil with the other, and stabs overhead three quick times. The first blow bucks off Lex's forehead, the second glances off the side, hitting the carpet. The third finds the eye, soft and wet. Achilles feels a primordial cry—mournful and panicked—travel up the big man's chest and clatter in his throat.

The chokehold breaks.

His voice dry and chiseled with fear, Lex whispers, "Arnold, help."

Lex crab-walks up the stairs. Achilles struggles to his feet, holding the wall for support. Blow shrinks deeper into the corner, pressing his back tight against the wall, that squat neck all but disappearing as he drops to his haunches, tucks his bad hand under his arm, and waves his good arm like a white flag. Achilles kneels before Blow and calmly extends his hand, palm up, holding it there until Blow returns his necklace. When he does, Achilles first pockets his locket, then throws Blow to the floor, forcing him onto his back, kneeling on his chest, choking and punching, slamming Blow's head against the floor until the dry thuds become wet. Blow's face contorts with each blow, the web of red spit stretching across his lips and breaking just as panic passes into shock. He looks as if this is the first time he's lost a fight, as if Achilles popped his cherry.

He is Bud, Lex, the shiftless kid in the Afro waving wildly at Wages. He is the teens hanging on the corners in southwest DC, drug dealers, death dealers. The man who mugged Achilles and his mom. Men who think that fucking makes fatherhood.

He is the other Achilles.

Face blank and black as a TV that has lost its signal, Blow writhes and coils, his limbs twitching as if electrified. And, and squeezing, and the other Achilles keeps squeezing, squeezing so tightly Blow's skin presses through his fingers like dough; squeezing until Blow, in his panic, bites the tip off his tongue; until Blow's movements are weak and dreamy; until his twitching is only an occasional jerk, like a lazy swimmer barely staying afloat; until his eyes bulge and his pupils zoom out and a shroud of calm seals his face and even his acne scars smooth out, and he stops crying, and even Achilles, finally satisfied, has stopped breathing.

He hears a shot. Lex stands at the top of the stairs, waving a pistol, his left eyelid curled around the mechanical pencil that pins it shut.

"Daddy, he's killed me," whispers Blow.

Lex fires again. Achilles scrambles out of the stairwell, down the hall, and through the back door. He runs down the alley, away from the car, and doesn't stop until he's sure he isn't being followed, by which point he is lost, wandering one dark unnamed street after another.

His stinging eyes made stars of the streetlights. He tried blotting his face with his shirt, but that didn't staunch the flow. He knew that head wounds bleed easily, so he wasn't worried by the blood or the bruises. When he stopped to study his reflection in the window of a rim shop, his head was framed in faint silver. But he deserved no halo. He had cut and ran. His shirt was sticking to his back like a wet rag. In the distance, blinking red and yellow lights. He limped down the deserted street in the direction of the neon oasis, a Kikkin Chikkin. Chikkin indeed sounded Kikkin, *Praise Jesus*. He pushed the door open. A blast of cold air. A golden bell jangled. Time for school, Sunday school, *Praise Jesus*. The security guard, hands out as if he were afraid to touch Achilles, escorted him back outside before he could get to the bathroom. He promised to buy something, offered to pay first, but the guard pushed him out. "Not like that you don't. You could infect somebody. No one wants to eat around you looking like that. Go on now. Get." The guard had the same New Orleans accent as Bud and Lex and Blow: "gone" instead of "go on," "git" for "get."

Achilles stood at the door. A woman at the counter ordered a large bucket of chicken, half mild and half kikken, all dark meat, a dozen biscuits, macaroni on the side, and a few of those peppers. Orange or red? She couldn't decide on the drink. Achilles drooled. The scent of fried chicken was strong now. The guard stood in the doorway, flanked by two friends, the smells and cool air wafting around them.

"Orange," the woman at the counter said, flipping her hair. "Large orange drink." She pronounced it "erenge." She wore a shiny black sleeveless shirt and her bra straps hung by her armpits. Handprints were painted across the back of her jeans, one on each cheek. She was dark-skinned with platinum dreads, heavy in the legs and ass. The last thing she needed was fried chicken. She was about one two-piece dinner away from the rip-cord being pulled on her raft. Merriweather would've liked her, being a thigh man. Achilles usually preferred drumsticks, and wasn't into women like her, but between the arch in her back and her manner of sashaying even as she stood, his gaze was drawn back to her again and again. She was scrappy, spunky, but he could easily see her kneeling, hunched over with her head to the floor as if praying to Allah, naked, slathered in Crisco, with an apple jammed in her mouth like a gag ball.

"Go on now." The guard pointed down the street. "Go on, zigga, get."

Hearing *zigga* again, Achilles felt loose-limbed, like he could jump on this kid and bite his fucking nose off, and if the kid hadn't had a gun, he might've done it. But who was he fooling? Last time he was faced with a gun, he'd run, and run some more. "Fuck you, zigga. Zigga," said Achilles, his mouth burning with the word. He waited for a reaction, refusing to back down twice in the same night. He knew he should let it go, but he didn't. This was why they always took turns being first through the door. Every contact—even peaceful ones—got them pumped up, and if you were first through the door twice in a row, you were liable to shoot somebody just because it felt like it was time to. "Yeah, zigga. Fuck you." He spat.

For a moment there was nothing to hear but the air vents and the fryer and the beeping cash register. All else had stopped, as if, as Achilles had always expected, that word was an irrevocable curse, a chant calling for destruction.

"You still here?" The guard shrugged. "Fuck you too, zigga."

And that was it. He'd used the word for the first time, *against another person*. Achilles had expected more. Anger, acknowledgement, maybe even fear, yes, fear, because for Achilles to use that word he had to be serious, dead serious.

Asked if her order was to eat in or take out, the lady at the counter popped her neck and said, "Zigga, I look like I can eat all that?" drawing the guard's attention.

The cashier yelled, "Bitch, I don't know your life!"

Achilles turned and walked away. Behind him, someone said, "Nawww! Let that zigga go. Something wrong with him, all bugged out and shit, all fly-eyed. He might even have the virus."

"Look at him, thumping his chest like a dumb monkey."

Achilles hadn't realized he was automatically reaching for his weapon sling, expecting it to be there to guide his thumb down to the butt of his machine gun. Two weeks ago, they'd all have had a boot on their backs and a steel circle in the base of their necks, except the one with the gun. Wages might already have shot him. Achilles turned to go.

"See him walking? He can't even return his serve."

"Clark Kent–looking zigga."

"Erenge" soda, pants drooping, oversized shirts. He wouldn't have fit in even if he hadn't been bloody. He didn't belong in there anyway, eating nasty, cholesterol-laden ghetto food. Halfway down the block, Achilles turned back to face them and screamed, "Bitch, you don't know my life!"

But they couldn't hear him. All three were inside, sliding into a booth. The one who sat alone facing the others scooted all the way to the inside of the bench, as if he was making space for someone. They laughed and dapped, slapping hands front and back. They were roughly the same height, all of their heads long and peaked at the top, their eyes round and deep-set, so much so that he wondered if they even had to use their hands to shield them from the sun. They had the same rawboned cheeks and satchel mouths. They weren't friends. They were brothers, the ziggas.

Who was a zigga? Was he the bobble-headed, loose-lipped brother posted up on the corner eating fried rice from a paper cup? The lifer who converted to Islam, finding in prison a newfound sense of security? Was it reserved for men, hulking, shifty, flitty-eyed simian males? Or was it the woman working the alley behind the head shop who started out cute, who blushed when her pimp complimented her bone structure, who lost fifteen pounds and three incisors in two months? Was it the elderly housekeeper, unless, of course, she was your housekeeper? Was it reserved for the servile and chimp-lipped? Or could white people really be ziggas, as Achilles had so often heard? Was it simply reserved for the fringe, those night eaters the mayor once referred to as soap scum because "They live at the edge of society and, ironically, the harder you clean, the more there are"? Or could it really be the first black executive of a major bank? What about Wesley Snipes? When he'd packed his bags for basic, Achilles would have said none of the above. Merriweather said *all*.

Ziggas! Zigger? Zigga. To form the word, the tongue curls up, then out, like it's releasing a burning seed. In Goddamnistan, kids working as street vendors often cried out, "Brother, Brother! My zigga, my zigga!" Achilles ignored them. Troy laughed. Wages looked embarrassed. Ramirez answered, "Que pasa, vato?" Wexler complained that they weren't black. But Merriweather would smile, give them high fives, say, "What's up wit you, my zigga?" Merriweather's reply to Wexler's complaint was always "Half of these ziggas darker than you, Mr. Love-Sexy."

Achilles admitted that much—Wexler resembled Prince and was light-skinned, while the Afghans were often brown from so much sun. Some even looked Asian. But overall, while Afghans and Iraqis couldn't pass for black, they certainly weren't white. He was stunned the first few days, discomfited by the sensation of being in a country where most people looked somewhat like him and the youth hailed him as a brother. It was more pronounced during their week in Baghdad, where he actually saw people with brown skin and kinky hair. What if his primary objective hadn't been to discern who among all these eerily familiar faces was evil? What would it have felt like to be, for once, among the majority? What if the question of black and white hadn't been so neatly replaced by brown and green?

But they were all the same to Merriweather: ziggas. Anytime they weren't fighting, that was how he greeted the young males, enveloping their limp hands in his huge paws, two quick pumps and a *What's up, my zigga?* They responded with smiles, as if they and Merriweather shared some common bond. They probably didn't completely understand what he was saying but recognized the tone as friendly, like dogs reacting to pitch. And his was so casual. What were they? Waiters? Sir, would you like a side of shrapnel with that grenade? Achilles wanted that confidence and connection, Merriweather's habit of acting as if theirs was the most normal job in the world, but he didn't have Merri's aw-shucks grin and using that word in front of other people didn't jive with him. He couldn't apply it to so many people, and make it sound natural to do so. A farmer is beating his mule: *That zigga's getting it.* A kid meandering through the market slips an apple up his sleeve: *That zigga's got skills.* A goat darts into the road and gets hit by a car: Achilles and Troy eye each other; laughing, Merriweather says, *That zigga got fuuuucked up.* The president fails to approve the budget for new safety gear: *That zigga better get on his job.*

Merriweather explained it: "Dick and W are obviously ziggas. They're like pimps, players, like the old Ice Cube song, "Who's the Mack?" The rest of these motherfuckers—well, if they ain't ziggas, they got no excuse to be treated this way. Look around. Their shit's all tore up, they keep their women in check, they live ten to an apartment, they roll six deep, every-one else thinks they know what's good for them, and every time they get a leader we cut him down. Who's that remind you of, except the pork thing, right? But even we got some crazy ziggas won't eat bacon," thumb-ing his nose at Jackson, who was a Seventh-Day Adventist.

Merri's talk greatly offended Ramirez, who said that the Afghans could blend into the barrio and accused Merriweather of being like a black politician and trying to claim everything for himself.

Merri looked to Achilles for support. "I'm like Paul Mooney. I say it a hundred times every morning to keep my teeth white." Pointing at ran-dom objects as he spoke, he said, "Say it with me, Connie: zigga, zigga . . ."

"Alright! I got it," Achilles had yelled.

"Leave him alone," said Wages.

Merriweather continued, "It's a beautiful word. It's our word. That's what connects us. You might think you're different or lighter or darker or smarter or better-talking, but to a racist motherfucker, we're all ziggas. That's why we're lucky. We only have one enemy. These poor ziggas got us here, the whole of Europe, plus they're fighting each other. Know-whatta-mean?"

Achilles didn't, but thought that one day he might, that he would feel a click, a switch flipping, and be able to speak this new language with new freedom. But after using the word at Kikkin Chikkin, all he felt was dirty, like he'd admitted to understanding something he didn't want to, the same way he'd felt for clearing up the confusion when the chaplain said he was going to try the Donkey Punch on Friday night. He brought it on himself by saying things like "I'm God's inbox," or "The Bible is God's Myspace," but it was still disrespectful. Achilles didn't know who was feeding the chaplain that misinformation, but the poor old man (who was Achilles's father's age and looked somewhat like him, except that both of his arms were covered in tattoos) thought that felching, the Rusty Trombone, and the Statue of Liberty were all New York cocktails. He imagined the chaplain inviting an infantry dog hot off a fireworks show back to the tent for a Rusty Trombone. To save him the embarrassment of actually hearing the acts described, Achilles informed Chaplain Weidman that they were slang for drugs and that someone was playing a joke on him. When the word got around that Achilles had said this, they started calling him Urkel and Carlton and every other black television character known as an oreo, but no one called him a zigga.

He removed his shoes and wrapped his damp shirt around his head before entering Wages's house. He went straight to the bathroom to wash his face. His left cheek was raw from being dragged against the wall, his right eye rimmed with blood. Raw hairless patches dotted his scalp; the right side of his face was a rainbow of black and brown bruises. Then there was the limp. He didn't know when or how he'd started limping. He shouldn't have come back. Wages couldn't see him like this. It wasn't pride. He simply didn't want Wages involved. If his friend saw Achilles like this, he'd get sawed off.

Blood dotted the porcelain sink, one spot then another, then another and another in greater concentration, until it was dappled like the ground under sudden rain. When he tried to clean up, the drops streaked across the bowl, long stripes trailing. He needed more water. Dots now stripes, stripes now streaks. Blood splattered on the toilet seat. On his arm, a gouge he hadn't noticed before.

As he undressed to shower, the locket dropped to the floor, hinges twisted and glass cracked. The photo of his mother's father, now badly scratched, popped out of the frame. Gliding through his slick fingers as he tried to reassemble it, the locket fell again, this time breaking open and revealing a small crucifix wrapped in cotton and hidden behind the photograph. The back of the cross was engraved *AHC for AHC*. He often forgot that he and his mother, Anna Holt Conroy, shared the same initials. He rubbed his finger across the tiny golden Jesus he had unknowingly carried around the world—and he'd thought his mother's faith was a new thing.

After his shower, he quietly opened the bathroom door and slipped into the hall. Wages was mopping the living room. Achilles reached for the mop, but Wages insisted on continuing, which was unusual. People should clean up their own messes, he always said, especially when anyone mentioned the possibility of being transferred to Iraq.

"Bethany's going into labor if I don't get this up. She's sensitive about blood being scattered around. Germs and all." He laughed. "She thinks I'm paranoid about not sitting with my back to the door or going to the window twenty-nine times a night, complains I sleep like a baby, up every few hours, but let her see someone eat without washing their hands. Boom!" He waved his arms around to indicate an explosion.

While Wages mopped, Achilles sat, curling and uncurling his fingers, stretching his toes, checking in with his battered body. After a few minutes Wages asked, "So what the fuck, dude?"

Achilles told as much of the truth as he thought it prudent to share: No, Troy wasn't at that house, though there was a guy named Tony who looked similar enough to confuse an old man with cataracts.

Wages wasn't convinced. "Does this have anything to do with why Troy was in that line? Is he into some shit?"

"No, he's not into anything," said Achilles.

"And you?" asked Wages.

"Just a barroom brawl."

"I knew that guy was a fucking cruncher," said Wages.

"Cruncher?" asked Achilles.

"You know: crunch, candy cane, Cindy." said Wages. When Achilles said nothing, he continued. "It's what every addict wants for Christmas, the perfect drug. They say it's not addictive. You can smoke it, eat it, snort it, or just hold it too long. It's what everyone's on. It gives them those cracks and crevices in the face. Fucks up your skin."

"This didn't have anything to do with that." Achilles had never even heard of crunch before. Sure, Blow had shallow fissures in his cheeks, but they'd looked like acne scars. If they were into crunch, how'd they lure Troy into a drug house? Probably the same way they'd lured Achilles in: Troy asked after his parents, and Bud took him to the green camelback.

"Come on, man. This is the first time you've showered in three days. You're living like you're on active. I wouldn't be surprised if you're sleeping in your boots. You've gone Renzo." Lorenzo hadn't showered or shaved for days at a time and ate raw garlic, claiming he wanted to smell like the Taliban, not like Ivory Soap. "What the fuck is up?"

"Nothing. I told you everything. I need to sleep." Wages left. It was obvious he hadn't bought the story.

Achilles felt riven, anxious, as if he had lost something, broken a bone that couldn't be set. Shame menaced him that night, shadowing him as if it had a life of its own. He had never lied to Wages about anything before, not even minor shit like farting. Sure, he'd never told Wages he was adopted, but that was different, private. He told himself that lying about the fight with Blow was an act of kindness, of consideration for Wages's new life. Wages would have demanded involvement—the starfish handed out more than plastic forks.

Before drifting off, he listened to his message from Janice, to see if maybe she'd changed her mind about Dale. "I'm just calling to see how you're doing," she said. "Wish you were here so we could go to the quarry. I went once without you and it wasn't the same. If I go, it's not the same as when you and I go. I know why *us* is *you and me*, not *I*. I've finally figured all that out: *I* and *me*, *who* and *whom*. I'm in a night class at Shippensburg taking English. I want my baby to be smart . . ." He hung up at the first mention of the baby, whom, until then, he'd managed to forget.

A heated conversation woke him in the middle of the night. He heard Wages grumbling and Bethany say "infection." A moment later the light came on, and Bethany tiptoed into the room wearing the 49ers cap she wore whenever it rained. Had it been raining? Was that why his face was so wet? This was the worst hangover he'd ever had. She pushed an ottoman close to the pallet Achilles had made on the floor and sat down. Her voice apologetic, she said, "Sorry to wake you, but we've got to take care of this. Kyle told me you refused to go to the hospital. You know, those cuts could become infected. We need to clean them properly and bandage you up. Is that okay?"

Achilles nodded, noticing that someone had slipped a pillow under his head and covered him with a blanket. His legs were stiff, his head thumping. He was momentarily confused. Feeling as if he was going to cry, he immediately sat up, hoping that would forestall any tears. "Nothing hurts, but if you want."

"I want." Bethany gave him a big smile. Her face was cherubic, the ever-red cheeks setting off the bright green eyes. She led him by the hand to the bathroom and sat him on the toilet. When she leaned forward to get a closer look at his cuts, her hair fell into her face and her breasts swung forward in her shirt.

She tucked her loose hair under her cap and went to work. Her fingers were cool and dry, her hands steady. When had anyone last touched him like this? He remembered the sixty-day shots and how he'd always hoped to get a woman, any woman, as the nurse. Bethany smelled like baby powder, her breath like almonds. His arms went limp as she bandaged his hands. When she reached for his ear, he felt her body heat as her heavy breast grazed his shoulder and pressed against his neck. Achilles would have taken a beating every day to come home to this.

Wages loitered in the hall, muttering. The bathroom was too small for all three of them. It was a tiny room with a shower instead of a tub and a medicine cabinet the size of a shoebox, a room so small, in fact, that Bethany stood with one foot in the hall.

"Be useful and get me some more alcohol," said Bethany, glaring at her husband. "And a cup of water." Wages left with a grunt. Bethany caught Achilles's eyes with her own. "You know he doesn't believe you. I asked him how he could let this happen to a friend. So he's grumpy."

"It was just a misunderstanding," said Achilles.

"Even I don't believe that. But, thank you," she said. "He's trying to stay up all night and party like a rock star and still go to work. He wants to live like he's twenty-one again. I know you boys like to stay up late and all, and that's okay. But whatever this is," she motioned at his face and the bandages, "I appreciate your keeping him out of it. He's not alone anymore, and he's quick to react." She leaned in, now close enough that her breath tickled his earlobe, "You know his temper, so thank you."

Achilles nodded, though he disagreed. Wages always had one chambered, but that wasn't a temper.

"First your father, and now this. Poor Achilles. You have it so hard." She clamped her hand over her mouth. "I forgot I wasn't supposed to say anything."

"It's okay," said Achilles. Coming from her it sounded nice, not like pity.

Wages returned with the water.

Bethany looked through her red nursing bag and pulled out two brown glass bottles. "One to help you sleep, and one for the pain you're going to feel in the morning, and you're going to feel pain." She gave him two pills and the water. After he swallowed, she said, "Lift your tongue and say ahh."

Achilles obeyed.

"Shit, Beth, he's not a chemo kid," said Wages.

Bethany shot Wages a look.

"Sorry," said Wages, throwing his hands up like she'd drawn a gun on him.

Bethany patted Achilles's arm. Her hand lingered as she said, "Forgive me. I get into the work zone." She stood. "That should do it. Get some rest, on the couch, on the couch." She repeated herself until Achilles nodded in agreement. "We're right in the next room if you need anything."

"Yeah, like you have a nightmare, or the Boogie Man comes, or some shit," said Wages. "You have more bandages than the Invisible Man."

He did. Half of his skull was swathed in gauze, as well as most of both hands, and his entire right arm was one cottony limb. Wincing at the pain in his ankle as he stood, he gimped his way back to his pallet on the floor, and was just about settled in when Bethany called out, "Are you on the couch?"

"Yes," he said.

"Just checking." Her voice hung in the air like perfume. His skin was icy-hot everywhere she had touched him. He drifted off to sleep imagining himself in the photos. Achilles and Bethany at Disneyland, the steeple of the Enchanted Castle rising high above them in the background. Achilles and Bethany at Niagara Falls, sipping hot chocolate dotted with marshmallows, while Rex, their lazy yellow Labrador, rests at their feet. Achilles and Bethany on a riverboat, the paddle pushing them to their destiny, roiling water behind, while ahead, a river as smooth as glass. Achilles and Bethany at the Elvis Chapel in Vegas. Janice objects, but it's too late because Janice already had a baby. Bethany was having his, and Janice shouldn't begrudge him that. She was pregnant for Dale for chrissakes, a stuttering, tobacco-swallowing mechanic too lazy to chase down any deer he doesn't drop on the first shot. But Janice is upset anyway, very, dark lines streaking down her face like she's a melting candle. Her crying tilts into a choking sob. Achilles puts a finger to his lips. "You'll wake Bethany. Shhh."

CHAPTER 6

I T WAS A MONTH BEFORE THANKSGIVING, TWO WEEKS AFTER HE'D ARRIVED in New Orleans, one week after the night at the camelback. He wouldn't involve his friend, no matter how often Wages asked about the fight. Achilles had finally admitted he was ambushed in the boardinghouse, though he couldn't remember its location. Nonetheless, Wages had put the word out. A few days before, Wexler and Merriweather had both called Achilles and left messages about "bringing the thunder." That's the kind of friends they were. They would have all insisted on being there, prosthetics and all, when Achilles went to Ready Pawn to take out a loan on his locket and buy an eight-round Mossberg with a clean black barrel and polished oak stock. They would have insisted on helping Achilles remove the dowel rod so that he could chamber four extra rounds. They would have helped Achilles pack the Mossberg in a big duffle on top of enough cardboard to lend the bag an innocuous shape, and cut a hole in the outside pocket so that he could fire it without opening the bag. They would have been in the car with him the night Achilles parked down the street from the green camelback and said aloud to himself, "No one is strutting out that back door. I'm going to show these motherfuckers what a real shotgun is."

In the past few days, he'd slept often, eaten seldom, and thought much about this moment. Parked two blocks away from the green camelback, he visualized the inside of the house, and ran through the plan: He knocks on the back door. Blow opens it and finds his face mounted on the barrel like a silencer, aka the muzzle muffler. Lex answers his questions about Troy and returns his watch, or gets Blow's head in his lap. In and out in less than five minutes and back at the quarry tomorrow night, though what he'd do there he didn't know.

Immediately after the fight he'd been upset that he had tried to kill a man and felt nothing. As O'Ree once said, "There's a difference between getting blood on your snout and developing a taste for it." Having been shot at more than he shot, Achilles wondered if it was possible to develop a taste for something you'd never had. Every evening some Afghan assholes tossed a few potshots at camp, the bullets usually falling several yards short of the wall. The Americans shot back, and of course there were the two firefights, but he never knew if he actually hit anyone. You just shot until they stopped shooting back. It wasn't like hunting, where you tracked the quarry down, bagged it, and ate it.

He rechecked the bag for the eleventh time, to ensure that the trigger was easily accessible. He would travel through the alleys to the back of the house, not that he was really worried about witnesses in this neighborhood. Even as Achilles sat there, a drunk teetered down the block, listing so severely he had to steady himself against the side of a truck. The bum's face was pinched and worn, marked with fissures like Bud's. *Bud.* Bud had better pray that *Nawlins* was a big enough city that he never ran into Achilles. He put his hands to the roof of the cab, near the smudge Bud had left, and said, "Hand to God. Hand to God, my ass." He cringed at the memory of Father Levreau's hands on his own. Why had he lacked the courage to shake him off, to shun the imposition of faith? Faith, as demanding and unyielding as the pain it was rumored to heal; faith, as costly as despair. Of all the prophets Levreau had mentioned, out of the entire Old Testament starting lineup, Achilles recalled only Jacob and Noah. Jacob he didn't know, but everyone knew Noah: the man who built a boat in the middle of the desert and left his friends behind to be swallowed by the bitter surf.

The truck swayed—the drunk was leaning against it, fumbling with his fly. Achilles tapped his horn. It was broken. "Motherfuck, I'm in here!" Losing balance as he tried to wave, the drunk put one hand to the window, leaving a greasy palm print. If ever a city needed a Noah. Achilles slapped the window and the man staggered off, singing. A flock of pigeons launched from a nearby roof. Watching as they scattered, Achilles raised his hands as if holding a shotgun and drew a bead on the bird closest to his car, following its trajectory—a soaring arc of alabaster wings eating the night—and firing just as it lit on a sign that read St. Jude Shelter and Community Kitchen, under which a crowd was organizing itself into a line.

Achilles smelled it before he saw it. The green camelback was a burned-out shell, the dirt yard cracked, the walls of the adjacent houses scorched. The second-story roof was gone, as was most of the first-floor roof, leaving the house open to the sky. The sidewalls remained, but the front wall had crumbled except for an untouched area two feet around the front doors, where the mailbox hung unscathed, unmarked by soot or flame. He flipped the lid up. Joe, Angela, and Raymond Harper had lived there, along with, in incrementally smaller letters, Angie, April, and Amy. Charred shingles cracked underfoot along the alley. The back wall had fallen completely off and lay on the ground like a loading ramp leading into a trailer. The kitchen, dark as a shadow box, had suffered only smoke damage. A few bottles and the ashtray and the take-out containers and the dishes piled in the sink, all coated in black ash, so familiar a sight that he expected to see Lex seated there, coated too. Achilles put the duffle bag over his shoulder and ventured farther into the house. The stairway lay on the floor like a broken accordion. Achilles climbed the wall to the second floor, his fingers burning and twitching with the memory of the fight, his sore ankle groaning, his anger rising.

Two of the upstairs doorways were obstructed by a densely packed mass of heavy beams and charred shingles, impassible now, let alone aflame. The third door led into a bedroom furnished with bunk beds as well as a playpen that was a knot of sooty tubing. He almost lost his footing on a squeaky toy, three baby dolls gnarled by the heat, their legs melted together, two of the heads joined at the hair, forming one stiff plastic web. He stomped on it until one head popped off and bounced into the hallway, where it caught the slant of the floor and careened off the edge. He listened closely but didn't hear it hit the ground. He set the duffle bag down and kicked the body, a Medusa with legs for hair, over the edge; he listened closely, but didn't hear that touch down either, which really pissed him off.

Feeling sorry for himself, he catalogued his grievances: How could Troy be so thoughtless? If his mom believed enough to slip crosses into their lockets and keep Bibles tucked around the house, how could she pander to his father's atheism all those years? And his father, for chrissakes, how could he die before seeing them again and leave Achilles holding this bag of shit? And if you adopted a kid or two, what was the point in forcing the papers on them? People didn't need to know everything.

He was back in his car before he remembered the duffle bag, and pounded the dashboard in frustration. He didn't want to do this anymore. He didn't want to go back into that house. He knew burned houses. Plenty. He had been in burned houses, searched them, slept in them, ordered them razed and retorched. He had been the one to burn them. He had called down the thunder. He knew that if the right ordnance came knocking, even the stoutest building crumbled like cake. But he didn't want to go back into that house and wonder again who had been trapped in those rooms. But that was stupid. It wasn't like Troy could die in a fire: he had survived a minefield.

A storefront operation in a block of shops that had been taken over by churches, St. Jude was sandwiched between First Bethel Apostolic and the Church of the Almighty Congregation, all three names stenciled in cheerful colors as if they merely hawked baked goods or dry cleaning services. He peeked in the window of First Bethel, the single room with industrial carpet installed halfway up the walls and folding chairs striking him as too earnest, too impoverished, to be a sacred space. A service in a converted store couldn't be the same as mass in a real church like St. Augustine, not that he even knew what that was like. God was blond in this part of town, both storefront churches displaying the same blue-eyed Jesus, like franchisees, the shelter's sign featuring a sandaled brown-haired man who must have been St. Jude. For a moment, he wondered how they even knew what any of these saints looked like.

Achilles scanned the line, seeing no sign of Troy or anyone who resembled him. Ignoring the grunts and the half-hearted objections, he pushed his way through the crowd to a door marked Volunteers. Inside, two teenagers sat at a folding table. They were Blow's age, no older than Troy at his enlistment date.

"Name?" asked the tall one.

"Achilles Conroy."

"Where'd you serve?" asked the tall one.

"Korengal," answered Achilles, wondering why it mattered.

"Is that federal?" asked the tall one.

"Yeah, I guess," said Achilles.

"Korengal?" muttered an old man he hadn't noticed before. "I had a cousin there."

The teens scanned the sheets spread out before them, meticulously running their fingers along rows and columns as if they expected to find Achilles's name hidden in one of the little black boxes. "You sure it's federal? How do you spell it?"

Achilles spelled it.

"And where is it?" asked the teen.

"Afghanistan," said someone behind him.

"I knew it," said the old man, lounging in a corner.

The tall teen shuffled his papers. "Knew that shit didn't sound familiar."

Achilles turned to see a large-breasted white woman with blond dreadlocks and a red paisley head wrap. She waggled her finger at the teens. "Tsk tsk! Korengal is in Afghanistan, seniors. It's SAT season."

To Achilles: "Were you really in Korengal?"

"Really."

"Doing what?"

"What else is there to do?"

Admiration shot across her face. "Really?"

"Yeah," said Achilles.

"How can we help you?"

"I was looking for somebody."

"Who?"

"A friend," he said quickly.

"What's he look like? We got a lot of somebodies here."

He reached for his wallet, but as a precautionary measure he'd left it at home before going to the green camelback. "Five eleven, one hundred eighty-five pounds, brown skin, brown hair." Half of the people in line matched that description. "Light brown skin and green eyes." That described the short teenager at the volunteer table. The woman nodded, waiting for him to finish, her eyes round as quarters, focused only on him, as if for this moment he was all that mattered. Her face was bright and open, honest. Her heart-shaped lips were glossy and garnet, as radiant as her head wrap. The bright colors, the dreadlocks, the figure—she was perfect, like an anime character.

"You're more than welcome to wait," she said. Her voice was deep and rich, sweet too, like honey and cream. "What's his name?" When Achilles hesitated, she repeated the question.

"Troy. Do you know anyone named Lex or Blow?"

"Sorry. You're looking for a bunch of folks."

"Yeah."

"Good luck, soldier." She extended her hand. "I'm Ines."

"Achilles."

"Really?"

"Who would make that up?" asked Achilles.

"You're probably right," she said. "Were you really in Goddamnistan?"

"Who would make that up?" asked Achilles.

"A lot of people." She nodded knowingly.

"Not if they were there," said Achilles.

"That's a tautology," she said.

The teens snickered. Achilles shrugged it off. He didn't know what it meant. Did she say Goddamnistan a minute ago? She couldn't have.

"You're serious," said Ines, facing him squarely. "Okay. Let me guess. You were in a hipster bar, someone insulted your commander-in-chief, and you decked the guy."

Achilles shook his head.

"Girlfriend dragged you out tonight?"

"No."

"On your own. That's unusual. Since you're trying to do the right thing, could you monitor the line? We're shorthanded. Just remind them not to push or fight. If they do, yell. There's always one off-duty cop, but he's inside because it's air-conditioned. What can I say? It's volunteer work."

"Sure."

Ines pulled a pen out of her hair and wrote something on her forearm. "We'll owe you one. Thanks."

At first, Achilles didn't see any problem with agreeing to help. He'd planned on watching the line anyway. The St. Jude line was no different from the St. Augustine line. They stomped and stammered loudly at the end of the line, but shuffled and whispered as they approached the door, avoiding eye contact. Within ten minutes of pacing, his eyes drawn to the intersections whenever anyone approached, he regretted his decision. His shirt was plastered to his back, the bandages on his arm damp, and his boxers bunched up in a damp wad. As the men filed inside, they straightened up and focused on Ines like BBs to a magnet, and she looked them in the eye and called them brother, all of them, black, white, brown, and the two yellows.

In Kabul, he'd known white people like her in the charities. Nicknamed NGOs because No Government Organization gave shit away, they were staffed by glassy-eyed Americans. "Brother! Brother!" an Afghan would shout, but they knew it was solidarity by circumstance. The white Americans were different, saying "brother" like they believed it, earnestly claiming kinship with all humanity. Most volunteers were idealists or opportunists running a side scam. Both camps scorned the soldiers, though the opportunists admitted that they profited from destruction because no matter how much food, medicine, and clothing they gave away someone else paid for it, and paid them to deliver it. Charity was big business. The desk pilots understood that, as did the smugglers—who were more fun to drink with—but most volunteers were naïve optimists, though they didn't think of themselves as naïve; how else could they be optimistic?

After a week in country, the volunteers would tell a sad tale about the day they realized Afghan kids imitated gunfire and artillery while playing with their toy trucks and planes. Isn't that why we're here? Wasn't that what most trucks and planes were doing in Goddamnistan? Achilles would ask. But he'd never push it. If he did, they'd start moaning about the army's deplorable recruiting tactics, their tendency to target neighborhoods like the one Achilles must have grown up in. They'd sigh for him, curse the government, saying what they assumed he couldn't, steadfast in their belief that Achilles was a victim, a sacrificial lamb on the altar of Democracy, not understanding that he hadn't volunteered to die for anything. He'd been indirectly drafted. But he let them talk. Liberal guilt was always good for a few beers.

After the shelter closed, Ines stopped to talk to him on the way to her car. They stood in the street while the off-duty cop extinguished the lights one by one until the building was dark. Achilles had thought people stayed there overnight, that maybe there was yet a chance that Troy might arrive. But of course he hadn't seen Troy. He hadn't really expected to. Ines was what he needed, a distraction from all the possibilities he couldn't admit to himself that he was even considering.

She thanked him for helping out, adding, "The students thought you were here for community service. It's rare we get a real live hero here."

Hero. Achilles smiled weakly.

"Volunteer often?" asked Ines.

"I just finished two paid vacations," said Achilles.

"That's right. Twenty months of shawarma," she said.

"And bitter beer," he said.

She made a lemon-sucking face. "Yuck! You were there." In a serious tone, she added, "When did you get back?"

"About a month ago."

She nodded knowingly. "Ah-ha! That explains the scars. What did you do?"

"Airborne Infantry."

"An airborne soldier saved my life outside of Jalabad. He carried me right out of a minefield. I wandered into it and froze. We were bringing medical supplies to a remote village, and I had to go to the bathroom. It was my first week in country and I wanted privacy, the ubiquitous American amenity. There I was squatting down and I look over and see the sign. He walked right in after me and carried me out. You believe that? Of course you do."

He *had* heard her say Goddamnistan. "Sounds like a murder-suicide pact."

Ines frowned. "He had a metal detector."

Her savior wasn't as crazy as Troy, but she'd think Troy brave. "There are units specially equipped for that."

"He had a metal detector," repeated Ines.

He smelled something burning and looked in the direction of the green camelback. She turned to follow his gaze. He stole a glance at her profile, the outline of her white tee pressing against the night.

"Are you here often?" asked Achilles.

"Tomorrow I'll be at the new St. Jude."

The next two nights, he went to the new St. Jude, a converted high school significantly larger than the old location. An immense brick building with a white stone foundation, its four turrets and tiny windows gave the shelter the appearance of a fortified structure. The classrooms were dormitories and the cafeteria had annexed the gymnasium. Troy wasn't there, but Ines was, because her work involved several shelters, and Achilles took the opportunity to learn about the other organizations, each night dutifully plotting them on his map.

As she explained it, "I coordinate the efforts between different shelters, churches, and NGOs, if they're willing to cooperate and their charters allow it. If their calendars and interests intersect, I team them up for lower pricing and better services. For example, if St. Jude wants to feed a neighborhood on the same day that St. Mark's plans a health clinic, I get them to overlap."

"So you know all the churches and shelters?" asked Achilles.

"Every single one."

"And you came up with this on your own?"

"Sure did."

"That's admirable," said Achilles.

"Why do you say that?" she asked, cocking her head to the side.

"It just is."

"So you're the measure of what's admirable?"

"I do know what I admire."

"We'll see if you're still around in two weeks, when your guilt wears off."

"I'm not guilty of anything," said Achilles, crossing his arms.

"Of course not."

"You?"

"Never. It's what we do. My friends, family, all of us. I attended a small school in the Northeast. You know how it is. You're young with a heart as big as the Hindenburg, and just as volatile. We joined the Peace Corps, went to grad school, to teach, or to New York. Every single person. Volunteering is best, a paid internship in an exotic locale. You help out without feeling any discomfort except the recognition of just how wealthy this country is. Then one day I asked myself why I was a thousand miles away when these black kids right here needed my help. I was just like all those white girls who do mindless shit to assuage guilt they claim not to have. You know how most white people are."

"Most white people," she said without a trace of irony or jest. There would be no oblique references, no mentioning that Tammy Wynette was his mother's favorite singer and Waylon Jennings his father's. There'd be no dropping a photo of his parents. Peace Corps, grad school, New York. *Most white people.* He could be most black people. I can play this game, *Praise Jesus,* thought Achilles.

After the fight, he had continued to sleep on the floor. But when Bethany came home, she would wake him, the little flashlight used to avoid disturbing him wielded with the opposite intention, the beam fanning his eyes. "The couch," she'd say. And he'd adjust his bandages and lie on it until she went to bed. He'd wised up in the last few days and started sleeping on the couch until she got home. If only it were covered in plastic, like Janice's mom's couch.

He wondered what Janice was doing, then pictured Ines. Was she an innie or an outie? Slipping his hand into his shorts, tremors rippled across his stomach. His hands moved faster, making short yanking motions until he added spit for longer strokes. He wrapped his thumb and forefinger around his cock, making the okay sign, and tugged, breathing faster, imagining Ines above him. Feeling lightheaded, almost like he was floating, he rolled over and entered the cushions, thrusting spasmodically.

"Achilles! The couch!" said Bethany.

He hadn't heard her come in, but should have smelled the antiseptics and alcohol trailing her like a ghost. She was taking her careful fencer's steps and using the little flashlight to find her way. He appreciated her trying, so he never let on that he usually heard each step because, however soft, it always became a slide. He imagined her scowling face behind the beam that hovered on his dick like a spotlight on a fugitive. He covered himself. She switched off the light.

"I'm sorry, I'm sorry," she repeated several times.

Hearing her bump into the wall and mutter a curse, he turned on the lamp, knocking over the starfish card. She was at the door and when she bent over to arrange her clogs, her scrubs pulled tight across her thighs, highlighting panty lines. He adjusted the tent in his blanket, searching for something to say.

She stood there a minute before finally saying, "At least you're not sleeping on the floor anymore." She nodded twice, that comment meeting her approval.

"Yeah," said Achilles after searching for a response. He sat up and gave a half wave.

"It must be more comfortable," she said. She stretched out *comfortable* like it was a cross between *comfort* and *affordable.*

"I like the couch," said Achilles. "But I guess that's obvious."

"Don't like it too much. We don't want any little cushions running around. Though that would be more comfortable, and better for your back."

"Always the nurse."

Her smile was tight.

"I meant looking out for people," Achilles said. "Nurses are good."

"I understand," she said. She put one hand on her hip, standing as if there was something on her mind, and she intended to share it. "He missed you guys. All the male bonding stuff. Growl." She scowled, obviously her impression of a man's face. "I thought it was an excuse to get away. Always seeing to this friend or that. But he's happier when you're here. Even though he drinks more. But seeing you here for your brother, seeing you together, I understand. You have something in common, but it's not anything you would have wanted. They say you can choose your friends but not your family, but that's not really true for you guys. I don't know what I'm saying."

"I think I do."

"Good night Achilles," she said, pronouncing his name correctly.

Her scent lingered. He understood what she meant. He felt the same way about Troy. He loved him, but sometimes he was angry, and other times jealous that there might be someone somewhere who knew Troy better, someone he trusted more, maybe even Wexler. Maybe Bethany felt out of the circle; it was a men's circle. It was a man's, man's, man's world. Only men could understand what they had chosen, and why they would gladly return. It was a family too, a family who stood by you even when it meant risking a limb they couldn't grow back.

"The couch," called Bethany from the bedroom.

"Yes ma'am," he called back. Women made you think. What was it like to have one always around and within easy reach? Did you stop masturbating? Was it like having an endless supply of beer in the refrigerator? If you wanted some sex, did you just go to the bedroom and get it?

"The couch," she called again.

"Yes ma'am." If only it were covered in plastic.

He retraced his steps, looking for any clues he might have missed when he was there. The baby-doll heads: smudged and disfigured, the limbs mangled, the eyes locked on his. He kept seeing the head rolling off the edge of the landing and into the space where the stairs should have been. Those tiny limbs forever tumbling, as if drowning. This image brought him to a halt as he was driving to the new St. Jude for the third day in a row. He yanked the wheel, jerked the car over to the side of the street, and called the morgue.

A man with a clipped voice answered the phone. Yet again Achilles described his brother: five eleven, 185 pounds, light-brown skin, green eyes. The man with the clipped voice read the description back to him: average height, average build, average complexion—he pronounced it "complected." He also said "ABM," which Achilles thought he remembered Morse saying.

"Hold on." The man sighed deeply. Achilles heard the phone drop, a chair creak, and the raspy groan of reluctant metal file cabinets.

On the sidewalk, the crowd swam by. How did so many people manage to avoid touching? A welcome shadow fell over his car as the St.

Charles streetcar came to a halt beside where he had parked. An elderly couple with a small boy squeezed their heads through one of the narrow streetcar windows, their tanned faces glowing in the sunlight. The man took photos, the camera glued to his face as if he were a Cyclops. The woman directed the boy's gaze toward nearby landmarks: the listless flag atop Jax Brewery, the Aquarium, and the Customs House. The child waved at passersby, who mostly pretended not to see him, as did Achilles when the child waved in his direction. The child persisted, his waving becoming frantic. Achilles cupped his cell phone tighter to his ear, looking straight ahead to avoid the child's insistence and the pedestrians' charades. The light changed, the streetcar lurched forward, the trolley pole sparking as it dragged along the overhead wires. The electricity in the air smelled like boiling artichokes. He watched the streetcar travel three blocks and turn up St. Charles toward the Garden District, an area of town he'd never seen.

When the phone was picked up again, a different voice said, "When you come down use the Rampart Street entrance, not the Tulane Avenue entrance. It's the one nearest the Superdome. There's a great big sign says Charity Hospital of New Orleans."

He remembered Troy on the side of the road a few hours after they'd driven over the IED, glowing, with the sun behind him like a sombrero. Troy, his smile big enough to swallow the sky. Achilles had let them all down. He should have driven more, canvassed, called the morgue sooner, or the hospitals, put up posters, put out a radio ad . . . Before he could reply, there was a muffled exchange and he heard the phone being dropped and picked up again. The clipped voice returned and muttered an apology. "He thought you were someone else."

Relief. His heart was still racing. The clipped voice continued. "Anyway, I'm sorry, but you'll need to come down here. There's too many guys fitting that description. Do you know where we are?"

Achilles hung up. He'd already heard the directions once and besides, he had his map. He gripped the wheel with both hands in an effort to steady himself. How could he have ever been mad at Troy? How could he have even been angry about things that were out of his control? He was only six, he couldn't have known. It wasn't like Troy had planned his arrival.

CHAPTER 7

A CHILLES STARTED HUMMING A FOUR-COUNT THE MOMENT HE ENTERED the cool, dim marble lobby of Charity Hospital. While waiting for the elevator, he thrummed his fingers against his thighs and tapped his foot, keeping cadence until he reached the subbasement and was in the morgue office showing a photo to the attendant, a white man with thick black hair, a dingy lab coat, and the kind of belly developed by years of eating at a desk. Between the smell of Grecian Formula and the antiseptic hospital odor, the room smelled like a barbershop. The man thoughtfully studied the photo. It was taken two years before at the Baltimore water park, before basic and infantry training, before their tour of duty. Troy smiles, the gap in his front teeth prominent, his green eyes razors in the sunlight. He wears flip-flops and shorts, no shirt. It was hot that day, or so they'd thought at the time. Against Troy's broad shoulders, the swim towel around his neck is a mere cravat. He has hair. There were more recent photos, but they were all from Goddamnistan. In them Troy is wearing his uniform, and Achilles doesn't want to open up the questions that would raise, such as why Troy couldn't simply be identified by his prints.

The man glanced at Achilles, then at the photo again, squinting as if noting the differences: Achilles was darker than Troy, almost six inches shorter, and had smaller eyes and a wider nose. True, he and Troy looked nothing alike, but most white people didn't notice. The man glanced at Achilles, and again at the photo.

"How long have you been a diener?" It was a term Achilles had learned from the German soldiers.

"They don't call us that anymore." The man worked his jaw like he was chewing on the words. "We got two you should look at. One's pretty rough. Sure your brother doesn't have prints on file? It would be much easier on you."

Achilles: "None."

"Follow me."

The viewing area was a narrow room barely large enough for the three chairs that sat facing the dull, mirrored glass in the opposite wall. The left wall was blank. On the right wall hung a bulletin board with posters for crisis hotlines and HIV prevention, and beneath that, an intercom with red, black, and green buttons. The attendant pressed the black button and requested D-782. Achilles pressed his nose to the glass but couldn't see anything. He pressed his fingernail against it and tried to recall the test for two-way mirrors. Was a space between the reflections a positive indication, or was it the reverse? Either way, he knew this one had two sides, and either way, from his side of the mirror, it didn't matter. It mattered even less from the other side. He counted the tiles on the floor and ceiling—sixty-five and twenty-two respectively. After a moment he heard the squeak of rubber soles on linoleum, the distinctive rattle of old gurney wheels, and the rustling of a sheet. The noise died down. The attendant asked if he was ready. Achilles nodded and fingered his dented locket, remembering that Troy had one just like it. The attendant rapped his knuckles against the mirror, then stepped back behind Achilles. His hands clammy, Achilles ordered himself to relax, unracking his shoulders and tightening his stomach as if preparing for an unavoidable punch.

Light spat and flickered in the room behind the mirrored glass. He could barely see the outline of a body, then it was overlit, then it was again dark. Finally, the sputtering buzz settled into a hum, and the room was blanched in fluorescent light.

D-782 was too short, too dark, and too thin. He looked nothing like Troy. Achilles shook his head, no. He exhaled in a rush—he had dodged the first bullet. *Breathe. Always remember to breathe.* No less than three military instructors had reminded Achilles of that, catching him with his shoulders hunched and lips pursed when out on the range. The attendant called for D-794 and the light blinked off. Achilles heard one gurney being wheeled out, another wheeled in. He watched the diener's reflection. His breathing was labored, the nametag on his chest rising and falling as if at sea, as if Troy were his brother. The faster that nametag moved, the more Achilles relaxed, like O'Ree had told him: "We're the opposite of most people, son. We must learn to be like a ship that grows steadier the more the sea storms." Was he ready? Achilles nodded. Another knock on the window, the light flashed on. This time a kid in a lab coat and head-phones, the one who must have transported the body, remained in the viewing chamber standing behind the gurney.

The white plastic sheet used for burn victims was folded back to the waist, revealing second- and third-degree burns over much of D-794's torso. The skin was mottled black and pink, except his raw, gnarled fin-gertips and ragged throat, which Achilles recognized as a sign a man had burned to death in an enclosed space while trying to claw his way out. One unburned patch of skin on the chest was the same shade as Troy. The scorched cheekbones were high, like Troy's. But the eyes were too close together, *Aren't they?* Troy had wide-set eyes. *The eye sockets are too close, right?* He inched closer to the glass, remembering Troy's uniform folded neatly on the bed with his helmet on top.

He knew it was physically impossible, but for a moment he thought he smelled the body. Breathe. *Always remember to breathe—through the mouth.* The eyes were definitely too close. The upper lip cracked like pumice as the kid in the lab coat nudged the mouth open, revealing gold teeth coated in ash. Achilles grinned with relief, ignoring the attendant's reaction to his smile. The attendant pressed the red button, and the kid in the lab coat gently pulled up the sheet, letting it float down and settle on the blunt contours of the scorched face. The light snapped off. Achilles put his fin-ger to the glass again, studied the gap between his fingernail and the reflec-tion and remembered—if there was no gap between your fingernail and the reflection, it was a genuine mirror.

Back in the office, the attendant searched for the visitor's log. Able to focus now, Achilles looked around the narrow room, which was furnished only with an old gunmetal desk and a rigid plastic chair. No file cabinets. This wasn't the man who'd answered the phone, the man who'd listened to Achilles describe his brother, then muttered "Light-complected ABM. We got one, but he's burned real bad." ABM—average black male. Achilles scowled, muttering "complected" to himself. It made skin tone sound like a psychological burden. It must be a New Orleans thing, like *cold drink* meant *soda,* and *reach me* meant *hand me.* On the wall was the same Dilbert cartoon he'd seen hanging up in the Forward Operating Base morgue. The characters were in a board meeting and the caption underneath read, *The Only Place Lower than Hell.* The idea that an office could be anything like hell always made him chuckle. Some people had it too easy. He laughed again, louder.

"Tough job there, boy," said the attendant as he rifled through the papers on his desk.

"Yeah." Though Achilles didn't know what was so tough about sitting around in an air-conditioned office all day. "How do you do it?"

"No, son. I meant yours."

Achilles winced. "You do what you got to do, right?"

"My captain used to say that in Korea. I believed it too, back then. But you'll tell yourself anything to stay afloat on a river of flaming shit." He found the log and waved it triumphantly. "I'll tell you what's a shame. It's a shame what these kids are doing to each other out there nowadays. Animals. Those dealers are animals. Someone should line them all up and shoot them, and their dogs. Civilians shouldn't be allowed to carry guns. That guy was burned up by his dealer. They even poured alcohol down his throat so he couldn't scream." His toned changed and he hunched his shoulders like it was campfire story time, like he was on *Scared Straight,* that old TV show that tried steering bad kids in the right direction by taking them to prisons and morgues, the eternal message always the same—*This could be you!*

"Imagine that! Alcohol in his throat so the minute he yells, the flames are in his mouth and neck, and he's ripping his own skin off trying to make it stop." The attendant beat at his chest, openhanded, pantomiming fruitless efforts to douse a flame. "Ever seen anything so gruesome? They call it baptism. Baptism!" He crossed himself twice. "Can you imagine hating someone that much?" He was still clutching the log, awaiting an answer in exchange.

Achilles shrugged again and shook his head. For all he knew, they did it to themselves. D-794 could have been one of those crunchers Wages had talked about, someone who burned himself up trying to light a pipe, like that old comedian Richard Pryor. "Yeah, it's terrible," he said as he reached for the clipboard. He listed Wages's address as his own, noted himself as next of kin, and marked their parents as deceased.

"Good luck." The attendant stared hard.

"What?" asked Achilles.

"I'm just wondering, do I want to see the other guy? Or have I already?"

"I don't know." He'd forgotten about his bruises and sore muscles, as he'd been trained to. The implications of that answer dawned on him. "I mean, of course not."

"Never mind." He clapped Achilles on the back, as if he understood his plight, as if something had passed between them. "Good luck."

There was no use saying he didn't believe in luck. There was no use explaining that Achilles's reserve wasn't luck. He'd often attended the sifting of the dead. Not even the first ones had been shocking: a cluster of civilians, a wedding party charred beyond recognition, only vaguely human in shape, and most importantly, absent familiarity—he couldn't have possibly known any of them. They were, as someone said, the only Gannies it was safe to turn your back on.

He reminded himself of why he was doing this. Troy had prints on file, and when they were run, their mom would be called. She would have to answer when the phone rang in the middle of the night because it could be Achilles with news of Troy, if not Troy himself. Too old-fashioned to have a phone in the bedroom, she would feel her way to the living room, her left hand grazing the wood-paneled wall and her right holding her reading glasses. Once seated in the green chair at the roll-top desk where she writes out the bills and reads the Bible—which she never even looked at when their father was alive—she'll turn on the lamp, pick up a pen, and put on her glasses, behind which her eyes float in the air like two blue globes. Then she'll answer the phone. After hearing the news, she'll call Achilles and apologize.

That was why he must be the first to know. But if he found Troy on a gurney, what could he really do? Apologize for letting her down? Again? When Troy first talked about signing up, his mother pulled Achilles aside and said, "Only you can talk him out of it. He'll listen to you." He'd expected Troy—who hated authority, listened to no one, followed no directions but his own—would be phased out within weeks. A drill sergeant would give him an order and he would walk off, like he did on every job. There was no way that Achilles, who thought his own cautious but easygoing nature perfectly suited for the military, was going to talk him out of it. How could he have expected that Troy, the free spirit, the wild card, the deck with three jokers, would fit in like he'd been born into chaos? "Every deck needs a joker," Troy always said, though he was anything but a joker, throwing himself into his duty as if all he'd ever wanted all his fucking life was for someone to be man enough to tell him what to do and have the balls to back it up.

"His heart is set on it," Achilles had told his mom. "You know how he gets." She'd nodded knowingly, sighed, as though she'd wished for anything except that answer, but expected it. He couldn't forget what she said when they shipped out: "The loneliest person in the world is a mother who outlives her children."

He sat in his car, on the top floor of the parking garage, watching two pigeons fight over a hamburger patty. He could just barely see the tip of the church steeple at the center of the French Quarter and a flashing red light that might have been Jax Brewery. The lot was at least two blocks away from the hospital, but he swore he still smelled D-794, and along with him gunpowder, rifle oil, garbage, diesel fuel, body odor, roasting lamb. He shoved three pieces of gum into his mouth. The rush of peppermint burned his tongue, and he started breathing through his nose again.

Later that day he was at Seaton's Diner, across from St. Augustine, when his mother called. She sounded hesitant when he answered, as if she thought she had the wrong number. After some small talk, he took a breath and asked, "Do you know any of these people he might be looking for?"

"No," said his mother.

"Isn't it in the envelope?" he asked.

"I never opened the envelope," she said. "Your father sealed them."

"Really?"

"We talked about this already. Yes, you're both Conroys. Troy Magnus Conroy and Achilles Holden Conroy. You're your father's sons and mine. Always."

"Geez." Achilles exhaled sharply. "That again." Hadn't she signed court orders or birth certificates? He wanted to scream, *Don't you even know their names? How could you possibly not know their names?* His sandwich arrived, a chicken club held together by toothpicks. The waitress regarded him strangely every time he ordered it, rushing it to the table like she didn't want to be seen with it. He'd forgotten why he called his mother in the first place, or if he was even the one who had called. "I gotta go."

"Wait. Your father left you some money, a lot of money. Seventy-five thousand dollars." She was gleeful, sounding like she had after discovering petroleum jelly was the antidote for the dry skin that afflicted him every winter. "I meant to tell you before, but I didn't know how much, and everything went so loosey-goosey with Troy leaving and all."

Where did his father get that kind of money? That was almost two years of net pay from a man who'd wanted to move for the last ten years but said he couldn't afford it. How he wanted to retreat farther up the mountain, complaining constantly about the city roping him in, the noose of new developments driving up property taxes. "How much?"

"Fifty thousand from his life insurance and another twenty-five from his pension. But if you need more, let me know. You'll get the rest when I go."

"Why are you talking like that? Where are you going?"

"I'm still going on my trip. But anything could happen, even here. Look at your father. You need to know how these things work. The papers are in the roll-top. Everything goes to the surviving heir. The lawyer can give you the details. Chuck over in Mercersburg. You remember him? He handled Troy's accident."

"I remember him." Accident? Chuck was the attorney who persuaded a jury to acquit Troy after he was arrested for driving drunk and running over Mrs. Dyson's two goats. His father bought the damned things too. They ate goat for months.

"Call him at his office. When you see your brother, tell him too."

"Okay."

"Come home anytime. You could start that hot dog stand now."

"Right," he said with a laugh. A hot dog stand had been his dream business in middle school, more for his love of hot dogs and fascination with the word *frankfurter* than for any true interest in business. There was a pause as if his mother expected a more detailed answer. Did she think he was still serious about that, or ever had been? "I have to go."

"Wait." After she gave him the attorney's number, she said, "Achilles, you know you were always my favorite, don't you? I always wanted you. You know that, don't you?"

She sounded like everything depended on his answer, so he murmured, "Yes."

"I just wanted to make sure you knew that. I'll let you go now."

Achilles picked at his food, constantly glancing out the window at St. Augustine, hoping Troy would walk by. He could tell him, *I'm the favorite, find your own way home. I'm the favorite.* If that was really true, how come Achilles always had to do everything Troy wanted to do, and not the other way around? He wondered about that as he dialed Chuck's number, identifying himself as Mr. Conroy to the receptionist. While holding, he practiced what to say: *I'm calling about the will . . . My father passed . . . My mom told me to call.* He settled on, *It's Achilles Conroy.* Even that sounded presumptive to him. How could he start the conversation without sounding money-grubbing? Chuck did it for him, saying, "Troy, I'm sorry for your loss. How are you?" In his low voice, Chuck stretched out *you* as if talking to a child. "Are you okay? Troy, are you there?"

Achilles shivered the way he did after biting ice, or, as the old folks said, as if someone was walking on his grave. "I'm here. I'm just . . . I'm here. I'm good." The younger waitress refilled his coffee. Her snug polyester uniform reminded him of a nurse's outfit. She winked every time she passed, like they were in this together.

"You sound good, but you were always a tough kid. I guess your mom told you about the will. So what are you going to do with all the money? You don't need to decide now, but I know your father would have wanted you to be wise and thrifty. It's quite a large sum, enough that with the right financial advice you could do well for yourself. I have a client who retired on half that amount. He lives on a Greek island, a little one, and he does some freelance consulting, but the point is he retired with only one hundred twenty-five thousand in stocks. I'll give you the broker's number."

"One hundred thousand?" Achilles heard paper shuffling.

"Legal fees aren't that high." Chuck laughed.

"Can you mail me a check?"

"You and your jokes. You have to sign for it. Achilles too, so just let him know. When can you come by? I just need your John Hancock. This is a lot of money."

Achilles slid the saltshaker from hand to hand. "How much after legal fees?"

"Two-hundred and fifty-three thousand seven hundred and twelve dollars and nineteen cents, give or take. When should I expect you?"

"Soon." said Achilles

"Where are you?"

"New Orleans," said Achilles, looking around him then hanging up.

Seventy-five GS for the oldest brother and three or four times that amount for the younger. He knew who his father's favorite was. But he'd known that all along. He'd known that ever since Troy came through the door.

When Achilles turned eight, he expected a golden Lab. For years, his mother said, *When you're ten*, but he didn't expect to wait until he was two-whole-hands old. He knew the puppy was coming because his parents described his gift as *Warm, friendly, and tireless*. His friends were going to be so jealous. His parents left early that Saturday morning, leaving Achilles with Mrs. Bear, the babysitter who let him take showers. They were due back well before 6:30 p.m., when the party was set to begin. At 5:30, as instructed, Achilles took his cake out of the refrigerator and placed it on the coffee table in the living room, where the paneled walls were festooned with streamers, balloons, and his name in winking, glittering gold letters. He sat on Mrs. Bear's welcoming lap and watched *Romper Room* until 6:15, when the first guest arrived. The last guest was there by 6:30. He knew the precise time because *Ren and Stimpy* was starting. While making Jiffy Pop for the hungry kids, Mrs. Bear chatted with the parents who waited with their children. At 7:30 they had hot dogs, then ice cream, but not cake, the adults insisting that his parents should be present when he cut the cake. At 8:30, when the party was scheduled to end, the parents began packing up their kids.

Wearing a pirate's eye patch, the one gift he was allowed to open, Achilles fell asleep on Mrs. Bear's lap. This was a first. Mrs. Bear usually insisted he was tucked in by 8:45. He was still on the couch at midnight when his mom woke him. Someone had put a pillow under his head and covered him with a blanket. "Hey honey." Her smile was strained, toothy. She guided him to the kitchen with her hands over his eyes, his outstretched fingers grazing the paneled walls.

"Surprise!" his parents yelled.

The kitchen was a bright, bright room, thanks to the white walls and fluorescent lights. Achilles threw up his hands to shield his eyes, peeking through his fingers at his parents, who stood flanking a little boy in a birthday hat.

"This is Troy," said Achilles's mother.

"Happy birthday!" said Achilles's father. He pulled a chair away from the kitchen table and motioned for Achilles to sit. Between the manic grin, the pompadour, and the exaggerated sweep of his arm, his father looked like a carnival barker.

Achilles went back to the couch and curled up under the blanket, his usual antidote for strange and disturbing dreams. Sometime later his mom awakened him, led him to the kitchen, and said, "Troy's having ice cream. You have some too."

Troy sat in Achilles's old orangesicle-colored Scooby-Doo booster seat, eating a big bowl of butter pecan ice cream, Achilles's favorite because of the salty-sweet and soft but crunchy confusion it caused in his mouth. Troy held his bowl close to his body like someone might snatch it, occasionally stealing a glance around the kitchen, immediately looking back down at his ice cream if he caught anyone's eye. He was about half Achilles's size, with wide-set eyes and a broad forehead, like an insect. His left cheek was bruised, and snot dripped from his red and runny nose right into the ice cream, which must have been his favorite flavor too, judging by the way he slurped it down. Troy had seconds, and Achilles had seconds. While they ate, his father leaned back against the wall, smoking and smiling, occasionally rubbing their heads. Troy had thirds, and Achilles had thirds, their bowls brimming with his father's generous scoops.

After his mother dropped a glass in the sink and stomped out of the kitchen and his father scampered after her, Troy spoke for the first time, in a hushed voice as if to avoid being overheard by the adults in the next room, barely moving his lips, squeezing the words out of one side of his mouth, so that if you stood on his other side, you wouldn't even know he was asking, "How long they going to let us stay here?"

Achilles shrugged. He was tired and overfull. "Not long, I hope," he said, not yet understanding that months would pass before Troy would accept that they weren't in a foster home. At that moment, confused, exhausted, queasy, Achilles wanted only sleep. He slipped down from the chair and made his way to his bedroom, where he climbed into bed, careful not to bounce or burp for fear he would barf. Behind him, he heard Troy's *yessirs* and *yes ma'ams*. What a suck-up.

A while later—or was it? He couldn't tell anymore—his mom woke him again. "Hey honey, Troy is having waffles," she explained as she led him to the kitchen.

Whether Troy had been out of the booster seat since Achilles last saw him, he couldn't tell. Troy sat before a plate of waffles, picking at them like a beaten boxer who refused to quit. Eyes fluttering, his chin would slump down to his chest and jerk aright whenever his fork clattered off the table. Achilles's father would pick it up, wash it with soap and water, and press it gently back into Troy's hand, like a gift. Achilles pushed the food around on his Justice League plate, sometimes revealing Aquaman, sometimes Batman, but never the Wonder Twins.

"You tired, Troy?" asked Achilles's father.

Troy snapped awake. "No, I'm fine." He stuck a piece of bacon in his mouth and slowly chewed.

His father looked happy and chipper, his mother serious. It was like they had exchanged bodies in the last hour. His father exclaimed, "Six and eats like a horse. He's a real Conroy. Let's have cake!"

Excited that the cake was to be again unveiled, Achilles said nothing about thinking that horses ate hay.

His mother flung open the refrigerator door with such force it banged against the counter and the glass jars rattled on their shelves. She slapped the cake on the table.

"Ann, please," his father whispered.

"Yes sirree! A knife." She yanked open the cutlery drawer, and after a moment's searching upended the drawer into the sink, picked out a knife, and tossed it on the table.

His father, red-faced, stormed out of the kitchen. His mother followed a moment later, saying over her shoulder, "Have all the cake you want Achilles, sweetie. All the cake *you* want."

Achilles opened the cake box. He'd snuck a peak earlier, but hadn't seen the whole thing. His name was spelled out in red letters with *Happy Birthday* in gold. Orange and blue frosting balloons clustered in the corners and a comet trailed by yellow stars underscored his name. The brightly colored decorations stood out against the white frosting. He hoped it was angel food, the best flavor ever! Troy grabbed the knife, wrapping his fingers around the tapered end of the blade, and waved it about like a conductor. Achilles, feeling heroic, leapt up and snatched it from Troy. The blade glistened. Rivulets of blood welled between Troy's fingers and dripped onto the cake. Troy squeezed both of his hands into tighter fists, but still the blood ran, like he was growing Wolverine claws. His parents rushed in when Troy wailed. Their eyes traveled from Troy's hand, by then bleeding so much that the corner of cake nearest him looked like red velvet, to the knife in Achilles's hand. He saw the shock on their faces, the misunderstanding, but he couldn't move.

"It's okay Keelies," said his mother, inching around the table to Troy, going the long way and sidestepping the entire time, as if afraid to turn her back to Achilles. His father raised two hands in surrender, and calmly said, "Put the knife down, son."

The short wooden riveted handle and long steel blade felt so dense, so heavy, his entire arm and the knife one leaden elbow pipe, a rigid burden affixed by a cruel fate.

"It's okay son. We can talk about it. Put it down."

The knife bounced off the table and onto the floor, clattering and streaking blood. His father kicked the knife away, backhanded Achilles. A thud. The first blow surprised him. His father had never struck him before, so he sat stock-still until the next blow knocked him to the floor. The base of his skull and jaw rattled, and he instinctively ran his tongue across his teeth to see if they were all there. Tucking his chin tightly into his chest, he tried to cover his ribs with his elbows, but the blows came from everywhere. Covering his head, he was kicked in the side, and covering his sides left his face exposed to his father's kicks, precise and snappy, cracking like a whip. One foot found his temple, another his stomach, and his breath rushed out in a whistle. Heaving, he scurried under the table and curled up to fight the contractions in his stomach.

Like playing Rock'em Sock'em Robots, he flinches when struck, but he no longer feels it. His father's waffle-soled brogans stomp back and forth, probing under the table, and behind them, his mother's red espadrilles squeak as she shuffles to and fro, like she's dancing, until suddenly they take flight, her legs dangling like willows until she wraps them around his father's waist. Achilles hugs the pole supporting the table. The metal is cold on Achilles's face, but he stays there, keeping his head away from the floor because he knows it's dirty. His father pounds the table, the vibrations traveling down the pole and rattling Achilles's head. Soon the metal is no longer cold against his face. He can't see his mother's shoes. His father must have taken off his belt because the buckle catches Achilles on the funny bone and he vomits, like a sissy. Someone yells, "Daddy, please. Daddy, please stop!"

His father's heavy breathing. His mother on her feet, her voice a knife. "You will leave now." His father's last kick, halfhearted. A brogan floats by Achilles's head like a blind, angry animal. His father's pronouncement: "I'll not have that kind of violence in my house. I didn't adopt a boy so he could attack my son, his brother, with a knife. Be a man, Achilles. Things change. Accept it. Be a man." The front door creaks open and slams shut. Two steps down the porch, slipping on the gravel. The opposite of the scrape and two stomps that cast the day off when he comes home each evening.

His mother, eyes swollen and bloodshot, sat Indian-style on the floor, something she always forbade Achilles to do because the floor had *little germs with big teeth.* She held her arms open to him, a gesture of forgiveness that made him cry, and cry he did, knowing, unable to explain, but knowing, that she took his sobs as an admission of guilt.

"I didn't mean it," he sniffed.

"I know." She remained motionless, arms extended, until Achilles released the pole and crawled to her. She hugged him and helped him to his feet, sitting him on her lap. Troy sat in the corner, his hand wrapped in a towel, tears fanning down his face. Had Achilles heard Troy yell *Daddy?*

Achilles pointed to the small puddle on the floor and his shirt and started weeping again in earnest. He could smell himself. "I made a mess."

"It's okay, baby. It's okay."

His arm swathed in one of the white towels Achilles was forbidden to use lest he get them dirty, Troy held his hand like he was in class waiting to be called on. Seeing him fixate on the towel, his mom wiped Achilles's face with her own shirt. "You can put your hand down now, Troy."

His mother hobbled from the table to the sink. She slipped out of her squeaky red shoes and kicked them, sending them tumbling loudly across the linoleum and onto the carpeted living room floor. Then, thinking better of it, she retrieved them and tossed them in the trashcan. Every so often, between wiping the table and floor, she'd run her hand down the side of Achilles's face and tell him it was going to be all right or pull him in for a hug. She eventually led both boys to her bedroom to sleep curled beside her. But Achilles couldn't rest and slipped from beneath his mother's arm and out of the bed. He tiptoed to the door, looking back just before he left and catching Troy awake. Troy quickly shut his eyes and snuggled closer to Achilles's mom. When certain that Troy would continue pretending to sleep, Achilles left.

A third of it broken off, the edges crumbled, the frosting balloons flattened, his name smeared, the cake was in shambles. He pushed the third that was broken off against the rest, wet his finger, and ran it along the fissure where the frosting met. He tried replacing the balloons. All stayed, save one. He tried to reshape the crumbled end, but it kept tumbling back down. Thirteen years later, he will stand before the minaret that remained as the last monument to a bombed-out mosque, remember this moment, and realize that he had always been puzzled that it was so easy to destroy things and so hard to fix them, that even the biggest building could crumble like cake. He will temporarily feel less anxious about the war, about the future, believing that to have plumbed his younger self meant all mysteries would eventually unfold. Neverending darkness was how he'd later describe the feeling he had on his eighth birthday. It was the way he felt watching the night sky from inside a bombed-out building, thinking about how peaceful it would be if the sun never rose.

In his room, Achilles propped two pillows against the wall and spread a blanket across the top. Sleeping in his pillow fort, he felt certain he wouldn't be disturbed anymore that night.

The next morning, his father placed Achilles and Troy side by side on the corduroy couch, their legs dangling, and sat on the ottoman facing them. "Things are going to be better for both of you." Troy nodded. Achilles mumbled, "Okay."

His father leaned forward so his hair fell across his eyes, curled his bottom lip up, and blew, making his white forelocks tickle the air like smoke. "What's happening?" he asked anxiously. "What's happening?"

It had been dark the first time his father did that trick, and Achilles had thought he was on fire. Achilles was supposed to say, *You're burning up, Daddy.* First he had to share his cake with Troy, now this. He looked down at his feet. Troy was wearing his red Superman socks.

His father tried again, curling his lips and blowing, but this time he poked Achilles in the ribs, and Achilles couldn't help laughing, even though it hurt a little to do so because his sides were still sore, and when his father chucked his chin and hugged him, his memories of the night before faded, the way landmarks dwindled in the rearview mirror, sometimes receding so swiftly he flinched and wondered if they had ever really been there at all.

"Things are going to be better than they've ever been before," said his father. "Troy, you have the home you deserve. Achilles, you finally have the brother you need."

They nodded obediently. His mother cruised by, her purposeful gait becoming a limp when she thought herself out of sight. She wore the same look as the night before, a mix of guilt and embarrassment.

His mother said they never had to be alone. His father said brothers had to stick together. Troy wanted to join the Cub Scouts, Achilles joined the Boy Scouts. Troy wanted to play t-ball, Achilles played Little League. Troy wanted to take judo, his mom made Achilles go too (though Achilles eventually switched to karate because it provided more opportunities to kick people). They didn't stick together; they were stuck. The ice cream and waffles had only been the beginning. That night, his parents did switch bodies, his father chipper, his mother suddenly somber. If their father went anywhere with Troy, even for a quick smoke and fire run—to fill up the tank and buy cigarettes—Achilles's mom made them wait for Achilles. By the time they were in high school, Achilles was a wind-up doll. Troy wanted to learn guitar. Achilles signed up without being asked. Troy wanted to run cross-country. Achilles went shopping for new shoes. Troy wanted to join the military, go Airborne, jump out of perfectly good airplanes. Next thing Achilles knew, he was dodging bullets and shitting sand and there was Troy, always smiling, always with the sun and the wind to his back. Troy, the one everyone thought older and wiser because he was taller. Troy, always raising Cain. Troy, not, as promised, always warm and friendly, but damned near tireless.

PART 2

LATE FALL 2004

CHAPTER 8

"**B**RING A FRIEND TO THE SCREENING," SAID INES. "YOU'LL SEE MY NEW Orleans." Did she think he needed medical attention? She said she wanted to thank him for his help over the past couple of weeks, but upon hearing *screening*, Achilles thought triglycerides, blood pressure cuffs, lipid tests. He imagined helping Mabel and Dudley—Ines's two longtime volunteers—escort the old and infirm to a mobile medical clinic and knew Wages wouldn't want to spend an afternoon doing that. Good thing Achilles agreed, because a couple days later he and Ines were on the St. Charles streetcar entering an area of town previously known to him by name only—Uptown.

With the wooden seats, manually operated curtain, wheeled popcorn machine, marble floor, and gilded marquee, it was like no theater he'd seen before. The feature starred an Icelandic band singing in a make-believe language, and included interviews with several eccentrically attired, dour musicians with thick accents. The film ended with one of their music videos. In it, a boy dressed like a soldier and carrying a drum marched across somber tidal flats, traversed black shale dunes, scaled ragged gorges, and hiked through tawny fields of waist-high grasses, picking up other kids along the way until a troop of them followed him, clinging to his heels like ticks, the whole gaggle in costumes. Some wore bear masks, some rabbit ears. Trailing the group was a little boy in a nutcracker outfit like the one Troy wore every Christmas, between the ages of six and nine. He surrendered it only after the pants ripped in half, but he cried about it and wore the hat for two more years. At the end of the video, the drummer boy led a charge up a steep, grassy hill that gradually tapered into a narrow spur. The audience could see that the promontory ended at a bluff hundreds of feet above the sea. The kids could not.

Knowing it was silly to worry about a video, Achilles nevertheless found himself looking away, and noticed the other audience members were rapt. He wanted to yell, to ask if they thought this brave. Ines, who had been wringing her fingers, started clapping. The drummer boy had gone over the edge. The other kids followed, flinging themselves from the cliff and flying into space, blue and wide. They took air for water, fanning legs and arms like swimmers, banking to the beckoning clouds, the winds teasing their hair, at ease in the palm of the sky. The boy in the nutcracker suit hesitated at the edge. Finally he stepped off the cliff into the ether. The camera cut back to the flying drummer boy, and the video ended without revealing what happened to the child in the nutcracker suit. Achilles tried to recall the final, swift image. Had he kicked at the air? Looked down? Floundered? Frustrated, Achilles didn't applaud when the lights came on.

Achilles's motto was *Look both ways before crossing a one-way street.* While waiting at a crosswalk, stand on the side of the light pole opposite the flow of traffic. Avoid crowded elevators. Back into parking spaces. At traffic stops, maintain a distance of half a vehicle from the car ahead. Drive with one hand on the seatbelt button. Never wear open-toed shoes, in case you need to run or fight. Always wear a belt because it quadruples as a tourniquet or maul or lariat or garrote.

The list exhausted and frightened him. This fear was heightened by the presence of Ines and her smile, and her tall, good-looking friend who stood beside them in the theater lobby, and all the fine-looking, smiling people crowded around them, blissfully unaware of what price the rest of the world paid for their conveniences. Sharp creases, wind-resistant hair, perfect makeup, gold bangles. Hushed tones, subdued nods, polite laughter. They all looked so happy. The polished wood floors, the colossal chandelier suspended from gilded chains, the etched box-office glass. Even the building looked happy, as if the ticket was worth more than the price of admission.

Running through his list, Achilles doubted he would ever be happy because he couldn't stop holding his breath. Even that was cynicism. He couldn't stop thinking about what he was thinking about without being cynical about it. The army taught him to hope for the best but expect the worst. Yet how he yearned to join those kids.

Looking at him, Ines's smile flattened, then rebounded, her own eyes starting to glisten. She placed one hand on each side of his face and gently drew her thumbs under his eyes. The overhead lamps reflected in the wells of tears along her bottom lids, making her eyes bright and lively bowls of light, framed by thick eyelashes long as pine needles, brown at the base and blonde at the tip. He'd thought them light brown, but they were amber irises, brass in the center and honey around the edges, speckled with pearl and peach and his reflection, really just the outline of his face, set in shadow by the chandelier glowing behind his head like he was on fire.

After the screening, they went to lunch with Ines's tall friend Margaret, who reminded Achilles of someone he knew long ago. She sighed frequently as if awaiting a train long overdue, and had a tiny, upturned nose much too small for her long face. Her skin was deep brown, and her large teeth perfect. She stood very straight, back and neck in one long, unyielding line. Ines and Margaret met with a gasp and an "Ooh girl" in the theater lobby, supposedly surprised by their good fortune. Achilles thought it extremely unfair that he would have to take the friend test before they'd even had sex.

They ate at Minette's, a small restaurant in the French Quarter. Along one side of the dining room ran a bar behind which men in black rubber aprons told jokes while serving beer and oysters, shucked just that minute, to the patrons lucky enough to sit there. Ines chose a table next to the window. While they waited to order, Margaret mentioned how much she liked the movie, as well as the videos that played before and after it.

Ines hadn't enjoyed the video, describing it as another example of "rich people indulging obsessions."

"You say that with such envy," said Margaret. "Has Achilles seen the servant show, the old *I-hire-folks-who-look-like-you?* Vaudeville isn't it, Achilles?"

"I guess," he said.

"This was his first trip uptown," snapped Ines.

The businessman at the next table cleared his throat as he slipped his blue credit card back into his wallet. Margaret sighed. She had a man's voice and was too dark for Achilles's taste but, understandably, men noticed her. Her height alone set her apart, and her skin looked downright edible. It was easy to imagine her in a *National Geographic* centerfold, saucers in her ears, a dozen rings on her neck, and a plate in her tongue. She wouldn't be able to talk so much.

They continued the discussion of the films. The opening short had featured animated birds. Achilles hadn't liked it. Margaret loved it. Ines called it a second-rate remake of *Othello*, with an eagle as Iago, but a raven as

Othello. "How can the modern retelling actually compound the racism? It's worse than Hopkins or Olivier tromping around with bootblack on their faces, mincing and waxing apoplectic when they hear of Desdemona's infidelity. So whipped, so afraid someone else has hoed their little field, tarnished their virginal porcelain saint. I root for Iago every time."

Was this what they learned in college? Achilles saw no comparison between the animated short and the game he had often played at home with Troy. Piecing together the story, he put his money on the Moor.

The waiter took their order, fawning over Margaret, who ignored his smiles and clumsy attempt to open her napkin for her without grazing her breasts. Asked if anything else was needed, she pointed to her fork with her whole hand, letting her fingers drop like she was showing off a fresh manicure. "Clean cutlery is always appreciated."

The waiter groaned apologetically and snatched up the fork with two fingers, holding it away from his body as if it were contaminated. Achilles took his elbows off the table. Margaret continued the conversation.

"Iago! I heard that," she said. That little turned-up nose made her look like a black person trying to act white. That was who she reminded him of, the rich blonde girls at the mall dragging their heels behind their parents, whining and grousing, attracting attention they claimed to detest, the cheerleaders wearing miniskirts and high boots and complaining about the stares.

"At Spelman I had a professor who abhorred that play and M.O.V. The only person hated more than that old black ram is the Jew. The Jew can convert, while neither the Moor nor his progeny can ever change their stripes. The message is obvious: Black must destroy itself to save society. The Moor must be sacrificed to his own black hell as punishment for lusting after the white essence."

"Crunch!" they both said.

"Achilles, what do you think?" asked Margaret.

He was thinking that Margaret was crazy but remembered enough of Wages's speech to say, "It's what everyone wants for Christmas."

Ines winked at Margaret. Margaret nodded solemnly. He expected a sigh; instead she slapped the table. "That's it exactly. Drugs and money have become religion. It's no accident that the very thing that kills us is what we most crave."

"Crunch," they said.

"So you liked it, Achilles?" asked Margaret.

He pictured the little boy at the cliff's edge, then Troy perched on the rail of the water tower they loved to climb. "I'd rather know the ending."

"Hmmph." Margaret.

"The little kid jumped, but it looked like he couldn't fly."

"That's precious, though in movies, as in life, things work out for cute white kids."

Margaret's portabello mushroom arrived, and Achilles's red beans, and Ines's prime rib.

"But is it dead yet, Inesha?" asked Margaret.

Ines took a big bite, working it from one cheek to the other like an oversized gumball. Margaret waggled her fork. "Bitch, they have better manners at the Playboy Mansion."

"I've seen you eat corn on the cob. You couldn't get a job in porn," said Ines, blowing out her cheek like a baseball player.

Over the few weeks at the shelters, he'd seen Ines drink beer from the bottle, sometimes holding it up to her ear to listen to the fizz, eat wings with her fingers, and drown her eggs in ketchup. But he'd never witnessed her carnivorous fever. His concern about her bleeding heart liberalism and dreadlocks, his suspicions that her progressive tendencies were an ill-fitting suit hiding a spare tire of guilt and consumption, and his certainty that her charity was a front were all drowned out by the sound of her chewing healthy chunks carved from the slab of beef dominating the table with its cool, gray marbled edge and oily moat of blood and butter. She made a point of chewing with her mouth open, as she later explained, only to irritate Margaret.

Margaret had other things on her mind, constantly asking Achilles where he had served and what he had seen there. He shared where he had been but politely declined to offer details. "Some things shouldn't be glamorized, and to talk about them does that." He'd learned that in the civilian transition class.

Margaret stared at him as if seeing him for the first time. Sucking her teeth, she pointed at Achilles with her fork and said, "Rugged. I like that. Siblings? Or are you an only child like Spiney-Iney here?"

Achilles had been trying to formulate a better critique of the movie. Expecting any question but that, he said, "I have a brother."

Ines cocked her head. "You never mentioned that. Are you close?"

"We served together."

"Really?" asked Ines.

"That's allowed?" asked Margaret.

"One unit in Iraq had three brothers."

"What's he do?" asked Margaret.

"Not too much," Achilles shrugged.

"He's been off active duty less than a month," said Ines, smiling.

"Where is he now?" asked Margaret.

"Our father just passed, so he's doing some things at home."

Margaret pointed her fork at Achilles and Ines as if to say they belonged together. She became less combative, and after lunch they parted with hugs. Margaret gave Ines a look that said, *We'll talk later,* and Achilles's hand an extra squeeze. "Sorry about your father."

When Margaret was out of sight, Ines said, "Ignore her. She's the only person I know pessimistic enough to call Monet's garden a breeding ground for mosquitoes. She's *bougie* bougie. Every time I see her I need a drink."

"Where's the bar?"

"Sorry, back to work." She apologized again for Margaret, making Achilles wonder if he had missed something important, if Ines was slumming, or if he had just blown a blind date. It wasn't the first time someone had hooked him up with a woman on the basis of race alone. Should he have asked for her number?

"I can help with the work."

She studied his face. "You really took a beating, huh? Okay. Only one. And only because you've been so helpful. And only because it was just Veteran's Day. Yesterday."

Achilles shrugged. Veteran's Day was for old people, but if was worth a drink, so be it.

She chose a tourist trap atop Jax Brewery, a restaurant decorated with paintings of housekeepers in mammy head wraps, life-sized inflatable alligators wearing wrap-around mirrored glasses, and a waiter who introduced himself as "Samuel Clemens, your captain on this here steamboat." The appetizers were priced as entrees, the coffee as cocktails. At least they had a corner booth with a good view. The blinking Jax sign he had only seen from a distance with Wages now hovered overhead like a halo. One window offered a view of the streets below, and the other the river, black and shiny like wet obsidian, the waves looking sharp and still.

He hadn't felt this excited about Janice; maybe she had been too easy. On their first date they ate fried rice in the food court and snuck into *Terminator 2.* The week before, they'd kissed under the bleachers, and the night before screwed at the Ass Station, the abandoned gas station out on the old county road. Maybe it was because Ines was worldlier. Before ordering her coffee, she confirmed that she liked the brand they used, and requested special milk and Baileys on the side, *and not that well substitute, Carolans.* Janice was happier than a frog in a swamp whenever a diner had little white thimbles of cream and, after each meal, stuffed a handful into her purse. Janice had flags and pandas and fireworks painted on her long nails. Ines had natural nails with a strip of white across the tips, simple and glamorous at the same time.

She leaned forward, her breasts momentarily resting on the table, heavy, real snake charmers. A Spiderman pendant lounged in her cleavage. Lucky devil! God, she was so beautiful. Chivalry had its perks. After opening the door to the stairway, he'd remained two paces behind her to ensure a better view. What could be more pleasurable than watching a fine woman walk uphill, a little bit of shake in every step? Maybe Merriweather was right about the steroids in chicken giving white girls big asses. A thick cotton t-shirt, faded denim jeans, dreadlocks, freckles, a head wrap—the classic rich hippy, the prototypical freaky white girl, except her clothes fit like she'd been poured into them. Ines: white woman with a black woman's ass. As Merriweather would have said, she had puddin' in her pop, enough Jell-O to make Bill Cosby blush.

"Guys don't take their friends here." She gestured toward the windows. "Views are considered romantic." He had passed the first test, so he kept quiet about how much guys appreciated a view if it provided a clear shot.

"No, Wages doesn't take me to any fancy joints."

She smiled. "You even go by last names on the outside?"

"Outside? You make it sound like prison."

"It is if you're a woman, and can't even go to funerals. American women are like a third sex. We have a little more freedom, but it's still demeaning. Did you know that one in seven Afghan women—"

"Die in childbirth." Achilles finished her sentence, adding that he'd once been posted to Rabia Balkhi, the renovated women's hospital, after hardliners tried to disrupt the construction.

She nodded, then continued anyway, explaining that Afghan women had to buy their own medical supplies—sutures, drugs, everything— before surgery. "I spent a year as a gender advisor with an NGO."

Achilles said nothing, even though he knew how the system worked over there, and that men had to buy their own shit too. Achilles decided not to ask what a gender advisor did. He pointed at her pendant. "You like Spiderman?"

"A gift from my cousin Sammy. His favorite superpower is webcasting. I told him he could learn that in school these days, but he didn't get it."

Achilles offered a half grin. "I don't know much about technology."

She asked, "What's your favorite superpower?"

"America."

"Hmmph! Mine is invisibility."

"That's not a superpower. I learned that in the army."

"Is that why you joined, to get superpowers?" she asked.

"Is that why you volunteered?" asked Achilles.

"No. I wanted to be like all the other kids in my school. If I'd been a man, I'd have been that soldier who carried me out of the minefield." She winked at him. "Selfless, like in the movies where you're leaning over a terribly wounded soldier, gripping his bloody hand, and he says, 'Go on without me, save yourself.'"

It wasn't like that at all. Most guys begged for help. Their biggest fear, once assured they would survive, was being left behind. Remembering Jackson's face, Achilles reached for the cigarette he usually carried behind his ear. He smoked less than two a week, but kept one on hand to stave off tears.

"He put your life at risk."

"He could see my footprints. He had a metal detector."

"It's just dangerous."

"That surprise you?" Ines was beaming, eyes bright and perky as she told him about her soldier's name, unit, and uniform. "He touched his hat—just like in a Western—and said, 'eleven-bang-bang at your service, ma'am.'" The chances were slim, but did Achilles recognize him?

He didn't, and wouldn't have admitted otherwise. He hadn't come this far all for her to applaud another Troy, whom he could easily imagine tipping his pot top like a magician. Were this a movie, Achilles would walk out. He disliked films anyway, especially porn, preferring doing to watching. He caught a glimpse of his reflection in the window and his stomach turned. His eyes were still bloodshot, chin scabbing over, face abraded. What was he thinking? That was probably why the old white couple sitting nearby kept looking at them.

Achilles's father used to tell him that lots of women would like him, *Lots and lots of women*, he always said with a wink. But Achilles hadn't been lucky that way. No one as hot as Ines signed his yearbook. He wasn't as bold as Troy or as smooth as Merriweather.

Ines's coffee and Achilles's tequila arrived. She moved with precision, holding her teaspoon above her cup and pouring sugar into it until it overflowed, counting to three before dumping the teaspoon into the cup. The coffee on the saucer she poured back into the cup. She licked her spoon and set it squarely on a napkin, then bent forward, her breasts kissing, to nose the cup, inhaling deeply before taking a sip. A pale peach quarter moon remained on the rim of the cup. Did it taste chalky? Sweet? Like those wax lips, one bite and your mouth was flooded with sugar?

Entranced by these ruminations, he lost track of the conversation for a moment, but his wavering attention refocused when she said, again without a hint of jest or irony, "You know how most white people are."

"Yeah, I know how they get." Achilles smiled, sitting up, sticking out his chest, flexing his arms.

She smiled back.

Soon enough she was talking about demographics, and how it should be illegal for recruiters to target inner cities where it was impossible for black kids to turn down the temptation of recruitment bonuses that exceeded their annual minimum wage, Mickey D's salary. That's what surprised Achilles about *most white people:* they constantly bitched about the world, even shit that didn't concern them. He let her talk without interruption, camouflaged in her awe, preferring her take on the war, her sense of the heroic and, as she put it, "tragic role of the soldier who needs a job, but not as a hit man. Right?"

"Of course," he said, wanting to use Merriweather's line—*Do you have any black in you?*—so she could say no, and he could ask, *Do you want some?* Was she the demure type who wanted to be ravaged or the aggressive mare who wanted you to don spurs and slap her ass? Did she say shit like, "Give me that black dick, give it to me Daddy"? Did she shave her pussy? What did it smell like? Did she swallow? Do anal? Had she been with a black guy before? Weren't most people in New Orleans Catholic? Did that make her a dirty virgin? He'd slip his thumb in when she came. He'd always wanted to do that. Yes. He'd slip his thumb into her ass on the first go-round, just to let her know he's a cave dweller. A spelunker (another word he learned from the Germans in the next camp). No, he wouldn't buck being her soup-kitchen commando. Besides, Merriweather always said, "When a woman kings you, wear the crown."

And he felt like a king, until she mentioned having noticed his fond-ness for certain jokes. Did he know more?

She must have overheard him swapping jokes with the volunteers at St. Jude. Achilles knew he should remain stone-faced, but being alone with her made him so giddy—yes, giddy—that he rambled off a list. What do you call a cleric on fire? Why shouldn't civilians carry guns? Why do blacks prefer the air force? How do you get an Afghan to take a bath? How many Kurds fit in a phone booth? What do you call a thou-sand Iraqis at the bottom of the ocean? How does an Afghan practice safe sex?

"He marks the camels that kick," said Ines.

"What's Afghanistan's national bird?" asked Achilles.

"Duck," said Ines.

"What do you throw a drowning Afghan?" asked Achilles.

"His wife and kids," said Ines. "Yadda, yadda, and what do you call an Afghan cleric?

"Holy shit," said Achilles. "You know them all."

She nodded. "And they're not funny, unless you have a soldier's sense of humor."

Ines slapped the table, spreading her long thin fingers as if to keep it from floating away. "Well?" She slapped the table again. "Are they funny?"

Of course they were. Did he have a soldier's sense of humor? Yes. They put the fun in funeral. They laughed when heads scalped by shrapnel were dubbed sundaes, or when tossing grenades became known as blowing kisses, while throwing up became known as tossing a grenade. They laughed in the hospital when Merriweather screwed on his roommate's foot, the one that looked like a giant ice cream scoop, and said "Transformer, motherfuckers. Take me to Baskin Robbins." When you were mad enough to punch a baby, there was little to do but laugh until the blood left your feet. But this was the interview, so he gave the inter-view answer: "Of course they're not funny."

"I knew you were different, but not that much." She winked. "Why aren't there any Walmarts in Afghanistan?" she asked, adding a sneer cer-tainly meant to make him think she believed what she was saying, but that he recognized as her disgust at the joke.

"Because there's a Target on every corner." Achilles snorted, unsuc-cessful in his attempt to hold back his laughter. "But I'm laughing at you, not the joke."

"Of course," said Ines. She finished her coffee and motioned for the check.

"You were serious about only one?"

Ines stared at him for a moment before saying, "I should probably see the other guys."

Achilles nodded. "It's nothing, really."

He insisted on walking Ines to her car—a beat-up Carmen Ghia. Before getting into her car, she reached out and touched the scratch under his eye. "So who's your brother, Odysseus?"

Waiting for his answer, she buckled in and when she turned back to him, the moon was in her eyes and he knew that he was the soldier who'd saved her life, noble and august, tall and true, and part of him rejoiced that Troy wasn't there to take that away. He said, "It was this or Hercules."

Ines said, "I guess it's no different than Biblical names, or us naming kids after famous Americans. How many Abraham Leroy Lincolns and George Washington Johnsons do you know?"

Achilles shrugged. He knew none.

"Exactly. Too many to count," said Ines, starting her engine. The car rattled like it was going to take flight, or disintegrate. The body was mottled with primer and rust, the original yellow faded to the color of earwax and the left taillight covered with an oversized bandage. It was the kind of beater rich kids tooled around in on weekdays, the kind of car a poor person would actually fix.

"When can I see you again?"

"I have a boyfriend, Achilles. As I said, I only wanted to thank you for your help and share a different side of Nola. I'll be seeing you."

"Do you have Margaret's number?"

"Of course." She scowled and drove off.

Back at Wages's he tossed and turned, albeit dressed. That feeling he first had when Wexler ran into the minefield, which subsided after his discharge, was stronger than ever in New Orleans. A kind of paranoia, it was the suspicion that his life was irreparably damaged, that everything he touched was scarred and singed. His grandfather always said, "Don't write checks your ass can't cash." After a few weeks in Kabul, Achilles knew he was writing checks that other people's asses were cashing.

It was like the book they read in middle school about the big dumb guy who pet rabbits to death because he didn't know his own strength, or understand his place in the world. When Achilles first read it, the book meant little to him, but he thought about the story during every leave and wondered how he and his friends would fit into the world now that they knew what they were capable of doing. Wages was at the casino. Wexler worked construction. Merriweather was looking for a part-time job with kids. No purpose. Unlike Ines.

Ines. The taut pull of the T-shirt across her chest, the gentle curve of her belly, the shake when she walked. Those glossy heart-shaped lips, kissing question marks. His dick in those lips, a kind of Cupid. His groin felt heavy as his cock thickened. He saw Ines bent over the sofa, ass poked up, cheeks blossomed out, looking back in shock as he rammed into her, biting the pillow to keep from screaming. He would pause for a minute and let her savor the sensation of being impaled by his meat sword. Then withdraw, and return so slowly she'd wonder if it'd ever stop coming, like a long train easing into a tunnel. She'd look back at him with that face that said she worshipped him.

Just as Achilles began kneading his dick, Wages came stomping down the hall. "Have you tried calling boardinghouses?"

Achilles couldn't see the bottle but heard sloshing liquid. He pulled the covers over his head.

"He has to be staying somewhere. Let's get oscar-mike, Connie."

Hearing his army nickname, Achilles perked up. His hand to his ear like a phone, he said, in a bad British accent, "Conroy's room please."

"I'm serious and you're doing a bad Slurpee slinger impression."

As his erection subsided, Achilles admitted it wasn't a bad idea. This was the time Troy would most likely be in. Over the next hour, they called every hotel to no avail. Achilles experienced the same intense disappointment he'd known at the green camelback. Wages also looked forlorn, like it was his damned brother missing.

"We tried." Why was he consoling Wages just because Wages had to be in charge of everything? It was four a.m. Bethany would be home any minute, see him getting drunk only hours before his shift, and give Achilles the stink eye. Hadn't she known he liked to drink when they married? Everyone else knew. He didn't cause trouble, but he had a high capacity for high octane, as he put it. Achilles cocooned himself in the sheet and dove onto the couch. "Good night!"

After a moment of silence, he peeked out. Wages stood there in his hunting hat and yellow ducky boxer shorts, holding a pint bottle of whiskey with a crazy straw in it, peeking through the blinds. He had the tiniest spare tire growing. Bethany's cooking.

Achilles asked, "Are you horsesleeping?"

"No, I was just thinking about some of the rooming houses I've seen." As he described them, they sounded like halfway houses. "Maybe we should stick to B&Bs."

"We called them under hotels."

"No we didn't. That's a different section of the phone book. I work in the hospitality industry now."

"You work. Exactly. Man, go to bed before Bethany comes in and gives me crosshairs."

Wages straightened up and waved the bottle, sloshing whiskey on his feet. "No one tells me what to do."

"I know, dude. I'm just saying, she'll be in here like 'Kyyyllle? A-sheel?' dragging our names the way women drag names out."

"Ma ma sa, ma ma sa, ma ma ma coo sa." That was Wages's version of *blah blah blah*. He removed the straw and drained his bottle. "I know you just want to detonate your heat seeker. Go ahead. Just don't look at pictures of my wife while you do it. If you do, leave five dollars on the table." He raised the bottle in a toast, and shuffled down the hall.

Achilles's hands slipped back into his shorts. Of course he wanted to detonate the heat seeker. It would be light soon, and whacking off during the day was desperate and adolescent. If he did it now, he'd forget about it by morning. Achilles wriggled his shorts down and conjured Ines again. The gummy smile, the deep shadow of cleavage, but he couldn't hold the image. He kept envisioning the boardinghouses Wages had described, and imagined Troy inside some ratty home in the Tremé district. He thought of Ines, then Troy. He wondered if they would like each other, and knew she would like Troy more.

Ines was his most exciting fantasy since high school, when a Japanese exchange student transferred in for one semester. She was slim and porcelain and had such a small mouth he wondered how she ate. He constantly imagined himself with her. Jacking off was easy with people he didn't know. With women he knew it was different. That's why he never fantasized in earnest about Bethany. It was like trying to put a spell on them or reach into their dreams. He would imagine them just so, arranging it so they were looking him in the eye when he came. Then they belonged to him. It had worked with Aiko. He imagined her thin purple lips making cooing sounds. On their first date, he discovered that they did. They were quite a couple, the only black and the only Asian in the twelfth grade together. (There'd been one other black kid in his grade for one year, but he lived with his grandmother, brought his lunch, and talked like the rest of them from the city. So, he didn't count.) Someone had called Achilles and Aiko the United Nations. Achilles didn't remember who said that, but he should have punched him. He thought it funny at the time. Aiko deserved better.

So did Ines, so earnest. Ines pressing her tits together like a pin-up girl. Ines shaking her ass like a popcorn pot. Ines, reaching back and spreading her cheeks like a porn star, sighing when he enters her, and how he loves to enter, watching the look of surprise on her face. He wanted to lick her from navel to nookie, make her crow and caw, flap her arms and fly off the bed with delight. He wanted to bend her over, crack her cheeks, wedge his nose into the arch with the asshole for the keystone, and feel her fat ass like a velvet vise clenching his cheeks as she came. He would. Yes. He would.

CHAPTER 9

For the next few days, Achilles divided his time between driving the neighborhood where he'd gotten into the fight and doing the heavy lifting at St. Jude. It was difficult to say which was more frustrating. Since the screening, Ines had taken to calling him Mr. Conroy. *Mr. Conroy, can you help Dudley move these books? Mr. Conroy, would you mind assisting Mabel with the heavy pots? Mr. Conroy do you have time to help Mabel sort these clothes?* But Mr. Conroy would not be broken. He had nothing if not endurance, and the patience of a sniper to boot. Besides, she said Mr. Conroy with such a smile.

The neighborhood where he'd had the fight was a different matter. There, they actually stopped smiling when he showed up, like he was a teacher entering the room carrying final exams. Old women waved him off with a shake of the head, kids ran away, teenagers ignored him. He even tried dressing in a hoodie and Army surplus fatigues. The response was the same. Achilles didn't understand what about his demeanor led anyone to think that he was a cop, but the third time he was accused of being one, it occurred to him to call Morse.

Wages advised him against contacting the detective, explaining that if anything happened to the residents of the boardinghouse, the police would blame Achilles. "I hate to pull the wings off your fly, but these motherfuckers are dirtier than dealers. They'll shoot you in the back and sprinkle crunch on you. They'll run you over, and call it *suicide by cop.* They'll pressure you for cash, then arrest you for trying to bribe a public official. You aren't from here. Avoid them. In New Orleans, people go into crime so they'll have some protection from the police."

"All cops aren't dirty," said Achilles.

Wages shook his head, "That's what I always liked about you, Brother. You rock that suburban optimism."

When he arrived at the police station, Achilles was surprised to hear Morse tell him the same thing. Achilles had barely started telling him about the camelback when the detective raised his hands and mouthed *Not here!* as he offered to take Achilles to lunch at the Bluebird Diner next door to the station. In a back booth, Morse explained that it was best to stay away from a scenario involving arson, a corpse, and a one-eyed man. "I don't doubt they had it coming, but . . ."

"I didn't start that fire," said Achilles.

"I'm not saying you did—" Morse paused while the bottom-heavy waitress took their orders. Judging by their banter, she knew Morse and liked him. Morse stared wistfully as she walked away.

"I should have never divorced her. Anyway, kid, the first piece of advice is never order a chicken salad sandwich in a place that serves real food. Would you ask for a massage when offered a blowjob?"

Achilles nodded his understanding. That's why the waitress at Seaton's always looked funny when he ordered. Morse called his ex back over to the table and, arm around her waist, changed Achilles's order.

"Eat well. No one's here for the weather. New Orleans has traditions, like red beans and rice on Mondays, always." Morse explained that Mondays were washdays, so a slow-cooking meal left time to do the wash. The beans could stay on the pot all day, simmering, seasoned with the leftover ham or sausage from Sunday night's dinner.

When the food came, Morse attacked it like a soldier who'd been marching all day. He applied Tabasco until red pools formed at the edges of the plate, licked his fingers like chicken bones, and sopped up sauce with scraps of bread. Achilles felt comfortable to do the same, except for the hot sauce. The vinegary smell burned his nostrils. Achilles also declined to wipe his plate with the bread, which his father had always described as countrified.

While they ate, Morse explained that Achilles needed to keep a low profile. "When it's gang related, one guy kills another, killer goes to jail. Two birds."

It made sense. Let the troublemakers fight among themselves, and clean up the mess after the fact. It wasn't too different from Afghanistan, in theory. What was unusual was the patience with which Morse explained himself. In the past, Achilles had twice been pulled over by cops who were irritated that he didn't immediately hang his hands out of the window and drop the keys. His opinion was solicited whenever Ramirez made a slow-jam

CD for his girlfriend, who was black. He'd been expected to know where the good soul food restaurants were that time they visited DC. Morse was different. He spoke as if Achilles had no idea what was going on in the city, and the more Morse talked, the more Achilles believed him. Morse's point was simple:

"You get into a tussle with a gangster, your record says gang-related as far as the department is concerned. Forever. Then your face goes into the bang-book, the binder that every beat officer memorizes. If you so much as run a stop sign, and you're in that book, you're going to jail. And that's if you get a record and not a toe tag. What if a gang leader catches wind that you're in that book? You're either with him or you're on his hit list. And kid, the way you present yourself, it'll be the hit list. You open your mouth and everyone knows you're not from here. Your parents brought you up good. You sound white. I'm okay with that, but to some people you sound like a victim. This city is consistently ranked as a murder capital. In 1994 there were 421 murders. Even we were shocked. After that, who is left to kill? That record hasn't been broken anywhere in America. Over one a day. At that rate, it isn't even front-page news anymore. You'll get the Saints' scores before you find out who was shot. Understand?"

Achilles nodded. New Orleans was even more dangerous than DC, and he knew what Morse meant by *some people*.

"This isn't *Scared Straight*. I know you been shot at before and I'm sure you can handle yourself, you got some guns on you and some serious experience. But this is different. You're not Charles Bronson. The city is safe unless you wander into exactly those few areas you keep visiting. So, if you get any more 'leads,'" he made air quotes, "talk to me. About this green camelback, because you've already filed that report, I'll send someone to investigate a possible sighting." Morse gave him his cell phone number, and a piece of paper with "Spirit House" written on it.

"Spirit House?"

"You got this?" asked Morse, pointing at the check as he stood.

"Sure. Spirit House?"

"They took in a family who lost everything in a fire a couple weeks back. A family with three little girls. Sounds like it might be the Harpers from your green camelback." He clapped Achilles on the back. "I'm in a good mood today. My son got shot. Only in the leg, and it will heal fine. But it's enough that he's coming home early, on his own two feet. I'm sure your mother wants to see you do the same."

He pictured his mother with her backpack on. She wasn't worried. "This was her idea. Can't you introduce me to the other officers and let them know that I'm only trying to find my brother?"

Morse scratched his head. "Achilles, do you know about the Stop Snitching campaign? The T-shirts, the DVDs, the website? It's the whole public relations kit-n-caboodle. The message on the streets across the country is that if anyone finds out you're a snitch, you're done. What do you think half of those murders are about?"

Achilles groaned, trapped no matter which way he turned.

"Just go to the Spirit and let me know if anything else turns up."

Achilles thanked him, and rushed to the Spirit House, another small storefront shelter with a few bunks. The Harpers were in the small backyard. The couple was much younger than he had expected, younger than him maybe. They must have started early to have three kids already. Between the rusty barbecue grill, tire swing, and patchy grass he would have thought it was their house, except for the mother's constant watchful gaze, as if assessing a danger only she could see. Achilles could see her in profile, a broad nose and round eyes. For some reason, her face made Achilles think that she liked to hug a lot. Whenever one of her daughters waved, she forced a smile and waved back before her mouth took on a grim downward turn at the corners. The girls chased each other around the yard, the youngest trailing behind, weighed down by her right arm, swathed in bandages, save for two tiny fingers.

The Harpers were open and friendly, which he hadn't expected, but which made sense considering that they put all their children's names on the mailbox. After learning that he was looking for his brother, they invited him to sit in a plastic lawn chair. They were a nice couple and spoke freely with Achilles while keeping their eyes on their three daughters. They'd never even personally met the landlord and didn't really like the place, but the price was right. They'd never seen Troy. The only thing they knew was that Blow and Lex also referred to each other as Holiday and Charles.

"It's a shame they can play outside here and couldn't in our own house," said Mr. Harper watching his daughters play. "All those damned barrels."

It did seem a shame that they would be safer only after being displaced, but at least they hadn't been chased out of their city, at least it wasn't uninhabitable and overrun by the military. "Do you know how the fire started?"

Mrs. Harper turned to face Achilles. The other side of her face was badly burned, the skin from the eyelid to lower cheek pink and brown, like raw, spoiled chicken. She had no eyelashes and the hair around her temple was gray, as if it hadn't burned but was dying nonetheless. "If you know something, please tell us."

Achilles shook his head. Did Mr. and Mrs. Harper still have sex? "Is it okay if I say good-bye to your daughters?"

"Of course," said Mr. Harper.

Mrs. Harper, who hadn't taken her eyes off of him, held his stare a moment more before nodding, as if she needed that extra time to measure him.

But Achilles was used to it. The first few weeks after their injuries, the scarred soldiers either avoided your eyes altogether, or stared as if daring you to turn away. Achilles had seen much, much worse than Mrs. Harper, and had seen it happen to people who didn't live next to druggies. But it was seeing her children that made it feel so unfair. He felt bad for them, for what they would endure with a mother who stuck out like that.

He shook their hands one by one, planning to give them each five dollars. Shaking hands with the little girl with the burned arm, he felt especially sorry for her, and gave her a ten-dollar bill. He remembered adults doing this when he was a child. But no amount of money was going to help. The little girl was doomed. How could she not be when her father and mother were willing to live next to two scum like Lex and Blow just because the rent was low? The father had said *The price was right* in the same tone guys used to explain why they bought cheap beer. It was at that moment when Achilles was holding her free hand, the ten-dollar bill clasped between the two fingers that poked out of the bandages on the other arm, her mother cooing *What do you say?* and her sisters now gathered around Achilles with their hands out for more, that the girls all turned as if Carmen Sandiego had arrived and he looked up to see Ines smiling at him, flushed like she'd been caught leaving without saying good-bye, as she flashed a small wave, like a Castaneda clap, and skipped through the door. But he gave them each five dollars more, in case she was watching from inside the house.

The irony was that Wages had taken to calling Achilles a player, even though Achilles always described Ines as *Nothing*. Wages would say, *Right, and Chinese people's eyes don't look like that when they're at home. Really, it's Nothing serious.* And Wages, unaware that Achilles did his admiring from a distance, always answered that no one did *Nothing Serious* more than two days in a row. Maybe that was true, but Achilles still didn't think of Ines as anything serious, or that she would become anything serious. She was an obsession, a challenge. A mission. The couch couldn't be a stand-in forever. His plan was simple: suit up, show up, look attentive, and act cooperative: everything that had gotten him through the military. That had worked with Janice, who was a checkout girl at Sak and Save when they first met. He was in the express lane and let the lady behind him go ahead because she had only one item. Janice cooed like that was the nicest thing anyone could do, so Achilles did it three more times. That was how long it took before she agreed to go to a movie with him. After that, even though she already had a boyfriend, they saw each other almost every day. But that didn't make it serious.

Achilles wasn't sure he'd even know what something serious looked like. He didn't think like that. He wasn't married. He was Achilles. Whenever he asked his father for advice about women, or rather on the two women he had dated other than Janice, his father always answered: "Son, what's your name?"

"Achilles."

"That's right. You're Achilles, not married. Enjoy being single. Believe me when I say it will be over too soon."

So whenever Wages nosed around at it, Achilles just shrugged and answered, *I'm Achilles.* And Wages said, *I didn't know you were such a player,* and Achilles would grin, as he did now, against his will.

After Spirit House, he had headed back to Wages's to clear his head and think through things as he only could somewhere he felt safe. It was a few hours after meeting the Harpers, and Achilles and Wages were in the latter's living room shooting the breeze and playing video games. Bethany was out fencing, so the Xbox was blasting through the stereo. Achilles hoped to see Ines at St. Jude later that evening, but all afternoon Wages had been pushing Achilles to stay for dinner. He even tried to introduce it as a wager into one of the games. Lately, Wages had been more insistent about Achilles eating dinner at his house, making Achilles suspect that Wages was, well, jealous or offended. After Achilles made the mistake of mentioning Margaret, Wages concocted a plan: Achilles was to invite Ines to the gun show, where Wages would show up and do the male version of *Ooh girl, what you doin' here?* At lunch, he would grill Ines: How many rounds before you have to change the barrel of an M60? Can you perform that operation by hand? What's quieter, the suppressed .22 rifle or the HK with the silencer? Wages was in the midst of *ooh girl* strutting, his hand dangling at his side, sashaying between the high-heel chair and the sparkling settee, when Bethany came in about an hour earlier than expected, sabers and épées in tow. Wages stared at her like an intruder.

"How was the match?" asked Achilles.

"It was only practice, but fun." She shared a few more details, her voice dropping as it became apparent Wages was ignoring her. "What have you guys been up to?"

There was a long spell of silence. Wages stared alternately at his hands and at Bethany with a forced smile. Finally, he said, "We're going out for a while."

"*Kyle*, I thought we were going to see Candy today. It's my only day off this week." She sighed, ruffling Wages's hair. "Never mind. You and Achilles have fun." She pronounced it "A-sheel." It was obvious she'd been to practice. She seemed more aware of her body than usual, her movements were precise, her step light as she left the room.

"Excuse me!" Wages stood and stomped off to the back of the house.

Achilles heard Bethany laugh and ask, "Are you hungry, baby?" Hushed harsh words followed. Glass broke. A short scream sounded, and ended immediately, as if muffled. Achilles stood, "What's up?"

"It's cool," Wages called.

Achilles sat back down, despite hearing what sounded like a quick tussle and the sound of smacking flesh. "Get up! Get up!" he heard Wages say as if through clenched teeth. Wages reentered the room first, waving one arm in front of himself like he was swimming, the other behind him dragging . . . Bethany by her hair. Achilles shot back to his feet so quickly he felt dizzy. Wages had a fistful of her hair; she held on to Wages's arm to keep her full weight off her scalp. She was breathing heavy and steady, but not crying. Achilles had to give it to her: she was tough.

Achilles raised his hands slowly, palms out, stepping toward Wages.

Wages shook his head. "No. She's the one who needs to do the talking. Tell him."

Bethany inhaled sharply, coughing. Wages waggled her head back and forth.

"Wages!" yelled Achilles.

"She's only making it harder for herself." He shook her head back and forth again. "Don't fuck with me. I'll break your fucking neck and burn this house down. I don't give a reindeer fuck."

"Bethany, what's happening?" asked Achilles.

Her gaze strayed across the ground, the wall, her feet, anywhere but Achilles.

"Say it," demanded Wages.

Bethany cleared her throat, "I'm sorry."

Wages jerked her head sharply. "Look him in the eye."

Bethany looked Achilles in the eye. "I'm sorry for mispronouncing your name, Achilles. I won't do it again."

"It's okay, Bethany. It's not a problem. Please let her go."

Wages nodded quietly like a man who was just asked if a large meal, the remnants of which remained on his table, had been satisfying. "Is that acceptable to you? Is it?"

Achilles nodded vigorously. "Yes. I mean, I didn't care in the first place."

The way Wages grimaced, Achilles understood that the more he protested, the angrier Wages would become. Bethany took quick, short breaths.

"It's not acceptable," said Wages.

"It's acceptable," said Achilles.

"Are you sure?"

"It's cool. It's not a problem. It's acceptable. It's very acceptable," said Achilles. "Let her go, please."

Bethany breathed deeply, her little belly creasing her shirt at the waist. It was the first time Achilles had thought of her as pregnant. When she had been tending his wounds, he thought of having a baby as more like a job to do and less a thing to carry.

Bethany was looking at him again. "Is my apology acceptable?"

Achilles looked away and mumbled his agreement. When soldiers were stuck together in cellars and caves and tents and shit went zulu-foxtrot and a squadmate went goofy, everyone acted like nothing had happened. But this was her house.

Wages lifted Bethany to her feet and sent her down the hall with a smack on the butt. When she pushed back against Wages, he held up one finger. "Don't."

"You want to go for a walk or something?" asked Achilles, gently shepherding Wages out the front door.

Wages shrugged. "I could use a beer."

They walked in silence for several blocks. His parents barely argued. It was often apparent that his mother wasn't listening, only nodding to keep the peace. His father usually grimaced and rolled his eyes so far back in his head he looked possessed. But he had rarely heard them raise their voices except for his eighth birthday. Wages, though, hadn't raised his voice either, not once. His look and demeanor had been that of the Wages he knew on active duty: a big rock in a small river. Never a tremble in his hands, not even when packing Quikclot in that gaping hole in Ace's leg or forcing Xavier's mouth open for the medic to insert the breathing tube. Not a tremor in his voice when directing them to fall back and cover him while he ran for Merriweather. He was calm even in house-clearing runs. The Afghans would be trussed up and kneeling with hands over heads, sometimes with hoods over heads, sometimes bound like smoked hams and shitting themselves, and Wages remained cool as a cuke, chewing on a protein bar. The hotter it got, the cooler he got. He'd repeat his question over and over, and when he shot the detainee in Jalaya, all he said, with a mouthful of chocolate, was, "Mohammed pulled the trigger when he reached for me. He jumped on that bullet."

Achilles respected that. He was always struggling to hold it together, thinking every day that he wished he'd never gone. Because he followed orders without complaint, he fit into the army, finally feeling a sense of belonging, but he didn't want to be there. He was ducking in firefights and thinking that he wished he didn't have a fucking brother, because if it weren't for Troy's ass, Achilles would be grilling a burger instead of eating beef stew out of a metallic envelope. He would have a job at the mill, the feedlot, or driving the mail truck. In Goddamnistan, marriage didn't seem like such a bad idea. He could go home every night to a wife—which was always a blank face, but any soft, sweet-smelling lady would do—eat whatever she had cooked, down a few Silver Bullets, watch *Cops* or play Texas Hold-em, maybe fix the mailbox, or even hang a tennis ball from a string so she'd know when she'd pulled far enough into the garage, and have sex later that night. That would be nice, sex later that night. Sex every night. But instead, he was in towns he couldn't pronounce, providing support for a team of engineers that were building bridges for the very sorry-ass fuckers that were taking potshots at them *every* day. If he had figured out a way home, if he'd had one chance to get back to the States, Goddamnistan would have never seen his black ass again.

But he survived it. Wages at the helm, steady-like, always calm, always good at keeping everyone on the level, even after a night at the business end of the tequila gun, even when getting flushed into the big shit. He was always like he had been with Bethany a few moments ago—a machine. Everyone who came up against the machine could make it work for or against them. Bethany didn't deserve that, Achilles didn't think. But he really didn't know. She was always nice to him. She'd tended his wounds with steady, warm hands and a look of concentration in her brown eyes, the left one a little darker than the right, almost black. Fencing kept her light on her toes, even with the added weight, and her arms were well toned, especially the triceps. She had a swimmer's shoulders and pronounced calves. Well proportioned she might be, there was the old saying: *No matter how pretty she is, there is always someone, somewhere, sick of fucking her.* Who knew how Bethany agitated Wages? Maybe she disrespected him in all those subtle ways women have of chiggering under the skin. When men gave in to that, Merriweather called it getting drunk on whine. But Bethany was pregnant. Maybe that made her forgetful. "Aren't pregnant women forgetful or stressed or something?" asked Achilles.

"I didn't tell her to get pregnant. Am I supposed to let her do what she wants just because she's pregnant? I don't think so. It's the opposite. There're about to be two of them in the house. If I let the big one go off on her own devices, they'll mutiny, the whole thing'll come down on my head. You can never regain lost respect. The psychological war is not the land war. You cannot regain lost ground, except through virtual annihilation and I won't let it come to that."

Achilles had heard this all before. If you can't break their backs, break their wills. If you can't break their wills, destroy their homes, kill their livestock, raze their buildings. In basic training they were taught that the Geneva Convention prohibited soldiers from firing large rounds at humans. Fifty-caliber rounds, for example, could only be fired at equipment, like belt buckles or helmets. Commit to a course of action and complete it, even if you have to put your head through a wall. Yes, Achilles had heard it all before, in one way or another. It was the only way to hold things together.

They passed a Middle Eastern restaurant, sandwiched between a Chinese restaurant and a Mexican restaurant-slash-liquor store. The window was plastered with the gyro posters that could be found in any mall, and one beer sign. It looked good enough. Achilles had sworn that he'd never eat another food court gyro, but here with Wages in New Orleans, Nola as Ines called it, it felt like a sensible thing to do. Maybe Wages would relax a little, and talk about whatever was bugging him, in case it wasn't really Bethany. But when Achilles paused in front of the restaurant, Wages shook his head vigorously, "We gave blood, we're not giving money, too." And, he wouldn't go into the Mexican place because the guy had hit on Bethany once, and today Wages would have to smack the refried beans out of Manual Dingo. When Achilles pointed to the Chinese restaurant, or more specifically, to the humming air conditioner mounted over the doorway, Wages said, "Rocket pockets! I'm not walking into that whorehouse."

You wouldn't have said that six months ago, thought Achilles. What? You expect them to have a drive-thru?

Achilles tried to think of something funny but couldn't. Wages was never really a joker. Everyone had a nickname in basic training: gays were ass monkeys, blacks were porch monkeys, and Asians were monkey eaters. Wages never went in for any of that. Wages never referred to his men as ladies, never went for the gay jokes, never went for easy targets like sand zigger and camel jockey. In fact, Wages rarely laughed, but Achilles always found him easiest to get along with. There wasn't any pressure to say anything clever, they could just hang out and drink and relax and chat. Achilles doubled his pace to catch up with Wages, who had gradually pulled ahead as he often did after heated moments, like he had to be alone at the very moment the rest of them wanted to be together for reassurance.

Troy would know what to say. He always did. Achilles dug through his memory for the advice meted out in the transition classes. They had attended a mandatory class at the Kyrgyz airstrip before being shipped home, the Soldier's Reentry Readjustment Workshop, also known as SRRW or the "Don't (Leave Bruises if You) Beat Your Wife Class." The workshop covered three main topics: how to respond to people who criticize the war, and thus your duty, patriotism, loyalty and honor; how to recognize PTSD and why one shouldn't be ashamed to seek help; and how to handle unanticipated family adjustments. He didn't remember any of it except *Think before speaking* and *Walk away before becoming mad enough to strike* and *Act, don't react.* Or, something like that. He didn't remember the exact words, only that it felt like the opposite of what they'd been paid to do for the previous twenty-four months.

He knew that with an ACOG sight he could reach out and touch someone up to eight hundred meters away. He knew that the M4 fired a 5.56 at up to nine hundred feet per second. He knew that when insurgents "surrendered," stumbling out of a smoky doorway with hands high, the second one out of the building was the one most likely to draw a gun. But he couldn't remember a reassuring thing to say if his friend's life depended on it. He had nothing for Wages except a hand on the shoulder.

They walked that way a few more blocks in silence. Soon they reached a broad oak-lined road with a grassy median as wide as a football field. The lane ended at a turnabout, on the center of which sat an important looking building made of large slabs of marble and heavy columns. The metal banner suspended across the road read City Park. He followed Wages across the grass into the cool shadow under the canopy of ancient live oaks. It was still humid, but at least the sun wasn't beating down on them anymore. The trees were tall and stately, the massive limbs stretching out in all directions, some outstretched like arms inviting passersby to join them on a walk around the park, others hugging the ground low enough to serve as benches.

Along the edge of a small lake, a row of vendors sold hot dogs, cotton candy, and popcorn. Achilles was drawn to the Lucky Dog hot dog stand because the cart was shaped like a large frankfurter. He bought a dog and offered his friend a bite.

Wages waved it away. "No meat on Fridays."

Wages bought some popcorn and walked across a footbridge to a small island in the middle of the lake. The embankment was longer than it was wide, and shaped like a face, with two barbecue grills for eyes, a boulder for a nose, a bench for a mouth, and below the bench, a beard of monkey grass dipped beneath the tide line, making it look like a giant taking a drink, sipping from the gently swelling tide. The water was opaque, and where shallow, the color of whiskey. It felt out of place, a swamp in the city. Seated on the old metal bench, Wages plucked popcorn at the ducks.

After the pigeons started intercepting their food, the ducks drew nearer Wages, waddling so fast that at each step it looked like they were going to fall over. The sun glanced off their gleaming, lustrous coats. The leader, a melon-chested drake with iridescent eggplant and avocado-colored plumage, ventured within arm's length of Wages, boldly warning off the pigeons with his robust, guttural call. Satisfied that the interlopers had taken flight, the leader marched back and forth along the perimeter while the smaller ducks ate. The pigeons warbled their protest. A nutria rat with slick brown fur dashed across a drainage pipe. A group of clouds clustered in the south, like huddled athletes waiting to take the court. A high school soccer team scrimmaged nearby. Achilles moved closer to the soccer fields. On another field, a kid practiced free kicks. The ball lofted and arced through the sun right into the goal three times in a row, like it was tethered to a string. Everything was so vivid that he would have thought he had just been in a firefight if it weren't for the fact that he could hear everything, the warbling pigeons, the trickling water, the wind through the trees. Wages came and stood beside him.

"I never was good at corners," said Wages. "Believe it or not, it was the pressure. You're out there by yourself, and everyone's looking for you to make a difficult assist or an impossible shot. At least you have a chance with a penalty kick. A corner is shooting into a crowd, hoping to hit the right person, while everyone jostles to jump on the bullet."

The high-pitched pandemonium of children's laughter drifted over to them, galloping above the bel canto of the ducks. On the field behind them, smaller children played soccer.

"That'll be you soon."

"What? I'll be young again? Go through this shit again? Fuck that." Wages spat. "You know she did it so I won't go back."

"What?" asked Achilles.

"Got pregnant. It's an emotional ambush," said Wages, lighting a cigarette.

What about the photos, the starfish card, the closet they were converting to a nursery? He'd thought Wages happy.

"I sent her money and all. She didn't need to work while I was away. It was better that she concentrated on school, on the nursing degree, and kept busy. She didn't have to work. She had it all. That's why I couldn't save any fucking cash. Still she went and did this to me. I got to get up at the fucking crack of my ass every damn dawn to search people and make sure they aren't stealing from a *casino*. I didn't wear a suit before except for a funeral. Now I'm sporting these secondhand undertaker jobs and vfw bingo shoes because my feet are killing me from that fucking shrapnel."

Wages held his hands palms up, like he was holding a bowl. "Eight years in. I was going career. I ran a clearing squad without a single casualty. I lead a team that rescued three pows. I took down a sniper. And now, I'm making sure someone ain't stealing from a casino? I'm protecting the bandits, like the first time wasn't bad enough. There's my supervisor, fat fuck, heaving and whatnot when he walks, can't even halfway fit his fat ass through the door—no lie—a fucking pumpkin on toothpicks telling me what to do every day. He's so fucking fat in the face and his cheeks are so

big and his lips are so little and his goatee so wild it's like having a conversation with a hairy asshole. I'm a fucking professional soldier. He pokes
me in the chest sometimes. But, I got a kid on the way. I worked so hard
to get out of that fucking old uniform. I started in the kitchen. Me!
Catching the bus home in a uniform. You could change, then your clothes
smell like that nasty dishwater. Imagine being on the bus with people asking you about hot slots." Wages shook his head. He ground out his cigarette, abrading the filter and scattering the tobacco until there was not a
trace. "You need a job? I can get you a job. I've at least got that pull."

"No."

"What's up with your woman?" asked Wages.

"Nothing serious," said Achilles, surprised by the sudden turn.

"Nothing serious doesn't happen three nights in a row," said Wages.
"Playah!"

"I'm just Achilles."

Wages laughed. "Right, Player. Nothing serious? That's always how it
starts. Then, you're stuck. It's not like I want anyone else. I just don't want
her making decisions for me. All the while before people were making
decisions for me. You know what I mean, especially with Troy's reckless
ass. People do shit, then suddenly you're obligated. Women will emotionally ambush you. The domestic I-E-D is 'improvised emotional device.'"

A woman walked by pushing a stroller with twins.

"Remember the Krugers?" asked Wages.

Achilles nodded. The Krugers were three brothers stationed together.
Everyone said it was a stupid idea, until two died on the same mission.
Then no one mentioned it at all. "Kruger" became synonymous with bad
luck.

"We're lucky, ain't we," said Wages.

"Luckier than most," said Achilles.

"What did Jackson always say?" asked Wages.

In unison, Wages and Achilles said, "God loves everybody, he just loves
some of us more." They fell into raucous laughter, bobbing their heads
like rappers as they listed everyone that God didn't like, chanting the
words to the beat of Jay-Z's *Hard Knock Life*, but changing the chorus to
Jesus Christ don't like that shit! Jesus didn't like: the Taliban; the young, orange-
bearded herder struck down trying to save his goat from being run over;
Nintendo; the local who scrambled off with an armful of their bootleg
DVDs and ran right into the minefield behind the school (everyone else

knew it was there); all insurgents, everywhere, all the time; flat-chested women; or Kurds: many had incurred the Lord's displeasure. On the other hand, God loved the Airborne, all Infantry, all Rangers, most Marines, some air force enlisted, three sailors, a few Canadians, good mess cooks, America, tits, Xbox, oral, and soccer players. By unspoken agreement, they didn't mention Ramirez, Lionel Dinkins, Merri's kid, or Jackson, who'd always hated that song.

One of the younger kids shooting the free kicks overshot the goal, and the ball rolled toward them. Wages adroitly used his foot to pop the ball up to his hand, holding the ball overhead until the boy was close enough to hear Wages advise, "Use less toe." Wages dropped the ball to his foot, balanced it on his instep, and lobbed it to the kid, who yelled his thanks. The kid scored on his next shot and beamed a smile at Wages, who waved back.

Wages pointed at the kids on the other field who were on their backs in a stretching circle. "Remember those three guys with their heads and feet all to one side?"

"No."

"Outside Faizabad. All lined up like hieroglyphics."

"Nope."

"The three, all looking south," said Wages, gesturing excitedly, moving his head and arms like a dancer in that old Bangles video. "Doing that sand dance. Remember?"

"Yeah," said Achilles, though he didn't.

"I knew I wasn't imagining that shit," said Wages, punching Achilles on the arm. "You going to be here on Turkey Day? We're going to her parents' on the North Shore."

"I don't know." That was still a couple weeks away. Achilles hadn't thought that far ahead. His plan B was reenlist. His plan A, he hadn't yet conceived. "Should I be gone by then?"

Wages grabbed him by the arm and shoulder and gave him the micro, a close stare. "You don't ever have to be gone. The pact stands. Wife or no wife, kid or no kid. There's a place for you like there's a place every time Bethany's sister gets fired or her boyfriend gets sick of her tired-ass pussy and tosses her out. I endure all her friends and all the crazy couple activities. Movie and dinner. Wine-tasting shit. Even ballroom dancing, once. I endure those dudes run by their bitches. You dial them up and the wife wants to talk to you first. 'How are you? How's Bethany? Did y'all see so-and-so movie?' Sometimes you just wanna talk to the man. I compromise a lot." Wages nodded until Achilles joined him. "So, don't insult me by saying you'll be gone. And don't worry if she looks pissy sometimes. It's like a nine-month period and, anyway, a woman's got to have something to be upset about. Besides, you're the godfather."

Achilles nodded. Did that include responsibility, or just fucking people up if they messed with the kid?

"Let's get that beer," said Wages. But instead of walking toward the road, Wages turned and walked closer to the lake. His back to Achilles, Wages said, "Don't worry about her. I'll say sorry, kiss her up, you know—flowers, chocolate, scrambled eggs—love her up, shoot her in the ass with the cat pistol to show her who's boss. It's not like I torqued her. A woman will always give you a second chance if you love her, right?" He faced Achilles. "I never did that before. I swear. You know that, don't you Connie?"

Achilles nodded. "I believe you, man."

"Really?" asked Wages.

"Of course." And he did.

Wages took three quick, deep breaths as if making a wish. He held the last one as he kicked an egg-shaped rock down the bank. It cut a path through the monkey grass and hit the water with a subdued splash. He nodded with satisfaction. "Yeah. Don't worry about her. She knows I love her. I just got to keep it under control." He kicked another rock and another, then tossed in a big branch that was sharp at the end and bent like an arm holding a knife. Without complaint, the dark water swallowed them all.

"Bethany's mom can really burn."

Achilles nodded.

"Let's head back."

"I'm in the other direction. I'm meeting Ines," said Achilles.

Wages looked remorseful, like he had miscalculated terribly, calling in the wrong coordinates for an air strike.

"I swear," said Achilles, even though he was lying.

CHAPTER 10

A FEW DAYS LATER, INES INVITED HIM TO DINNER, AND AFTERWARDS TO her place. Her spacious studio in the Warehouse District was nicer than the restaurant in which they had eaten, a soul food restaurant where Achilles had loaded up on hot sauce, licked his fingers, and, because in Nawlins it was an insult not to, wiped his plate clean. With the industrial wood metal accents and exposed brick, it could have passed for an art gallery and was decorated like one. Portrait-sized black-and-white photos of King, X, Carmichael, Hosea Williams, Huey Newton, and Bobby Seale graced the foyer walls, each one labeled with a brief bio like museum displays. In the halls, Gandhi, Cesar Chavez, the Weathermen; in the living room, Camus, Sartre, Baldwin, Ellison; and, in the kitchen, Martha Graham, Sojourner Truth, Harriet Tubman, and Toni Morrison.

"Big family," said Achilles.

"Before I hung them, my friends called it Uncle Tom's condo," said Ines, leading him through the apartment.

Ines's one-room studio was larger than Wages's entire house. The bedroom was cordoned off by an embroidered tapestry, and the bathroom door was pebbled glass. Very little privacy. The transitions between living spaces were marked by changes in the floor: hardwood in the living room, tile in the kitchen, a rug in the sleeping area, polished concrete everywhere else. When he pointed that out, she complimented his keen eye. There was no point in explaining that he was used to reading the ground when on foot for trapdoors, and from the air for hot zones, safe LZs, weapons caches. So he merely nodded at the compliment. It was the kind of apartment Achilles had only seen in magazines. Obviously, her nonprofit business was doing well. He praised her apartment with reserve. Women were turned off when guys were too easily impressed. As she gave him the nickel tour, he pointed to the curtain around the bedroom and said, "The specialists' area."

She continued explaining how she had chosen the fixtures.

Tell no jokes. He didn't want to fuck up when finally in sight of the prize. Persistance had paid off, but the apology cinched the deal. *Sorry if I offended you by asking for that number. I thought it was a blind date,* he'd said, neglecting to mention that he'd often been set up with women on the basis of race and that it never went well.

They settled into the sofa about a foot apart and slid closer with each drink. Achilles knew the strategies: make her laugh, maintain eye contact, convey confidence through open body language. Be interested but aloof, humble but cocky, bold but sensitive. Humorous. He could think of nothing funny and unoffensive. Maintaining eye contact was easy enough. He couldn't take his eyes off her. But it was hard to make the move. A pattern emerged. She spoke, he nodded. She smiled, he nodded. She nodded, he nodded. No matter what Ines said, Achilles agreed, murmuring assent while imagining her naked. Did she have moles? Did those freckles go down her back? Would he have trouble unsnapping the bra? He hadn't been with a regular woman since Janice, who did that herself. When he finally leaned in for a kiss, she turned so quickly it was obvious that she had long been waiting for him to make a move.

Their lips met, his hands found her body, outlining her form in the air, running his fingers down her neck to her shoulder and arm and then across her belly, each pass venturing closer to her breasts. Her lips were softer than he'd imagined, and her tongue sweet, like her piña colada, and shy, gliding across his lips but never entering his mouth. As their kisses grew more intense and her tongue bolder, he grabbed her breast and they fell onto their side as one, lying the length of the couch. He would go down on her. It was sex karma, earning him the right to do what he wanted.

After one long, breathless, lip-locked spell, she took his hand. "It's shaking." She kissed his fingers. Smacking her lips, she said, "You should wash your hands before you hurt somebody."

He remembered the spicy meal and how his fingers had tingled from the peppers. He went to the bathroom and took a piss. The pain hit him while he was washing his hands. He tried washing his dick in the sink, but it was too late. On the bulb of his penis, exactly where he'd touched himself, a purple, star-shaped blister had erupted that looked and stung like he had an STD. He slapped the wall. "Are you okay?" Ines called out.

"Fine," he said, slathering on cucumber-scented lotion. It took quite a bit of cucumber to cool down. He flushed the toilet again before he went out. Ines was smiling as if she knew the answer when she asked, "Why do men always flush before they finish peeing?"

The curtain was pulled back, revealing a woman's bed: two box springs piled high with pillows of various shapes and thick, tasseled spreads, all red and gold, like the tapestry. Before he reached the bed, his dick was burning again. After a few minutes of kissing, he was perspiring heavily and worried about sweat dripping into her eye. The CD had ended, and the only background music was the wind against the windows, their breathing, and the sound of their bodies grazing against each other, the rub of jeaned thighs, shirts chafing against the bedspread, the gentle strum of hands caressing faces. The more excited he became, the more his dick burned. His movements grew more pronounced, aggressive, and she responded, moving faster as well. Together, they pulled her shirt off. His hand on her breast, an asterisk. She squirmed out of her pants, writhing as if shedding skin. He kept his pants on to hide the blister, not to mention that the burning threatened to snipe his erection at any moment. Ines reached into his fly, cupped his balls, and tugged twice. He came in her hand.

She froze like a thief caught in the act. He looked down at his feet. As Ines slowly withdrew her hand, he offered his shirt as a towel.

"I guess I have the touch."

He heard Margaret laughing about this over tea, her manly voice, *I knew a guy at Spelman, who . . . Blah blah blah . . .* Ma ma sa, ma ma sa, ma ma ma coo sa . . .

"It's okay," said Ines. "It's early."

He nodded, absentmindedly rubbing his fingers on her belly and kneading her leg.

"Are you going to eat me or something?" asked Ines.

She was bold. He wasn't yet in the mood, but that would get him off the bench and back into the game. "Okay."

Ines pinched his cheek and sat up, her breasts swaying as she laughed. "I meant the way you were squeezing my leg, it was like you were . . . but you meant . . ." She doubled over, holding her sides, her back heaving, her shoulder blades fluttering like sprouting wings. She pointed at him again, eyes wet, "You're such a darling. You were going to do it. You must have thought, 'Damn that bitch is demanding!'"

The laughter took the edge off, and Achilles made his move. It was quick like they were hungry. From the moment he put the condom on, until the moment they came, they never let go, saying nothing. After a nap, he went down for seconds. The light played on her body, all curves and arcs, gentle saucers and bowls, the flattening of the thigh where it met the bed, the hollow of the hip. Ines glowed like she was carved out of moonlight. He traced the gentle bends of her body, the earlobe so smooth save for the piercing divot, the highbrows high and regal, the gentle swoon of calf into ankle, the tip of the toe, the rising swell of thighs that gently bowed to her pelvis, the arc of her momentous ass, momentarily arrested by the bed.

She was a land he wanted to survey, to settle, to colonize. Were there shortcuts? A tickle at the diamond of the neck, a nibble of the toe, a run of licked thumb down the spine until it crashes into the warm embrace of her ass? She was flesh perfectly punctuated, all commas and question marks. Soon his dick was hard again. They did it again. Afterwards, they spooned. This was a new sensation, one he enjoyed. He and Janice brushed the dust off. In Goddamnistan, they wrapped sheets around themselves and shooed him out, frowning because the longer he stayed, the less they made. Sometimes he and Aiko held hands afterwards, but never for long because the only place she was willing to go where they could be alone was her garage. So they were always in a rush, trying to fit everything into the twenty minutes between school and when her mother arrived home. He pressed his nose into Ines's armpits and neck, inhaling and holding it in, the he way he would around opium smoke, curious about the effect. He put his ear to her back and listened to her heartbeat.

"Why'd you pick New Orleans?" she asked.

He felt the vibrations travel through his head and down to his throat. "I knew people here I hadn't seen in a while."

"How long are you staying?"

"How long do you want me to?"

"A black male volunteer that's not being forced to do community service? You're a role model."

"What was that?"

"You're a role model."

He liked that. "Is that why you want me to stay?"

"I never said I wanted you to stay."

He pressed his ear firmly against her back. "You thought it. I heard you."

Ines laughed.

"What about this boyfriend?"

"What about him?"

"Is he still around?"

Ines scanned the room. "Not now. But he's not gone either." She sat up. "Just because we had sex doesn't make us a couple. Are you one of those brothers who thinks he owns a woman after sex?"

Achilles shook his head. Was this related to gender advising?

"I'm joking. I said that because I thought you were stalking me. You weren't, but that's how it looked."

He laughed.

Ines sat up and patted the bed, excitement in her eyes. "What was your favorite kid's book?"

"I don't remember."

"Tell me something about yourself."

Achilles shrugged. "I talk all the time."

"But never about yourself."

"My dad was a manager at the mill, and my mom a housewife and part-time bookkeeper. Not much to it. I say what's on my mind."

"Tell me something new. How should I describe you on Facebook? Should I say, 'Hi mom, I'm bringing someone over for dinner. You'll like him. He only says what's on his mind'? Actually, she might like that."

Achilles smiled. He had only heard of Facebook, but she planned to tell her mom. Would he even be around long enough to meet her? What was she like? He knew only that she lived Uptown, on the river side of St. Charles, near that fancy theater.

"How did you get your name? Tell me again."

"With only a knife, my father killed a bear named Achilles, the strongest and smartest prey he ever hunted. My triple-great-grandfather, a Greek, was said to be a descendant of Achilles. My mother liked the name." After each tale, they laughed.

It wasn't Tyrone, or Tyshaun, or Tyrell, but he would've preferred John, Mark, Luke, Matthew, or Troy. Kids teased him but adults liked it. The drill sergeants told him he'd have to earn it, but his father said, *Never question your birthright.* Of course Achilles had read the books, but had never understood the part about the birthright. Achilles was his father's idea. His mom wanted to name him Price, after her great-grandfather, a fearsome middleweight boxer. His father had wanted to name him after a warrior, not a mere fighter. "Honestly, I didn't even know how to spell it," his mother always joked. His father had always dreamed of playing pro football, and attended Georgia Tech on a scholarship, so when she saw Achilles spelled out, she thought she'd been tricked into naming him after a muscle. She wouldn't put it past her husband, because they had funny names on that side of the family: *You know you have a distant cousin named Bicep.* After a month of reading, she decided Achilles was a good name, better than Price. But, there was no point in telling Ines all of that.

He carefully untangled himself from Ines and tiptoed to the kitchen for a glass of water. The light from the refrigerator illuminated the pictures on the wall, a houseful of strangers, not that different from his home. Sure, the Conroys looked good in the photos on his mom's nightstand. There was the year they dressed as the cast of *The Wizard of Oz*. His mom was Dorothy, his father the Scarecrow, Achilles the Lion, and Troy the Tin Man. Dressed in full costume and makeup, they posed in the barn. They looked happy, like people in a magazine ad. Next to that was his parents' wedding photo, which obsessed him. Would he have liked the young man with the bull neck and brick jaw, the young woman with the button nose and bouffant? Would they have liked Achilles? It was hard to guess, because in all the photos in the house, Achilles is a magic trick. One minute he's not there, the next he is. For an encore, see Troy.

Ines's invitation to another screening filled him with dread. He imagined another obscure art film and Margaret, her every grin a reminder of his hair-trigger incident, pointing at him with her whole hand, shaking with the palm down, like she expected a kiss. Fortunately, she wasn't there because it was a real screening. The Common Ground Collective, as Ines called her charity, cosponsored a picnic and medical van at Iberville Park, a single city block where houses had been cleared away and a small playground, now rusted, had been installed in their place.

When Achilles arrived, Ines's two longtime assistants, Dudley and Mabel, were setting out the food. Dudley piled Mabel's lap high with platters, and she wheeled to one of the folding tables, carefully arranging the food in neat lines. They bickered constantly, he accusing her of being too slow, she accusing him of piling too much weight on her.

"This is a wheelchair, not a pickup."

"You got a mighty big cab, and a hell of a lot of cargo space." Achilles found it hard not to laugh at that. Mabel was quite heavy. A large, short woman whose oversized tits spilled over her lap like two small, fidgety children, she smiled easily, and when she stopped to snack, she used her breasts as a shelf, her plate as stable as if it were on an airplane tray. Whenever she passed Achilles, she would say, "He's just mad because I can wheel faster than he can walk." Achilles helped them carry a few loads for the sole purpose of being a part of their obvious and infectious joy.

"Thanks for the hand, son," said Mabel. Her voice was deep, and *son* reverberated. If things were otherwise, would he have spent summers with someone like Mabel? Achilles looked down at her, the dark spots on her cheeks, the thin elastic pants, the bumper stickers on the back of her wheelchair. They were only recently homeless, according to Ines, losing their house after forty years of marriage because her diabetes treatments had broken the bank—and failed. She was scheduled to have one leg amputated the following week.

When they were finished, it looked like a real barbecue, the tables piled high with ribs drenched in gooey sauce, steaming piles of fried chicken, and several huge bowls of potato salad that were so cool to the touch that Achilles had gladly carried them all. There were a few dishes he didn't recognize, but couldn't wait to taste. There were also several large bowls of fruit that went largely uneaten throughout the afternoon). A desk next to the van held flyers with exercise and diet tips, and cookies for all the brave kids.

After the food was arranged and the technicians had set up the medivan—red as a fire truck and outfitted with an awning—Mabel rang a cowbell. Flyers had been posted for weeks but no one wanted a checkup. A few kids grabbed some chicken and darted back into the shade, but the adults stayed hidden from view. All the people who were milling about on their porches and stoops not long ago had vanished, and now, save for the medivan generator, it was as silent as if a tank battalion had rolled into the center of town. When volunteers knocked on residents' doors, music stopped and chair legs skidded to a halt.

Then Ines arrived, wearing a brightly colored African dress and matching head garb. She greeted Achilles with a quick smile, distracted by the fact that there were more volunteers than patients. Using the van's PA system, she reminded everyone that they had been eating fried fish and oyster po-boys every Friday, that they needed their cholesterol checked, that they needed to stop being selfish, that their health was not their own, but belonged to their children and grandchildren. "Show thanks for your life by respecting it! Come on y'all, this isn't Tuskegee!"

A few people chuckled, and Achilles laughed along with them. He didn't get the joke, but after spending the time with Mabel and Dudley, after seeing Ines wearing such an outrageous outfit, he felt almost happy.

At the sound of Ines's voice, curtains parted and venetian blinds ruffled. First singly, then in twos, people poured out, flocking to her like sparrows to St. Francis. They followed her dreads, the kente cloth, the brilliant yellow head wrap shining like a torch. They saw her clear, bottomless eyes and knew they could talk to her. And those who didn't come right out, she coaxed out, and for those difficult to coax, she enlisted the neighbors. And the deputized neighbors did their duty, rounding up their reluctant friends. First among the volunteers was Bud. Achilles restrained himself as Bud hopped from door to door, joking and laughing, the African medallion dancing with each step. He watched Bud help a man in a wheelchair down the stairs and refill water cups for a group of old women, each of whom he addressed by name. And, he watched Bud greet Ines like an old friend, and her smile in turn, and when that moment came when they stood in a triangle at the cookie and flyer table, and Ines introduced them, Bud grinned a grin of someone beyond firing range, his smug tongue sitting there like a target.

"This is Bud, a Common Collective regular. The other volunteers gave him a rough go at first, but he's doing fine now."

"That's me. I like to help," said Bud. "And, I don't hold no grudges. That's one thing I like about myself."

Ines gently prodded them back into the street to escort more people to the vans. Bud limped off with a swagger, giving Achilles the thumbs-up. He imagined wrapping his fingers around Bud's neck, and imagined Margaret hearing the story later and telling Ines, *Girlll, let me tell you somethin' 'bout dose here black men.* Ines drifted to the other end of the park, shaking hands, kissing babies, and hugging old ladies. She was always on duty. She'd said he was like a bulldog, her constant companion; however, she was the one who was indefatigable. He would have let evolution take its course. He said, *Feed the homeless to the hungry.* She said, *You and your soldier's humor.* He said, *Legalize drugs and let the weak weed themselves out.* She said, *The people aren't weak, they are hurt. They have endoracism.*

Endoracism?

Even after she explained it, he was doubtful. How could someone be racist against himself. Besides, wasn't "endo" another name for pot? That was more likely the problem. He tried to imagine scenarios in which he didn't hire himself, or paid himself less. Less than whom? His other self? In the end he pooh-poohed the idea and let slip, "So if I hang myself, does endoracism make it a lynching?" She did not laugh. Ines was a woman who would look a prostitute in the eye and say, "Come to the shelter, sister. Take your body back, and your life will follow." She would look a junkie in the eye and ask, "Brother, why are you killing yourself?" They rarely had an answer, but they rarely turned away. Neither could Achilles.

At the end of the day, as the salad was packed up, Achilles kept his eye on Bud. He waved as the van drove off, then went to the house he had seen Bud leave earlier. The door was answered by a girl no more than seven, wearing pigtails with big blue Babar barrettes. Her ears were pierced with red studs and she wore a red polka dot sundress with Little Red Riding Hood embroidered on the chest. Bud appeared behind her, a Babar book in hand, his smile fading once he saw Achilles.

"Hey Dauphine, sugar, this is just grown-folk talk here, you hear. Go on, baby. Go back and watch TV. I'll finish reading to you later."

Bud claimed to have shown the flier to someone who said Troy might be at the camelback. He didn't remember who told him, but he swore it was the truth. "I didn't have nothing to do with it. I swear. I'm clean now." Bud raised his hand. "Hand to God. I'm clean, and I didn't even know those boys. I just heard people stay there."

Achilles pushed Bud against the house. Dauphine drew the curtains back.

"It's okay, baby. Unky B tripped," said Bud. "You know he gets the itis."

Achilles made Bud lead him back to the green camelback. Bud was silent this time, no singing, no banter, and, surprisingly, no begging. When he pulled up in front of the burned-out shell, Bud shook his head and whistled.

"Goddamn man. You did that? You in the army? You a cop?" He looked worried now, hesitating when Achilles ordered him out of the car. Achilles ripped the mailbox off the wall and read the names aloud to Bud: Joe, Angela, and Raymond Harper, and in smaller letters, Angie, April, and Amy. Bud didn't recognize the names, and flinched when Achilles slammed the lid. Bud was right to worry. He was lucky he wasn't a muzzle muffler. Two months ago, he'd have been whining about the gun at his cheek while Merriweather asked, *What's wrong? You want some lipstick on it?* Two months ago, he'd already have a burlap sack over his head and quick-cuffs cutting into his wrists, turning his hands numb, and his karakul, that fuzzy hat that looked like a beaver's ass, would be under someone's boot.

If he was spunky—like the butcher in Lai'pur—he might have his kurta stretched over his head and his salwar down around his ankles. If he wore a pakul, the round hat—like the carpenter in Khost—it might be lit on fire and tossed like an angry Frisbee. If he were the suspected insurgent in Nangarhar, his wife's burqa might be ripped open or her hajib removed, her flawless coppery skin reflected in twelve dilated pupils. His kids might be dramatically, theatrically removed from the room, but not taken so far away that he couldn't hear them cry. If he were the Jalalabad schoolteacher reported to have Al-Qaeda ties, his dog might be shot and his Koran might be pissed on, after a few pages were ripped out, balled up, and hackey-sacked. He might be stripped. If he survived that, his goats might be slaughtered and dragged through the mud, by the other villagers. He might be beheaded before the mosque. He might be hung in the town square.

But before that happened, shamed that his wife saw him piss his pants, he might accuse her of infidelity and stone her, or only cut her nose off if he felt generous. Were he the stonemason in Konar, he might slit her throat with an ornate Khyber knife. He might throw petrol on her hair, light a cigarette, take a few deep drags, toss the cherry at her bound feet.

But Bud wasn't in Afghanistan. He wasn't the unfortunate host of a squad assigned to stabilize his country. He was only Unky B, an old man who needed to get back to his granddaughter. He was in New Orleans with Achilles who, after learning that Bud didn't actually know any of the people who had lived in the house, lost all his steam. Achilles who, after punching Bud once in the neck and forcing him into a headlock, felt his own voice break as he whispered *Shhh, it's just like sleeping.* Achilles who, after tearing up as Bud curled into a ball at his feet, his medallion in the dirt, helped him up, dusted him off, and drove him back home so Unky B could finish reading *Babar's Little Circus Star.* Achilles who sat there in the park, in the car, in the dark, for almost an hour, was suddenly tired, amazed by the things he had seen so far in his short life, wondering why he was such a coward and where the other Achilles was when you needed him, who even now heard Troy, saying, *I could have come alone.*

Troy had never *needed* him, as he made clear after the Khost suicide bombing. Achilles discovered a dead teenager in the shadow of a roadside stand at the edge of the blast radius, reclined against the wall like he was napping, his embroidered Kashmiri hat covering his eyes, one sandal on, dusty feet akimbo, a half-eaten piece of bread in his lap, his body unblemished, save for the flies at his open mouth and a brilliant red dot on his left temple. One slender nail must have caught him dreaming. The wall behind him, the ground, his clothes, were all unmarked, nothing else showing any sign of debris from the explosion, as if he wasn't even in the blast radius. Achilles wondered if he had been killed elsewhere and placed here to make it appear that he was a bombing victim, but the dirt was undisturbed by tire tracks or brush marks, except a single trail of footprints leading to and from a small brick kiln almost a hundred yards away, which explained why his hands were caked in mud. Achilles leaned in for a closer look.

"He picked the wrong side of the building to take a break on," said Troy. "Smells like he's been here for a while."

Achilles nodded. He hadn't heard his brother walk up.

"But they smell like motherfucking dogs when they're alive." Troy scanned the horizon, and then the ground in the immediate area, looking for tracks. "Poor fucker. I'd want to go out fighting. Maybe for a regular guy this is the best. You spook him?"

"No," said Achilles. When an army had suicide in the arsenal, the rules changed. In past weeks, three Americans had died trying to help wounded Afghans who had been booby-trapped. So, they only spooked the injured, giving a prick or prod, from a safe distance, if possible. Sometimes they used sticks, sometimes they just tossed rocks. If alive, they called the medics, maybe. The locals sorted the dead.

Achilles took aim as Troy threw one, then two rocks at the feet. The kid yawned and sat up, stretching as the ladybug at his temple flew off. They watched him return to his kiln, dragging his feet, his shadow trailing in the dust behind him.

"Why didn't you shoot him?" asked Troy.

"Why didn't you?"

"I was the spook," said Troy. "I thought he was fucking dead."

The kid was at the kiln, stirring mud. He propped the lid open with a stick and lowered in a brick, shielding his face with his free hand. He saw them staring and waved.

Achilles waved back.

"I guess it's not too late," said Troy, looking around.

"Fuck that. You're kidding, right?"

Troy wouldn't shoot an unarmed man, but he was right. They could have shot him and gotten away with it. Achilles kept seeing that ladybug flutter off. He should have fired. What if Troy had died? He'd have to continue on, even though he'd no longer have a purpose for being there. No one had to explain what it meant when Humvees crawled back with black bags tied on the roof like kayaks. He couldn't imagine riding back to camp with his brother strapped overhead like excess luggage.

Troy walked off in the direction of their squad, busy overseeing the locals clearing away the rubble. "I could've come alone."

Achilles had called hospitals looking for anyone with the names the Harpers had given him. He was, he hated to admit, officially at a dead end. Troy would have handled it better, extracted information from Bud. Troy would have screwed Ines the night they met and already moved on to one of those cougars he was into. Maybe after seeing a picture, he would go after Ines's mom. As he said, *The daughter is the mother's business card.* Troy would have it all locked up. But would Troy have spent so much energy looking for him?

CHAPTER 11

ACHILLES THE DOGGED, SHE SOMETIMES CALLED HIM. AT OTHER TIMES, Achilles the Determined. When he corralled the men into a line, Achilles the Enforcer. After walking toward gunfire and breaking up an argument at the corner, he was Achilles the Brave. He would have applied these same attributes to Ines. He often watched her from across the room or down the hall, waiting to see her flinching, to catch her stepping back when a homeless man approached, to find her rubbing her palms against her pants after shaking hands. She never did. She lived her politics. He couldn't find a chink in the armor of this strange white woman who said she loved the world and lived like it too. The only creeping question, and one that he didn't really want to think about but had to consider as a possibility, was that she was interested in him only because he was black. He knew not to ask. Merriweather always said, *Asking a woman why she likes you is like asking her why she's with you is like saying she shouldn't be.* But after meeting her mother, how tempted Achilles was to ask, even though at that point he wasn't sure he wanted to know.

His curiosity was peaked when, on Ines's bookshelves, he discovered *The Delesseppes in the New World.* On the back cover was a family tree that ended with Ines. Before he could open it, she angrily slapped the book out of his hand, rebuke in her eyes. *Respect my privacy!* But the damage was done. America was only a chapter in her family's history. The names alone were stunning. Rich, stately names. French names, Old World names. New Orleans had so many names: the Big Easy, Nawlins, Nola, the Crescent City, the Boom-Boom Boomerang, Mardi Gras City, Birthplace of Jazz, Sin City, Voodoo City, Hot Chocolate City, the Lucky Charm. Ines's family had even more exotic appellations: Gautreaux, Beauvais, Jaquillard, Larmeau, Mouleroux, Villemeur, going back at least three centuries. By the time he met her, Achilles knew that Ines's mother wouldn't like the name Achilles Holden Conroy. He was right. She even scowled as she said it, as if between her front teeth—as sharp as guillotines—she'd caught a bitter black currant. Was it a Creole name? She didn't think so. *A-sheel*, as she pronounced it, was a Cajun name. "I knew some Cajuns in the lower Ninth Ward. They sure could throw a party." She gazed wistfully at the ceiling for a moment. "They were brothers. One was named *A-sheel*." She pointed to his table tent for emphasis.

It was almost two months after he'd first walked into St. Jude and his first time meeting her immediate family, which consisted of her mother and her uncle Boudreaux, who lived together in the Garden District, as far from the Ninth Ward as Paris was from Algiers. The Delesseppes family home was a stately stone Georgian mansion, constructed in 1806, when they migrated from Toulouse. They'd brought from France a Mopani dining table so vast that when they were sitting alone, Achilles called Ines on her cell phone to ask how she was doing. *Fine, with you here.* Intricately patterned tapestries and family portraits labeled like museum pieces lined the dining room walls, joined during the meal by a staff of white-coated, white-gloved attendants who, between courses, stood in the shadows of the room as still and silent as tombstones. Achilles was seated across from Ines. Mrs. Delesseppes sat opposite Boudreaux, where she could see the portrait of her recently deceased third husband hanging over her brother's head. "Two lawyers and a doctor," she said. "Not necessarily in that order."

Troy would choke on his drool if he got one look at Ines's mother. Even Achilles was enchanted by Mrs. Delesseppes, still as striking as her daughter. A graceful woman with hair like Jackie O, her right forearm suspended haughtily at her side in defiance of gravity, as if carrying a purse, her long legs confidently sliced the air. Like Ines, she had ripe lips, and when in thought, she bit the lower lip hard enough to leave two tiny indentations, an *M* in Morse code. If he ran his tongue over those two faint lines, neat as stitches, would they feel slight as a whisper, pronounced like gouges, or nothing at all? He was mesmerized by her melodious Southern accent, the carnivorous smile, and the deeply channeled shadow of her bosom. *There* was gravity defied.

"Those Cajuns had a quaint shotgun, with fleurs-de-lys stenciled in the front windows," said Mrs. Delesseppes. "I remember it clearly. They lived below the industrial canal."

"Really? When were you in the lower Ninth Ward?" asked Boudreaux, always smiling, always drinking, never drunk.

Mrs. Delesseppes answered her brother in what sounded like French, eliciting the censure of her family.

"Mama!"

"Heloise!"

She ignored them and asked, "Tell me *A-sheel*, how do you find New Orleans?"

Achilles hesitated. Most people seemed to assume there was no more natural destination than Nawlins. When people did ask, he usually mumbled a line about school or work or friends. Fortunately, Ines cut in.

"Achilles, Mama, like the warrior. And, you didn't answer Uncle B's question."

"Certainly you don't mean like the heel. It's *A-sheel*," said Mrs. Delesseppes. "Trust me, darling. I've lived here all my life."

Ines huffed and winked at her uncle, plopping her elbows on the table. "Well? When did you see the lower Ninth Ward from anything but an *aeroplane*?"

Mrs. Delesseppes regarded her plate for a moment. "Bogalusa is no longer a reliable source for sausage. I must instruct Monique to start shopping at Basheman's again." She pointed to Achilles's empty plate and snapped her fingers.

Before he could object, a servant in a white coat as tight as a straightjacket was at Achilles's side, serving tray in hand. The servant's neck spilled out over a bowtie tied so tightly that Achilles knew if he pulled it, the man would explode.

"*A-sheel*, did Ines tell you we always outlive our men?" asked Mrs. Delesseppes.

And that was only the entrée.

The waiters held their breath like marksmen as they served course after course. After the oysters Rockefeller came turtle soup, then grilled andouille, then crabmeat mirlitons. The main course was a Creole bouillabaisse: lobsters, oysters, mussels, and scallops cooked in a tomato-based broth garnished with a yellow violet and swathed in wisps of steam, so spicy and sweet that Achilles had an urge to raise the dish and slurp the last drops trapped by the cursive *D* etched in the bottom of the wide, shallow bowl.

And for dessert, Mrs. Delesseppes asked, "Where is your family from?"

When Achilles said Maryland, she replied, "Oh, the southern state with the identity crisis."

Achilles had never thought of the "old line" state that way, and didn't know how to respond.

"Mama, have you talked to Aunt Harriet recently?" asked Ines.

"You know, dear, I've been so busy, I haven't time for charity, dear. I'm already paying Sammy's tuition for that fancy school in Atlanta. And for Saturdays, I've taken to attending morning mass. Besides, tears age one prematurely." Mrs. Delesseppes zeroed back in on Achilles. "How long has your family been in Maryland?" She stretched out the last word, tasting each syllable, Mare-ree-land.

"Generations," said Achilles.

"His grandparents are dead. His father just died, when he was on the way back from active duty. I mentioned this." Ines looked to Boudreaux for help.

Boudreaux nodded solemnly.

"I meant before then. I don't mean to upset. It was only a casual question." She dropped her hand to the table, ending the discussion, then tapped her fingers as if to say, *For now.* "You know she does things just to spite me. Like writing on herself. Look at that horrid black smudge on her arm. Pitch. Pitch, I tell you. I raised her better than that."

After dinner, Mrs. Delesseppes suggested they *retire* to the drawing room, where Ines cringed when her mother handed Achilles *The Delesseppes in the New World,* which she had commissioned to document their *many cultural and commercial contributions to the New World.* Achilles didn't dare meet Ines's stare as he made a show of licking his finger and settling into a chair to leisurely peruse the very book Ines had slapped from his hands only days before.

Parasols, stiff collars, buttoned boots. Blurry kids. A few death masks. Old shops and bars with French names. Delesseppes Brasserie. Café Delesseppes. Businesses. Delesseppes Tackle and Feed. Delesseppes & Son. Delesseppes & Co. Delesseppes Chicory and Tobacco. Delesseppes & Delesseppes Ltd. Stately couples in horse-drawn carriages. Large estates. Farms. In the middle of the book, a few Asians, and then a few Spanish, or very light-skinned blacks of the kind he had never before seen. Button boots, walking sticks, and horses with regal accessories.

As he leafed through the pages, Mrs. Delesseppes recounted the family history. The Delesseppes bought pews for slaves when St. Augustine was built in 1842. Ines said they should have bought their freedom. The Delesseppes first invested in Jax Brewery when it still made beer, and again when it became a tourist attraction of cultural and historical import. Capitalistic self-interest, said Ines. The Delesseppes fought in the battle of Chalmette Plantation, as they called the Battle of New Orleans. On the wrong side, according to Ines. They had varied *relations of note*, whatever that meant, but Mrs. Delesseppes was proudest of her father, Paul Delesseppes. Paul, or Papa P as they called him, was the first councilman in St. Bernard Parish with African American blood and a leading critic of the plan to blow up the Caernarvon Levee. Ines giggled, then whooped until her cheeks shone with tears. Mrs. Delesseppes steadfastly continued her advance, making it clear that her family had a long and proud history. Ines conceded only that it was long, making it clear that unless you wrote it, history was hateful. Boudreaux, between sips of bourbon, murmured his agreement with both of them.

Mother and daughter flashed perfect teeth. The conversation waned, the remainder of the hour like watching a poorly dubbed movie. Eventually, Achilles understood that Ines and her mother got along like snipers. If he followed Boudreaux's example, and stayed out of the line of fire, they would only shoot each other.

It was his first time around old money. The rich kids he'd known—or known of—from childhood lived in gated communities where the homes were built from one of three standard floor plans, and they all had identical front yards of bermuda grass cut as neat and clean as carpet. Each front door was one of four acceptable colors. In the Delesseppes' neighborhood, each home was unique but they all fit together. The houses in New Orleans were older, larger, self-confident. Not unlike Mrs. Delesseppes.

Still reading, Achilles found himself stealing glances at Mrs. Delesseppes. In some photos he saw her resemblance, and in others none at all. She and Ines both looked remarkably like Papa P. His skin was very light, lighter even than Troy's. White, actually. If they were always free, as Mrs. D had contended, how did they get the black in them? In 1850, *Do you want any black in you?* were fighting words. Had a free black married into the family? Were there free blacks? What was it like being a free black in a country where slavery was legal? Achilles would have never left the house.

Hearing that her grandfather Paul was coming over, Ines gathered their jackets and hustled Achilles out the door. Mrs. Delesseppes bid farewell with a smile and a queen's wave, standing in the driveway until they made the corner, her raised hand a stubborn weathervane.

Achilles knew he'd made a bad impression on Ines's family. He had been one step behind everybody; how else would he know which fork to use first, or to spoon soup away from his mouth?

"Sorry baby," she said, "for the who's-your-momma interrogation. The family name, genealogy, and we-kill-our-men-young-she-wolf talk. And *A-sheel*." They were in Ines's car and she shifted angrily, making him think that he wouldn't mind her taking him for a spin when they got home.

"It doesn't matter." Of course they would be curious about him. Of course Mrs. Delesseppes wanted Ines to have a man with letters behind his name, and not SGT. Of course they would be proud of their history. They remembered when the Vieux Carré *was* New Orleans. Theirs was a lineage he found as vast and incomprehensible as owning a tract of land that extended beyond the horizon. Theirs was history personified, like entering in the middle of a play in innumerable acts.

"She knows how Achilles is pronounced."

Achilles shrugged, of that long cured. "I know what they mean."

Her voice tight, Ines said, "What if some guy at a shelter was like, 'Yo, A-sheel, gimmie some more ham'? Why should she be different? That's what's wrong with her. No one stands up to her. If you don't earn her respect now, you'll never get it."

"I just met them."

"It's like that saying, 'Speak your mind even if your voice shakes.'"

In her profile, he saw Heloise Delesseppes, and imagined her at Ines's age. They had the same luscious skin, smooth as cream, accented by sparkling freckles, and highlighted by honey eyes that glinted silver and pearl. The same long frame, and finely tapered fingers. The same stubborn streak, deep veins of opinion. They were bulletproof.

He made a pistol with his hand, kissed his index finger and pointed. "Think fast!"

"You got me." Ines put her hand to her heart. "I'm sorry. I'm so embarrassed. We're just so fucked up and old-fashioned sometimes. All the New Orleans shit, you know: good hair, bad hair; the 'we're Creole, not mulatto, or octoroon, or quadroon' crap. It's disgraceful, shameful, and unforgivable. They're like dinosaurs; it's a prehistoric mentality. It won't be the first time they scared someone off," said Ines.

"They'll have to pry my cold, dead fingers off your ass."

"You don't know them." She paused, then added, "I guess dinosaurs are still polluting the earth."

"Huh?" asked Achilles.

"Never mind. You know that's creepy," said Ines.

"Don't worry. It takes a lot more than that to scare me."

"Who said I was worried?" asked Ines.

"You did." Achilles chuckled. He thought it sweet when she was salty.

"Humph," said Ines. "Really?"

"Seemed that way," said Achilles, retreat in his voice, recoiling from her tone, unsure now if she was angry with them or him. He was frustrated to have squandered that precious moment when they were united against their families.

"I thought you didn't scare easily." Ines glanced his way.

"I don't. Cold, dead hands," he said.

Ines made a show of shivering, and shot a kiss back. "It's not those cold, dead hands I want right now."

Achilles's leg jumped. She was nothing like her mother. Ines billed herself as a global citizen from New Orleans by way of New York. She drank beer from the bottle, and once, when drunk, had burped the ABCs. Ines's concern and embarrassment brought home the full weight of the afternoon, the stress that crawled over him as he wandered the long, wainscoted halls—lined with daguerreotypes and Boudreaux's mounted butterfly collection—looking for a bathroom. He felt like he had accidentally wandered into a museum where each display reflected his ignorance. As he'd passed the kitchen, the double doors momentarily parted and let escape exotic fragrances. His gaze following his nose, he glimpsed the kitchen staff, and realized he was the darkest person in the house who didn't work there. He wouldn't have noticed that before dating Ines, who was always pointing out skin tone, race, and sex—*gender*—in movies, on TV, and in public interactions. Indians were replacing blacks, she claimed. She complained about black women, like Beyoncé, being "caucasized," a word she pronounced with vehemence, spitting it out as if it were sour. That was the tone he had just heard. The anger suffusing her voice was directed at her family, not at him.

They'd left in a hurry, she explained, because she refused to acknowledge her grandfather, who fled to St. Bernard to pass: He left as Zulu and returned Comus. She told Achilles how her aunt Harriet had Sammy out of wedlock by an addict who pimped her, how Achilles couldn't know what it was like to go to a soul food restaurant in Harlem and have the server explain the menu, then retreat to the racist, backwards city where you were born because it's the one city where you don't have to explain what you are, and then realize that your name was all that ever mattered.

"I can't see Paul. I know I'm supposed to feel sorry for him, but I want him to suffer the way he's made us suffer. He's a coward and opportunist. Anyone who abandons their family doesn't deserve them. Why should he have it both ways?"

Except Paul, how Ines's family was fucked up he didn't exactly know. Achilles didn't care if they were Creole or quadroons or whatever. He couldn't figure the math anyway, and the more he saw Boudreaux drink, the more Achilles thought of him as a macaroon. Achilles guessed that Ines would tell him in her own time. He understood that people could be embarrassed for reasons clear only to themselves.

Right then, right there, on St. Charles Avenue, was the first of many moments he regretted not admitting he was adopted. After each visit they made to Magazine Street over the next few months, Ines left in a funk, and he wanted more and more to offer his life as proof that it could be worse.

The majority of their time together they spent limbs locked. They fucked. A lot. Until sore. He, blistered. Her, a little raw. Afterwards, they'd lie on their backs, slick as seals, with only their hands and feet touching and watch the shadow of the fan blades grow long and faint. He swore steam rose from their bodies. And it only got better. Everything he'd read about, she was up for. She was open but in control, and made that clear the night she wrested his head from between her thighs, already polished with sweat and saliva, and said, "You go at sex the way you walk."

"The way I walk?" His erection subsided. His dick didn't like the way that sounded.

"Remember when we went to the movies? You saw the marquee, and led me diagonally across the lot, through that short alley, between two moving vans, and jaywalked. A straight line to the goal."

He rolled back on his haunches.

"Watch me," she said. "Don't touch me except where I put you. I'll tell you if I need help. Otherwise, don't touch me. You'll want to do something slick-like, like stick your finger in my ass or something. Every time you do that, you reset the meter. Be patient. And you shouldn't drive anywhere until the engine is warmed up anyway." She took his hand, squeezing two of his fingers between her own, moved the fingers back and forth across the outer edges first, ruffling the faint downy trail below the navel before brushing along the shorter, bristly hair between her legs, at one point moving slower and slower, his hand just grazing just teasing, then faster, then tracing the fingers straight up the center, parting the folds, her back bucking as she did, and slipping in only the tip of his finger, and Achilles bit his lip at the heat as she made larger and larger circles around the outside, her other hand strumming up and down until his breath was as shallow as hers, shorter and shorter her breath, faster and faster the fingers, until she was rigid and then melted, and he was as long catching his breath as she was. His hand. *His* hand. And his hand, feverish with the memory of her skin, spent all that night stroking his chin, bowled like an oxygen mask.

After that, he knew their bodies were made for each other. He hadn't felt this for Janice. He melted at Ines's smile, and just the sound of her voice on the phone earned a salute. Achilles was unaccustomed to so much downtime, but found himself feeling less guilty as time went on. For one thing, didn't helping Ines mean that he was always looking for Troy while she was working? For another thing, Troy was a grown man, wasn't he? He was probably fine and would show up when he was good and ready. There wasn't any guarantee he was still in New Orleans anyway. Achilles deserved some R&R, didn't he?

But the biggest reason the guilt receded was because he was happy. He had never before had such access to the female body. But he didn't think that was why he was happy. His first week in Goddamnistan, he realized that he had been happy at home but had never known it. He missed Janice, the mill, the cool quarry water, everything that up until then he had thought he was doing to pass the time until his real life began. He'd had nothing but time, and it felt like a burden, like the proverbial rich man whose fortune drives his insomnia, except that Achilles's fortune was time, and he was always looking for ways to spend it. That first week on rotation, before he learned to shut it all away, to hope for nothing, what he wouldn't have given to be home helping his father weatherize the house or cut the grass or shore up the barn, but once home, all those tasks lost their nostalgic luster and he wanted a rifle in his hands and a pack on his back and to be doing something that mattered. Anyone could cut grass, but not everyone could clear a room in 5.2 seconds. Then, after the funeral, he'd have given anything to do that again, running the mower along the drive while his dad warned him away from the rocks, as he did every single time, even when Achilles was home on leave. He had not realized at the time that maybe *Watch the rocks* was another way of saying *I love you.* He'd learned to take whatever pleasure came his way, and Ines was all his. No kids, no ex-husbands, no crazy brothers.

Of course it helped that he'd never known a woman more comfortable with her naked self. Even prostitutes around the bases covered up after the act. He wondered now if that was to keep him from getting more than his money's worth. With Ines, it was different. She would spring out of bed and roll a joint, or sweep, or read, or make phone calls nude. That was something Achilles could never do. To be nude on the phone was impossible. Besides, to whom would he talk nude? Since he'd stopped returning Janice's calls, he didn't have many telephone conversations with any woman other than Ines. It would seem gay to be naked on the phone with his friends. It would be too creepy with his mother. He didn't even like it when Ines was nude while talking to her own mother. Other than that, everything was perfect, and his only concern was what to say when his brother did show up.

He imagined that after finding Troy, they would drive straight home. Troy would be exhausted from his search, but appreciative, in his case meaning quiet but responsive, unlike their last ride home when he had been sullen. He was rarely sullen, but when opting for radio silence became nearly catatonic, prompting Merriweather to once say, "I fucked noisier pussies!" When they squeezed through the front door, their mother and aunts would cheer and clap, welcoming Troy home, but more so applauding Achilles's tireless efforts. Kisses and hugs, cries and sighs. His mother wouldn't be wearing that backpack, not around company. Their names up in glittering letters, the party would finally begin. They could even have that parade Janice had mentioned. Sure, Troy had a Silver Star. But Achilles had Troy. Instead, Achilles received a voice mail and one text message: TROY ON WAY FROM NEW ORL!!!! ANY MINUTE NOW!!!!

A dozen exclamation marks! When he called her back, the line was busy, of course. Thirty minutes later, his mother's line was still busy. She and Troy were probably talking to each other, laughing the whole thing off, as Troy did so well. Achilles had been out on the road for almost two months, but it felt like two years. All of that crap and he didn't even get a phone call. He counted them, twice. Eight exclamation marks!

When he finally spoke to his mother, she didn't sound like the same person who had sent the text message. She was so composed he wondered if it was for his benefit.

"He must have gotten one of your messages," she said. "That's the only way."

"Yes ma'am."

"He would have done it for you. And know what else? You were successful. You were there when it mattered. I was counting on you, and you came through. Your energy and faith and belief." She had big plans. She's going to cook for her sons. She's going to have that extra room built on the back so they can put in that pool table their father always threatened to buy. She's going to let them have a dog. They could build a kennel out back, or have the dog in the house, if they want. Every prohibition was lifted, every pledge affirmed, every courtesy extended. Though, of course, this didn't mean that she expected them to move home. No. *Not at all.* She'd *never* suggest such a thing. Preposterous. They were soldiers now, men. Their country might call them to serve at a moment's notice. In fact, Achilles didn't even need to come home now. No, she was only saying that they would always have a house to come home to. Always. A comfortable home. The home they always wanted. Their home, really, because, as she explained with a smile in her voice, "No one is going to be around forever."

He said he would leave the very next day, but he dreaded returning home, recalling those few nightmarish days, the lame laugh tracks, the preposterous comic books, the cheesy British accents. He packed anyway.

Having heard that in the seventies it was a backpacking haven known for the hospitality of the natives, he had often wondered what Afghanistan looked like in the deep sleep of peace. How would New Orleans feel now that it was only he and Ines? Now that Troy had resurfaced and headed back to Maryland, would Achilles have the same vertigo as on his first day home, when he awoke and didn't know what to do? Surprisingly, he didn't. The morning after his mother's call, he felt free, a little nervous, like a puppy testing the leash, but free. So when Ines called that morning and suggested a *staycation,* he agreed. One more day couldn't hurt. She shuffled a deck of souvenir cards featuring the top fifty-two New Orleans landmarks, and they each selected two. Because they did this over the phone, she had to tell Achilles what he had selected via *the sexiest proxy in the city*: Jackson Square and Café Du Monde. Meanwhile, she'd selected the Zoo and Café Du Monde.

His last trip to the Quarter was a blur. He and Wages had made the obligatory stop at Pat O'Brien's and the Dungeon, then spent the afternoon daiquiri shop hopping, so Ines said he was still a Quarter virgin. They went first to Café Du Monde for hot chocolate made with real milk, and beignets—the blessed French pastry flash fried and dusted with confectioner's sugar. Ines called it sacrilege when Achilles ordered his without sugar. She ate hers proper, so that the first bite released the dulcet steam trapped in the center, coating the tip of her nose and making a mustache. In a deep voice she said, "Kiss me, dammit." And he did, quickly, suddenly shy, stealing a kiss that tasted of sugar and chocolate and lipstick. She dipped her beignets in hot chocolate and watched the sugar float on top, clumping up and clinging to the side of the mug. He followed suit.

Ines looked at Achilles's ashy hands, pulled a bottle out of her purse, slathered his hands with lotion, and massaged it in until his hands were smooth and gleaming, even the knuckles shimmering like wet coffee beans. She did this without skipping a beat in the conversation, and when she finished, his hands were throbbing. He hadn't known that nonsexual contact could be so intensely pleasurable, so intimate. In high school, in an attempt to segue into seductive slang, he'd once told Aiko, "I was thinking about you last night." In response, she'd blushed and said she was thinking about him too. After much coaxing and whispering, she admitted that she'd imagined walking with him and holding his hand and laughing, *much laughing, smiling*. He'd thought she was joking. Now he understood. Everything in his body ran loose, his limbs slack and free, blood pounding in his temple, the vein in his thumb thrumming.

After Café Du Monde, they sat on a bench in the center of the Quarter, in Jackson Square, a park girdled in ornate fencing, and beyond that bordered by a courtyard of eighteenth-century townhouses skirted with baroque wrought-iron galleries. Behind the park stood St. Louis Cathedral, its white stucco walls glowing in the sun like an enchanted palace. On the other side of the park was a queue of horse-drawn carriages, Jax Brewery, and, above the ridge, ironically, the Mississippi. Rock doves darted from finger to finger of trees that rose from the ground like hands reaching for the sky. Leaves purled in the background, tourists submitted to caricature artists, and the shadow of Andrew Jackson's statue chased a sun-seeking golden retriever across the lawn.

Ines's smile was a flame, igniting all it touched. Old men saw her and proffered toothless grins, babies stopped crying. Even the retriever occasionally ventured into the shade that had crept over their bench to offer his cold wet greeting. And everything Ines anointed with her smile Achilles liked, including the golden retriever, when he usually preferred Labs. He was proud to be with this woman with a smile like fire, spreading as if carried on the wind. Ines touched his hand and pointed to the petal of a black-eyed Susan pirouetting across his shoe. He picked it up, placed the spot of yellow in his palm, and blew it back into the wind. A tall, slim man loped across the park, turning away as soon as he saw Achilles. Achilles sat up and stared. The man was light-skinned, but his shoulders were too narrow. A few minutes later, another man who looked like Troy passed. He wore a blue suit and loafers. Troy had never worn a suit in his life, not even at their father's funeral.

"Observant Achilles." Ines kissed him on the neck. "That's what I like about you. You're so vigilant."

Achilles shivered, his body thumping from the kiss, his mind still split between Ines and Troy, between his pleasure at being with her and his resentment about his brother not calling, a resentment that grew by the minute. He so wanted Troy to call. Achilles had earned that much. The man in the blue suit passed again and winked. Achilles pulled Ines close. She hummed softly against his neck. "I feel safe with you," she said. "I know there won't be any unpleasant surprises."

They rambled and giggled, talked of where they'd been and where they yet hoped to go. Her voice made every destination appealing, though he was satisfied with the Vieux Carré, which thrummed with energy. In the background were two yellow-rumped warblers playing in a fountain and a steamboat's paddle and stack, the latter lightly smoking and red at the tip, like a cigarette recently stubbed out by a beautiful woman.

Gone were the coffee can planters, the crumbling cornices, and the mindless litter. It wasn't the New Orleans he'd met with Wages. It wasn't the same city at all. The only thing missing was Troy. He could at least call to say thank you. If not that, at least hello.

"Flak jacket, babe," said Ines with a wink. It was what she said to him when he looked tense.

Achilles sat up. What a smile. It wouldn't hurt to stay one more night.

She called "twisting" the only tangible skill she'd learned in college, a skill she employed on a semiregular basis, often on Saturday nights. She liked to smoke on the roof of her apartment building, pointing out her favorite spots in the city every five minutes and pointing them out again five minutes later. Though he had only smoked once before, in high school with Troy, and the nearly incapacitating paranoia lingered for several days, Achilles had been joining her, finding it pleasant. While his physical tolerance was unchanged, he was sufficiently accustomed to spikes of paranoia.

Wearing sheets like togas, they climbed the fire escape to the roof. After it kicked in, and he felt the cottonmouth, the hyperconsciousness—he could hear his stomach growl, his heart beat, his blood rush—all he could think was, *pancakes or eggs?* It was upside-down day, when they would eat breakfast food for dinner, and Achilles couldn't decide what would be better.

The sun had just set and the weather was perfect, warm but with a cool breeze off the river. Someone a few floors down was watching *Saturday Night Live* with the window open. The building only had seven stories, so they were low enough to also hear the hum of cars and the occasional drunk at the sports bar across the street cheering on the Saints. He could feel the wind on his neck, so slow it was like a hand gripping him and working around to his chest in short, frisky bursts.

Pacing as she spoke, she started talking about work, which she often did before the high kicked in, noting random aggravations and slights. She was morally offended by the reluctance that charities had for working with each other, which she blamed on faith-based initiatives. Achilles followed her purposeful strut as she walked with her head forward and down, almost as if she were dictating to an unseen secretary.

The Saints must have scored, because a cheer erupted from the sports bar. Horns blared. "Are you listening?" she asked after the noise died down, clapping. When she clapped, her thighs shook. He was getting another hard-on.

She mirrored his lascivious grin. "This is serious." She stepped over to the parapet wall and looked out over the horizon. "You can't not love this city, no matter what it does wrong. It's like a wayward sibling, a spoiled little brother. It's like a prodigal son, except you always return to it." She pointed toward Lee Circle, where a streetcar trundled round the turnabout. "See there, that streetcar? From that corner where it turns up Carrolton down to the zoo is the island where I grew up. That's how I think of it now, as an island. It's a small town. Sooner or later, everyone you know will cross paths. Don't you love it here?" She toked.

Achilles walked over to Ines and put his hand on her ass. "I like it here."

Smoke sputtered out as she laughed. "I like you liking it there. But what about here?"

He stuck his nose between her breasts. "I like it here. These are great, perfect. I don't even know why other women bother to put breasts on in the morning."

She laughed and pushed him away.

"Careful," said Achilles, swinging his arms in an exaggerated manner, as if he were at risk of going over the edge.

"What about you? Why don't you talk about yourself more even when you smoke?"

"I talk about myself all the time."

"Hmmph!" said Ines. She straightened to her full height. Her startling profile was set off by the billboard across the street, the white of her sheet eating up the black background. She was so sexy. Sometimes he just wanted to bite her, to just bite a big fucking chunk out of her ass. Ines stomped once, then twice, as if testing out the floor. She rounded her shoulders and paced back and forth with heavy, tromping steps. "You hulk a little, hunched like you're under pressure, like there's something you've got to hold so tightly, hold it until it hurts you, like you've been kicked in the stomach, like you're carrying a secret and you think if you squeeze it tight enough, it will become a diamond."

"Bullshit," said Achilles. "I don't walk like that. That's how you walk when, when, when you're stoned."

"You can take the flak jacket off."

A troop of rollerbladers towing a boombox in a baby stroller stopped at the intersection and performed the dance routine from "Thriller."

"See." Ines closed her eyes, took a drag, and held it in so long that Achilles gently pinched her to make sure she was still breathing. A car cruised by blasting a local rapper. Achilles recognized the song but didn't know the artist's name. Ines laughed and bobbed her head to the music. "I'm wrong. You don't walk like that. But why don't you talk about yourself?"

To avoid appearing as if he was holding back, Achilles forced himself to meet her gaze, staring directly into those amber eyes. If, at that moment, she asked him the wrong question, he would give her the right answer. He would tell her everything. "Like what? What do you want to know?"

Ines twirled a dread and hummed. "Why do you walk like that?"

Achilles swallowed, eyes big. Where to start? Ines placed her hand over his mouth. "Don't be mad. I'm just joking. What's your favorite superpower?"

Achilles whispered, "Flight." They'd already had this conversation, but unlike the frustration he felt repeating himself to Janice, this felt comfortable and familiar, their shared history a source of pride.

"Right, because invisibility isn't a superpower. I asked you this already. I was stoned then too. What about not sleeping or not eating for the rest of your life?"

Achilles bit back the answer to her earlier question.

"Well?" asked Ines. "Food or sleep? What goes?"

"That's no contest," said Achilles. "You can't do anything while you're sleeping, and while you're sleeping you don't know you're sleeping, so drop the sleeping. No one spends that much time eating anyway."

"What about dreams?"

"I don't remember them anyway."

"Good answer. In Nola, people spend a lot of time eating. But I agree with you. I hate people who say they'd give up eating, like that means anything but that they're stupid. I'm always like, 'If you can give up eating, you have no big-picture view of life.' Next question. What would you do if you were invisible and didn't sleep?"

Sometimes when he was drunk, his mind was so clear it surprised him. This was one of those moments, and he was surprised to have it stoned. Without hesitating, he said, "I'd be a bra. I'd sneak around and hold your breasts up for you." As soon as he said it, everything he'd thought about moments of drunken clarity faded. Whenever he drank too much or got stoned, stupid shit buzzed around in his head and slipped out of his mouth. Buzzed. Buzzed like drunk. Buzzed like bees. Like bees in a hive, his words flying out. The image made him laugh. Like bees in a hive, except the bees were his words and they bit him as well as the people around him. Why couldn't he have thoughts like this all the time? He laughed again. Ines was staring at him. How much time had passed since he'd made that comment? Had he said it, or only thought it? What were they talking about anyway?

"You finally laughed. Bzzz. Bzzz." She made antennae with her fingers. "Shh!" She cupped her ear. "Bzzzz! Bzzzz!"

He laughed again, and she laughed with him, and she buzzed and he laughed harder for that and he could tell that somehow she liked this

comment about her tits, even if he had only said it to himself. It occurred
to him that maybe Ines was like his friends who got political when they
were stoned. Because she was political all the time, this was her chance to
be silly.

She sprawled out in a lawn chair, her legs splayed out, the toga hiked
to midthigh. She fingered the hem on the sheet, running it between two
fingers as if checking for defects before waving it, softly slapping it against
her leg. "Huh!" she said, smoothing it out, looking surprised to find herself wearing a sheet. "You know who hosted my first toga party?"

Achilles shrugged, not wanting to hear a story about frat boys and keg
parties.

"My mom. She suggested it instead of a bikini beach theme. She said
togas were classy because they were classical." Ines stared at Achilles.
"Didn't she think about how much easier it is to fuck when people are only
wearing sheets? Fuuuuck! Or did she?"

Achilles didn't know what she was thinking, but picturing Mrs.
Delessseppes killed his buzz faster than falling from the roof would have.

What did Ines's mother think? Janice's mom had been welcoming,
but her brothers less so, once smashing in his windshield, slashing the
tires, and writing, on the side of his car, *I'LL CUT YOUR ZIGGER DICK OFF.*
Achilles had been pissed. He'd spent a lot of time and money on that
car. *Stop whining,* said his father, *Men eat anger and save it for later. They use it
on the field.* Achilles did precisely that, taking Janice's older brother's spot
on the varsity team. That was an unusual situation. Race had never really
mattered when he was growing up, but this was the South, and before
meeting her, he'd been worried that Ines's mom might not like him
because he was black. Now that he had met her, he still wasn't so sure. One
drill sergeant had always made him repeat himself. Merriweather sometimes teased him until he cursed, them mimicked his curses. Janice had
once claimed to have better rhythm. She did. So did Ines.

Shaniqua, Tyrene, Laquisha, Amina, Diamond, Jazzmyne, Aunt
Jemima. Black women. Like that plump bird at Kikkin Chikkin. Tough,
determined, hard to crack. Attitude and flak. Loud. He flirted with them
in gas stations and supermarkets. He'd smile at them, even ones with tattoos. They'd smile back, eventually. Black women. More bark than bite.
Necks popping, gum chomping. They heard his suburban accent and
thought Achilles smart or brainy or trying to act white. Black girls.
Enigmas. He hadn't met a single one throughout all twelve years of school.

He'd slept with Wexler's sister Naomi that time in Atlanta, but he was drunk and on leave, and she lived there. He'd never really known one, not really. Sure, he knew Aunt Esther on *Sanford and Son*, the mother on *Good Times*, Florence on *The Jeffersons*, and that lesbian in the *Color Purple*. But only from Naomi did he discover that BAP was as disparaging as *chickenhead*. Black women. Mysterious and powerful. The only one he had even eaten with, outside the military, had been Ines's friend Margaret, and now, apparently, Ines, who was so smart and classy.

Apparently? Yes, *apparently*, because only now did it occur to him to wonder why Mrs. Delesseppes had said *varied* relations, and not *black* relations? What did that mean?

"What?" asked Ines as she stood to shake the sleep from her limbs, which usually reminded him of a sprinter approaching the starting line, but this evening brought to mind a charismatic about to catch the Spirit.

In fact, thought Achilles, in the South, was there even a difference between being black and having black in you?

Another huge cheer erupted from the street. Apartment windows slid up, car doors flung open, people yelled into the air. Horns. Noisemakers. Aerosol horns. People poured out of the sports bar screaming, a tangled mass of faces painted purple and gold, their pounding feet audible, a rapturous hoard barking themselves hoarse. The Saints had won. The game was over.

They were ecstatic, as he had felt about the buzzing, the bees, and the breasts. He remembered that when they were little, Troy was afraid of bees, always running to Achilles to shoo them away, always relying on his big brother to protect him. Yes, always relying on Achilles, older, bigger, darker. Ines sashayed over. Whistling, she said, "The flak jacket, babe, the flak jacket."

What did she mean?

CHAPTER 12

THEY WERE IN A WADI IN LAI'PUR WHEN A SOLDIER THREE PACES BEHIND, shoulders swaying like he was on a boat as he listened to his MP3 player, tripped and fell, his shadow shrinking so naturally, so casually, that had it not been for the rifle reports—and they heard reports all the time— Achilles would have thought him clumsy, or another victim of heat exhaustion, or that he had merely stopped to adjust his laces. Dust flew as the new recruits scrambled for cover, firing to the four winds, some aiming, some on their backs shooting wildly over their heads, throwing bullets like salt after birds, and Achilles saw that fallen soldier nearby, one of his buddies lying over him, shielding him, the tiny white headphones still in his ears. As Achilles watched those fluttering brown eyes—the same color as his—close for what was certainly the last time, he called for Troy, who yelled that he was O.K., and thought, *Why are they shooting at us?* Even as he steadied his rifle and aimed at the far ridge, his limbs were alternately tingling then numb, his ass clenched so tight it hurt, and he was struck by the fear that he'd never, ever, ever, shit again, a sensation he felt when Morse called, nearly dropping the phone as the detective asked to speak to Troy.

"Mr. Conroy, your brother is looking for you," said Morse, his usually stentorian voice light, somewhat like the saccharine tone intended to lure a dog one was tired of chasing, a dog who thought it all a game.

"Are you still in New Orleans, Mr. Conroy? Your brother Achilles is here too. Mr. Conroy? Troy Conroy?" Morse confirmed the number. He had dialed correctly. Moved by Achilles's determination, Morse had done a little legwork, put a man on the case who found out that there was an inheritance, and that Troy had called about his.

True, Achilles had occasionally felt an envy that turned his stomach and left a sour taste in his mouth, like the film that remained after tossing a grenade. On rotation he had often wished he was still big enough to kick his younger brother's ass, especially when Troy sauntered out to the murder pool to mount up like he was riding a bull. In high school, he had rarely delivered messages from all the girls that called after Troy. But wanted to harm him? Never. Or had he?

The thought roused him, frisked him, and he felt exposed, as he had when Wages cinched his wrist in a vise-like grip and barked, "Why the fuck is this watch on Kabul time?" He had the physical sensation again of being shot at as Morse repeated himself.

Simple, old-time police work, Morse called it. And there was Achilles stuttering into the phone that he hadn't known about any inheritance when he filed the MP report, and he hadn't claimed to be his brother. The attorney made that mistake, and no, he still hadn't seen his brother since the day after the funeral. And no, he wasn't angry about Troy inheriting more money. And yes, the bruises Morse had seen really were from a fight with a stranger. And Morse hmm-hmm-ing and uh-uh-ing, finally saying, "I understand. I believe you, Achilles, but you need to come down so we can talk and update the report."

Surely Morse was wrong, Achilles protested. He had a text message with eight exclamation points. Achilles had spoken to his mother. She was buying a pool table and planned to build a kennel. She tried to contain herself, but she was happier than he'd ever heard her. "My mother talked to Troy."

Morse cleared his throat, taking on the avuncular tone he had used when they went to lunch. "Achilles, I spoke with your mother. She didn't talk to Troy herself. She bumped into the attorney's receptionist in the parking lot at the dentist's office."

Achilles fought the urge to vomit.

"I'm very sorry, Achilles."

Wages would have tried to fit it all into the new theory of life he'd picked up from the VA nutcrackers he had seen since the Bethany incident. His new vision concerned the Zulus and some kind of warrior purification ritual. Supposedly, until a warrior completed the ritual, he couldn't reenter society without soiling everything he touched. Achilles had agreed with him at first, desperate to find an order to things, an unfamiliar wistfulness overtaking him as Wages started his story. "Listen up good, Connie, this is like the Bible, but it's better because it's true, and it explains the dreams."

Achilles had listened as attentively as at a briefing but understood nothing, even as he studied the wooden African mask now dominating Wages's mantel for clues. The ovular brown face with slit eyes and pointy teeth stood over the room like a sullen guard. The hair was brown fur, but the beard was red, made from spent shotgun shell casings. Achilles couldn't make heads or tales of Wages's new theory. First, Achilles didn't dream. Well, he knew he dreamed, but fortunately he remembered nothing, so why did it matter? Second, what did an old African tribe have to do with modern warfare? Third, when he thought about Ines, he considered himself lucky. If he was soiling things, if he hadn't really reentered society and Ines was punishment, Achilles would die if things got any better. He'd just fucking pop-lock, like the otherwise healthy soldiers who died unexpectedly in combat, usually of sudden heart attacks. He had blown Wages off, but as he dialed his mother's number, he suddenly wasn't so sure.

Like that old song said, "*Getting shot at wasn't too bad, it was getting shot that shook you up.*" If talking to Morse was being shot at, talking to his mother was being shot. In the few days since announcing Troy's imminent return, she had accepted it and the joy was apparent in her voice, turning his belly cold and his tongue stony. His heart beat in his chest like a dying fish as he hastened to speak, to assure her he was there, he could hear her. He pictured her at her desk before remembering that she forwarded the house phone to her cell and could be anywhere.

"Are you at the house?"

"No."

"Where are you? Are you on the way back yet?" she asked.

"Almost."

"Almost here? Or almost on the way? Keelies? He'll be here any minute."

"Did you actually talk to him?"

The connection was poor. Or was it his hearing? "No, but . . . You see . . . Perfect isn't it . . . That's how I know he got your message. Achilles are you there?" He assures her he is still there, that it's great, it's wonderful, it's stupendous, it's terrific to hear that Troy called Chuck Riley over in Mercersburg about his inheritance. Yes, he agrees, it's miraculous, there is a God, but . . . "Mom! Did you actually talk to him?"

"No."

"Oh Mom."

"I saw Lisa, Chuck's receptionist."

"Why didn't you . . . Why did . . ."

"I was excited, and I didn't want you to think he only cared about the money."

This was a point that, embarrassingly enough, he had considered. He explained how the attorney had mistaken him for Troy, but she argued. "It's not like Chuck doesn't know Troy's voice," she said. "It's not like you wouldn't clear that up. Right? So you better get oscar on the mike or whatever you call it over there, because he'll be here any minute now."

It was one of the first times he understood how some guys could take off running across the desert, gulp a grip of Tylenol, bite a barrel. Maybe Wexler had known it was a minefield.

He liked to think of himself as an honest guy, but he was starting to think he'd never really told the truth when it mattered. When Lamont Jackson caught shrapnel that sheared off the back of his helmet and head clean-like, easy as scooping ice cream, and his brains looked like, well, a pickled walnut, he asked Achilles if he was going to make it, and Achilles was so transfixed by the sight of the open skull, so certain he was cursed to see this side of a friend, he couldn't answer. He tried nodding. Everyone was talking and yelling and screaming, but they couldn't hear shit, and neither could Achilles. Jackson was mouthing the words. All Achilles had to do was mouth the words *Yes, you'll make it*. He couldn't. He half-nodded. But Jackson had that look in his eye like he knew Achilles was lying, and, worse yet, he forgave him for it. That was the real burn, that a dying man held forth grace for Achilles, the living, who hadn't the courage to be forthright and tell him, "Yes, say your prayers or meditate, or think of your mom, or conjure the memory you want to take home with you, because you sure don't want it to be Sergeant Achilles Holden Conroy fly-eyed and crying and sweating on you, about to shit his own pants, you sure don't want it to be the crumbled remains of the bombed nursery we crossed yesterday, each brick a tiny headstone, you sure don't want it to be the sound of men crying and running scattershot in the dark, screaming for their mommas—and not like babies, but like only men can scream—and you sure don't want it to be the decapitated Muslims killed by other Muslims and left on the side of the road, because the townspeople who move to bury the dead are judged coconspirators and dispatched to join them, because to attend to them is to sympathize, to confer dignity is to abet, because compassion is outlawed, and you don't want it to be Lionel Dinkins, who took the brunt of the blast—acrid, pungent, something you should never smell—and you don't want it to be the way the sand under your back is hot, so hot it's like it's baking you through the flak jacket, or the corn that suddenly aches like a scorpion stung your toe because of how your boots pinch at the end of the day because your feet have swollen to what seems like twice their normal size, and it can't be the swishing of your pants as your legs twitch because that's too much like running, which you'll never do again, and you don't want it to be the sound of your feet flopping in the sand, it's too much like the sound of sifting, and you'll wonder what's being left behind, and you don't want it to be the sound of your own tears, with your heart beating too loudly in your ears and your sobs echoing in your chest, because you never rest well when you cry yourself to sleep."

But he didn't say any of that. He stared blindly and swallowed often, even though his mouth was so dry each contraction was like forcing a sharp chunk of burning granite down his throat. But he had to say some-thing, so he said to Lamont, "Remember how you told me that your mom used to put jelly between your pancakes and still let you put syrup on top?" And he held Lamont Jackson's hand, and the tighter Jackson squeezed, the tighter Achilles squeezed. And he said, "You know how you told me that your lady's dog used to get upset when you spent the night, and would piss in the hallway, and you won't be mad about it when you go home?" Jackson grinned widely. "Jealous devil. My Jody's a dog." The grin faded and he said, "Don't leave me." He tried to speak again, but no more came out, and an Afghan kid in the background was laughing and Jackson squeezed Achilles's hand tighter and Achilles squeezed back and felt the sun biting his neck, the sand in his mouth, in his socks, his ears, it was like there was sand every-fucking-where, even in his goggles, there was even sand in his ass, and it was so fucking hot he was gonna shit glass, and the kneepad straps pinching his knees, and helmet strap slicing his Adam's apple, and his belt cutting his waist, and his pistol butt digging into his ribs, and it felt like everything that was supposed to be protecting him was choking him to death, and he said to Jackson, "Know how you say, 'When we get back to the barracks and drop this shit off, it feels like we can fly'?" And Lamont nodded and went still, but his grip grew so tight Achilles was a long time freeing himself.

And after the perimeter was secure, when they reassembled in the silence of the aftershock—Wages calmly directing with his hands; the laughing Afghan kid defiant to the end, smiling even as he dropped to the ground clutching his neck, knees to the dirt in a soft puff of dust; Merriweather with blood on his fingers and a glazed look in his eyes, putting the blade away wet, as casually as zipping up; Wexler leaning against the burned-out hulk, sobbing, spitting on Merriweather—Achilles looked at Troy, who had switched seats with Jackson, and was just so glad that they were alive, and the sun was dead behind Troy's head like a halo, so Achilles couldn't see his face, and he was so happy Jackson had switched seats with Troy, and that whole fucking thing drove him fucking crazy, the whole thing, the idea that somehow by Troy being there it was impossible for Achilles to really give a fuck about anybody else in the squad, because it was like there was a tax and someone always had to pay it, and as long as it wasn't Achilles or Troy it was okay, and he knew he shouldn't feel that way, he knew he should want them all to make it out, but he knew they couldn't, he knew, somehow, in a way he couldn't explain, because he'd never believed in ESP or clairvoyance, but he knew that of the eight that started, only four would survive, and no matter what happened at each formation of prayer group, he could never muster the words *Let's do it* or *We got this* or *We put the fun in funeral*. He could only say, "That's right." And that was the look he must have worn as a mask while Jackson died, a tense smile that said, *It's as bad as it looks, and it probably feels even worse, but at least it's you and not us.* And in the soup kitchens it was the same, and he realized that as a kid it had been the same, that if he'd asked his teachers or his friends or his neighbors, "Am I going to make it?" They would have said, "You'll be fine as long as you never, ever, ever leave home, because here we all know you and treat you like one of us." Maybe that was the look the neighbors had had at his eighth birthday party. Had they already known about Troy that day? That thought burned him like no other. He could never show his face in Maryland again. Pity was fatal.

And it was pity Jackson had shown. Oh how Achilles burned as they trundled off with Jackson strapped to the roof, baking like a fucking potato, someone screaming for Wexler to shut his whiny vaginy, Merriweather murmuring "We don't get down, we get even," and Troy chastising Achilles for breaking protocol to stay with Jackson instead of pushing into a defensive position, whispering, "Asshole! You could have been shot. For fuck's sake, Keelies, don't start trying to be a hero."

With each passing day he wondered how to tell Ines, knowing this deceit amounted to infidelity. He would be branded, and Ines would be forced to wonder: if ever their lives diverged, was she also in danger of being psychically killed off, of being denied the emotional afterlife deserved by all those with whom one once shared a bond of affection—thumbed photos, the random wistful sigh, the occasional mention. She would have to ask, *If you could kill your family, where does that leave me?* God, would she be upset. When Achilles told her that his mother had died, Ines cried so hard you would have thought she knew Anna, and she never forgave herself for being out of the country when it "happened."

He hadn't planned it this way. He'd only wanted to protect their relationship from the bad luck haunting him like a phantom limb. Everybody liked freaky white girls, and he couldn't be blamed for having been turned on by the dreads and dashiki. He couldn't be expected to walk up to a woman and say, "Hi, I'm Achilles. I was adopted by white parents because mine didn't want me and my brother's missing." He had often asked himself what he would have done differently had he known Ines was black, or at least had black *relations*. He had just as often answered, *Nothing*, even though he had been quick to tell Naomi under the cover of night, in a raspy murmur, wondering if he would die before knowing who he really was, and afterwards swearing her to secrecy.

Besides, if he didn't find Troy, he would have to bear Ines constantly asking, "Have you heard from your brother?" Even if he could persuade her not to ask that directly, he would still see the question reflected in her eyes during family gatherings, in church, and whenever one of them received the piece of king cake with the baby in it.

Wages would understand, but he called Wages less and saw Ines more, until his life was riven into the old friends who would never know who he had become and the new friends who would never know who he was. Everyone, truly everyone—his mother included—had tacitly agreed to stop mentioning Troy on the phone except for the brief awkward pause at the beginning of calls when each waited to hear if the other had news. The less he spoke to old friends, the better he felt, until some days he could believe that normal was all he'd ever known. He had always clerked at Boudreaux's firm. He had always eaten boudin with breakfast, and spent Saturday mornings seated on the carpeted floor leaning back on the sofa, reading the comics aloud while Ines rested her legs on his shoulders. He had never been given up for adoption or gone to war.

Not that he wasn't proud of serving his country, it was just that no one else cared. Iraqi and Afghanistan vets weren't spat upon like Vietnam vets, but they certainly weren't greeted with ticker tape parades. He'd seen a commercial where returning soldiers were applauded as they walked through an airport. What a joke.

Vets didn't exist. It wasn't as much a war as a campaign issue, a mere budgetary concern, and if so many had died, and continued to die, it was only because no one had accurately forecasted the ultimate cost. The nonwar had continued so long without him it didn't seem like the same war. But he knew it was the same war, officially or not, "Mission Accomplished" or not, whenever he spoke with recently returned vets. They understood that after digging out of the dirt overturned by mortars, the sand in your mouth tasted like sugar. He refused to discuss Afghanistan with anyone else, especially the voyeurs. There were the morbidly inquisitive, people who thought they could comprehend, secondhand, how death trumps reason, as if they could understand how often the dead appear to be grinning, or that if you stare too long a dead friend looks more and more like a stranger, while a dead stranger looks increasingly like a long-lost friend. There were the gung-ho civilians who couldn't point out Kabul on a map, but swore that if it wasn't for fallen arches or tennis elbow, they would zip right over there and singlehandedly cap every towel head. (When he wasn't around, did they say sand zigger?)

Republicans patted his back, hawks strutting like pigeons, as if inviting him to award them a medal. Weepy Democrats said, "You should have never even been over there," and apologized for the terrible things "you must have been forced to do." As if there were someplace in the world where, when people shot at you, you didn't duck and, if armed, shoot back.

Worst were kids like Ines's little cousin Sammy, who regarded him with such awe, when Achilles knew it wasn't a matter of bravery, skill, or grit. He was simply lucky—lucky that Geary's Humvee caught the IED on the Khyber Pass, lucky that Howser's chute malfunctioned over the Kurdish airstrip, lucky that Merriweather was assigned to point that day. Lucky to have been shot with nothing more than a camera.

He occasionally looked at his old photos to remind himself that he had done something that mattered. He'd come to understand how Wages felt, how it demeaned you to take orders from a fat coward. Some days, when Ines wasn't home, he took his old battered black ammo box out on the corner of the condo deck, where he could feel the sun on his toes and watch the ships travel their steady courses while thumbing through old photos. He had three favorites: one in the 'Stan, one in New Orleans, and one in Maryland.

In the 'Stan: Achilles, Troy, Merriweather, Wages, Wexler, and Jackson stand shoulder to shoulder in the shadow of the Herc that will shuttle them to Dubai for a little R&R. Their faces are gaunt, pants loose, smiles brazen. Even in the shade they squint, except Wexler, who, with one eyebrow raised and a left dimple deep enough to swallow sunlight, flashes the look that earned him the name Sexy Wexy. They've all casually slung their MI6s over their shoulders, except Merriweather, who stands with his rifle butt to the ground, leaning on the barrel as if it is a cane. Troy's face is a bit smudged, but for once he is nearly as dark as Achilles, who remembers the date and time of the snapshot; Chan, the PFC from Kansas City who took it for them; and feeling like he finally belonged.

It's a favorite photo because Wages is sober; Merriweather is happy, eager to see his first beach; Wexler—with his long, slim neck—does look like Prince; and Achilles and Troy finally look like brothers. Achilles locks the ammunition box whenever he begins to drift upriver, following the tugboats headed upstream, wondering how different their lives could have been, and if different meant better, and if better meant normal, like life with Ines, the star of his favorite photo from New Orleans.

It's an informal shot taken at Ines's cousin's wedding reception. Mrs. Delesseppes has hastily herded the wedding party into the center of the parquet ballroom at Gallagher Hall. Ines wears a strapless red satin gown and her dreads are woven into three thick braids like a gold headdress. Again, and over and over, Achilles watches other men watching Ines, window-shopping, and swells with pride. He waits until a cluster of two or three men direct their common attention at her, then walks over and runs his palm down her back, and she stand as straight and tall as if in formation. He feels equally officious in his tuxedo, the first since his prom. Ines insisted he purchase one because *men don't rent clothes.* Achilles and Sammy wear matching cummerbunds. In the photo, Sammy stands between Achilles and Ines. Simultaneously, as if instinctively, as if magnetically, Achilles and Ines reach for each other to hold hands behind Sammy's back. This is the moment the shutter winks: everyone else is staring at the camera, but Ines and Achilles have eyes only for each other.

Later, she didn't so much as frown after missing the bouquet, but she glared when the garter dropped like a scud missile, the impact scattering men across the parquet halls, the echoes of their footfalls fading into awkward laughter, the tone of embarrassing relief surprisingly similar to the chatter in the wake of a near miss. On the drive home she said nothing at all. It was the first of three weddings that summer, and Achilles tried dutifully to appear to be dutifully trying to catch the garter at the next two weddings. Weeks passed before he finally understood that reluctance to catch a garter is considered natural, but sprinting across the room like someone has yelled "Fire in the hole!" appeared a reluctance to be with her for the duration. The *duration*. She often speaks of the duration. She never utters the word *marriage*.

Instead, she says, "We'll be your family."

"We'll make beautiful milk-chocolate babies."

"Uncle Boudreaux will gladly give you away."

And he replies, "Yeah! The old BB is just dying to give me away. But you know, men aren't given away. We run shit."

She says, "You wish. You know what I mean."

And he does, not that she ever utters the M-word, nothing closer than that Morse code, the double dashes that appear after, lost in concentration, she bites her lower lip. No, no M-word. Instead, she claps at cans clattering behind cars. Near bridal shops, her purposeful steps shorten to a saunter. And whenever a home makeover or newlywed show comes on, she yells, "Hurry honey, come here."

He says, "Will those chocolate babies be yummy or bittersweet?"

"Will they be solid or hollow?"

"I can't even spell *marriage*."

Her laughter, ignited by a snort of disbelief, is explosive. She commands him to *be serious!*

"I am," he says. He really can't spell marriage, that's not his name. And he leans in to taste her smile, biting at her lips, as red and ripe as plums, marking them with two short dashes of his own.

And slowly, like an incantation, she says, "IDC, IDC, IDC, Ines Delessseppes Conroy."

Ines Delessseppes Conroy! Mrs. D would like that even less than A-sheel. "Not to worry," she said. Her mom would come around. "I promise you that."

PART 3

SUMMER 2005

CHAPTER 13

FOR OVER SIX MONTHS, ACHILLES HEARD NO NEWS OF TROY. THEN, LATE one evening, while in bed with Ines watching a home decorating show, he answered his cell phone to hear Kevin Wexler say, without even a hello, "I saw Troy."

Hearing Wexler's voice, he went out onto the balcony, which stretched across the length of the condo and overlooked the Mississippi. Once outside, with both French doors safely shut behind him, he asked, "Are you still in Atlanta?"

"Yes."

"At your sister's?" asked Achilles.

"Yes."

"You sure?" asked Achilles.

"When I called his name, he ran."

Achilles snapped his phone shut just as Ines turned on the bedroom light, something he constantly asked her not to do when the heavy drapes were open. One night, he'd even marched her down to the street below their balcony to prove how much a burglar, or rapist, or any other psychopath would see through those sheer curtains she so adored. He stressed that any criminal of opportunity recessed in the darkness could see them, case the condo, or take a potshot. Achilles shook his head as she crossed the room, the hem of her T-shirt caught in her underwear. He moved to the dark end of the balcony.

A bellowing air horn drew his attention to the Mississippi. He heard the waters shouldering their banks, but what he could see of the river under the full moon was nearly flat, a field of shallow black bowls with silver brims. He leaned against the rail and ran his fingers across the balusters while a black tugboat with a shiny hull and one broad, chalky stripe glided by, the dark water betraying little hint of its passing, only a few silver rims of water wriggling into ribbons. The tug was headed toward Algiers, the twinkling lamps across the river. In the moonlight, the coiled chain on the aft deck was a glistening black wreath and the anchor at the rear of the boat a wink of light. Achilles spun on his heels and went back into the condo, past the waist-high vases of dried larkspur and emerald hydrangeas in the living room, past Ines's favorite print, a life-size rendering of Kali, and stopped at the bedroom. Everything was as he'd left it. The light was off. Ines was in bed looking at television, and even Ricky, the stuffed koala, stood balanced between her feet. Achilles pointed to the phone in his hand as if it were a witness and began, "A guy from my unit . . . a funeral."

"Oh no. Who?" asked Ines, turning down the volume on the tv.

He thought about it for a moment before answering, "Kevin Wexler."

"Were you close? What was he like?" asked Ines.

"He was fine. I told you. We don't have a pack of secrets about some crazy mission where we slaughtered a village of retarded babies or something and ran around with their heads on pitchforks. We don't know all the secrets the news doesn't tell you or the government keeps away from you."

"I didn't mean it like that," said Ines, turning the volume back up.

"I don't mean that you did. I'm sorry." Achilles sat beside her on the bed, taking her hands in his. They'd never had a major argument, and he wouldn't be able to leave if he thought she was upset with him. All the stares she got. What might she do for revenge? "We got a shitty hand. It's like you said about your three months in Kabul. 'The crazy thing about a war isn't that none of the stereotypes are true, it's that all of them are.'"

"I understand."

Achilles patted her hand, but knew she didn't. She couldn't. She was the most intelligent person he knew, and it was true she had, in her words, a heart the size of the Hindenburg. That had taken some research to confirm, but he knew it to be true. Nonetheless, volunteering in the ghetto wasn't the same as being from the ghetto. Volunteering in Goddamnistan wasn't the same as being posted there. What would she say if he told her about Jackson, or that Afghan kid defiant to the end, smiling as he hit the ground clutching his neck, or Merriweather, putting his blade away without even wiping it off, as casually as zipping up? Would she think he had deserved to lose his foot? What about Wexler running into a minefield, and Troy going after him?

He was on the road within an hour. He carried little: the carry-on Ines had loaned him for the suit he'd almost forgotten, a rucksack he kept stuffed with a few pairs of underwear, and the black hooded sweatshirt he wore as urban camouflage. Ines had packed almond butter and honey sandwiches, pomegranate juice, a gift for Sammy the Stargazer—whom she foisted on Achilles whenever Sammy came home for a three-day weekend—and a card addressed to Naomi Wexler in perfect script, the letters as fluid as water, cursive that belonged on the Constitution.

He was on the twin spans, just beyond the New Orleans city limits, when the rain struck, sudden and vengeful like a prophecy, and he hydroplaned. He drove slower after that. He had promised Ines he would drive carefully and call her when he arrived, no matter the time. And before that, that he didn't scare easily, and after that, that he wouldn't fuck other women. His father had made him promise to look out for his younger brother. And before that, that he wouldn't cry when he was lost, and before that, that he would take a punch from someone else before kicking himself for running away. His mother had made him promise to return alive, at all costs, telling him squarely, "Son, don't be a hero." And before that, "Never go into Pennsylvania without an adult." And before that, "Hold *his* hand and look both ways." And after that, the army made him promise to support and defend the Constitution of the United States of America against all enemies; to bear true faith and allegiance, etcetera, etcetera; to obey the orders of the president, etcetera, etcetera, et-fucking-cetera. He had promised Wages to deliver a package to his mother and Bethany, *if circumstances warrant*. And after that, after Merriweather overdosed on crunch, Achilles, Wages, and Wexler stood in the ratty linoleum hallway of Walter Reed Memorial Hospital, somber as pallbearers, and declared that if any of them saw any one of the others going down the slippery slope of addiction, they were to forcibly intervene, no questions asked. Their hands clasped, his arm one of the three spokes in that wheel, itself a silent promise. They hadn't *survived all that shit just to come home and get hooked on this shit*. Still, Achilles felt odd about showing up at Wexler's house at four a.m. Surely Wexler had expected this when he called, but during the drive from New Orleans to Atlanta, Achilles's fear that he wouldn't find Troy, now missing for almost a year, was slowly eclipsed by the fear that he would.

He made good time, pushing himself, driving like he was on convoy, moving at a constant speed and stopping only when necessary. Finding his way through downtown to Grant Park, where Wexler's sister lived, was easy. Barely a month had elapsed since he and Ines drove to Atlanta to visit her nephew Sammy the Stargazer, but the city seemed taller, surging skyward in a frenzy of construction. Cranes perched over skeletal skyscrapers, their pulleys lost in the mist. Downtown, a web of repaved roads: slick, black tongues of tar studded with orange barrels. In the rain, expansive concrete foundations gleamed like giant slabs of melting ice. Even in Wexler's neighborhood, new brick homes with antique touches dwarfed historic clapboard duplexes, and mere blocks away a glassy new midrise condominium sparkled like a gem. The city was shedding its skin.

Wexler lived with his sister in a craftsman-style bungalow in Grant Park, a historic neighborhood, according to the sign. The house was old but well maintained, a row of potted sunflowers standing sentinel over the porch. Even at night, the mustard trim around the windows and the violet balusters lent the house a warm, feminine air. Achilles parked in the driveway behind a fancy four-door sedan. Before he had extinguished the headlights, Wexler was clomping across the porch like those G.I. Joe action figures Achilles played with as a child, articulated only at the hips and shoulders. A thick scar ran across the side of Wexler's neck where the landmine had lodged a children's toy, one of the die-cast ambulances passed out to establish rapport with the local kids. Achilles had expected that by now, over a year later, Wexler's movements would be natural. Watching him lumber down the stairs, gripping the handrails and almost imperceptibly feeling his way with his feet, step by step, Achilles told himself, again, that there was a difference between bravery and stupidity, and that running into a minefield was stupidity. He quickly grabbed his bag, wanting to meet his friend halfway.

Wexler was slight, shorter than Achilles, and his skin was much lighter, almost the color of pale cedar, like Troy's. Before their tans had set in, people had thought Wexler and Troy were brothers. Wexler had the light step and braided muscles of a runner, which he was, but he looked thinner, if that was possible. His face was drawn, cheekbones sharpened as if by hunger, and when he raised his arms to give Achilles a hug, his shirt rode the waves of his ribs. But when Achilles felt Wexler's forearms press against his shoulder blades, he knew that his friend's strength had not faded one bit. Wexler squeezed even tighter, and Achilles's eyes began to swell, so he dug his chin into Wexler's shoulder until Wexler pushed him away.

Wexler clapped him on the shoulder. "Ape arms."

Achilles pointed to the fancy black sedan. "You're coming up in the world."

Flashing his Love-Sexy grin, Wexler said, "My cousin's. It's in the witness protection program."

Achilles was puzzled until Wexler explained, "He's hiding it from the repo man."

The laughter felt like a release valve, felt like the good old days when they would drink down a weekend of R&R without sleeping, felt good enough to ignore the shallow creeks running across Wexler's cheeks, and Achilles's new habit of averting his eyes.

"Where's Chief?" asked Achilles, surprised that Naomi's beagle wasn't yapping at their heels.

"He's gone."

A knot pulled tight in Achilles's stomach.

"Just old age. He was up there, you know." Wexler winked and pointed up, his voice light. "Hey, you brought the rain."

"Eee-yeah, baby. Here comes the thunder!" said Achilles, mimicking the battle cry that announced air support. They hunched their shoulders and peered up at the sky and listened attentively, nostrils flared, Wexler bent back at the waist as if leaning against an invisible wall. They saw the three flickering red lights on the belly of a jumbo jet, a squadron itself, and heard the engine, a low, distant rumble scraping the sky. Antennae atop skyscrapers blinked their secret, stuttering code through the clouds. A swarm of gnats snapped around their necks. The smell of jasmine mixed with the scent of fresh-cut grass mixed with lingering exhaust. Though a few feet from the car, the warmth radiating from the engine pressed against their thighs. A dog barked, another answered. In the house across the street, a light blinked on, yellow behind the faded curtain, followed by whimpering, the rattle of a chain, the clattering of a glass pane in a slamming door. Soon the jet had passed, that sound funneling into a distant point. They strained, but all that remained to be heard was the rain and humming gnats and breath. And though it was a bright night, the raindrops materialized only inches from their face, always too late and too close and too fast to blink in defense, but blink they did, catching the rain in their eyes until lightning sliced the night, illuminating Wexler's eyes, round and burning, as when Troy had carried him out of that minefield. Achilles plucked Wexler on the back of the head where the cross on his Trojan would have been and said, as they'd always said after a touchdown, "They shoulda punted."

Wexler shrugged, his eyebrows knitted. Achilles pressed his tongue behind his lower lip, poking it out, doing Troy's impression of a drunken camel, coaxing his friend into thin laughter, and promising himself to never again utter, "Here comes the thunder." As he searched for something reassuring to say, something Ines would say when she caught him intently watching the lines at the shelters, the burden of the unmentionable set in, and he remained silent as Wexler stepped aside to usher him up the porch stairs.

The living room, painted sage, was as orderly as a footlocker. The magazines were stacked in neat pyramids: *Essence* on the bottom, *Jet* and *TV Guide* on top. At Achilles's house, that pile would have contained *People*, *TV Guide*, and *Readers' Digest*. His mom had ordered a subscription to *Jet* when they were in middle school. Smaller than a comic book, it seemed appropriate for children. After she discovered that each issue included a weekly swimsuit centerfold, each little glossy mag appeared on their desk sans pinup. "Jet" became their code for "porn." They later found the missing centerfolds in their father's winter chest. It was funny to see that magazine here, nestled innocently between the other publications. Beside the magazines, the remote controls on the black lacquer entertainment center were arranged in squad formation, the bottom of each one flush with the front of the television. Wexler had remained fastidious, as they had all been once, believing that to have an item out of place was to be out of place was to invite disaster; they would sooner stand downwind during target practice. But Achilles knew it wasn't Wexler's home by the row of potted sunflowers lining the porch, the embroidered placemats, the burnt-orange bathroom walls, the smell of sage, and most importantly, the open blinds in every room. He recognized Naomi's touch, earthy and open.

He could smell her—nutmeg, which was also the color of her skin, and his. A first for him. She'd thought him freaky because he couldn't stop staring down when they had sex, his eyes drawn to the immeasurable symmetrical shadow pulsing between them. Then, doing the William Tell trick, he'd shot Chief in the leg, grazed him really. He was reckless during the few days the squad spent in Atlanta on the break between earning their silver wings and Goddamnistan. He had learned to live without food or sleep or water or fear and felt a certain power, as if he had fingers of fire. He'd expected the feeling of invincibility—the other Achilles—to last until he reached the FOB, but it began to fade in that kitchen as Naomi pushed the placemats aside to tend to Chief, his breathing worried, his black eyes spinning wildly, as if looking for a reason. When she'd poured peroxide on his leg, his claws on the healthy front paw had tapped the kitchen table, *click, click, click.*

That same sound he heard now, sitting at the same table as Wexler fiddled with the matching glass salt and pepper shakers, sliding them from hand to hand, clacking them on the table as he explained to Achilles how he had seen Troy near the lunch bucket across from his jobsite, and how he had called Troy and chased Troy and lost Troy in an overgrown alley that cut between a row of abandoned homes and a large housing project called the Bricks. But surely it would be different when Troy saw Achilles. It would be different when he saw his brother. "When he sees you, it'll all be over," said Wexler.

"Yeah," said Achilles. It would all be over, whatever that meant. He pressed for details. How did his brother look? What was he wearing? Had he lost weight? Or teeth? Wexler had only seen him from a distance, and remembered little. There were no more details, other than the map Wexler had made.

That Troy had run from Wexler forced Achilles to face a possibility that had been bugging him. What if Troy was avoiding Achilles? Vowing to be smarter this time, he cautiously unfolded the map, as if afraid of what might pour out, as if to damage it would spill the truth, or ruin his luck, when he was so close. Across the top of the page, block letters spelled out OLD 4th WARD. There was a *T* circled where Troy had been spotted, and an *S* where Wexler worked and, near the middle of the map, an area highlighted and labeled THE BRICKS.

Wexler said, "I made up the spare bedroom, but you can only stay until Sunday night, when she gets back." He said it quickly. Though his face was visibly relaxed, he started clacking the shakers again. *Click, click, click.*

Achilles nodded. He couldn't be in Atlanta any longer than Sunday. He had work Monday morning. Today was only Wednesday. That gave him long enough, he hoped. Boudreaux probably wouldn't mind if Achilles took another day off, but he didn't want to ask for any more favors, not after the DUI, which had roused Boudreaux's ire because he'd repeatedly warned Achilles off that stretch of road.

"I think she's still mad," offered Wexler.

"I apologized," said Achilles with the same air of exasperated finality as his original apology. He seldom openly expressed regret, so when he did, he felt that it was beyond mere atonement; his shouldering the blame and burden should be accepted as the final word, the final fistful of dirt on a grave to which no one should ever return, and of which no one should ever speak. Besides, he'd been assured that Chief was well trained, and could remain still for long periods. There would be nothing between them now anyway. In recent photos, Naomi wore an Afro. Wexler said she'd gone granola, but that was too much. She'd never get a job with that hair.

"There's something else you should know." Wexler paused.

When Wexler still hadn't said anything a minute later, Achilles said, "I know you're gay. And Naomi is your cross-dressing boyfriend."

Wexler laughed weakly. "Yeah, I turned faggity after you sucked me off."

They fell silent, gay jokes falling flat when there were only two of them.

"Going to any groups?" Wexler asked this like he was talking about a playoff game.

"You?" asked Achilles.

"I go to PTSD sometimes, but ain't no crazier than when I went in. Speaking of crazy, Merri's going to run a marathon and the VA got him a thing he can run on and he's not talking about exploding melons anymore. I guess you've seen little Wages."

Achilles was glad to hear that Merriweather was moving on with his life, that he had stopped picturing everyone who crossed him as dead, their heads burst open like melons, an image borrowed from *Day of the Jackal*, a French film in which the assassin used large fruit for target practice: "Blow the seeds out," Merri would say. He deserved to be happy. In a world so hungry, a world that took so much, a man deserved something good in exchange for a foot. As for Wages, Achilles hadn't seen him since that time at the casino a few months back. Little Kyle he'd seen only once, shortly after they brought him home. Whenever Wages called, Achilles claimed busy. Achilles suspected that Wages still thought the Bethany incident was the reason for their parting. Achilles wanted to tell him otherwise, but to bring it up would only reinforce Wages's suspicions. That, or they'd have to start hanging out again, and Achilles just didn't see how to make that happen. If Wages was in the room, Troy was in the room, then they all were, and then Achilles would have to introduce them all to Ines.

Wexler flashed a photo of Wages's son, insisting it was the cutest baby he'd ever seen. Achilles agreed. He didn't know exactly what babies were supposed to look like, only that they shouldn't resemble the crushed infants he often saw when accompanying Ines to clinics: glazed in sweat, distended eyes, urgent, yurling cries, persistent twitching, even in sleep their tiny limbs flailing as if drowning.

On the drive to his jobsite, Wexler explained that several roads had been recently renamed after flowers to lure suburbanites into town. Achilles ran his fingers across the map, memorizing the terrain. He'd never seen the Fourth Ward, but he'd been with Ines enough to know exactly what it looked like. The corner store stocks tawny-tipped lettuce and lottery tickets. Near the front doors sit two barrels of ice, one filled with malt liquor named after animals and weapons, the other filled with syrupy drinks in little plastic jugs with foil tops, drinks with names like Red Jungle Punch, Yellow Jungle Punch, and Green Jungle Punch. When you buy a pack of cigarettes—they sell singles as well—they won't give you matches. But they do sell several types of lighters, which is important, because at the counter they have a display case stocked with screens, pushers, and straight glass pipes: everything needed to pretend to satisfy your crush—*pretend*—because they will tell you the pipes are novelty items. They also trade in insults: *Learn English! No, you learn English!* As they toss your change on the counter, the mouth sometimes says, "Thank you." The eyes often say, *Dirty motherfucker.* Half of the stores are run by Koreans, the other half by men who resemble, at first glance, those he was sent a quarter-way around the world to kill.

Outside the store, squat houses mired in moats of wrinkled concrete rimmed with crabgrass, stripped of copper and wire. Potholes are de facto speed bumps, large enough to swallow tricycle tires, but that doesn't keep children out of the road. Streetlights are shot out. The neighborhood is bordered by a cemetery, a factory (possibly abandoned), a waste treatment plant, and railroad tracks or a highway. And indeed that was the Old Fourth Ward, except there was no waste treatment plant and there were two highways—the Connector and Freedom Parkway—so that the neighborhood was both bordered and bisected by high-traffic roads impassable by pedestrians. It looked like the Tremé District in New Orleans, or DC, or inner-city Baltimore.

They reached the jobsite in the dark morning hours, just before five a.m. Wexler worked for his cousin, Tony Sharon, renovating a historic Victorian home four blocks from the King Center. It was the tallest house on the block, with three floors and an attic bristling with narrow dormers sharp as steeples. Like all the houses on that stretch of Medgar Evers Avenue, from the second floor you could see the eternal flame hovering over Dr. King's tomb, mere blocks from where he was born.

Wexler rambled as he led Achilles through the house and up the stairs, ducking under hanging plaster and high-stepping over debris. The interior of the house was being dismantled to save the antique fixtures such as wood trim, solid wood doors, and stained-glass windows. He followed Wexler up to the attic, brushing cobwebs aside, stepping cautiously from joist to joist like he was crossing a river on rocks.

From one dormer, Wexler pointed out the gingerbread houses and embroidered lawns of Inman Park. "Cross those tracks and you're in Inman Park. They jog, we run. There, B&B means bed and breakfast. Here, it means boarded up or burned down."

From another dormer, Wexler pointed out the vacant lot across the street. "That's where the lunch bucket parks. Where I saw him." In the dark there was little to be seen except a billboard-sized silhouette of MLK's profile at the far end of the lot.

From the third dormer, Wexler pointed out a complex of scarred cinderblock buildings surrounded by a brick wall and painted the same shade of red as the clay upon which they stood, as if they had grown out of the earth. "That's Banneker Homes, aka the Bricks. People are posted up at the entrance twenty-four seven, or one-six-eight as they say around here. When someone dies, they just dump the body outside the wall and call the police. Don't go in there. For true, Chief. Someone gets shot or falls off a building every other week. That's how they settle things. Don't go in there. For true."

Wexler pointed out the last dormer. "That's the cemetery. It's historic." He tapped his temple. "I like to come up here and watch the traffic right before the sun comes up, when you can hear it better than you can see it. I think about going to another country, not like we did, but just to see how other people normally live. Shopping, talking, reading, whatever, in another language. It's weird the first time you see people doing the shit you do, but in a different language. Someone said there's an MLK boulevard in every city with blacks. There's blacks in France and London. They have one? Probably not. There wasn't one in Valdosta when I was a kid. I know it's not true, but I'm curious. They say it's always the worst street in the city. That can't be true either. Look around."

Wexler's voice dropped like he was in the confessional. "It doesn't look like much now, but wait a year. New street names. Flowers grow from shit. See, the neighborhood is changing. You have to watch it like white people." He tapped his temple again. "They watch, they wait, and pounce when the time is right. That's why my cousin Tony is successful. Other blacks are moving out. For them, success means moving away. But Cousin Tony bought these houses, just like the white folk. He's going to be rich because he's thinking like a white person." He swung around to face Achilles. "How do you plan to do this?"

The Old Fourth Ward was nearly fifteen blocks across and twelve blocks up, much larger than the Tremé District, too much ground to cover on foot, yet it made little sense to drive from house to house. By the time he started the car and drove a block and parked, he could walk. So his plan was, "Watch, walk, and wait."

"I mean, what if he doesn't want to go?" said Wexler. "Are you going to check him in?"

"Check him in?"

"Look around. It's not a vacation destination."

"Who says he needs to be checked in? Who says he's got the crush?" asked Achilles, pounding the joist closest to him. A cloud of pink insulation drifted between them.

Wexler pointed at him. "You just did."

"You're twisting shit. How can you know what my brother needs?"

Wexler raised his arms in surrender. "It might be more complicated is all I'm saying. I'll do whatever you need, but there's one thing I wanted to tell you earlier. I'm born again."

"Again?" asked Achilles. "What went wrong the first time?" An ambulance crawled by, the siren loud and frantic.

When the sound died down, Wexler said, "You know you're not the funny one."

Achilles raised his arms in a gesture of surrender.

"I didn't mean it like that." Wexler clapped his hands together, interlacing his fingers. As he spoke, his hands shook slightly, like he was praying.

He said, "I want to help. I will help. But it's just that I can't do any more crazy shit."

"Who said crazy shit?" asked Achilles, knowing that Wexler was referring to the boardinghouse fight, which had grown in Wages's imagination. "I don't even have a gun." Noting Wexler's disbelief, Achilles added, "Really."

"Okay. It's just that I don't want to make it a situation where force is the answer. This isn't a battle of wills."

So this was the new and improved Wexler: all fore, not enough head. Whatever happened to "react or die"? What kind of pussy shit were they learning in PTSD counseling? Was the same thing happening to Wages? This was worse than that Zulu hoodoo. They used to say people didn't need shrinks; people needed friends. For Christ's fucking sake, was Wexler really reborn? They used to say, "My M16 is my G-O-D." Achilles was the only veteran among Ines's friends, the wild one, Brick they sometimes called him, a name he wore with more pride and bravado than he'd ever felt on duty. His military swagger set in. Achilles put a finger to his temple and said, "Every fucking thing is a battle of wills."

Wexler said, "This shit gets in the brain. Crunch affects people on an animal level. It's like possession. Think *The Exorcist* or *Night of the Living Dead*. They get like zombies. Believe me. Most people can't even quit cigarettes."

Achilles raised his hand to silence Wexler. Achilles wasn't naïve. Maybe Troy had the crush. Maybe he'd gotten flushed into some bad shit hanging around with his black family. But that was only a possibility, and Achilles wasn't going to treat the probable like the definite. He knew Wexler would back him if ever push came to gun, but said, "It's cool."

"Brrrlll." Wexler blew air across his lips, as if to brush off Achilles's remark, shook his head, gave Achilles the finger, looked flustered, said "Fuck," and crossed himself.

Achilles shot the finger back, as he used to during PT when Wexler would glide by grinning, his stride as smooth as a moonwalk. "How'd he ever outrun you?"

Wexler snapped his head back, as if dodging a live wire. "He had a head start. Fuck man. I called you."

Achilles felt awkward. He was being a complete dick to the friend who'd called him, put him up, taken him to where Troy could be found, a friend who was a brother in his own right. But Wexler owed them. Troy had saved his life, and, after Jackson died, Troy had soothed Wexler. It was

Troy who pried Wexler—kicking, screaming, biting—off Merriweather. In fact, Troy had calmed Wexler first, like Wexler was his brother. Achilles didn't hold that against Wexler, nor did he resent all the other times it seemed Troy was more concerned with Wexler, nor did he resent Wexler's obvious attachment to his brother, but for some reason Wexler's almost matronly caution was always Achilles's trigger, or was it just that whenever he was around Wexler he felt like yelling "bring the thunder," screaming "drop the money shot," throwing rocks, blowing chunks, drinking whiskey with a crazy straw, and shooting himself in the head with the tequila pistol?

The orange Hummer drove by again.

Wexler laughed. "That's who I need to be praying for."

"Oh yeah?"

"Yeah. He's the HZIC around here, runs the Bricks. Knows all and everybody, got his finger in everything: drugs, hookers, dogfights, numbers, welfare, daycare."

Prayer? Whatever. But what if Wexler was right about Troy being on crunch? Did it even matter? Everything would collapse when he found Troy. Telling Ines had seemed easier when he thought there wasn't any chance of finding him. But how to speak of the living? He tried to push that thought out of his head, but it only reminded him that he'd promised to call, *no matter the time*. He stepped into the dormer farthest from Wexler and dialed.

A rush, a tingle in his neck, when she answered. He adjusted his pants, excited by the sound of her husky morning voice, needles and all, as she mildly admonished him for taking so long to call. While he was driving, Tropical Depression Twelve had been upgraded to Tropical Storm Katrina. She said she might be joining him in Atlanta, then assured him she was only joking. Her family hadn't even evacuated during Betsy. "We can always go to our place in Lake Charles," she said. "Hell, we didn't even leave for the Battle of New Orleans. But that's all right. How are you? How's your friend's family? The name was Kevin Wexler, right? In the rush to get you on the road, I forgot to get the address."

He looked at Kevin Wexler, who stood in the opposite dormer, probably listening to traffic and dreaming about visiting some other country, unarmed. "Baby, I'll call back about that. I just wanted to let you know that I made it."

"Okay. I love you," said Ines.

"Think fast," said Achilles, unconsciously extending his index finger like the barrel of a gun.

"Okay, Mr. Cool." Ines laughed as she hung up.

Achilles joined his friend in the dormer and tried to follow his gaze. Water dripped from the ceiling, collecting on a skewed window ledge in a star-shaped puddle that swelled until one single drop slipped over the side, taking the rest with it, then more water collected, forming another star-shaped puddle. Under the only working streetlamp, the sidewalk was a stage awaiting a performer. But it was intermission, the slice of morning when the crunchers were already in, and the workers weren't yet out. Cars hummed through puddles. Downtown, a succession of streetlights went out, one after the other, as if extinguished by the wind. A hazy orange aura lay on the horizon, as if the distant trees had burst into flames and a fire was headed across the city, straight into them.

Achilles and Ines had visited Atlanta for Sammy the Stargazer's birthday. Sammy had prominent front teeth and the stubborn stance of a spoiled kid. Achilles and Ines bought tickets to Six Flags over Georgia; the amusement park seemed a good choice for a fifth grader. But the surprise was on them: Sammy, who attended a fancy boarding school in the suburbs, wanted to be an astronomer, and demanded, truly demanded—teary-eyed as he proclaimed his adult status—a trip to the planetarium at the Fernbank Science Museum. "It's my birthday after all!" Ines said Sammy was granted latitude because of his *condition*. Achilles asked her to repeat it three times, finally giving up because all he could make out was that Sammy had "ass-burger" (which sounded like something Merriweather would say, until it dawned on Achilles that maybe he'd been molested—at which point he kept his distance). Achilles was pissed. The tickets weren't cheap, and he'd been looking forward to a few rounds on the Cyclone roller coaster. Instead, he found himself at a museum enduring an animated dramatization of the Big Bang, complete with celebrity voices.

The Fernbank lecturer, wearing socks with sandals and smelling of patchouli, compared the Big Bang to conception, calling it, "Another explosive genesis, but driven by enzymes. A flash of light is emitted at conception, a burst that is far too bright to be explained by chemistry. Boom! There we are. And so our body is created in a big bang, like the universe. Likewise, it starts to cool and contract in old age." He lowered his voice, as if delivering a pickup line. "In this vast universe, there are solar systems, and in these solar systems there is us, and in us, there are additional solar systems. We are each interconnected beings of light." Achilles noticed, not for the first time, how Ines perked up when she was intellectually stimulated, as if aroused. His anxiety that he would never be an intellectual was cooled by the fact that he felt equally moved, being in that moment entranced by the possibility that all was as it was meant to be.

At the same time, the Fernbank lecture had left him spooked, much in the same way it chilled him to hear Ines, stoned, hold forth on water and earth as living things. If the world were alive, it would be a mirror reflecting him at every turn, and he simply couldn't abide that. He didn't like the thought of a living being that large and always in motion, and breathing, and watching, for surely it would see him and know what he worked so hard not to think about, surely it would harrow his secrets and kindle his fears. If the world were alive, wouldn't that be like a parent who knew your every move? Wouldn't thoughts be weapons? Wouldn't that make karma real? Wouldn't there be danger in his joke, "Everyone wants what they deserve. Me, I'm hoping not to get it."

In retrospect, it had been a good time. Like she had with New Orleans, Ines breathed life into Atlanta. During that trip, they'd visited the Coca-Cola Museum, eaten prime rib at Bones, strolled Phipps Plaza's marble halls. Now he was stepping over beer bottles and dog shit. Armed with Wexler's map, Achilles noted the new street names, which definitely didn't match the neighborhood. Medgar Evers was surrounded by Carnation Avenue, Gladiola Street, and Peace Lily Way. Achilles corrected the map as he circled the block. If a house appeared abandoned, he went inside. If not, he knocked. It took over ninety minutes to do all thirty-five houses on the first block. There were sixty-five more blocks, not to mention the old paper plant and the abandoned cotton mill. He wouldn't be even halfway finished before Sunday, when he had to leave. He battled his discouragement by trying to stick to the plan and treat it like a road march—one foot after the other, orderly, insistent. But he couldn't shake the feeling that when he was on one side of the block, Troy was on the opposite side, that they were like the blades of a propeller, and he soon found himself backtracking and making figure eights via the grassy alleys, like a gambler who thinks that one more time around and the wheel will pay.

Alleys fed even narrower side streets that poured into broad thoroughfares like Auburn Avenue, which was once the African American Main Street, according to Wexler. The decline appeared irreversible, like

New Orleans's own Tremé District, which Ines had explained was the oldest black neighborhood in America (and St. Augustine the oldest black parish). The Fourth Ward felt different because at least commuters passed through this neighborhood, whereas in the Tremé, you either lived there or you were lost. In both cities, old men spoke and young men stared. But Atlanta had more black history on display, the neighborhood dotted with plaques memorializing bygone glory. One minute he was in a Section Eight complex, the next he was on a path identified as Freedom Walk. For a time it seemed the only businesses were pawnshops, churches, and funeral homes. Then came King's tomb and torch. Achilles detoured from his path, venturing into the paved courtyard surrounding the tomb. A group of schoolchildren held hands, heads bowed before the eternal flame. Catty-corner from the MLK center, a row of burned-out homes, and across the street a statue of Gandhi. A few blocks later he was facing a six-foot-tall cast of John Wesley Dobbs's head. The plaque read: "Give us the 3 BS—the buck, the ballot, and the book." Behind the sculpture, winos slept in the shadow of a replica of a slave castle wall. As he passed the winos, one spoke: "What's up, young blood?"

The tone and timber of the man's voice reminded Achilles of Bud and Father Levreau, and the blaxploitation movies he had recently discovered and enjoyed but Ines detested: *Dolomite, Shaft, Black Belt Jones, Truck Turner*. Pimps, pushers, prostitutes. "It's vaudeville," declared Ines, "blacks in blackface." But Achilles saw black men leading a revolution, cleaning up their neighborhoods, meeting the government on their own terms. The fabled *Spook Who Sat by the Door*, of which he had only heard, *Gordon's War*, *Coffy* (Grier had serious high-beams): where were they now? Afros and picks with fists, fly suits, and high fives; the seventies were a golden age of brotherhood. The men in the shelters often talked about it, a time when everyone was a brother or sister, a time when there were *young bloods* because they were all of the same *blood*. He felt a heightened sense of fraternity as he answered, "I'm fine, old-timer. How are you?"

"Good, brother, but I sure could use a quarter, a dime, anything to help a brother get something to eat." His eyes were red, but his hair was thick and wooly. He was plum-cheeked and thick-ribbed, his body round, not chiseled and angular like those on the crunch diet. He could work. Achilles handed him some change, a bargain for such a precious lesson, or a refresher course. You couldn't talk to some people without being asked for money.

What would Ines say? Achilles asked himself as he entered an abandoned house and found himself staring down at two squatters immune to the flashlight shining in their eyes, splayed out as if they had fallen from a great height onto the soiled bedspring, a raft in a sea of food wrappers and glossy jack mags. *Brother, do you think you can hide from your true nature? Brother, why are you killing yourself?* Achilles told himself, *Self, they're not weak, they're just hurt.* He couldn't conjure her compassion.

These men before him were self-destructive, meaning weak. Through the ratty aluminum foil covering the window, a few dusty blades of light stabbed the darkness. At the foot of the bed were bits of fur mixed with balls of puffy mattress stuffing. Beside it, a tub turned toilet, attended by flies. On the floor in the corner, a third man, curled into a ball, with a bundle of newspaper for a pillow, hugged a Krazy Kreme donut box to his chest, a column of ants trekking back and forth across his arm and circling the sugar ring around his mouth. Feeling like a vampire hunter, Achilles ripped a large strip of foil off the window. The man on the floor beat at the ants.

"Hands up! Heads down!" Achilles yelled in Arabic and Pashto, as a joke. But as he said it, his right hand reached for his sling and his heart started racing.

Two of the guys retreated to the corner, hiding their faces like bad dogs. One man in a black POW-MIA T-shirt rolled off the bedspring and onto the floor, turning clumsily, the exposed steel toes of his unlaced boots knocking the floorboards until he reached the shadows. Achilles hefted the flashlight like a baton, ready to strike. *Unarmed is disarmed! It's like sticking your ass up and yelling "chowtime" in San Fran!*

The man in the POW-MIA shirt sat up, one hand raised to shield his eyes from the light. His voice hopeful, he asked, "Lionel?"

Achilles, who had nearly begun hyperventilating when he realized he was unarmed, shook his head.

When the man asked again, Achilles said, "No!"

"You seen him?"

"I don't know anyone named Lionel," barked Achilles.

"If you see him, let him know I'm still here."

"Yeah, sure." As he searched the other rooms, he moved with caution, his adrenaline high, his fingers twitching. He was surprised to find it otherwise deserted. Why did they all congregate on the same mattress? He passed that room on the way out. The man in the POW-MIA T-shirt was trying to stick the foil back up, muttering. He pressed it against the glass, but it flopped down. He tried smoothing it out with his hands, and it tore. He spat on the window, and tried again, but it fell. When Achilles heard a sob, he cast the flashlight toward the window. When the beam crossed his face, the man flinched and slapped at his cheek as if an insect had landed. "Lionel?"

"I'm not Lionel."

"You seen him?"

"No," said Achilles.

"Tell him I'm still here. Tell him Norm is here."

Achilles turned away.

"Sure, I will. I'll tell him."

Once outside, using one hand to steady the other, he made an X on the map, having checked the last house on the block. He had recorded the creases in overgrown lots, the runs that cut through otherwise impassable alleys, the winding trails that wound across vacant plots and between houses. Ultimately, every path led back to one place. Every street that ended without warning—Medgar Evers Avenue, MLK Boulevard, and Malcolm X Way—dead-ended at Banneker Homes, suddenly colliding with that brick wall as if it had been planned this way, as if the housing project had fallen from the sky whole, like a box trap. When Achilles finished correcting the map, the Bricks stood in the center like a bitter black heart.

CHAPTER 14

WAGES AND TROY SOFTLY HUMMED "MAMMAS DON'T LET YOUR BABIES Grow Up to Be Cowboys." Merri muttered the Psalms. Wexler said, "It looks like someone ripped a pillow open." From where Achilles lay, he couldn't see Wexler's face, but knew that Wexler was referring to the puffs of clouds scattered across the horizon, white wisps sweeping westward, occasionally revealing the low, full moon. The squad's position in a shallow cave offered a prime view of the piedmont below, dotted with brush and squat red dunes with low vegetation rounding their bases, like receding hairlines. The mountains on either side of the plateau vanished at the horizon long before meeting, forming a huge channel leading to the end of the earth. Gradually, the clouds retreated to the edge of that channel, bunching up like a blanket, revealing the moon high above, one perfect circle. Three goats crested a dune and stopped, as if they too admired the view.

And it was breathtaking, this valley laid out before them like a tapestry, the gently undulating land, the high ridges on either side, and in the middle of it, one small village of only five buildings illuminated by flickering oil lamps, the only sign of human life, and above it the biggest sky he had ever seen, a dark sheet with that perfect sphere of light in the center like a watchful eye. The next morning a thin layer of mist hugged the hills. Watching the rising sun burn it off, he recalled the dawn vistas from the highway behind his home, the trees wavering behind a veil of fog like the shadows of people who weren't there, the three rocks in the lake lined up like the back of a mythical beast preparing to surface, and it was all so stunning that as he fell asleep in that cave beside his brother, as he had those first few days before Troy's bed arrived, it was hard to believe someone out there was trying to kill them.

How had it started? Everyone blamed someone else. They were walking along, then a landslide, and next thing they knew, someone was firing at them. Then, as Merri later described it, it was quiet as the night before Christmas in the mofo. They tried to move a few times, but every time they did, the firing started again. Wages called it in and they waited for the money shot, watching that sunrise, all of them, side by side, tuned in like it was the best movie they ever saw. And Achilles forgot for a few moments that he was on Mission ZF1983—his birth year—and that he was trapped by bad decisions or fate or intel no more accurate than the maps on a child's place mat.

He felt equally trapped in the stifling attic at Wexler's jobsite, hemmed in by the fear—foolish, he knew—that he needed to see Troy before Troy saw him. He was also unsettled by the suspicion that with all his drug talk, Wexler was hiding something; and he was angered by Ines's sudden decision to come to Atlanta, which he resented because he'd need to stop his search and find a hotel room. "Doesn't your mother need you?" he'd asked. Her answer: silence. His thought: *Who ever heard of a little rain driving people out of town?*

The lunch bucket was setting up in the partially paved lot across the street, the doors unfolding upward like quilted silver wings glinting in the sunlight. He watched the lunch line grow in clusters—the sheetrockers coated in white dust; the painters in their dappled whites; the masons in their gray, dusty overalls; and Wexler, who stood alone, yet spoke easily with everybody. A gaunt gray dog, ears tattered like pom-poms, wandered the lot, dodging kicks and stopping to sniff the occasional rock tossed its way. An old man sucked a packet of mayonnaise like it was a pig's foot, licking each finger when done. Others did the same, collecting and trading condiments, which he hadn't seen in New Orleans. But he was always at locations where food was given away.

At the edge of the lot, at rapt attention, stood a man draped in desert BDUs that hung on him like curtains. The pant legs, rolled up to midcalf, rattled around his thin shins like bells. Achilles moved from dormer to dormer, scanning near and far, looking at everyone again and again, as if studying a check for an extra zero. A sheetrocker had Troy's profile, a painter his gait, a mason his habit of pulling on his earlobe when waiting in line, and a beggar the same tilt of the head just before telling a joke. When the men in line around him laughed, Achilles's throat constricted as if he'd swallowed a pinecone. A gold Hummer cruised by and in its wake the bubble of laughter collapsed, lips tightening and necks twisting, as if it were a hearse.

Wexler came up with two Styrofoam containers, offering one to Achilles. His mouth watered at the smell of fried food, but he wanted to remain light, coiled, and ready to spring.

"I don't eat that crap anymore." He'd long ago said good-bye sloppy joes, pot roast, cheesy hot dogs; hello muffuletta, jambalaya, stuffed mirliton.

Wexler patted Achilles's stomach. "Can I make a wish?"

It was true, he spent less time in the gym and more time in the kitchen. But it was hard not to. Until Ines, he'd never known what it meant to really want to be with somebody, to have somebody just for him. To get up and have a common routine, to be in the same circle. He and Janice were never completely in the same circles. "Life is good."

"Yep." Wexler stood in the sunniest dormer and ate, chewing loudly, attacking the chicken like a big cat. He always ate like he was happy to be alive.

Achilles kept moving around the attic, watching the surrounding streets, examining every profile. When the lunch bucket folded up its wings and trundled off, there was still no sign of Troy. The workers drifted off. The homeless men who had been standing at the edge of the lot swooped in, kicking the dog out of the way.

Achilles sat on an overturned bucket across from Wexler. Achilles had been up all night and felt the fatigue setting in as soon as the lunch bucket left. His muscles were smoldering, aching, and burning. "He's here. I can feel it."

Wexler nodded knowingly.

"This has nothing to do with religion."

"You'll find him," said Wexler. "The creator has a master plan. The Lord moves in mysterious ways. Sometimes we have to be tried before we can be really blessed, like Jacob or Job. You'll see. My pastor says that sometimes you have to suffer to be tempered, like the iron in a forge becomes a fine sword. You'll see. Soon we'll all be delivered, like the Israelites out of Egypt. My pastor says we're the chosen ones. My pastor says God loves black people, and God has a plan for everybody."

So did Hitler, thought Achilles. "Leave that alone already." He pointed at Dobbs Plaza in the distance, where winos slept in the shadow of that slave-castle wall, and beyond that, at a new church, as if people could pray their way out of poverty. He made a sweeping motion with his hand as if to say *Behold*. These people were fucked up. It was always the same. The pushers, pimps, and preachers all drove fancy cars while everybody else rode the two-dollar taxi. The big sell: get high Friday, get laid Saturday, get forgiven Sunday. God was the gravy that made shit sweet as sugar. "This shit isn't mysterious."

"I know it's not your thing, but I've been praying for him. Look around this neighborhood. He needs all the help he can get. So, I pray for him."

"Thanks," said Achilles, the way he said it when Sammy gave him a CD he already had. Avoiding Wexler's eyes as he left, Achilles took the stairs one at a time, his steps heavy. Outside, the last few people scrounged through the scraps abandoned by the lunch crowd: bread crusts, potato chip crumbs, warm dregs of pop. At the end of the block, a malt liquor sign blinked a question, a menthol cigarette sign winked a response. A pregnant woman carrying a baby on her hip, dark *V*s on the backs of both of their shirts, pushed a stroller piled high with newspapers, and perched atop that pile, two bags of crushed cans. If this was his plan, God hated black people.

The man in the BDUs rummaged through the fifty-gallon drum that served as a trashcan, his arm in up to the elbow so that only the shoulder patches were visible: the Infantry badge, the Airborne patch, and as Achilles saw when he was close enough to read it, a nametag that read CONROY.

Achilles took the man by surprise, throwing him facedown to the ground, kneeling on his back, and pulling the jacket below the elbows so that the man's arms were tangled in the sleeves, making it hard for him to fight back. Achilles leaned on the back of the man's head with one hand and grabbed an ear with the other, pressing his head into the ground, his mouth into the dirt, suffocating him, pressing harder the more he kicked and easing up when the kicking stopped. The procedure was simple: induce panic, take control, set parameters. "Where you'd get the jacket?"

The crowd was initially stunned, but the spell broke when Achilles spoke. A few stepped forward, muttering about their rights. They were the same crew that had been lurking along the bushes while the lunch truck was there.

Achilles put his hand up. "Army business. Step back or you're obstructing." He returned his attention to the man beneath him. "Where did you get the jacket?"

His response was drowned out by the crowd, which had now coalesced around the old man who'd eaten the mayonnaise packets. He had a neatly trimmed beard and a shock of gray hair brushed back like Frederick Douglass. He cleared his throat. "This ain't the army. I was in the army. And you can't come around here like that. This here is America." "Amerca," he pronounced it.

"Preach on," a few murmured their assent. Others shouted, "This ain't Virginia Beach."

"Where'd you get the jacket?" Achilles asked again. "That's all I want to know."

"The purple house. I'll show you. The purple house."

The crowd stepped back when Achilles yanked the man to his feet and marched him off in the direction indicated. Someone said, "He ain't all that tall no way."

Achilles pushed through the crowd flashing his military ID, the men moving back like it was radioactive, except one old guy who called out, "That don't scare me none. I was in the real war. Smells like a con to me."

Conroy meant "wise advisor," according to their father. According to one drill sergeant, it meant they had to carry a lot of shit. According to another, it meant nothing. "You have new brothers now," he told them. "We are all your brothers. You are now 11-B, one and many." Basic training and infantry school were combined into five phases named after colors, but Achilles thought of them in three stages: crawl, walk, and run. They learned to get by on little water, less food, and no sleep, and to carry only the bare necessities when possible, which was why Achilles was surprised as he went through the bag in which the man had found Troy's BDUs. They were in a purple house right behind Wexler's jobsite. When Achilles had found it empty before, he hadn't thought to search the odd bags scattered throughout. There were several pairs of dirty socks and underwear, three T-shirts, another pair of pants (too short), a blank address book with the F-section torn out, and the same photo of them all on the way to Dubai, enough stuff to suggest that Troy might have hung around for a while. "How long has this been here?"

"I found it in the Bricks."

The occasional black brick stood out like a rotted tooth. The top of the wall glinted, crowned with broken glass. There was no grass and no shade, only parched clay and cracked asphalt, nothing to catch the sunlight bearing down on the roofs and heads of the kids posted up at the entrance. They were as young as ten, the oldest not even twenty from the looks of it. They were joking, rambunctious, invincible; like in Afghanistan, Baltimore, DC, New Orleans, the poorest laughed the loudest. Ines knew how to speak to them. "Just look them in the eye and say hello. That's all folks." It's easy, Achilles reminded himself. He showed them his picture of Troy, and they only laughed harder, without moving their mouths, with steady shark's grins. They lounged like they had no bones in their bodies, leaning at impossible angles as if made of rope, loose-limbed and slack-jawed. They looked at the blood on his knuckles and waved him through. As he passed through the gate, they laughed even louder, like they had seen this before, as if to say, *You'll be right back, running so fast your sneaker soles will melt.*

They thought they were tough. Tough was the little boy who snuck into their tent to steal food; tough was the sniper who shot two members of J9 before Wages neutralized him, a boy who had barricaded himself in his minaret, a boy barely as tall as his rifle, a boy who had affixed a pillow to the wall behind him to absorb the recoil. Tough was Wages, who walked away from that without looking back.

Achilles walked the inside perimeter of the housing project first. He was surprised that Wexler had been so adamant that he never enter the Bricks. People weren't tossing bullets like it was the Wild Wild West. It was quiet. A white kid in a black hooded sweatshirt walked a pit bull. A few kids played king of the mountain on a picnic table in a roofless gazebo. An overturned slide lay under fingers of kudzu. Like his sergeant said, "The earth will soon eat us all." All the buildings, except a smoke-damaged one in the back, appeared occupied. The complex was broken into nine square blocks, like a tic-tac-toe grid. Each block had two two-story buildings with a parking lot between them. Hand-printed signs were posted on the telephone poles: "Don't let them change our name!" Across a few of the signs, someone had scrawled, *They already killed them once.* These streets hadn't been renamed. MLK and Medgar Evers ran north to south, Malcolm X Way and RFK ran east to west. As he completed his walk around the perimeter, he saw the orange Hummer. Beside it, the boy in the hooded sweatshirt was talking to a man in a letterman's jacket, large and angular, as if made of cinderblocks. A man wearing a red Atlanta Braves baseball jersey sat in the back of the Hummer. The kid left, without the dog.

As Achilles approached the Hummer, the big guy in the letterman's jacket held out one hand like a traffic cop. He had a tattoo of a pistol on his palm, drawn so that Achilles was staring down the barrel of a revolver, like those decals that read, *This Property Protected by Pistol.* The dog pranced back and forth and whined. The man muttered something and the dog barked a few times, but Achilles wasn't worried. Janice's brother fought dogs in the old garage bay at the gas station, and Achilles knew what to look for. Even if he hadn't seen the kid turn the dog over, Achilles would have known that it wasn't the big man's dog. The dog wasn't in a defensive stance and didn't position his body in front of the man. His ears were loose and his shoulders hunched like he was more anxious than anything else. The pit bull was a pet. He had his ears and tail and no scars. He seemed concerned about the kid who had just left.

Achilles held up the photo. The big man shrugged.

The man in the red jersey still sat in the backseat. Achilles slipped the photo through the half-open window. "Have you seen him around here?"

The window lowered, and the guy in the red jersey returned the photo. He had copper skin with freckles. He wore his auburn hair in cornrows, the rows on the side of his head woven into a diamond-shaped pattern and the braids extending almost to his neck. "This is the city of five-dollar whores and two-dollar hits. There's a lot of folk around here, comin' and goin', one-six-eight. What's so special about this one?"

Achilles held out the photo again, holding his hand out until he felt awkward. "This one's my brother. Look again. They found some of his stuff around here."

"Brother? Ain't we all?"

"No," Achilles shook his head deliberately. "We all ain't."

The man laughed, opened the door to stretch his legs, and took the photo again. "I might have seen him around, but I can't be sure."

"How long ago? Within the past few days?"

He nodded. "Maybe yeah. If I see him I'll let you know. You're over at the old yellow house on Evers Ave, working with Tony Sharon and those crunchers, and Kevin Wexler with the scar." The man pointed to his neck. "You know, the little one who looks like Prince."

The big man guffawed.

The man with the cornrows leaned back into the car and stared straight ahead, as if signaling the end of the conversation. With a slight motion of his chin he directed the big man to close the door. Achilles leaned on it. "So you've seen him?"

The big man stepped closer. Achilles held the photo out again. Troy's smiling face hung in the air between them. The dog whined, kids laughed, a window slammed.

The man with the cornrows stroked his chin. He spoke through a big grin, bearing his gold fangs. "Don't this make your brown ass blue?" He took the photo, studied it for a moment, and handed it back. Leaning forward, resting his elbows on his knees, he said, "You need to give up the ghost on this shit. Crunch crushes. The crush crunches. I seen a big fucker," he spread his arms for emphasis, "a bodybuilder, looked like Lee Haney, get on his knees and gargle mayo. He had that crush. See, maybe this ain't your brother. Maybe this is an animal." He cocked his head to the side, studying Achilles, who said nothing.

He continued. "You can't take him home. Listen to your pretty talk. You got shit. He slips up, pawns all your TVs and shit. Then what? He gets in that hole, they come gunning for him. He's dying for the bullet, but you get your potato peeled. Then what? He hits your liquor stash. Fa-fa-flash-back. He hits the locker room and comes back to your place with a crew of hos, and they fence your shit. Then what? Or you go on a three-day MLK vacation and this zigga turns your shit into a whorehouse before you can say 'I have a dream.' Then what? RICO Act, *brotha*. That's *your* shit on the six, eight, and ten. That's *your* shit stacking the shelves at the cop shop. All *your* favorite shit becomes the property of your least favorite uncle. And you still have to pay taxes."

Achilles inhaled deeply, and deeper still. And held it. *Remember to breathe.*

"Pretty-talking zigga like you, you know you got matching sheets and an old lady who don't want to deal with this shit, who does not want to contend with these muchos problemos. I hope I'm not making your record skip. I admire the way you come after your kin. That's righteous. It's straight country. Too bad it's probably a waste of time. Most of these cats end up ziplocked, on the shelf at the cop shop, or on the six-eight-ten. But I'll keep my eyes open. We'll talk again." He smiled wide enough for Achilles to see that the jewels in his teeth spelled *Devil Dog*, a glint that in some circumstances was an invitation to a bullet, and shined brightly enough that with an ACOG sight, he could reach out and touch him from up to eight hundred meters away, at night.

"We will," said Achilles, stepping away from the door. *Ziplocked?* He smiled, picturing the bastard's grinning head as a ripe melon rolling off a high counter, as Merriweather liked to put it.

"Not even you want to ante up for this. For true." Wexler even knew their names. Pepper was the man with the cornrows. The big man in the letter-man's jacket was Cornelius. Even after hearing that Pepper knew his full name, Wexler remained calm, telling Achilles, "My grandmother used to say, 'Even a crooked limb can cast a straight shadow when the sun is right, and ain't no one with good sense won't stand in that shade.' The dealers do some good stuff around here. They keep people from breaking into cars and houses. It isn't like there's a lot of opportunities around here."

As he spoke, he worked steadily, up on a ladder removing strips of crown moulding with the care of one peeling back a bandage. His move-ments economical and precise, he moved along the ceiling two inches, removed a nail, pried the moulding out a bit, moved down two more inches, removed a nail, and pried the moulding out a little bit more. Achilles had heard the term "dental moulding," but only while watching Wexler did he realize that the notches indeed resembled teeth. Wexler said to himself, "Nope. Not a lot of jobs around here. Even the local laborers only get a few hours of work at a time, and they're paid hot shit."

For the past few months, Achilles had gophered part-time at Boudreaux's law firm on Camp Street. He envied Wexler's focus, that he had a job actually doing something, not running errands for his potential uncle-in-law; that his only coworkers were the day laborers that helped load lumber for a few hours every few days, not guys like Keller, who insisted on speaking to Achilles in slang. After the film *Big Dog City* was released, downtown came uptown, and the vernacular went mainstream. For the last few months at the office, Achilles had been haunted by under-handed references to drugs because the white-collar workers had started talking like rappers. "Hello" and "What's up, man?" were replaced by a catalogue of hip phrases that they tossed around like enthusiastic tourists armed with a new phrase book.

They stopped sharing rides to lunch and started *rolling to the joint*. "Call me" became *hit me on the hip*. Achilles said, "Hello." They said, *What up, folk?* If Achilles made the mistake of saying, "What's up?" they said, *You know how we do it.* And when he stopped nodding and starting saying, "No, I don't," they laughed. And when he said, "No really, explain it to me," they only laughed harder, Keller's sharp cackles ricocheting around the law library like trapped birds. Only a few years older than Achilles, Keller was a prodigy, the newest partner, a shining star, so Achilles said nothing, not even when Keller's favorite celebratory catchphrase became the *Chapelle Show*'s infamous *Fuck your couch, Zigga.*

It didn't take long for the saying to catch on throughout the office (in Keller's words, *Hitting the corners faster than a paralegal afraid of being fired*). After a fruitful deposition, once the deposed was out of earshot and the recording equipment powered down: *Fuck your couch, Zigga!* After hanging up with the DA's office: *Fuck your couch, Zigga!* After a successful court appearance, the young turks charged into the building like linebackers into the locker room, ties loose instead of helmets off, doing everything except patting each other on the ass, yelling, in harmony: *Fuck your couch, Zigga!*

He imagined them trying that at Kikkin Chikkin, but he never mentioned any of it to Ines. Where would he begin without appearing accusatory and ungrateful? How could he explain the problem without inviting Keller or someone else to ask, "Why can't we use zigga if you can?" Never mind that Achilles had only used it once; he was indicted by every black person who used it routinely, and he had no logical answer for why his white coworkers and bosses shouldn't use it except that it made him uncomfortable. But how could he explain that without sounding like he was whining? How could he explain it without Ines thinking he wasn't man enough to handle himself? Then there was always the chance that she might go off the chain about it, fly down there for an emotional drive-by and leave Achilles feeling like a child, when he was no one's victim, no crybaby, no snitch.

Besides, it's not like they knew he heard them making those jokes behind closed doors. And he liked some aspects of the job. He enjoyed going to the courthouse to look up deeds and delivering documents. It was easy work, and he liked the uniform. Maybe Wexler was smart to work alone, but in the army no one did anything alone; they operated as a team, a group, a collective, a brotherhood, and there was security in knowing your team had your back, that even if they wouldn't die for you, they wanted to live badly enough to return fire. So you forgave them every other deficiency, because man knows no trait more valuable than loyalty. He knew Wexler was loyal, but his rant about drug dealers having no other options was ridiculous. Even Ines didn't think that. *They should be lined up and shot!* she always said. "That's the dumbest fucking thing I ever heard you say. Poor drug dealers can't get a job. What the fuck?" barked Achilles.

Sighing, Wexler moved along the ceiling two inches, removed a nail, pried the moulding out a bit, moved down two more inches, removed a nail, and pried the moulding out a little bit more. He stuck his finger in one of the many holes in the wall and ripped off a strip of wallpaper. "I know you're thinking, 'Why not just tear it down? Why not tear it all down?'" Wexler tapped his temple with his finger and said, "But people like old houses. When it's put back together, this will be better than anything new you can buy, because they don't make this stuff anymore." Wexler set down his hammer and crowbar and glanced around the room with a smile. "This is history. Do you know how many people it took to put this together? And it was hard work back then. Manually operated drills. No such thing as nail guns. If you knock it all down, you'll lose the good with the bad. And there's a lot of good that went into this house, too. Can't just come in and say you're going to knock out a busted wall. Whole thing might cave in on you."

Wexler really had changed. Standing there with his friend, Achilles felt very lonely, lonely for Ines. He understood Ines. He didn't understand Wexler and being born again. He didn't understand the new Wexler. Achilles didn't even understand himself when he was with Wexler. He wanted to shout. He wanted to shake Wexler, shock him out of his calm. They needed necessary fun, to go to the strip club, or pick up some hookers, or shoot at somebody. It felt unearned, unjust, unfair that Wexler, always the most excitable of them, should have the gravity, tranquility, and certainty that had for so long eluded Achilles. Wexler was at home in his skin, as was Ines, but Ines centered Achilles while Wexler's right-steady rudder confused him, made him feel abandoned, as if Wexler had set sail on a ship now vanishing over the horizon. Wages had a baby. Janice was married. She still called every couple of months, and he still ignored her calls. He spoke to his mom, at least briefly, every two to three weeks. She was still planning that trip. And his brother was living his own life, and his father was gone. Maybe everyone had moved on except him.

The clerk took one look at Achilles's license, praised his foresight, and promised him a nice room, one with the ice and vending machines nearby but not close enough to be a disturbance. The small room had a kitchenette, a shower with a tub, and two double beds. Western was the theme: orange cowboy hats woven into the brown carpet, paintings of horses gracing the walls, the curtain-rod metal molded to resemble knotted rope, and beyond the drapes, the balcony offered a clear view of the parking lot and highway. After sunset, the soda machine glow suffused the room like red illume, the lights they used on night missions, not that he planned to sleep in the room. Satisfied that he had made adequate preparations for Ines's arrival, he returned to Wexler's house, where he had the use of a bedroom but usually dozed off on the couch, undisturbed by Wexler on the loveseat, curled up like a cat and snoring like a dog.

"Connie, Connie, Did you hear that?" Wexler whispered every morning around zero-ass-thirty back when they were on rotation. Achilles scrambled for his gear the first few times it happened, holding his breath, his ears out for things going bump in the night, but eventually he suspected that Wexler heard nothing, that he was only recruiting a partner for late-night conversations, and Achilles's cot, unfortunately, was closest. Achilles imagined him tiptoeing through the tent, whispering in everyone's ears until someone awoke, so he started ignoring him, and soon enough it was Troy and Wexler up talking through the night, sometimes getting silly and switching peoples' boots or uniforms or underwear, though never in the field, of course.

So when Wexler woke him at zero-dark-thirty the night he'd gone to the Bricks, Achilles mumbled, "Go back to sleep, maybe Troy's up," reminding himself not to be alarmed in the morning when he couldn't find his mess kit, or lucky charm, or boots.

"Connie, Connie," Wexler insisted, whispering that he needed to talk, explaining that he hadn't actually seen Troy, nor had Troy run from him. He'd received a call from the morgue after some poor guy showed up with Troy's ID in his pocket. "It wasn't him, but it got me worried."

Wexler sat on the arm of the sofa, his silhouette barely visible. In Goddamnistan, people routinely disappeared. When Wexler went into the minefield, Achilles's first impulse was to drive on, to claim he had no idea what happened. He'd felt weighted by resentment, but now felt somewhat justified. "I was wondering how he outran you."

Wexler gestured at his leg and neck.

"I guess I meant why," said Achilles. "Is that why all the drug talk when I got here? What else do I need to know?"

Wexler shrugged. "I was scared, man. I didn't want you to feel that same sick feeling, Connie. It was like we were back there again. The whole drive to the morgue I was losing my shit. That same fucking night I started having crazy dreams again. Men were shooting dead fish. Into their veins."

Achilles patted Wexler's trembling shoulders, a gesture that said *I understand*, which he couldn't bring himself to say, but nonetheless was true.

CHAPTER 15

A CHILLES WAS AT THE GRADY HOSPITAL MORGUE WHEN IT OPENED, SHOWING a photo to the attendant, a kid who looked to be barely out of high school. Marcus, according to the nametag, carried a cigarette behind one ear and a pencil behind the other. Marcus vaguely remembered Wexler, or rather a slim guy who resembled Prince. He showed Achilles a picture of the body Wexler had viewed. Found beside the Bricks, the man was much older than Troy.

Marcus studied Troy's photo again, thoughtfully, his eyes moving between Achilles and the picture.

"How long have you been a diener?"

"They don't say that anymore." Marcus looked at Achilles. "You say this is your brother?"

Achilles nodded. "Yes."

Marcus held the photo up so Achilles could see it. "By blood?"

"Adopted."

Marcus appeared to weigh the probability of that being true. His tone apologetic, he said, "We have two more from that area. No, four. Two more just came down. You done this before?"

"Two tours in Afghanistan."

Marcus jerked his head toward the door, motioning for Achilles to follow.

Some morgues had gurneys parked in large walk-in coolers. Others, like New Orleans, had the silver wall of drawers. Grady had both: on the right were the drawers, and on the left were two large walk-in coolers, the kind usually found in restaurant kitchens. A long metal grate ran down the middle of the tile floor. The tiles were the reddish-brown terra cotta that hid dirt and blood. For all the fluorescent lights overhead and absence of shadow, it still felt too dark. It was remarkably clean and shiny, all the steel reminding him of his middle school cafeteria. He'd been in eighth when Troy was in sixth, and so hadn't let Troy sit with him.

Referring to the clipboard, Marcus led him to the drawers. Well-oiled, the action was fluid and silent, and the drawers slid out smoothly as if designed for comfort. Achilles scanned quickly, looking first for skin tone—not too dark to account for the sun or too light to account for an addict's nocturnia—then glancing at the face and moving on.

Two men were too old, one too young. They were all fresh. None had an autopsy suture. Marcus was considerate. He lifted the sheet enough to reveal the face and then looked down or at the body, anywhere but at Achilles. After each body that wasn't Troy, Achilles tried his usual ploy to buoy his mood, telling himself that he was lucky, that they'd won again. But each one left him breathless, fatigued. He felt lethargic, as if he was breathing underwater, as if oxygen was a salty viscous fluid he had to work to keep down, heavy in his lungs, and the more he inhaled, the lower he sank. Achilles was thankful that Marcus didn't offer him water or a chair, or acknowledge the chemicals.

In the walk-in, eight gurneys were lined up, dusky feet sticking out, and in the corner, one gurney with a smaller body. Marcus showed him one, a handsome teenager with auburn skin, deep-set eyes, broad lips, and one neat hole in the chest. He said, "The rest are all identified. Shoot-out. Family's on the way down. These three here are brothers, sixteen, seventeen, and twelve."

Achilles pointed to the smaller body in the corner.

"He's not related. That's a kid who's been unclaimed for a while. Smoke inhalation in an abandoned house. He goes to Potter's Field next week." His breath hung in the chilled air.

"How does someone claim him?"

"ID and paperwork. Sometimes a church will sponsor a funeral for an unidentified kid. Sad thing is no one reported him missing."

The dead wanted nothing more than to be left alone, or at least that's what they used to say. He and Marcus regarded the small form cloaked in white, barely bigger than Troy had been when he came to live with them, maybe as tall as Sammy the Stargazer. Achilles studied Marcus, just a kid himself. Downy sideburns stopped at the meat of the jaw, bald chin, faint mustache; he wasn't even shaving yet. "An unmarked grave?"

"We still say Potter's Field, but the indigent and unclaimed are cremated these days. We hold the ashes and bury them all together once a year," said Marcus. He shivered and suggested they leave the walk-in. Out in the hallway, Marcus briskly rubbed his arms. "It's cold in there. It's cold in there," he repeated, his voice hollow, his dark skin ashen. He appeared on the verge of tears. "He's dead, you know, but still, it seems like someone should get him." Marcus laughed. "I hoped you were here for him. Not that I wanted your brother to be here. I just wanted someone to come for him. Your brother's lucky. I work here, and I couldn't do it."

"How long have you worked here?" asked Achilles.

"About three months. It pays better than dishwashing and I get a lot of time to study. I'm used to it. You know what I mean."

"I know," said Achilles, knowing Marcus didn't mean a word he said.

Looking embarrassed, Marcus stepped closer to Achilles and, dropping his voice, said, "I know this is unusual, but I could copy the picture."

"O.K.," Achilles nodded.

Marcus copied the photo, and Achilles wrote his cell number on the bottom of the copy. Marcus pointed to the area code. "Shame if it hits y'all."

"What?" asked Achilles.

"That hurricane. Haven't you heard? It's headed straight for y'all."

Achilles had thought Ines was overreacting. It was nothing, according to Wages. *Happens all the time. It's hurricane season.* It was probably nothing to worry about. Feeling a mere thank-you insufficient, he shook Marcus's hand, closing it in both of his.

"Hopefully, I never see you again." Marcus grinned awkwardly.

Achilles mustered a smile and another thanks.

His tone measured, Marcus asked, "Does your brother have the crush? I ask because if he does and he's around the Bricks, you need to watch Pepper and his crew. Everything leads back there. But it's crazy. If you go in, keep your tens on the inside." Marcus balled his hands into fists for emphasis.

Achilles wanted to tell Marcus to quit while he could, before it changed him, to let the dead bury the dead—only they had the strength for it—and that he needn't blame his tears on the cold, that it wasn't too late for him, but Achilles just nodded and thanked him again and slipped out, exhausted.

Was it the antiseptic atmosphere of the hospital, all white walls and gleaming metal? Was it that the morgue was in the basement, tucked away like a secret, so far underground that the exposed pipes dripped condensation, the air so cool and dense he could feel the weight of the earth overhead? Was it the sense of inevitability that accompanied death in a war zone? How could he have squatted to eat a pork chop out of a pouch, smoke a cigarette, and swig an entire canteen of water in the same room as three dead insurgents while rocket impacts sprinkled them all in mortar, then, after the thunder came, after the Apaches shat a steaming pile of missiles in the faces of the hajis and their artillery, walk out of that same building, water sloshing in his belly, gnawing at a chocolate bar and laughing— until he cried—at Merriweather's knock-knock jokes about *the real money shots*, yet the little boy Marcus said was destined for Potter's Field remained seared in his mind, as did the body he had viewed at the first morgue? He remembered thinking that D-794, the burn victim in New Orleans, must have done it to himself, but now he couldn't forget him. The one clean patch of skin on the chest, the fingertips worn to the bone.

In New Orleans, the gurney had been wheeled in by a kid in a lab coat and headphones. He'd been wearing orange skateboarding sneakers with thick soles and had put a lot of effort into looking bored, not unlike Marcus. Was that how Achilles had appeared to the locals? Had they thought of him as a kid in funny clothes but with a gun? What had they thought about him when he was overseeing the cleanups after bombings, safe behind his Oakleys while wives and mothers examined limp fingers for wedding bands and looked for matching shoes they hoped not to find? His own hands shook at the thought, his mind racing wildly as he tried to imagine how others had seen him, something he hadn't dared consider while active. Too weak to walk, he sat on a parking barricade. The concrete felt good. It was cold, cooling first his butt, then his thighs. He unclenched his fists and placed his hands on the barricade as well, taking a few deep breaths.

Every Achilles, all of them, missed his friends. Achilles the Stubborn. Achilles the Suited. Achilles the Cynical. Achilles the Goofy. Ines had nicknames for his every mood, more than he could remember; hence, he was also Achilles the Absentminded. Achilles thought of himself as versions one, two, and three: the dutiful son, the reliable brother, and the soldier, all of which were reconcilable. But the new Achilles, the Ines Achilles, who was that? And what about the other Achilles, from the minefield, from the fight? Where did he fit? The only thing they all had in common was that every Achilles missed his friends, all of them, and being able to talk to them without saying anything.

What's going on? Will the ball club win it? Do you think they have a chance? What's the deal? What's new, man? What you know good? What's happening? He tried it with Wexler, tried explaining that he needed to talk, that the morgue had freaked him out, that corpses again gave him crazy legs. *Where's the nearest bar? Isn't Atlanta the strip club capital? What about Magic City? Ptah. Women! Isn't there a shooting range nearby? Let's head to Columbus and hit the Benning Brew Pub. Is a game on?* And, finally, "Fuck, man."

Wexler said nothing.

They were in the living room, where Wexler, always moving, always busy like a small dog, was folding laundry as patiently as he worked at that crap house. He had to lay the clothes out on the ironing board because he couldn't bend his chin to his chest.

In the yard next door, three kids dressed like superheroes played hide-and-seek, their high-pitched voices drawing Achilles to the window again and again. Two of them were about seven or eight years old, the third about five. The small backyard in which they played offered little cover: a rose bush, a pine tree, a stump, and a rusted-out Lincoln Continental Mark v riding cinderblocks. The five-year-old was most often It. While he counted, the tallest of the three, Spiderman, having figured out that the little one never looked up, would climb the tree, carefully keeping his face away from the sap and the sharp needles. The other older kid, Batman, would carefully tuck his cape into his belt and crawl under the car, leaving Achilles holding his breath. The youngest one, Wolverine, would count—one, two, three, four, four, four, seven, eight, nine, twenty—then wander the yard for barely ten seconds before he started crying, poking himself in the face with his plastic claws as he tried to wipe the tears away.

When they let him hide, Wolverine always stood at the edge of the rosebush and closed his eyes, as if that made him disappear. Achilles had often seen that, under fire, had always thought it a natural reaction to fear, never realizing that maybe the person just wanted to disappear. Troy had done it when Wexler ran into the minefield. Wexler had done it when Wages shot the sniper. Achilles had done it when Troy followed Wexler, swore to never look away again, but did it again when Merriweather was shot.

The two older boys started jumping on the roof of the car, yelling, "Where's Tony? Where's Tony?" Tony, aka Wolverine, was on his back under the rusted-out car, and as it began to rock and wobble on the cinderblocks, he bit his lips to suppress a laugh.

"Are you fucking stupid?" yelled Achilles.

The kids froze, looking around for the source of the yelling. Achilles lifted the window higher and stuck his head out. "Get off the car, idiots."

The kids shot him the finger and starting jumping again. Achilles started for the door, but Wexler stopped him, placing both hands on his chest and saying, "Breathe."

"I'll stick those fingers up their asses," said Achilles.

"They're kids. And I have to live here."

After Wexler talked to the kids, he got a couple of beers. Achilles was breathing heavily, almost crying.

"What's wrong with you?" asked Wexler.

"What do you mean?"

"The kids, the flowers. What the fuck?" asked Wexler.

"Flowers?"

"*What flowers?*" said Wexler in a mocking tone. He removed a bouquet from the trash and handed Achilles a card. "Who's Ines Delesseppes?"

The card was printed on heavy paper with a seashell embossed on the cover. It read, *To Naomi Wexler and Family, Our Deepest Sympathies for Your Loss. From Achilles Conroy and Ines Delesseppes.*

"You can't understand second chances. And what if Naomi was here? Are you trying to hurt her again?" Wexler pointed to the flowers.

"When I came up here, I mentioned a funeral."

"Mine!" Wexler thumped his chest. "You can't be serious. Don't we know enough dead people? That's some fucking high school shit." Wexler stomped across the room, the pictures on the mantel rattling with each step. He slumped into the La-Z-Boy, holding his head in his hands. With his small frame and frown he looked like a child in time-out. All three of the kids next door were now jumping up and down on the roof of the car, yelling, "That's some high school shit!"

"I had to come, but I couldn't tell her why. What else could I do?" In hindsight, there was a lot he could have done. He could have said his friend was sick, or in rehab. He could have just said that he had to go because he was a man, and he had shit to do.

Wexler jumped back up. "There are things you don't lie about. On second thought, I guess you wouldn't know. It all makes sense."

For someone reborn, Wexler was overreacting. Achilles wanted to say, *Doesn't Jesus have your back?* Merri said it too, later adding, "And now he's got my foot." But Jackson used to say stuff like that too, and look where he ended up. Sometimes Achilles repeated these sayings to Ines, all these nifty little aphorisms his friends spouted at the most unexpected times. "No need to order Chinese," she'd say. "Achilles the Fortune Cookie." All the fortune, half the calories.

Wexler kicked the sofa. A bird cawed; the dogs across the street answered. Then it was silent except for the shuffling of Achilles's feet. The kids next door yelled, "That's some fly school shit!"

"How'd I die?" asked Wexler.

"That never came up."

"How did you describe me?" asked Wexler.

"I said you were a good guy."

"That's all?" asked Wexler.

"You are," said Achilles.

"Did you tell her I look like Prince?"

"No."

"Buttcake."

Achilles tried to explain that it wasn't about Wexler. He hadn't told Ines everything. As Wexler ranted, Achilles looked around the room, as tidy as if two women lived there. Unlike Wages's place, there was no clutter. He wondered, not for the first time, if Wexler was gay, which would explain why he was so dramatic and sensitive. Wexler was still his friend, but he wondered.

"So what if she doesn't get it, she could still forgive you," said Wexler. "You're not giving her the chance."

"She wouldn't understand. She has a fancy house, and family paintings, and butterflies mounted in the hallway, and waiters and cooks. She pretended to be white. Her family had slaves. It's survivor guilt. They're part of the talented tenth."

"Like Special Forces?"

"No." Achilles explained that the talented tenth were the blacks who were supposed to go out, make money, and come back to save their community.

"Whatever! You're lying to her," said Wexler.

"Her family had slaves. They were rich. She helps people because it's easy. She can afford to volunteer. She says she doesn't want to be like white people, but she is. That's why she says it. That's how she tricked me."

"Tricked you?" asked Wexler. "She helps people. Who cares about motivation? And if it's so bad, why are you with her?"

"She's only with me because I'm dark enough to upset her mom." Even as he said it, Achilles knew he was wrong, but he couldn't stop himself from trying to save face. They had owned slaves. So what? Her wealth did frustrate him, though, because she didn't care about money in that way that only rich people could. She never looked at prices. She didn't even check the total before handing the cashier a credit card. Achilles sometimes found himself envying her family history, and her skin, lighter even than Troy's, the passport that let her be what she wanted when she wanted. He thought then of how Ines complained about being mistaken for white and being teased by the darker-skinned kids growing up, and he felt guilt and confusion not only because what he'd said was not then true, but because of how often in his life he had suspected that it *was* true but hadn't had the words to express it.

"I'm not surprised." Something shifted in Wexler. "The way you grew up."

"The way I grew up?"

"Troy told us that you didn't go to church, that you were adopted by white people."

"Us who? When?"

"After you shot Chief, he explained that you were reckless and angry. He mentioned it again toward the end, to explain why you volunteered so much and why he had to follow you. That's why Wages looked after you. Well, he would anyway, he's stand-up. That's why Merriweather always gave you advice."

"I was following Troy," Achilles protested.

Wexler continued as if he hadn't heard Achilles. "Troy mounted up like he wanted to, but he makes everything look easy and sound like your idea. I swore I'd never tell you. I'm only saying this because I want you to know I understand that it's strange for you, but you need to find Jesus. Only he can help you."

A loud crash shook their feet, followed by a scream as the car in the yard next door fell off the blocks. The kids circled it like it was a bonfire, skipping and cheering, the youngest one yelling, "Fly school shit!" Achilles counted the heads, holding his breath until he saw Spiderman and Wolverine clamber up the hood, and Batman, his cape trailing behind him, leap onto the back bumper, holding a stick to the sky like a sword, proud as a knight who had just slain a dragon.

It simply couldn't be true. Had he missed the signs, like Ines's race, and the doubts he felt about his own envy when Morse called? No. It wasn't true. Troy was always first in line, and giving Wexler that bullshit excuse was his way of making it appear necessary, and therefore easy.

"You gotta tell her," Wexler said. "You won't get away with this, Keelies."

"What's that mean?"

"Don't make that face. You know I got to tell you if you're wrong. I don't think you're going to get away with this."

"Are you cursing me like you cursed Merriweather? You know that's the last thing you said to him."

The blood drained from Wexler's face.

"You know it is," said Achilles, feeling betrayed by both Troy and Wexler. And Wages. And Merriweather. And Jackson. Next Wexler would tell that story about footprints in the sand. They were all in it, which explained why Wages lied about Merriweather's kid. They were all having a good laugh about Achilles. Troy assuming his avuncular tone when they all met up at zero-dark-thirty for a final gear check, Troy's grin a silent signal saying, *Here we go again, Achilles out to prove himself,* like a parent overseeing a child's first attempt to climb a slide. That casual shrug he always offered as a last word now an indictment. He saw it again: Jackson strapped to the roof, Wexler groaning like the time he had dysentery in Gardiz and hiding his face under Troy's protective wing, Troy with his arm around Wexler like they're at a horror movie. Is that why Wexler and Wages were so eager to help him find his brother? Did they feel sorry for him? Was that why Wages offered his couch for as long as needed? What they thought was shame was merely prudence. Troy couldn't understand; his name was at least normal. Did they think they could understand what it's like to have the teachers treat him better only after meeting his parents but the basic training cohort eye him curiously for that same reason? Well they were wrong, all of them. Achilles didn't need anyone's pity. In fact, he needed no one.

Achilles stood in the window studying the night sky, the river of dancing light flowing down Peachtree Avenue and the waxing moon so low he could hang his coat on it. He was in a hotel room with a beautiful woman—for whom he hadn't paid—who said she loved him. He beckoned Ines to the window, put one calloused finger to her cheek, as Sammy had earlier that day at the planetarium, and said, "Your freckles do look like stars."

She laughed. "Don't make fun. He's just a child expressing his feelings. You know that's not easy to do." She winked and turned away.

The quarter moon resembled a smug, cockeyed grin. Arrested by the traffic signal, the river of dancing lights was only the usual drunken gridlock that appeared every Saturday night in a big city. He jerked the drapes together, pulling so hard that one end of the curtain rod popped off the mount. She said nothing as he rehung it. After Ines fell asleep, he studied her face, her cheeks flushed with Cabernet. Was that a dipper in her right cheek, and Orion in the left? Or was it the other way around? In Goddamnistan, he always watched the stars to make sure they weren't moving.

The museum lecturer had said the stars were lights from the past, sometimes dead before you saw them because of the time it took light to travel through space. Incomprehensible distances. That thought seized him, and he was gripped by the same panic that strangled him awake his first nights at the FOB, when screaming mortars, stars very much alive, pounded the earth. Pushed by the same terror he felt at the edge of that minefield when he stepped outside himself—which he surely did, he saw it happen as clearly as if he were watching his own shadow step off on its own accord—he started for the window to check the sky for some sign, some reassurance. Still unsettled, he wanted to wake Ines and rock her back to sleep, run his finger from her brow to the tip of her nose, give the constellations new names, but he knew the one thing you never tell a woman is that you need her, and that you're scared to lose her, especially if it's true. So he'd just quietly slipped under the bedspread and pulled the sheet over both of their heads, locking her into his pillow fort, inhaling the scent of her shampoo.

Still, he told himself that he wasn't afraid to lose her. He had lost more and lived through worse. But whenever he imagined life without her, his joints hurt as if grating against shrapnel, as if ground against glass, as he felt now, alone in Atlanta.

After Wexler's hissy fit, Achilles decided to spend the night at the hotel. When he returned, the line at the check-in counter extended out the door. Almost everyone waiting in line was from the Gulf Coast, and complaining loudly about price gouging and the trip. The drive, usually seven hours, had taken them fifteen, even with contraflow. His mom called to ensure he wasn't trapped in New Orleans. The call was brief, and no one mentioned Troy. They'd long stopped using his name. Would it be the same with Ines, or even easier because no one knew her? Sitting alone now in that hotel in Atlanta, thinking back to the last time they'd been in a hotel, he thought maybe it was cowardly not to admit one's feelings. In the room, he dragged his feet on the carpet, opened and shut a few drawers. Dust rose when he slapped the pillows. He jumped up and down on the bed and rolled around in the covers. It was his first time being alone since moving in with Ines. His first time alone, ever.

New Orleans was on every channel. "Tropical Storm" had been dropped. The cyclone tearing across the Caribbean was known by one name: Katrina. The governor of Louisiana declared a state of emergency, and Mississippi was planning a massive evacuation. A couple days before, he'd sent Ines a text message with the hotel's address, but that was the last time he was able to get through, or receive a response. He tried calling Ines every few minutes. *All circuits busy.*

An argument erupted in the parking lot. The motel must have filled up. Every parking space was taken. People streamed from their cars to their rooms, some setting up for car camping while others appeared to be negotiating side deals. From the window, Achilles watched the panicked travelers with a smirk. They could easily pitch a tent in the strip of grass and trees that ran between the motel and the highway. If he hadn't been waiting for Ines, he would. He'd travel light. Curl up in a branch. Tuck away in the attic of one of those abandoned buildings down where Wexler worked. If it wasn't for Ines, he'd do a lot of things differently, starting with laying five fingers across Keller's face the next time he said, *Fuck yo couch, zigga.*

But there was Ines, and if he had told her the truth, she'd be in Atlanta, safe. If he didn't hear from her by morning, he would go to New Orleans, contraflow or not, walking if needed. He would tell her he loved her, introduce her to his mother, give up drinking. Catch the garter at every wedding.

In his bag he found a bottle of rum he'd bought earlier and one of Ines's elastic ponytail scrunchies. A few long hairs were tangled in it, and when he held it up, they caught the light, turning a mix of purple and peach. He held it to his nose, and his thoughts slowed and his breathing grew deep and steady. *All circuits busy.*

It was the last Friday of the month, upside-down day, the night they would have had breakfast for dinner, turned the AC as low as possible, and snuggled under the comforter, pretending it was winter. He longed for

Ines's soft snore, her purr his metronome, lulling him asleep with a rhythm steady enough to set his heart by. Deeper in his rucksack, he found his original map of New Orleans, complete with Wages's legend. There was the X where the church was located, and a circle representing a one-mile radius. Outside the circle sat the Garden District, Uptown, and Esplanade Ridge. Like distant planets, he had known them in name only until he met Ines. He ran his finger across the city until he found their street and, in case anyone should ever see it, drew an asterisk instead of a heart. And to think, when she had first called and mentioned the possibility of leaving the city, he'd felt as if she was crowding him. *All circuits busy.*

CHAPTER 16

H E WASN'T SUPERSTITIOUS, BUT HE WANTED TO BELIEVE THAT HIS CHILDISH wagers paid off. If he made the traffic light without accelerating, if he had correct change, if he reached the automatic door before it closed, Ines was okay, and soon enough, she was at the door, chewing gum, which she did only on road trips, and wearing her driving outfit: a sundress and no underwear.

He lifted her skirt, but Ines had other ideas, like putting flowers on Wexler's grave or taking Naomi out to dinner. She remade the bed, wiped down the bathroom counter, filled the ice trays. She tested the taps, ruffled the drapes, stopping only when she saw the empty rum bottle in the trashcan. Appearing satisfied, she plopped into the chair beside the bed. "I had a tree planted in his name. It must be terrible to bury your child. It must feel like the world's upside down. Did the flowers arrive?"

"Oh yes."

"Did they like them?"

"Oh yes."

She jumped up again. Turned on the television, flitted about, making minor adjustments while the news played. She moved the table six inches to the left, centered the chairs on it, opened the drapes and closed them, all the while with her eyes on her hands, but her head cocked in a way that let him know she was listening to the news. The anchor, a middle-aged white man, was reporting from the foyer of an office building on downtown Canal Street, deserted save for the wind pushing a lone shopping cart across the bus lane. Palm trees bowed unnaturally, rain swept horizontally across the street. After the lamps, chairs, and pillows had been moved the half-inch Ines felt they required, she stopped in the middle of the room and surveyed her work. The room looked the same to Achilles.

Ines pointed the remote at the TV. "Bang bang. That's better. Let's get Sammy."

By agreeing to drive there in Achilles's truck and let him sit in the middle of the bench seat—*an aptly named space, Achilles thought*—they persuaded Sammy to spend an hour at a small traveling carnival on Buford Highway. Sammy had resisted because *Fairs are for kids*. Achilles concurred, wanting to check the little bastard back into the library he came from. But Ines was insistent, whispering, "He doesn't have a father, and therefore feels compelled to act like an adult." So, Achilles found himself wandering between food trailers, barkers, and flashing lights, none of which interested Sammy, who didn't want to take a spin on any of the rides, rickety erector sets so shaky they scared even Achilles, especially the Kamikaze, shimmying like a lame Huey raining pain. Sammy wanted no fried candy bars, cotton candy, or funnel cake because *Candy's for kids*. But when he saw the big blue bull's-eye flashing over the shooting gallery, he tugged Achilles's hand, referring to himself as a marksman.

The shooting gallery barker, stumbling as if drunk, motioned Sammy over, flashing crooked teeth. "Easiest game on the boardwalk."

Surprisingly, Ines handed the pompadoured barker a clutch of tickets, more than one game's worth. Sammy made a show of picking up each rifle, weighing it, sighting it, and replacing it before he settled on one. He tucked the butt under his armpit, pressed his cheek against the stock, pinched one eye nearly shut, closed the other, and missed ten shots in a row. He tried another rifle and went through the same routine, this time waggling his tongue, still hitting nothing, hearing nothing but the trigger and the soft thunk of pellets striking the sandbag behind the target. The barker said Sammy only needed to warm up. Ines handed over more tickets and rushed off to replenish her supply. Sammy tried again, and missed again. Ines returned and nudged Achilles.

"I thought you didn't like guns," said Achilles.

Ines whispered, "Yada, yada, yada, I know, Mr. They're-fun-as-long-as-they're-not-pointed-at-you. This is a game. You can teach him the proper technique, to be responsible. He needs the distraction. He's upset about the storm."

"No he's not."

Ines raised her eyebrows, the Groucho Marx impression that was her nice way of saying, *Obey.* Achilles taught Troy how to shoot, then got into trouble when Troy shot a rock and the pellet ricocheted into his face. Praying Sammy didn't hurt himself, Achilles nested the rifle butt against his shoulder. "Hold your breath for two counts before firing."

Sammy looked up at Achilles, losing his grip as he did so. Achilles readjusted Sammy's posture. "Stay focused. Eyes on target, always, in all things in life."

"Thanks. I'm going to win now." Sammy's smile was big and bright, and so was Ines's, her face lit up like Christmas. Was this what it felt like to have a family?

Sammy missed again. "Is this loaded?"

"Of course, son," snapped the barker.

"He's not your son," said Ines.

The barker started to say something, looked at Achilles, thought better of it, and said, "Sorry ma'am."

Ines nudged Sammy, who, eyes down, said, "Apology accepted."

"Well?" asked Ines. "Is it?"

"Yes ma'am," said the barker.

"Answer him." Ines glanced at Achilles as if to say, *You can deal with him or me.*

"It's loaded." The barker pursed his lips.

Sammy asked, "Are you sure?"

"Yes sir," muttered the barker.

Sammy pushed his shoulders back, held his neck straight, and tried again. Spurred by Ines's intercession, Achilles hefted one of the rifles, a lightweight BB gun with misaligned sights. He handed it to Sammy. Sammy turned the gun around and stared down the barrel, just as Troy had when he first handled a rifle. Achilles placed his hand over the end of the barrel and snatched the gun away. Sammy froze.

"Never, ever, ever, ever," Achilles paused, "ever look down the barrel of a loaded gun. Never ever, ever, ever point a gun at yourself or anyone else, even as a joke."

Sammy nodded timidly.

"What's the first rule?"

"Never, ever, ever, ever," Sammy paused, "ever look down the barrel of a loaded gun. Never ever, ever, ever point a gun at yourself or anyone else, even as a joke."

"Smart ass," said Achilles before he caught himself, and when he glanced at Ines she was trying to stifle her laughter too. Dropping to one knee, Achilles guided the butt to Sammy's shoulder. He smelled like baby powder. "First, Kentucky windage, because this isn't zeroed." His voice dropped to a whisper. "Aim for a fixed point above the ducks."

Sammy was a quick study. He hit the target three times. Ines handed the contrite barker more tickets. "Again!" Achilles remained on his knee at Sammy's side, guiding his little hands and adjusting his posture, as his father had done for him, and as he had done for Troy. Soon Sammy had shot the six in a row needed to claim a prize. He chose a koala and, being too old for toys, awarded it to Ines to keep her other stuffed koala, Ricky, company. Sammy gave Achilles a hug, his short arms straining to wrap around Achilles's waist. Ines gave him a kiss on the neck, her cheek wet. Whirling teacups, the spinning Ferris wheel, laughing parents, screaming children, dancing neon. A clown in one dunk tank, a blonde in another. Achilles breathed in the traces of Ines's perfume, the smell of alcohol on the barker, the aroma of funnel cake, and the smell of Sammy's jawbreaker and held it all in as they walked away.

After they had gone a few feet, Ines squatted so she was eye-level with Sammy. "You remember what I always tell you?"

"I'm a man. I'm no one's son but my mother's," said Sammy.

"That's right," she said, looking up at Achilles. "Can you believe that? Son? Can you believe that?"

Achilles grunted.

"The barker's nineteen? Twenty? Sammy's nine. Every Southern white man thinks every black man is his son. But if you ask them, they'll say that race doesn't matter, son. They ignore the implications of that paternalistic attitude."

If he said nothing, she would fade out. His mother used that trick with his father. Ines spoke loudly enough for passersby to hear, and they were within earshot of the barker, whose black pompadour and Doc Martins reminded Achilles of his goth friends in high school. He glanced over her shoulder to see if the barker was listening.

"Noooo." Her eyes narrowed. She stuck her chin out, like a boxer luring her opponent in for a punch. "Did you just look at him?" Ines put her hands over Sammy's ears. "Did you just check in? Are you worried massah might think you gettin' uppity?"

Before Ines, he had never known how much some black people talked about race. He told her on several occasions that he'd fought side by side and trusted his life with *whites;* even using the word in that context sounded strange to him. "All white people aren't bad. Sammy is a kid." A white couple passed with a stroller, speeding up to put distance between them.

"All white people aren't bad? Is that a proverb? You're like a bad fortune cookie. I'm not talking about all white people. I'm talking about right here, right now. Being a young black man without a father, Sammy doesn't need some half-drunk trailer-park trash calling him son. Your jokes are fine, but the world is not the suburb you grew up in. The same cop calling him 'son' will be the first to draw his gun when Sammy is eighteen and makes a wrong turn. He has to learn now, or be shocked later. He's not the sarcastic type. He doesn't have your sense of humor."

At least he had a sense of humor now. Earlier she accused him of hiding behind deep irony and fake disaffection, whatever that meant. She had been snippy ever since leaving Nola. "I'm sorry. Forget I said anything."

"Okay." She sighed.

He sighed.

"So, we're supposed to forget? We're supposed to forget because they don't mean anything by it, and all white people aren't bad? Look around, that's all I'm saying. On the job, in the stores, everywhere. We're followed by clerks while some white kid is the one shoplifting; we're pulled over by the police while some white kid whistles by with a trunk full of guns, planning to shoot up his school. Character assassinations against black athletes while corporate criminals bilk investors out of millions. And you say they're not all bad, but racism is the bus that runs us over, every day, and while maybe only the racists are driving, every white is along for the ride: every one that makes more for the same job, that gets called in for an interview when Ashante doesn't, every one that then moves to a better neighborhood, sends their kids to better schools, then to colleges, then their kids get called in for an interview when Ashante Jr. does not. They're not all bad, but they're a hell of a lot luckier. And you want Sammy to forget, to go back to that white boarding school thinking there's something wrong with him because he isn't treated like the other kids. Or complain and be told it's in his head—*Race doesn't matter. We're all the same and don't let anyone tell you otherwise.*"

"He offered Sammy a free round."

"That's white nice. They double-charge you, then give you a discount. They take your land, then offer you a reservation. They enslave you, then emancipate you."

What about his parents, and everything they had done for him after he was abandoned by his *people?* They weren't riding a "racist" bus. Wages was scraping by, just like Achilles's parents had. After the factory burned down, Achilles's father took a job at the school as a football coach. His mother worked part-time as a bookkeeper at the mill, which employed blacks in both the factory and the yard. If only Ines could meet his mom, she'd understand there was no bus bursting with white people careening down the road, taking out black pedestrians. The image was upsetting, the suggestion ludicrous. Ines made it sound like white people had it easier just because they were white. Achilles knew better. He knew *a lot* of white people, and none of them had ever mentioned this privilege to him. Being white wasn't keeping down the rising property taxes his mom paid because of all the rich people moving in from DC. And, things were getting better; he'd heard that Illinois elected the fifth black senator in U.S. history. Besides, people shouldn't name kids Ashante, not if they wanted them to get jobs.

They walked toward the truck, Ines storm troopering ahead. Cars swooshed down Buford Highway, dashing between the ethnic restaurants that dotted this area of the city.

Sammy asked, "Are we leaving already?"

Achilles and Ines looked down at Sammy, then up at each other. "No."

As they walked back toward the spinning lights, Marcus called. Achilles ignored it, turning his phone off for the rest of the time they were at the carnival. On the way out of the parking lot, they saw the barker taking a smoke break. Achilles waved some money at him. When he came over, Achilles slammed the door into him and punched him three times in the nose, stopping only because he heard it crack.

Getting back into the truck, he said, "He won't be driving any more buses."

Except for Sammy saying "Cool!" and Ines shushing him, they rode back to the hotel in silence.

Over the next couple of days, Ines was glued to the tube. "Flak jacket, babe," he would say, hoping to get her away from the television. His comment was not well received. Ray Nagin, the mayor of New Orleans, had issued a mandatory evacuation. While Ines cursed at the TV, Sammy was unaffected by the news coverage, moping around and asking to go outside. Broken levees and stranded citizens meant nothing to him. At one point, he saw a floating car and yelled, "Cool!" That was the extent of his interest.

The three of them were piled on the bed, picking at the pizza they'd ordered for breakfast, when Marcus called again, prompting Achilles to claim he had to run a quick errand, and to see a few of the fellows before they left town.

"Take Sammy," she said.

On the way to Grady, Achilles dropped Sammy off with Wexler. At the morgue, Achilles followed Marcus back into the cooler. The unclaimed child was still in the walk-in, next to another gurney. "Still no kin. He'll be cremated soon." Marcus pulled back the sheet on the other gurney. "I'll leave you alone."

Achilles stepped closer to the body. Multiple blunt force traumas, abrasions on the upper-right forehead, abrasions on the lower-right fore-head above the eyebrow, multiple contusions on the right cheek and lower nose, back of head. Abrasions on his chest, lower coastal margin. Contusions on the left arm, elbow, forearm, wrist, upper inner arm. Contusions and abrasions on the right elbow, foot, toes; hemorrhage on the rib area and leg. The left temple was concave, skull flattened, as if he had been struck with a brick or another heavy, blunt object. Eyes swollen, lips cracked. Teeth knocked out. Finger pads filed down. Deep fissures ran up the cheeks.

A sheet attached to the gurney detailed the injuries. "Bone fractures, rib fractures, contusions on midabdomen, back, and buttocks extending to the left flank, abrasions, lateral cuts on buttocks. Contusions on back of legs and knees, abrasions on knees, left fingers, and encircling to left wrist. Lacerations, right forth and fifth fingers. Blunt force injuries, pre-dominately recent contusions on torso and lower extremities."

Achilles looked again. The mole on his right cheek was lost in the bruises. The shoulders were broad enough, reaching almost to the edges of the gurney. There were faint lines across his cheeks. He was thin, almost as thin as Wexler. Almost as thin as he had been after jump school. He was rawboned in the face and shoulders, the skin stretched tight over the large jaw and cheekbones and oddly protruded shoulder, the skin appearing borrowed and two sizes too small for his frame.

Through all the bruises, Achilles couldn't make out the cut under his eye sustained when they wrestled Josh; the scar on his neck that their mother's cat gave him one of the many times they teased it and forced it into the house, where it would get in trouble; the v-shaped scar from the minefield, his only war injury. Achilles lifted the hand—the birthday scar on the palm was there, as was the scar above his eye where the pellet caught him after he shot the rock. There was the cut on his bicep from the water tower ladder. Achilles touched his face, cold and firm. The skin didn't spring back, remaining depressed as if still bearing the weight of Achilles's touch. One tear landed on Troy's chin. *Not now!* Achilles held his breath; that tear was all he would allow himself. His brother was a hero. He went into a minefield after Wexler. Troy wasn't reckless. He was brave. He was here, and must be avenged before being mourned. As Merriweather would say, "We don't get down, we get even."

He took Troy's hand, running his finger along the long scar on the palm, and he switched the tags, putting the child's tag on Troy. He closed the door silently behind him, as if to avoid waking anybody. Marcus leaned against the wall staring at his shoes and twirling a cigarette.

"What happened to him?" asked Achilles.

"Abrasions consistent with the use of restraints. Manner of death is homicide." Marcus flipped through his clipboard. "Found outside of Banneker Homes two days ago."

"Banneker Homes?"

"Benjamin Banneker."

"Benjamin Banneker?" asked Achilles.

"The Bricks. He was dead before the ambulance arrived. Broken neck, crushed vertebrae, probably from a fall. One set of bruises is postnecrotic. It's like he fell from a building, twice. Seen a couple like this before, caught up with Pepper and them."

"Poor kid."

"Hmm?" said Marcus.

"That's not my brother."

"Are you sure?" Marcus grunted.

"I'd know my brother. That's not him. But thanks for calling." On the way to the elevator, he passed a group of old women shuffling down the hall, a young boy enfolded in one of their arms; a father and mother and two daughters huddled together as if seeking protection from the elements; another family in their Sunday best, another in capris, a group of men in sweats and bandanas, a kid with a red lollipop ring around his mouth: all the men stood with narrow eyes, their mouths tight, like dams.

Achilles hurried past them and to his car, his arms limp, numb from the wrist down as if the nerves had been cut. He beat them against the steering wheel until he could feel again. He took out the photo he carried in his wallet, the photo of him and Troy at the amusement park. His favorite photo he didn't have with him. It was from Pennsylvania. They had crossed the County Line Highway, which they were forbidden to do, and snuck out to the old water tower. It was the first time Achilles had figured out the auto-timer on the camera, before which self-portraits were assholes and elbows.

That day, Achilles climbed to the top of the water tower. Troy cut his hand on the rusty ladder and chickened out halfway. Achilles had escorted him down and cleaned the wound with spit, to prevent lockjaw. On that day, like so many others, he was brave when it mattered least. Helping Troy down from the tower had been easy, but Achilles was elated to have saved the day. He'd wanted to mark it with a photograph. In the photo, both of their faces are blurry from fidgeting; only they know who they are. Achilles, ten, is still taller and stronger. Troy, eight, hasn't had his first growth spurt yet. They stand side by side in their secondhand Tuffskins. It's a sunny day, and they squint against the light, so bright that it washed out the flash. The candy bars melted in their pockets. How sweet they were, the chocolate sticking to their hands. He licked his right off, but Troy rubbed some on his cheek and held his sticky palm next to Achilles. "Now we look like brothers."

Troy, ever present. When Achilles, his baseball bat in the trunk of his defaced Ford LTD, high-wheeled it to Gary's Cycle Shop to confront Janice's burly brothers only to discover they weren't working that day, Troy was there. When Achilles buried Buster, the rabbit he kept hidden behind the house in a makeshift kennel of cardboard and milk crates, Troy was there. When Achilles's father lost his temper on that birthday, Troy was there, his quavering voice, scored with fear, pleading for their father to stop.

Wexler and Sammy were playing cards on the front porch. A sheet of gray clouds hung low in the sky. Achilles honked from the street. Wexler waved. Achilles honked again.

They waved him up to the porch and returned their attention to the game. Achilles trotted up, marched Sammy to the car and buckled him in, then stomped back to the porch.

The floorboards creaked as Wexler shifted his weight. "He's a natural card shark. Better than the Duke," he said, flashing his grin, as if to say, *All is forgotten.*

Shot through with love, Achilles closed the distance and wrapped Wexler in a bear hug. When Achilles at last felt his friend hug him back, he said, "Thank you."

Stepping back, he opened his mouth to say good-bye, but settled for raising his hand. As he walked back to his car and pulled away, he didn't look back, careful to avoid seeing Wexler make those stiff turns and limp back into the house. He didn't turn even to look in the rearview mirror when Wexler called, "Connie, wait."

As they drove off, Achilles said, "Remember what I said earlier, right Sammy?"

Sammy nodded. "Brothers keep secrets."

"That's right. And where were we?" asked Achilles.

"We were talking to Merrywhen, Mary . . ."

"Merriweather," said Achilles.

"Merriweather. Right!" He smiled with satisfaction, settling back into the seat.

"Because?" asked Achilles.

"Because of the funeral. Because Wexler is dead."

As he drove, Achilles snuck sideways glances at Sammy. In the hotel lot, Sammy asked, "Why does your friend walk like a robot?"

"He was in the wrong place at the wrong time."

"And where were you?" asked Sammy.

Troy asked a lot of questions too. *Why aren't my palms the same color as my skin? Why isn't my skin the same color as yours? Why is Achilles so much darker than the rest of us? Why did our parents give us away? Were we bad? Can they take us back? Why do we have a menorah if we're not Jewish?* Achilles was embarrassed by these dumb questions to which even he knew the answers. *The skin in our palms has less melanin, is thicker, and has keratinocytes. We're black, but our parents are white because their ancestors evolved in different climates. Melanin comes in two types, pheomelanin, which is red, and eumelanin, which is very dark brown. I have more eumelanin, which was determined by four to six genes that I inherited from each parent. We didn't do anything wrong. No one can take us back or return us. We're not on loan like library books or returnable like merchandise. And, that's a kinara, not a menorah.* Achilles had answered with disdain, realizing now that he knew the answers because he had asked the same questions.

There were also unasked questions. If he'd been Troy's complexion, would girls have liked him more? If he hadn't had a brother, would he have been his father's favorite? He'd envied his brother, his ease, the way the air parted for him, the way Troy wasn't followed in the store or pulled over when their mother sent him on an errand, or triple-checked at the bank, all things that Achilles never told his parents about because they never happened when he was with them, and they never happened to Troy. So it had to be Achilles's fault. Yes, he'd envied his brother's skin, his "light-complected" genes. Yes, he'd begged, entreated, pleaded with Troy to tell no one that they were adopted so that his brother's skin could be his own.

CHAPTER 17

SOME ARE BROWN, MOST ARE BLACK. SOME ARE SLEEK, MOST MATTE. SOME textured, most flat. A few have bright splashes of color for the younger crowd, on others are earth tones for the mature customer. The greens vary from light to verdant, the browns from oak to mahogany, the camouflage from desert to woodland to traditional. Long barrels, bolt action, breach loaders. Large caliber for game. Target pistols for sport. Air rifles for children. Being a sporting goods store, they stocked oddities like a fluorescent orange shotgun, a handgun with plastic ribs lending it the futuristic look of a laser pistol, and a selection of gift sets with matching knives, holsters, and ammo bags, all nested in festively colored molded plastic inside cellophane-wrapped boxes adorned with glossy photos of bucks and buxom women. Achilles settled on a black .260, a handsome machine with clean lines, a smooth wooden butt, and none of the superfluous attachments that make cheaper rifles and pistols more attractive to kids. It was pricey but reliable, important because he hadn't time to zero the sights. The rifle was one that aficionados consider well made, manufactured by an Eastern European company with the unofficial slogan *Preager Velond Pistols, Intl.—When the shooter wants to send the very best.*

Not all agreed. Among his friends, five loved Preagers; four thought them acceptable. They also disagreed on the best SAW. Three said RPK because it was a lighter gun. The rest liked the Browning because it had more firepower. It was a moot debate, because they were assigned the RPK. They argued anyway—what else was there to do when there was nothing around to shoot at? They also disagreed about the best heavyweight boxer of all time, the most realistic version of *Madden NFL,* and what to do if killed. Most said, "Burn my body." Jackson, Wexler, and Ramirez were holding out for resurrection. This conversation started the week before

Jackson died, prompted by another squad humping a fallen friend across three clicks of mountainous terrain.

Wages said, "I don't care if I look like a bag of smashed assholes. Mail me back to Nola. I don't care what's left."

Merri said, "Mamma don't need to see me all like chicken parts and shit."

Jackson said, "If nothing's left but smoking nuts, ship those salty apples home."

They did. Jackson's corpse traveled with them for a day, getting a whirlwind tour of southeast Goddamnistan, as Dixon dubbed it the day of the IED. Jackson's body was with them when Wexler lost his mind, when Merriweather got shot, and when Wages took out that sniper. A rough forty-eight, and halfway through it, Merriweather suggested the tax, the only thing the squad agreed on. Merri, who prayed silently each a.m., tapped Jackson's black body bag and said, "I know they're treating you well up there, my man." He later followed with, "What are we doing? We need to tax these fuckers."

Their first consensus. *Tax those motherfuckers. Fuck interrogation and dropping mofos off for AI. If I get smoked, level the place, go Vietnam on them, get medieval, like the Crusades and shit. Get jiggy-Jihadi-Hutu-Tutsi right back at them.*

Dixon said, "Yeah baby. I like the cut of your chin."

Wexler, who usually kicked dust on the topic, chimed in. "Torch it all."

"That won't get you into heaven," said Dixon.

"It will make us feel better," said Troy.

"Right on! Eat that anger. We don't get down, we get even," said Merriweather.

Can you go to both heavens? Can you bring the virgins to our heaven? Jokes circled the room, including mention that Hitler killed ten to one. At that Wages cut them off: "Everyone is going home, in one piece." It was decided, though—manifest extreme prejudice.

As Achilles planned to. Would he have told Troy? Yes, and Troy would have joined him. Troy had heart, prey drive. Achilles always knew he could trust his brother without question. He remembered their big fight over the truck, tumbling down the driveway. Their mother running outside screaming, their father on her heels with his rifle, laughing once he saw that it was only his sons who had provoked his wife's howling anger. And why were they fighting? Their father chuckled at the explanation. Their mother cursed and pushed—yes, pushed—them into two separate rooms and asked them again. Two hours later, their answers remained the same. Troy (on a Britpop kick) was like, "Because Achilles is a right faggot." Achilles (on an NWA kick) was like, "Because Troy is a spoiled punkass bitch." As far as Achilles knew, the truth died with Troy, as did the day they skipped school to go into DC for the Chuck Brown performance, and how the garage window really broke. What about all the habits he didn't have to explain (mayonnaise on eggs, that he shit every night at four a.m. local time, how *Jet* magazine gave him a hard-on)? What else did only Troy know about him? What had he forgotten about himself that died with his brother? Which of those things, if any, could he tell Ines? He would make a list and carry it with him.

He would begin with the minefield. That night, Achilles was driving, Wexler was riding shotgun, and Troy and Merriweather were in the back. Jackson thudded against the roof on every rise in the rough wadi, the dry riverbeds that served as roads. "We've got to tighten those ropes," said Merri. Wexler howled, threw himself out of the vehicle, and started running, dragging his pack behind him. It was a quarter moon, so there was little light, and using their flashlights could attract unwanted attention. Achilles got out of the vehicle and called after Wexler in a hushed voice, hearing in response only steps in the sand and brush. Achilles stopped Merriweather from giving chase. It would only make Wexler run farther, and Wexler was the fastest of the four of them. Just that morning they had been intact, all of them, laughing and joking. They had passed some kids playing in a pile of rubble and Wexler asked about average lifespans, yelling and repeating himself to be heard over the engine: "How long do Afghans live?" Merri laughed. "Until we find them."

The faint glow of the moon illuminated the mountain range at the edge of the horizon. The occasional bat flew by, and they could make out every star in the sky. It was one of those moments when Achilles was drunk on the idea that if a war hadn't been going on, this might be one of the most beautiful landscapes he had ever seen. Instead, he wanted every inch of it razed, every tree stripped bare, every building leveled, every rock crushed. A flash of light silhouetted Wexler as a tree of roiling red and orange flames sprouted. He grabbed his neck and fell down. It was dark again. A sheet of squawking bats passed overhead. It had happened so quickly no one had time to blink or shut one eye, and they were all

momentarily blinded. Merriweather cursed. Troy shook his head mourn-
fully. Enter now the other Achilles, stage left. A man named Achilles
Holden Conroy spun on his heels, climbed into the driver's seat, hit the
hot start button, and patiently awaited his mates.

As he watched himself, the other Achilles pressed the hot start button
again, and the starter barked. He waved the others in. The *other* Achilles
slapped the side of the door. Merriweather and Troy took small steps
toward the vehicle. The *other* Achilles put it in gear. "That's it. Let's go
now."

Troy was almost at the vehicle. Merriweather was reaching for the
door handle. Then they heard Wexler's curling cry. The other Achilles's
murmurings that there was nothing to be done and Merriweather's nods
of assent be damned, Troy charged out there—red illume between his
teeth, as soldierly and surefooted as if on asphalt, across the rise and
through the shallow bowl—hefted Wexler over his shoulder, and on his
return, with his left hand—the jump-shot hand, ATM hand, jab hand,
shooting hand, pitching hand, cue-stick hand, wanking hand, the scarred
hand—patting the back of Wexler's legs; mouth full of fire, he can easily be imagined in silhouette on a recruitment poster or in a movie trailer;
more emotional than that scene in *Platoon* when Willem Dafoe, peppered
with bullets, is left behind to die at the hands of the VC, sparking Achilles
to wonder how he was going to explain this, fingering his pistol, wondering if he could live up to the old saying, *In the final assault, save the last
bullet for yourself,* that question remaining on his lips until Troy lay Wexler
in the sand at Merriweather's feet like a peace offering, at which point the
other Achilles, who'd remained in the driver's seat until now, came to
watch as Wexler was bandaged. The two Achilles stood side by side,
shoulder to shoulder, and the other Achilles said, "Goddamn him to
Christ." On the drive back, whenever he looked back at Wexler, he imagined him strapped to the roof.

On that night so hot they wore it like a robe, tossing that little body
over his shoulder, Goliath saved David, leaving Achilles only angry. And
after Troy took walking through a minefield as proof he didn't even need
to duck when people tossed bullets, Achilles felt resentment, wondering
how different it would be if he were also so confident. After the morgue,
he knew it wasn't the confidence he'd wanted, or the reassurance that Troy
would have walked into a minefield for him. He'd wanted Wexler left
behind that night, so that everything could remain normal, so his brother

wouldn't take luck for latitude. Achilles loved Wexler *like* a brother, as the saying went. But Troy *is* his brother. There was *like;* there was *is;* and, there was his fear of *is* becoming *was.*

For two nights, Achilles followed Pepper while Ines slept. Everywhere he went, people smiled when Pepper arrived and sighed when he pulled off. Even the cops treated him well, leaning in the back window like groupies after autographs. Pepper traveled primarily from the Bricks to a house in East Point and back, making an occasional detour at an old apartment complex named Hollywood Court where dogs were fought in an abandoned nursery. The second night, the police stopped Achilles. The truck was still registered in Troy's name, which they found suspect enough to make Achilles ride in the police car while they went on another call.

The nursery was too crowded and the house in East Point was a gated community in a sea of subdivisions, surrounded by flat land providing little cover, so Achilles broke into the church being built near the Banneker Homes. The bell tower provided a perfect line of sight, and room to maneuver as needed because there was no bell, only a large speaker mount. After firing his second shot—he planned to get off at least two—he would cut the barrel off the gun, drop it into his backpack, and walk away. Why would the police set up a roadblock or search pedestrians over the death of a drug dealer? If anything, they should reward the shooter.

Ines was antsy, threatening to return to New Orleans, so he decided his second night in the tower would be the night. He waited a long time before the golden Hummer finally appeared. The bodyguard limped into the building with the fire damage. Wexler had said his name was Cornelius. Achilles preferred to think of him as the accomplice. A white cargo van pulled up. Accomplice loaded two muzzled pits into the van, tapped the side of the vehicle, and it pulled off. He leaned against the wall, smoking and picking at his nose. Achilles sighted on the back door of the Hummer and waited.

The clickety-clack of high heels bounced off the wall. Two prostitutes passed the entrance to the Bricks, slowing as they neared the guys posted at the entrance. The guys at the gate didn't even look up, understandably so. It was a hip-hop version of Jack Sprat. One was large-breasted but fat enough that if she lost the weight, she'd lose the bait. The other was thin as a stick and walked as if she was on stilts, teetering as if she might topple over at any minute.

Meanwhile Accomplice paced around the car, occasionally checking his watch. He moved with an exaggerated gait, a walk meant to announce his street cred, but which was so extreme he was the caricature of a street hood, the hop in his step something you'd see in an SNL skit featuring a white comedian doing his best impression of a B-boy. Finally, he got into the car and drove off.

Around two in the morning, the Hummer returned with the van close behind. Again, Accomplice loaded two muzzled dogs, tapped the van, and it pulled away, lights off until it hit the street. This time Achilles crawled to the other side of the tower to track the van's progress, but it disappeared from view at the highway on-ramp. The bodyguard paced around the Hummer again, talking on his phone while he did his pimp walk. He stopped at the edge of the light, gesticulating wildly, holding the phone up to his mouth as if it was a walkie-talkie, yelling into it before slamming it shut and pocketing it, dropping his cigarette in the process. He lit a cigarette at the wrong end and fumbled with two more, successfully lighting the fourth only after he leaned back against the wall. He held the first breath so long that only a wisp of smoke slipped out when he exhaled. He French-inhaled and slapped the air in front of his face. Still leaning back against the wall, he crossed one leg over the other. Achilles dropped his sights to the man's legs. One shot could take out both knees, and Achilles was good with a gun. His father had made sure of that. His father's only rule: *Don't kill anything you can't eat and don't maim anything you don't kill.* Two rules roundly disregarded in combat.

Achilles waited, the feeling shifting from neutral to impatient. He had to keep reminding himself that he didn't want the driver's knees, he wanted Pepper's head; he was aiming for apricot, as the snipers put it. Patience was the key. He had known this moment was coming as soon as he heard that Troy was found outside of the Bricks. For all Achilles knew, Accomplice was involved, or another foot soldier, but nothing demoralized a group more than spilling the brains behind the operation. The bodyguard was pacing again, and as he walked thoughtfully, head down, in the shadow of the wall, it became clear that the swaggering step was merely camouflaging a limp.

Merriweather walked like that. When they went to visit him at Walter Reed Hospital, they were reminded of everything that could have possibly gone wrong for them but didn't. At one point, Merriweather and Wexler had ended up in the same room. Achilles finally understood the meaning of the word *irony*. How had their luck changed all at once? They survived a baker's dozen of snipers, mortars, IEDs, artillery, RPGs, bombs, land mines, claymores, numerous troops in contact incidents, missiles, grenades, friendly fire, and suicide. Then, barely a month before they'd be done, Jackson catches the IED, Merriweather unzips the kid, and Wexler, upset at Merriweather, runs off into the dark and ends up in a minefield. While he's being carted off, the last thing Wexler says is, "Merriweather won't get away with it."

Wexler was right. A couple days later, Merriweather was shot in the ankle while the squad moved in on a residence where Taliban sympathizers were known to be hiding. But he took it like a man. After Wages ran out to the road and dragged him to cover, and Troy packed the wound with Quikclot that stopped bleeding but burned like hot sauce on the devil's ass, Merriweather said, "I don't know what's fucking worse, the bullet or the so-called first aid."

They laughed, but Achilles was thankful he'd never needed Quikclot. When they later went to see Merriweather show off his new foot, each time he adjusted the prosthetic, Achilles saw the permanent burns the Quikclot left on his calf. But no matter to Merriweather; he clipped his prosthetic on and strutted around the room like he'd never strutted before, a dip in his walk deep enough that you could miss the limp, if you didn't know him. Wexler later claimed he hadn't meant what he said, that Merriweather had just been in the wrong place at the wrong time. That was how Achilles preferred to think about it. That's what he told Sammy.

But Sammy's second question was even more disturbing. If Wexler was in the wrong place at the wrong time, where had Achilles been? On the sidelines. He'd watched Wages dragging Merriweather, leaving two ruts in the dust and a trail of blood, the right foot skipping and twisting like a caster, picking up dirt like a dropped popsicle, and he couldn't make himself take one step out of the alcove where he was hiding. Even when they were within arm's reach, Achilles hesitated, afraid of being shot in the hand.

Troy was different.

Pepper finally exited the car. Achilles preferred to think of him as the dealer. Achilles held his breath for two seconds as Dealer walked around the car, as if inspecting it for damage, gesturing wildly at Accomplice, who momentarily blocked Achilles's views. Sweat stung his eyes, and he took several slow breaths to steady his hands, quickly rearranging himself, tying his shirt around his head to catch the sweat and adjusting the folded gym bag serving as a makeshift tripod. Dealer was now on the phone, pointing at Accomplice as if relaying a message. He smiled as he did this, his gold teeth glinting. How much had those cost?

In one morgue, a dealer's teeth had been yanked out after he was killed. He wondered if someone would lay claim to Pepper's Devil Dog mouthpiece. The thought of putting someone else's teeth in his mouth was disgusting, even if they were gold. Maybe they would be mounted like a trophy.

They were now laughing, rapping together, bobbing their heads in harmony, more like friends than employee and employer. Now they leaned silently against the hood, side by side like old buddies. Dealer clapped Accomplice on the leg, saying something that made them both smile. Achilles heard the tap-tap-tap of his own feet against the unfinished plywood. *We don't get mad, we get down.* Wiping his burning eyes, Achilles held his breath again for two seconds, and then two more, and then ten, but nothing banished the tremors that traveled from his hands up his arms, down his back and to his legs, or the shameful suspicion that it was tears, not sweat, burning his eyes. He willed himself to pull the trigger. It's not like he didn't know exactly what the result would look like.

He had felt this way after turning a corner and coming face to face with a man holding an AK-47 in one hand and an infant in the other. Achilles had stepped back around the corner, rifle chest-high, and counted to ten. When he'd looked, they were gone, as was Pepper.

A couple of hours before sunrise, when the streets were quiet, the Hummer gone, and his pants dry, Achilles snuck down to the apartment where they kept the dogs. The eye-watering stench explained why Cornelius lit a cigarette each time he entered the apartment and spat each time he left. Dog crates were stacked in the living room, two rows per side. It was an ugly apartment with exposed block walls and the cheap fixtures found in barracks. A mattress leaned against the wall in the bedroom. The bathroom was relatively clean, save for two dead puppies wrapped in plastic bags in the tub and fast food containers stacked neatly next to the toilet. Rusty surgical implements were piled on the kitchen counter: shears, scalpels, razorblades, a propane torch, a shoebox filled with alcohol and gauze. In the corner stood a short wooden sawhorse with heavy straps attached to each end and padding taped to the spine. At the far end of the counter: Troy's rucksack, empty except for the remnants of his blue envelope.

The pits were muzzled and in various stages of modification, some fully processed, others with only tails and ears clipped. A small white one appeared untouched, but when Achilles stepped closer, it hid its face in the back of the crate, revealing testicles bound in a leather strap. There were a few wretched mutts probably used as bait dogs. A terrier mix wagged his tail and followed Achilles's every move, padding from side to side, panting. Eventually, she would be thrown into the ring with a new fighter to build his confidence. Janice's brothers made good money from dogs. Pepper was diversified.

Achilles freed the terrier mix first. It was a scrawny gray dog with big eyes like those greeting cards featuring bug-eyed puppies. He let a tawny pit bull puppy out of his cage and it bolted for the terrier, which ran back to her cage. The tawny puppy whined and pranced. The terrier ventured closer. Soon they were playing, skidding all over the linoleum. Achilles opened the cages one by one, hoping for more of the same, but the fighters herded all the bait dogs. The terrier, whimpering now, hid behind Achilles, and when he turned to looked at her, she pissed. An adult blue nose knocked into Achilles, growling, trying to get to the wide-eyed terrier. Achilles pulled the blue nose away from the bait dog and toward the door. The bait dog went back to playing with the tawny puppy. The blue nose slipped out of his grasp a few times, and every time it did, it ran after the bait dog. Finally, the bait dog retreated to its own cage, followed by the tawny puppy. Achilles ran down the blue nose and pulled it toward the door. It was anxious about going outside, and kept planting its feet firmly in the carpet.

"There, there." Achilles petted it between the shoulders. It was a regal, full-chested, bowlegged dog with a lustrous silver-gray coat. Achilles scratched it under the chin and tickled its thin pointy ears. Each time Achilles grazed the left ear, the dog sneezed and shook its head. When it was calm, Achilles straddled him. His heart knocked against its ribs and Achilles felt every breath on his thighs. Gripping the scruff of the neck, Achilles yanked him up on hind legs, took one of the razors, and stabbed the blade into the dog's throat. He whimpered and twitched. Pinching the blunt end tightly between his thumb and two fingers, he drew the blade across the throat. The blade was not as sharp as he would have liked, and Achilles pushed hard to penetrate the hair and skin, thick as auto upholstery. It was like cutting leather with safety scissors, the line ragged and rough, more hacked than cut. The dog kicked and squirmed free, knocking the razor loose when Achilles was only half finished. The dog coughed through the wound, hyperventilating, its scrambling feet kicking the razor under the sawhorse as it ran for its cage. Achilles slipped in the blood as he yanked the dog out of the cage by the hind legs, half walking it, half dragging it to the kitchen, where the other instruments were. He finished with a straight razor. Throat clean open, it ran to the corner and dug its head into the carpet, legs running at full speed, like it could push itself through the wall. After half a minute, its legs slowed, then stopped, twitching only occasionally, like dogs did when dreaming. Achilles wouldn't have believed so much blood was in a dog, or a person, if he hadn't already known.

The first was the hardest, and he didn't do a good job, but he warmed to the task, as if someone he didn't know had stepped out of the shadows and taken over while Achilles sat on the counter to take in the view.

The other dogs were writhing over each other like maggots. He felt stronger, like he had absorbed their spirit. It was as if his entire body was expanding and contracting with their every inhalation. He selected the largest of the dogs, a pit-Rottweiler mix with short ears, a brown snout, and a black brow. To keep it still, he dragged it to the kitchen and used his knees to pin it against the cabinets. The dog shook its head wildly as Achilles plunged the blade into its throat and pushed through. It broke loose and ran into the bedroom, hiding between the mattress and the wall. Achilles tackled it. The dog turned over and scratched him. He was strong. Achilles tucked his head into his arm to protect his face and shoved the scalpel into its eye, up to the hilt. Warm urine and blood pooled at his feet and quickly soaked his shoes. It expelled its last breath and its head lolled to the side, the good eye following Achilles.

The third was easier than the first; its skin was thinner. They wore fear and confusion like long overcoats restricting their movements, dragging behind them, tripping them up. Achilles's every hair danced like an antenna. The air was water, each breath wind and wave. He felt their motion from across the room, sensed which way they would turn, where they would run.

The fourth he barely saw, automatically squatting a little to drop his center of gravity so he could easily work his forearm under the neck, stabbing and cutting simultaneously, like slicing a tire. It struggled beneath him, the writhing between his legs no more than eddies in water, like he was standing in a river that would soon run dry. As it did, he lay it down gently.

The fifth he chokes with his belt.

He heard a noise in the hallway, stepped back into the shadow of the kitchen, and leveled the rifle at the door before realizing it was only children in a nearby apartment arguing. There was one adult fighter left, and Achilles had just grabbed it when the front door was kicked opened, and a high-pitched voice yelled, "Use the force, zigga!"

A young boy stood in the threshold. Judging by his expression, he'd expected to find someone else in the apartment. He was little, no more than six or seven. He looked at the panting dog at Achilles's feet, at the rifle, at the other dogs scattered around the room like soldiers dropped where shot. The kid might have felt the way Achilles did when they stormed the Al-Jok stronghold to find it silent, save for the flies, and empty, save for the scores of corpses scattered in the courtyard, like a scourge had run through, like God had delivered some old-time religion, as Jackson put it. That was his saying when someone was dying for a bullet: they were itching for a switching or praying for some old-time religion.

"Where's Cornelius?" asked the kid. "I thought I heard shots."

"He'll be right back."

"They sick?" asked the kid.

Their eyes met. Achilles nodded "Real sick."

"All of 'em?"

"No." Achilles pointed to the bait dogs and the three pit bull puppies, and a dog he hadn't noticed, the same brindle he'd seen the white kid in the hooded sweatshirt walking a few days back. He picked up the tawny puppy and fondled its ears. "These ones are okay. In fact, they're going out for a break. You wanna help?"

The boy nodded. "This is like a war movie."

"Right. Do you want to be in it? Can you be my lookout?" asked Achilles, hoping to keep the kid close until he left.

"For ten dollars."

A rectangular bulge pressed through the kid's front pocket. "Are those cigarettes?" asked Achilles.

"One dollar," said the kid.

They smoked, the kid taking surprisingly deep drags, Achilles looking at the carnage, wondering if he could add two more bodies to the pile.

After stubbing out the cigarette, Achilles opened the bedroom window and gently dropped the remaining dogs outside. When they were done, he paid the kid an extra fifteen dollars for what remained of the cigarettes, because *kids shouldn't be smoking*. The kid thanked him. "Now I can buy three packs."

He considered snatching the money back, but there was no point. He put his backpack into Troy's rucksack, slipped the rucksack onto his back, and stepped out the window. Outside, the white kid in the black hoodie chased breathlessly after the dogs.

On the way to his car, he passed the same prostitutes. They straightened up at his approach, walking tall, kicking their legs forward like swimmers leaning against the side of a pool. The fat one had thick lips and a tempting smile, an inviting moon face and rich brown skin the color of Naomi's, skin you wanted to lick. Her full and snug breasts sat side by side instead of leaning out for air, but her belly was low and hard, like she was pregnant, too pregnant to fix it. As they passed, the thin one winked. Achilles turned in the trail of their perfume and slipped into a shadowy doorway to watch them. They paraded a few more steps before the thin one looked back and whispered to the pregnant one. They dropped their shoulders, shortening their stride, no longer high-stepping. The one with the belly put her hands to her back, kneading the area around her kidneys. She stepped gingerly. As they turned the corner, she cupped her hands under her belly and whistled. She was definitely too pregnant to fix it. Where would that kid end up?

Back at the hotel he showered, washing the blood off his face and chest and hands and wrapping clean socks around the cuts he hadn't noticed at the time, the scratches on his hands and arms, the gouge above his eye. He looked almost as bad as the night Bethany tended to him. He slipped into bed, Ines turning at his touch, pressing into him. He gently pushed her onto her stomach, lifting her ass as he straddled her. He emptied the tube of hotel lotion on his dick, spread her cheeks, and plunged into her ass. She tried to pull away. "Why didn't you warn me!"

Sammy flopped in his bed. She switched to a hushed tone.

He slipped his arm around her neck. "Don't fucking move." He worked his way in deeper, his dick growing harder every time she flinched. "Tell me you like it."

She mumbled and bit his arm. He tightened his grip on her neck, pinching the skin in the crook of his arm. "Tell me you like it."

She started breathing slower and deeper, her ass relaxing.

"Tell me you like it."

"I love it."

The dogs run through his head. Ines bucks back, pressing the top of her head into his neck, her body rippling beneath him, her legs kicking out as she collapses onto her belly. He yanks her hair like a bridle, jerking the reins of the chariot, pulling until her back is arched and her tits jet out like the figurehead of a ship. She snorts, sharp exhalations in short breaths.

"Harder!" she breathes. "Harder! Faster! Faster! Faster!"

The more she says "Faster!" the less excited he becomes, rushing to finish, pace quickening, his eventual grunt of relief lost in the clapping breasts. He collapses. Every time he thinks he's pushing through a wall, he's tumbling over a cliff, like that last kid in the music video.

"Is that it?" she asked. He clasped his hands together to keep from punching her.

After sex, she usually lay on her side and pressed her cold feet to his warm belly, and he rubbed them. He reached for her feet, and she jerked away.

As she turned over, she asked, "What happened to your face?"

"I was mugged."

She sniffed. "By a pack of cigarettes?"

Let her leave. Why was he ever worried about her? He went to the bathroom for a wad of tissue to wipe the shit off of his dick. He hadn't felt a thing at the time, but saw that his face was scratched much worse than it was at the camelback. Bethany would have taken care of him. The mirror framed a slice of Ines, glowing under the hot blade from the vanity bulbs. She had gained weight, and the freckles made her skin look splotchy in some areas. In others, he wasn't sure if it was pimples or freckles he saw. She was a stranger to him, which made him feel a stranger to himself, like he was scattering, becoming smoke, like he needed her to touch him all over to reconnect the parts, to make sure he was all there. He needed a message; she would agree. But he couldn't ask. It's easy to take what's wanted, not ask for what's needed. Sammy was snoring, a million miles away. A bomb could hit, catching them all in this dream. They'd never know.

CHAPTER 18

IN THE FIFTH-GRADE PRODUCTION OF *BILLY GOATS GRUFF,* ACHILLES WAS CAST as the troll, a role Troy reprised two years later. On the opening night, nervous Achilles forgot his lines. The stage manager whispered them from the wings, but Achilles couldn't hear under the green wig, so he edged closer to her, and in doing so upset the bridge and the kid playing the youngest goat. After the show, his mother said, "You're too handsome to be under a bridge anyway." His father said, "Son, you were great. So you made a little mistake. That happens to everybody. When you make a mistake, you have two choices. You can ignore it and go on with your life. Or, you can acknowledge it and go on with your life. So what if a whiny little goat falls off a paper mâché bridge? Sometimes the screw-up is the best part of the show."

But his father never explained what to do if the screw-up hurt somebody, and the shit floated downstream, which Achilles feared was the case the next morning. For a long time he lay under the covers listening to Ines snap at Sammy. Ines's walk held the key to her mood. Her steps were slow, heavy, dragging: announcing anger, disappointment, and hunger.

Next thing he knew, he heard a yelp and peeked out to see Ines shaking Sammy by the hair. Sammy was yelling about a Mrs. Babcock. Ines screamed, "No one volunteered for this! In elementary school, no one said they wanted to be homeless or on crunch or stuck on a fucking bridge to die of dehydration!"

Ines jerked Sammy with each word she yelled. The drapes were twisted around her arms, and as she shook him the curtain rod quivered and finally collapsed, flooding the room with light and silhouetting them against the window like paper dolls. Sammy had one hand to his neck and the other on Ines's arm. She slapped him four times in quick succession before pushing him to the floor. Sammy emitted one high-pitched squeal, hugged his knees to his chest, and rocked back and forth, whistling like a teakettle.

"I'm sorry. I'm sorry," Ines kept saying, dropping to her knees and reaching out to Sammy, who scurried away, squeezing himself between the chair and the wall as swiftly as a salamander. He started babbling. When she reached for him again, he squealed like a gerbil; this time so loud and sustained that Achilles had to cover his ears and the guests in the room next door stumbled out to the hall, mistaking the sound for a smoke alarm.

Ines was crying silently, mouth open, body heaving, gasping for air. A string of saliva ran between her lips as she pointed to the television. On the screen, images of New Orleans underwater flashed by. People stood atop the arches of undulating highways rising from the murky waters like the humps of mythical beasts. Achilles held Ines until her breathing steadied. With his other hand, he rubbed Sammy's neck and back while Sammy rocked back and forth chanting, "It's o.k. Mommy's here. Come to Mommy. It's o.k. Mommy's here. Come to Mommy. It's o.k. . . . ."

Sammy peeked out from behind the chair and Ines turned away, motioning for Achilles to do the same thing. Ines and Achilles remained facing away from Sammy for fifteen minutes, silent, until Sammy fully emerged and climbed into bed.

Achilles helped Ines up to the chair and kneeled at her feet. He took off his shirt and wiped her tears. "What happened?"

"The news. It's terrible, Achilles. Bodies are floating down the street. People are stranded. And Sammy said, 'They were warned. Sometimes people are in the wrong place at the wrong time.' Apparently it's something his teacher, Mrs. Babcock, said. I lost it. Maybe you can talk to him when he wakes up. He's always hearing it from me. He should hear something positive from a black male."

It was late afternoon, the streets quiet, as if all Atlanta were inside watching storm coverage. Sammy had slept for three hours, which Ines explained was normal after an attack. Until that afternoon, Achilles hadn't believed that Asperger's was real. He assumed it was like ADD, that Sammy needed a father to kick his ass. But the distant gaze and eerie tone when mimicking his mother had convinced Achilles otherwise.

Achilles had driven Sammy into the city, and they were walking along Highland Avenue. They turned down a residential street where all the trashcans were lined up like parade spectators, *or Katrina victims*, thought Achilles. Sammy wanted pizza and cheerfully pointed out every neon sign, whether it said pizza or not. It was amazing how quickly kids rebooted. They came to Johnny's Pizza on Highland, where a bum was collapsed on the sidewalk near the door. Achilles lifted Sammy to his shoulders, stepped over the bum, and went inside.

"You're strong."

Achilles grunted his thanks, preoccupied with how to fill his appointed role as positive black male role model. Could he say anything positive because he was black? Or did he need to say something black and positive? He had a beer while they waited. It was a new-old restaurant, with black marker scribbles scrawled on the wall to give it character. The cashiers and waitresses had jagged haircuts designed to look accidental. Beside the oven, a guy with *Boss* tattooed on his neck assembled pizzas with the slow, gruff movements of a mechanic, dropping everything from six inches above the counter, like army cooks. They'd ordered a pizza with everything except broccoli. Sammy didn't like broccoli, unlike Troy, who'd loved the stuff. They had to keep his hands out of the basket in the grocery store because he gulped it down at every opportunity, pretending to be a giant eating trees.

At the table next to them, a little girl with a clear view of the front window kept tugging at the father's sleeve and asking, "Soon?" Her father would answer, "Yes, honey." A baby dressed in blue slept in a car seat beside the mother.

Sammy drained his soda.

"You know your auntie I didn't mean anything by all that commotion in the hotel room," said Achilles.

"She sure seemed mad," said Sammy.

Achilles fought the urge to laugh. Wasn't Sammy supposed to say yes? "I mean, sometimes we hurt people we love and we don't mean to. We hurt them because they're the only ones in striking distance. She wasn't mad at you. She was mad at other people."

"But she pulled *my* hair."

Achilles chuckled. The girl at the next table tugged her father's sleeve again.

"She was very, very mad." Sammy chuckled too. "She pulled my hair very, very hard. My cheek burns. I feel like one of those duckies at the carnival."

Achilles laughed so hard his belly ached. "Sam, your auntie I wants people to get along better than they do. She wants people to care more than they do. She wants the world to be a better place than probably it ever was or will be. She believes these things strongly. She believes we're all . . ." Achilles paused. We're all what? We're not all the same. We're not all equal. She was irrational on that point. The world had never been peaceful, fair, just. A quick history of warfare proved that. The little girl at the table beside them started sobbing softly and was soon inconsolable. As her parents tried to calm her she only grew more upset, shaking her head, her pigtails bouncing with each sob. She started talking loudly, but her words were hard to understand. Achilles could only tell that a promise had been broken, and she could not abide it. Achilles slid Sammy's soda to the dark end of their booth. "Your auntie I wants us to get along." Achilles interlaced his fingers for effect. "She wants us to be better people."

"Is this like when the guy at the museum said we're all related and we all come from the same particle before the Big Bang explosion?" asked Sammy.

"Exactly."

"Or like when Auntie I says if you think of the whole world as a prison, there's no such thing as a cage-free egg?"

Achilles took a second to sort that out. "That's what your auntie I believes, that everything is connected."

"Then why don't we help them if they're not bad?" asked Sammy.

"Who?"

"The people in New Orleans," said Sammy.

"I don't know, Sammy. I don't always know what your auntie I means."

"So, we're all part of the same particle, except them?" asked Sammy.

"Them too. We're all like family. Family looks out for each other, right?"

"Cain killed Abel," said Sammy.

"What's that?"

"When I ask for a brother, my mom says Cain killed Abel."

Achilles wasn't ready for kids. He'd pictured Ines pregnant, but he wasn't ready for kids. He always imagined them as receptacles. He never imagined them asking so many damned pointed questions. "I'm pretty sure that was an accident."

"No it wasn't," said Sammy. He looked like that kid in the video, the one stuck at the edge of the cliff. It was the expression, as if he wanted to believe but needed a little help.

"Okay, so it was on purpose, but he didn't know any better. They were the first brothers, like a dry run."

"Was he angry? My teacher says anger is one letter away from danger!"

"Is that Mrs. Babcock?"

Sammy nodded.

"What happened that last time you quoted her?"

"I said the flood cleaned the city up, then Auntie I went into a rage and started squeezing and slapping, and I was running and kicking and getting away, and she pulled the drapes down for everyone watching to see her pulling my hair, and—"

Achilles put his hand up. "Enough, Sammy. I was there."

"I also quoted you. Some people are in the wrong place—"

Achilles put his hand up again. "Sammy, don't repeat everything you hear, and don't share everything you think."

The waiter brought the pizza to the table next to them but the little girl wouldn't eat. "You said you called them and they were going to come get him, and he's still there, and he might be dead now, or runned over by a car." She started crying again.

Her parents maintained their poise, but the way the father cut his eyes made it clear he blamed his wife for allowing a scene he wouldn't tolerate at home. The little girl wailed again, this time waking her brother, who joined her.

"I called them, Ingrid. You hear me?" The father sounded exasperated. Achilles and the father briefly made eye contact. The father offered an embarrassed grin, but scowled with his eyes. "The ambulance will be here any minute."

"It might be too late. A car might have run him over."

Achilles realized they were talking about the homeless man sleeping on the sidewalk outside the restaurant. Achilles couldn't eat because he couldn't avoid wondering how long she would care so deeply and what would eventually cool that heart of fire. Would the frustration and the fear and the impotence of this afternoon be the first step to saying, *Fuck it*? That was the way of the world. You bought cigarettes from a kid; the kid bought more. It was like you were always placing a losing bet, but kept gambling pieces of yourself away in the hope the house would eventually slip up. Maybe it was easier to care about things you couldn't fix, like world peace, than to care about people who were present and needed you.

The waitress came over wearing her best smile and asked if she could get someone another soda. That didn't work. Achilles leaned toward their table and said, "Ingrid, he's only sleeping. I talked to him when I came in. He's just very tired."

Ingrid looked up for the first time. She sniffed twice, so quick and hard that her nostrils clapped. "Really?"

"Yes, really. He's only resting."

She sat up, clapped once, and grabbed a big slice of pizza. The mother whispered her thanks. The father smiled, genuinely this time, and gave him a thumbs-up. Achilles felt guilty about covering the father's lie, but the little girl was so happy. Besides, it was no worse than lying about Santa Claus. As they left, Sammy looked up at Achilles and asked, "That's what Auntie I means, right?"

"What's that, Sammy?"

"What you told the girl," said Sammy.

"Thanks."

"What's for dinner?"

"You just ate."

"I like to plan ahead."

"How about upside-down day?" asked Achilles.

"Like pancakes for dinner? Really?"

"Really," said Achilles.

"Can I put jelly between them and roll them up?"

"You can do anything you want, Sammy, but isn't that for kids?"

"I am a kid."

After Sammy buckled himself in, Achilles yanked his seat belt to ensure that it was properly latched. Sammy tapped him on the hand. "Do you have a brother?"

"What's up, Sammy?" asked Achilles.

"I don't have a brother. I'd like you to be my brother," said Sammy.

"Oh yeah. I said that the other day," said Achilles.

"I mean for real, not a bribe for keeping a secret," said Sammy.

Achilles snapped his fingers. "Okay. Bang! It's official."

"You don't sound like you mean it."

"I do, Sam my man. I really do."

They found Ines checking the drawers, slamming each hard enough to shake the TV. The television blared, voices distorted. Her eyes red and puffy, she pointed at the TV. "They're killing us. They're saying shit like the flood is cleaning up the city. They won't let the survivors cross the bridge to Gretna."

"Flak jacket, babe," he said.

"The Gretna police have set up a roadblock, a fucking barricade—Sammy cover your ears—and are threatening to shoot anyone who tries to cross the bridge. They're saying—Sammy!—fuck you. Die! They survived a natural disaster to die now. Do you know how long it takes someone to dehydrate?"

He knew exactly how long it took someone to dehydrate or drown or asphyxiate, as well as bleed to death from a stomach wound or severed carotid.

"Not now." Ines continued, "We know some of these people Achilles. We know they're not all criminals. And the few who are, can you completely blame them? For five centuries told they don't deserve to be alive." She felt that was the crux of being black in America: it was a crime to assert your humanity, to speak your mind. According to her, it had been like this since slaves demanded their freedom, and even now a black person couldn't speak their heart and mind without white people feeling threatened. "And it culminates at this moment, when it's a criminal act to cross a bridge that leads from certain death to safety." She pointed to the TV as if to say, *Behold!*

The city was waist-high in water, but he could see enough landmarks to guesstimate the location of St. Jude, the house where he'd been ambushed, Wages's home, the school across from Wages. He wondered where Wages was, but knew he was okay wherever he was. Wages certainly wouldn't be among the people stranded on the overpasses. He wanted to look away, but they cut to a wide shot and the Superdome appeared, like a capsized ship, and behind it a sodden city center. Jesuit High School sat midscreen, and though he couldn't see it, he knew that meant that Wages's little duplex was underwater. Of course Wages would have gotten out. As the camera panned across the city, across the water coffin, he saw the burned-out camelback, Jax Brewery, the new St. Jude, Charity Hospital, where the morgue was located. Surprisingly, he felt angry.

Ines crouched on the bed, butt to haunches, looking like a statue of a lion, regal, or one of those weird winged tigers, the pose reminding him of the difference between the two of them. He wasn't sure about the image, but if he asked, she would know. Looking at the evacuees, he remembered that day at St. Augustine when he wondered why so many of them wore jackets and coats in the heat, not realizing they simply had no safe place to leave them.

The people on the bridges and boats and roofs looked like all the people he had worked with in the last few months in the shelters and stores and movie theaters. He'd always thought America's poor weren't really that poor. They didn't live three generations deep in one stone apartment. They had running water and electricity. Their schools and nurseries weren't bombed out. America's poor had cars with stereos and phones with cameras. America's poor had cable TV. America's poor had credit. They had opportunities and choices. But looking at the TV, it appeared that while America's poor had a better standard of living, they were largely the same as the poor elsewhere in the world—powerless to decide the basic direction of their lives. Like when the KPT tells an Afghan village, *Sorry, road come this way.*

"I'm going back now," said Ines.

He'd often faked the funk with Ines, like mumbling the lyrics to unknown hymns. But this, he agreed, this was too much. Even so . . . "You can't help everybody."

"Everybody I help matters. Like the starfish."

She loved to tell the story of Loren Eiseley walking along the beach, throwing starfish into the surf. A man tells Eiseley, *Why bother, this beach is strewn with stranded starfish. You can't help them all.* Eiseley tosses another starfish into the sea and says, *Helped that one.* Achilles liked that story, but this was different. "The city is closed. You can't get in. It's impossible."

"Impossible? Where is my Achilles?" She held her arms above her head. "We've got to try. That could have been us."

"You evacuated. You took precautions."

"I could. Not everyone had the choice."

Achilles nodded. He had so little time to do what needed to be done. "Let's leave in the morning."

She initially scoffed at that suggestion, accepting only after much pleading on his part. He tried to explain that while people were evacuating they shouldn't have to fight the stream of rescuers coming in. And it was late afternoon already. It would be better to drive during the day because they didn't know the extent of the damage to the power lines. Ines packed and set their suitcases by the door. In the morning, all they would have to do was shit, shower, shave, and hit the road, dropping Sammy off on the way. After they'd agreed to wait, Achilles excused himself to *run an errand.*

Marcus wasn't working, and the attendant on duty was locking up when Achilles reached the morgue. But it didn't take much persuading; Achilles merely explained that he'd received a phone call. The man unlocked the door and ushered Achilles into the morgue. The shooting victims were gone, as were the other bodies he had seen. The kid destined for Potter's Field was still there, but Troy was gone. Achilles checked each drawer twice.

"My brother was here three days ago," said Achilles. "Where is he?"

"Claimed?" the attendant said, his patience wearing thin.

"He couldn't have been claimed. No one knows he's here."

"He's here, he's claimed, or he's waiting to be transferred to Potter's Field."

"Where are they held for that?"

The attendant lead Achilles down a series of narrow halls into a section of the morgue that was a bit warmer. Being underground, it wasn't hot, but it clearly wasn't air-conditioned like the other section. After sorting through a series of keys, he unlocked a door leading to a small room no larger than a walk-in closet.

The shelves were lined with wax-coated gray cardboard boxes the size of magazine holders. Each one had a single white label in a metal frame, and the shelves were labeled by month, like an archive. Achilles ran his fingers along the labels, high and low, scanning the dates. He found one dated the day Troy would have been brought in, but as he removed it from the shelf, he noticed one beside it with the current date. "Is . . . Is this the day . . ."

"It's the date they're cremated. We bury them once a year."

"God, how do you know who is who?"

The attendant shrugged, "They're unclaimed."

"How many this week?"

The attendant shrugged again.

Outside, Achilles called his mother, holding his breath as she answered and immediately started complaining about the county's decision not to repave the local road, the taxes going up for the dump, and the speed demons who had taken over the highways. That off her chest, she asked

Achilles how he was doing. Before rushing off the phone, all he dared say was, "Been better." As much as he'd dreaded the sorrow he expected to hear in her voice, this was worse.

He and Troy had argued the day before Troy enlisted, Achilles calling him a coward. He thought nothing more of it until the next day, when they were supposed to go to a movie. Troy didn't show. Achilles checked the fridge, where the family left notes for each other, but there was nothing but the running grocery list: bread, Velveeta, butter . . . He never guessed that Troy was at the recruitment office, but when he returned to the hotel and found Ines gone, he didn't need a note to know where she had gone.

Sitting on the bed in that empty hotel room, as the sun faded and the shadows crept across the floor, across his feet, then up his legs and chest, at last swallowing his head, a new sensation settled over him, one he couldn't name.

Were it only so easy to have never been, or vanish, to really be invisible, singed, the pink of his muscle showing where the charred skin had cracked off, Achilles bleeding out with Jackson holding his hand, murmuring heartfelt but pointless reassurances; Achilles's parachute burning out over the airstrip—at that height, even water is a solid surface—a hole where his Adam's apple had once been; Achilles falling in Kurdan, one clean shot catching him in the middle of his favorite song; Achilles drowning in the Khyber Pass; Achilles asphyxiating in that camelback; Achilles trapped in Wages's attic; Achilles incinerated by the foo gas at Mosul; Achilles ambushed in Logar; Achilles's vehicle hit by the RPG in Konar, one remaining hand carefully bagged by Private Kevin Wexler; Achilles in the Black Hawk that crashed in Qalat; Achilles falling to hostile fire in Zakel; Achilles in that accident in Marjah; Achilles electrocuted in Jelewar, the smell hanging in the air for three days, being disturbingly enough not unpleasant, if you didn't know what it was; Achilles struck by indirect fire in Kheyl; Achilles shot by that sniper on Paktika; Achilles killed by the suicide car bomb in Tagab; Achilles killed by the accidental discharge at Camp Bulldog; Achilles killed by friendly fire in Gardez; Achilles killed by a satellite-guided bomb at Takur Ghar; Achilles killed by a fall in Shkin; Achilles catching the brunt of the suicide bomber in Helmand, the makeshit bomb in Zhari, the missile in Zabul; Achilles decapitated by the flying door, his arm torn off by a .50-cal round, the limb accidentally misbagged, which no one notices until Mrs. Henry Lee receives her husband's remains, finding among them Private Henry Jones's arm; Achilles blinded by a Browning as it stovepipes; Achilles walking into a minefield with Troy nowhere near; Achilles killed by a self-inflicted wound in Deh Chopan, in the latrine; Achilles no more, like the rest of them, in less than the time it took to light a cigarette, open a beer, unlock a door, cock a gun, rally up. If only it were so easy.

After he enlisted, Achilles's father took him out alone. They cleaned up the rifles and marched through the wood behind the house, stalking silently. It was deer season. Three days of hard rain followed by a freeze had left the ground too hard and leaves too brittle for them to stalk quietly. So they'd waited for another light rain to soften the earth. The early October air was brisk and the ground right, firm but not too hard, making it easy to move stealthily through the leaves, the only sound that of their legs occasionally rubbing together. They wore bulky, water-resistant hunting bibs, waddling to avoid making unnecessary noise. Trekking single file, they hugged the shadows of the pines, avoiding the open areas where the sun fell though the bare limbs of the fallow white ash and beech. Only ten minutes from the house, the tree line stopped abruptly at a new chain-link fence with No Trespassing signs posted on it and, beyond it, a row of concrete slabs lined up like a giant hand of solitaire. His father kicked the fence, cursing. His nose was red from the cold, and congested, so the curse sounded more like a quack. Turning to Achilles, he said, as if it were his fault, "I'm sorry, son. Bad intel." He pointed to a young tree on the other side of the fence, a few branches distorted from growing around a metal post. "That's my damned tree. Look what they've done to it."

They turned back, his father no longer stalking but stomping through the brush, his polyester legs sawing the air, his upstretched arms balancing his rifle across his shoulders. Walking like that, with his head down to watch the ground and his hands up, he looked like a recaptured POW being marched back to camp, his mind preoccupied with dreams of freedom. Did people in Iraq hunt? Did hunters in Iraq wear camouflage that so closely resembled military garb? Achilles wondered if he could really shoot someone. At the house, his father exchanged the rifles for wire clippers and bolt cutters, and led Achilles back to the fence, where they spent the next few hours cutting the fence down. "I guess this is why we haven't seen any deer running through here lately," was his father's only explanation.

Why did he care about deer running across their land? Only the week before, he'd stopped Troy from shooting a six-point buck in the driveway because it wasn't right to kill them when their natural habitat was being destroyed. *Shooting a deer in your yard just ain't hunting.*

It started to drizzle, but they continued working until they had detached the fence along the entire length of the property. As they worked, his father reviewed the advice he'd shared over the years: the night sky is brightest along a river, slow steps and shadows are the next best thing to camouflage, and defeat starts in the mind. Afterwards, he set up some cans and bottles for target practice, choosing a low berm far from the tree line. *Shooting a tree isn't hunting.* After that, his father walked him back to the house, his arm around Achilles's shoulder, telling stories about his days as a Yellow Jacket.

Overalls still on, they went to the VFW. Achilles had only been in the VFW to use the bathroom during the Fourth of July picnics, and each time he did he went the long way around the dimly lit bar so that he could run his fingers over the sawdust-coated shuffleboard table and, if no one was playing, slide a few of the weights around; then he would stab the dart board a few times, right in the center; finally he'd sink the cue ball, winning the big match in his mind, and emerge from the dank wood-paneled bar into the sunlight, hands aloft like a champion. He'd imagined being outside the VFW door at eleven fifty-nine at the end of his twentieth year. When the clock struck midnight, he would go in and play shuffleboard and pool, darts even, while drinking boilermakers—canned PBR with a shot of Jack tossed in. It was an image that meant freedom, but that night it felt like anything but.

His father held the door for him. "Let's have a cold one, or two, or six."

Their eyes met as he edged through the door, squeezing past his father's large frame. "Thanks, Dad."

"Go on in, son. You're old enough for war, you're old enough to have a drink with your old man, I fucking say! When y'all get back, your photos go on the wall with ours!"

When he stepped inside, the customers roared like Achilles was a gladiator entering the coliseum. Some sang old army cadences, some chanted his name. But for the next hour, Achilles fidgeted anxiously as the regulars kept him pinned into his booth, shaking his hand and buying him beers. He appreciated the attention, but the nicer they acted, the more he felt like a visitor, and the more he felt like a visitor, the more he thought about where he was going. That scared him. He was going home that night, but home didn't feel like home anymore. In his head until then it was always the house at the end of a stretch of slick black asphalt with no dividing line, no lights, no lane reflectors, and a dense tree stand hugging both sides. There was no other traffic on this road. It was always dark, the sky gray, the air wet. It was a straight road that vanished into the distance. Had it curved or rippled, that would have been okay. But in his mind, straight as a rifle barrel. The only landmark was his parents' home, which up until then had been the terminus, but now felt like a way station because now this road stretched well beyond that house and faded into the horizon where it merged with the night, becoming one undifferentiated question.

So he nodded at the regulars and drank the beers and watched men play pool while, in his mind, that road kept stretching farther and farther out into the distance until a warmth set in, a tingling in his fingers and numbness in tongue as the alcohol went to work and for one split second he thought that he understood why they all drank so much. Jake with the bum arm; Harry the barkeep and his garage full of porno magazines; Terry, who carried pictures of his dead dogs instead of his children in his wallet: each had a road in his head, and they were scared to know where it led.

On the way home, his father stopped the truck on the side of the road and said, "I know why you did it. Thank you. You were always the cautious one, and there's nothing wrong with that." His father patted his head, and Achilles loved him so much he would have cried right then if he wasn't afraid it would ruin the moment.

His father belched. "When your mother flaps her gums about where you've been, what do you say?"

"Out with Dad."

But all she said was, "I hope he fed you."

That night the family went to Lawrence's Steakhouse, a chain restaurant with wheelbarrows and old bicycles hanging from the ceiling, and walls covered with old photographs and posters advertising long-forgotten products. They went to Lawrence's once or twice a year, usually for a festive occasion, but tonight they ate in silence, everyone except Troy pushing their food around on their plates until his mom asked again if they had everything on the list. Achilles and Troy sat on one side of the booth, their parents on the other side, with the list on the table between them.

Achilles and Troy nodded. Black shoe polish, small squares of paper, pencils, foot powder, foot cream, eight pairs of black socks, for starters: it was a long list, but they had everything. And stamps? asked their father. Yes, they had those too. Their father nodded solemnly, "During your first week they're as good as cigarettes in prison. You might even be able to trade them for KP duty."

He returned to his food, chewing slowly. They rarely ate out, but their father made an exception for Lawrence's because their filet was, "The best filet your mother didn't cook. The only time I'll eat it made by someone else." He said this repeatedly, even though their mother never cooked filet, or any other cut of steak. After the belt on the bandsaw snapped back and hit him in the face, breaking his cheekbone and four teeth, their father refused to have an implant made because he discovered that his workers didn't have dental coverage under the new owner's insurance plans. The mill closed down shortly thereafter, and his new insurance plan through the school didn't include dental at all. So he ate his steak very slowly, working the left side of his mouth, his chin up so that no one could miss the scar on his cheek he wore like a war wound, his gaze wandering off as if he were thinking back to his own preparations for basic training.

He'd been adamant that they never join the military. On more than one occasion he told them that it was the randomness that nearly drove him mad in Vietnam, asking them to imagine if the Wizard had given brains to the Cowardly Lion and courage to the Tin Man. The cowardly private who hides if he hears a rooster crow triggers a booby trap and the brave officer leading every charge never gets a scratch. The next week, it was reversed. You'll try to crack the code but there is none. In a large-scale armed conflict, there's no relationship between how a man lives and how a man dies. He'd adamantly repeated this after Troy came home on 9/11 threatening to do something about *this terrorism crap*, but when the enlistment contracts showed up on the fridge a year later, affixed by the Lacrosse Club magnet and covering the family Christmas photo, their father limited his comments to practical advice like, "Change your underwear frequently and your socks even more frequently." Achilles, who until then had limited his comments to "the army doesn't take virgins," said nothing.

That night's advice was, "Keep your head down. You've done something wrong if the drill sergeant knows your name. I mean it, Troy."

Troy stared at his father with a mouthful of food, giving him a look that said, *Just wait.* They had been clashing all month, all summer really, ever since Troy graduated and demanded his adoption paperwork. Troy later said he only wanted to piss off their father. But really, both boys were ready to go somewhere.

Between meeting Janice at the quarry, his English class at Shippensburg Community College, and his part-time job at the lumberyard, Achilles was bored to tears, literally, one afternoon the drops collecting in the bottom of his goggles, blurring the edges of the two-by-ten he was ripping and then dotting the sawdust and woodchips along the rim of the table saw after he pulled off the safety glasses thinking he felt blood on his cheek.

His supervisor Kent, who had once worked for Achilles's father, rushed over and hustled Achilles to the eye-wash station, reminding him to wear eye protection always; he could be blinded in a second. *Blinded!* Could Achilles imagine that? A young boy like him without any vision, nothing to see, no future, no women, nothing of the world to be? It didn't sound fair, but it could happen. Kent had seen it. Could Achilles imagine that? Achilles could, which was exactly why he found himself in tears over the forty-fifth piece of wood that day, one more in a long line of lumber that had started his junior year in high school and had no foreseeable end in sight. Troy was threatening to go away to college, but all Achilles could see was one eternal line of timber. The world ended where I-80 intersected with I-74, just dropped off, and so when Troy stuck his DD Form 4/1 on the refrigerator without a word, Achilles went straight into Hagerstown and signed up. Here was a chance to serve country and family.

"Talk Troy out of it," his mom had said, cradling Achilles's face in her hands but holding his attention with her eyes.

"O.K. I'll try."

Three hours later, wearing the smug grin he'd worn all the way home, Achilles stuck his contract on the refrigerator next to Troy's and said, "Check that, bitch!"

"I'm gonna take a dump. Want to join me?" said Troy.

Their mother ripped the contracts in half and called the recruiter. Their father took Achilles aside and said, "It's good that you're going with him, but it would have been better if you had talked him out of it. You have no idea what you've signed up for."

And they didn't. Basic training was a breeze, infantry school a gale, and jump school admittedly a squall, but nothing—no berets, no blue cords, no silver wings—prepared them for the actual devastation on the ground in Afghanistan: the odd children's sandal amidst the rubble, the leveled towns, rank subterranean jails, marble-eyed refugees, the constant odor of death. Goddamnistan, however, adequately prepared Achilles for the Gulf Coast. They had both been visited, as Merriweather would have put it, by Old Testament–style devastation. "What you alone witness, you alone bear," Wages once said. Achilles had raised his beer in happy accord but secretly laughed it off, eyeing that African mask on his friend's mantel with suspicion, as if it were the font of the new Wages's steady supply of aphorisms. But now, Achilles understood, there being no one to nod when he nodded, whistle when he whistled, sigh when he sighed at the towns completely razed from end to end, every tree naked, every building again a blueprint; yards where trees stooped under great metallic nests, the trunks sometimes hunched as if weary, as if exhausted, surely thinking that now that the waters have receded, they have paid their dues; the lot where the house was nowhere to be seen but a sofa, love seat, and chair remained neatly arranged around the coffee table, as if the occupants had just popped into the kitchen during a commercial break. As he neared New Orleans, law enforcement waved his military ID through roadblocks where civilian volunteers towing boats and campers were turned away. He wondered how Ines had gotten through.

PART 4
LATE FALL 2005

CHAPTER 19

A THIN LAYER OF SLUDGE COVERED THE LOBBY FLOOR, BUT THEIR CONDO
had suffered minimal damage, aside from the odor. There was no sign
that Ines had been there recently. The surrounding streets hummed along
their gutters as if in heavy rain, pooling in some areas. He half walked,
half waded to the higher ground in Uptown, which had fared rather well.
There was the usual storm damage: missing shingles, trees stripped bare,
signs in the street. But most homeowners in that area had boarded up their
windows, avoiding the worst of it. The flooding wasn't as bad either; many
roads he could walk instead of wade. Every half-mile he was stopped by
Army National Guard troops and subsequently released with a warning to
beware looters and snipers. None of the soldiers knew what condition the
Delesseppes' home was in, which was surprising because when Achilles
reached it, there were a lot of people in the front yard.

The house had suffered little damage. Most of the roof shingles had
been blown away, as had the shutters and part of the porch railing, but at
least the house was standing, and it didn't look like the water had reached
high enough to damage the main floor. Mabel was in the yard wearing a
big smile on her face, directing everyone to form two lines, one for food
and one for the phones. She greeted him with a hug, wrapping her arms
around his waist and pressing her face into his stomach. She looked up at
him, dropping the smile like it was a tiring act, but said nothing.

"It's good to see you, Mabel. Where's Dudley?"

She squeezed tighter, pressing her face harder against him. Voice muffled, she said, "We got split up. They put me on a handicapped bus and
him in a cargo van. He's gone home."

Achilles hugged her back, bending to press his cheek against her gray
hair. He waited until she let him go, which seemed like a long time, long

enough that he melted into the embrace and the now-familiar scent of cocoa butter.

"She's around the corner." She jerked her thumb over her shoulder.

There stood Ines on the side porch handing out cups of juice and water to the people lined up in the yard, graceful as a queen bestowing favors. The line wound around the house and to the garage out back, where Ines had set up a mobile and satellite phone bank. Achilles watched, stunned as always by her grace. Ines laughed with the men, joked with the ladies, and hugged the children. Each time she smiled at someone or grazed their hand, they stood a little taller. Wages had the same touch. Giving that man a fork had been like giving him a hand. A little girl tripped in front of Achilles. He helped her up. She dusted herself off and the doll she was holding, comprised only of the torso and one leg. She held it by the foot, wielding it like a hammer. A few feet away stood another little girl holding the other leg with the foot jammed into the head. She held it by the leg, waving it like a mace. Achilles called her over and handed them each five dollars. The girl who had tripped took hers, but the other glared. "There ain't no stores open," she said before snatching the money from his hand. "This won't even buy a bottle of water."

Achilles gave her a few more dollars, and when he looked up, Ines was gone, the screen door rattling in the doorway. He followed. Inside was lit only by candles, but intact. All the paintings and books had been packed up and moved to the attic. Moving from foyer to living room to hall to dining room to kitchen, as he turned each corner, Ines vanished around the next like a ghost.

He passed Mabel again, who had wheeled up the makeshift ramp built off the back porch and rolled by with a tray of sodas and water on her lap. Unaware of being watched, there was not even a hint of a smile on her face. He passed Margaret seated at the desk in the family room, writing in a large book, taking notes as a weeping woman seated across from her spoke. Margaret barely waved, as if she didn't recognize him. She looked tired, her hair rough at the roots, a few streaks of gray showing at her temple. Was that gray hair or dust? He couldn't tell. Only Mrs. D managed a smile for Achilles, but not a nice one, saying, it seemed, *Your face. Darling, haven't you grown beyond this rugged look?*

When he caught up with her in the kitchen and asked if they could talk, Ines drew aside the blinds. Only a few feet from the window people stood waiting in line for the phone bank.

"Sure, Achilles. What do you want to talk about? What's on your mind?"

The two little girls screamed by, waving their doll parts overhead. The queue billowed and in their wake resettled into a looser, lighter, chattier arrangement.

"Can I help?"

She asked him to carry a few boxes, wheel an old lady home, move a few more boxes, and each time he finished, she said, "Thank you, Mr. Conroy."

As the sun set, people bunked where they could, in the yard, in the garage, in the basement. Achilles followed Ines up the stairs to the maid's quarters in which she now slept, having given her bedroom to a young family with children. She stopped him at the landing, a purgatory in view of both the room above and the hall below.

"Where can I sleep, then?"

"At the condo. Isn't that where all your stuff is?" said Ines.

"You can't stay here alone with all these people."

"I don't need your protection from these people. I don't need a soldier."

"You can't be—"

"Achilles," Ines said, cutting him off, "I don't need a soldier. I need a man. You can't always be in soldier mode." She handed him a business card. "If you want to soldier, see these people, they came by looking for local guides."

"Can we talk? Please?" he whispered.

A stranger at the base of the stairs called up to them, "Is everything all right, Ms. Ines?"

He looked to be in his mid- to late thirties, tall and thin with a beer belly. He had the light skin and green eyes common among so many local men, or Creoles as they called themselves. His hair was slicked back, his shirt tucked in, and pants rolled up neatly and evenly on each leg. He probably thought himself a lady's man. "Mind your own business, asshole," said Achilles. "Or do you want to come up here and find out for yourself?" Achilles held his arms out in invitation, itching to beat him black, and then blue.

"Achilles!"

"Okay, is everything all right, *Ms. Ines?*" said Achilles.

"Yes. Thank you, Raymond," she called down, and stormed upstairs, Achilles behind her keeping cadence.

When they were in the maid's quarters, he shut the door behind him. "Raymond? Raymond?"

"Who's Kevin Wexler?" she asked.

"That's different," said Achilles.

"Very. Very different. He probably doesn't sneak out after you fall asleep and come back to treat you like a dog."

If that was what this was about, he had it handled. Like Wages said, a woman would always forgive you if she loved you. "I'm sorry, baby."

"Really?"

"Yes."

"That's different, then," said Ines. "That changes everything. Do you want to fuck me in the ass again now, or should I close my eyes first?"

"Let me explain," said Achilles. As he tried to think of something to say, the sound of the girls playing drifted through the window only to be drowned out by a helicopter, that wobbling noise soon giving way to the vibrato of a small plane.

"I'll help you." One by one, finger by finger, she enumerated his sins, starting with the first and greatest: There was no obituary for Kevin Wexler, no information on Kevin Wexler at any morgues, or viewing or services for Kevin Wexler at any funeral homes *anywhere in Atlanta*. Then there was the matter of his despondency, remove, and callous behavior in Atlanta. You hit a man for no reason. Then there was sneaking out in the middle of the night and using Sammy as cover. Sammy wouldn't admit anything, but she knew he was lying. Achilles smiled to himself at the revelation that Sammy could be trusted. He'd do something special for the kid the next time he saw him, if there was a next time. She demanded to know about the scratches on his arms. He said he was mugged. She demanded to know why he slipped out in the middle of the night. He said he went to see off a friend who was in town for Wexler's funeral. She demanded to know why couldn't she go too, if that was the case.

For that he had no answer.

"Don't you get it? My mother didn't evacuate. Achilles, I went to Atlanta to be with you, to support you. Don't think I didn't trust you. I didn't want to check up on you, but you were acting strange, and you sounded funny, so I was looking for ways to help you bear the loss of your friend. But I should have been clued in by that phone call you got. Your grieving voice sounds exactly like your lying voice."

My grieving voice sounds like my lying voice. This felt true to him, revelatory even, like an apt description of his life from the outside looking in, but not an insult. It certainly wasn't a reason for complaint.

But it was the crux, the center of Ines's frustration. In the end, they'd had rough sex, but she hadn't used the safe word. There'd been no obituary, but she didn't doubt that someone had died (no one would lie about that). She even admitted, reluctantly, that Sammy, though a bad liar, was never prouder than when covering for Achilles.

"He grins, screws his mouth to the side, looks down, rocks back and forth, and babbles about the May weather. Sometimes I ask him what you did just to amuse myself. But this," she points to him, her hands grazing his wounds, the sticky fingers skipping across his skin. "This, Achilles, is too much. Can't you see that? It's like a regression. You've got that hulking, brooding war thing going on again and I don't know why. I don't know when you're joking anymore, or who you are since that trip to Atlanta. I feel like we've just met for the first time and you're not the person I've known."

But he is that person, isn't he? The medivan volunteer-blood-donor-progessive-liberal-bleeding-heart soldier. The person who cares about social justice and fairness and equity. It's her list, but he insists that he is that person, the person she thinks he is, and then it hits him full on, like being barely missed, just barely, and knowing it, the way it wakes you in the middle of the night for confirmation, it hits him, that he is really that person to her, that Ines was never slumming. Just like he thought she was someone else, she was only dating the person she thought he was, the person he had to be.

"That is me!" He is that person he insisted, reciting her list and banging the wall to punctuate each word. This is the first time he has raised his voice at her. Ines has backed across the room, eyes wide, eying him suspiciously, an unrecognizable look on her face, one he has never seen before but if pressed would describe as a mixture of fear and disgust. Was this the same way Bethany looked that minute before Wages grabbed her? He felt like those kids who charged headlong up the water tower and once up there freaked and froze, terrified of that one misstep on the way down.

To Achilles, she said, "I'm sorry. There are many soldier modes." She pointed to the dent he made when he punched the wall. "This just isn't the one I need now. Maybe you should call those people who need guides." He leaned in to kiss her, but she turned away.

"Does this mean you're not coming home?"

Ines walked to the window. "I've thought about this for a long time. You know I care about you—"

"But not enough to come home?"

"That's not it."

"Not enough to be with me. Not enough to want to be with me. You mean you care about me as a friend? Like a charity case? Or the way you care about Mabel and Bud. Is that it?" He stood and pounded his fist for emphasis as he said each name. "You care about me the way you care about the Harpers or Dudley."

"That's mean, Achilles. That's not right," said Ines, her hands on her hips.

"That's how it sounds to me."

"I mean about Dudley. You know Dudley's dead."

Achilles sat back down, shaking his head. "Mabel said . . . Fuck. I don't know what the fuck is going on here. She said he was at home. If she won't tell the truth, I'm not responsible."

"That's it, Achilles," said Ines, pointing, her finger trembling before leveling out like a divining rod pointed straight at his heart. "That's it. The anger. The violence. You need to see somebody. You're in a space where you attract trouble if you're left on your own. Like the mugging in Atlanta."

"That's my fault?"

"People attract what they deserve. No. I mean we attract what we . . . deserve. Yes. Anger, hate, love. We get back what we give, nothing more and nothing less."

"I haven't given you anything. So you won't come home?"

"That's not it. You're carrying stuff with you that you obviously don't want to tell me about, and I understand that. But you have to tell some-body. You have to face whatever is eating at you so you can be *here*." She put her hand on her chest, "Present in your own heart, in your own life. You can't be a community of one."

He'd had a response prepared, but she said "community" as Wages had said "community," as Levreau had said "community," and he forgot what he wanted to say. "I have a community. I'm a soldier."

"Isn't there more than one way to be a soldier, Achilles? More than one way to be brave? Isn't facing yourself the best way to be brave? Getting back to your community. Maybe you need time to think. Maybe it would be good for you to be with Charlie 1, to be with other soldiers." She touched the card in his hand. Her fingers were sticky with the juice she'd been handing out, and she smelled like cookies and soap and deodorant.

He tore up the card and intertwined his fingers together tightly, so tightly his nails turned pink. *Remember to breathe.* Did this mean they were breaking up? Him without her. Her with someone else. Both ideas horrified him. Merriweather once said, "I don't hit women. That's not power. Besides, that's what a lot of them want. That's how their daddies showed they cared, or didn't. Some of them will try to make you angry enough to hit them. They'll talk shit about you, about men in general, about your dick, whatever. I don't fall for it." Achilles had blown that off, never believing a woman might want to be hit, or understanding why a man would hit a woman. But he thought he understood now, and Merriweather was wrong. There was power in force. He could grab Ines and take her out of this house, make her go.

That's all it took.

One quick smack to shock her, but only on the butt, not the face. The face reddens on its own, the smile—she loves that he loves her ass—becoming a look of confusion as the sting traveling from her ass to her brain gains in intensity and she realizes it's not a love tap. *Get your fat ass downstairs, break a right on Tchoupitoulas Street, and don't fucking stop stepping until you reach the condo,* he demands, his hand clutching her jaw so tightly that when he releases her face it takes moment for the blood to return. *Hup! Hup! Hup!* He barks like a drill sergeant as she fumbles with her bag. *Leave it! You can come back for that shit.* He ushers her out the door into the stairwell. *Hup! Hup! Hup!* He chops the air, his hands flashing like tracers. *Go! Go! Go!* He stomps. Flustered, fluttering, her hands at her neck and then at her sides, no time to think with everything happening so fast, no time even to cry, breathing heavy, her eyes wide and crotch growing wet. Like a buck pushed to charge a stronghold, unable to make sense of the calm voice in his earpiece amid the confusion of the flares and mortars and charges and rockets and grenades and gunfire and random screams, unable to distinguish north from south or friend from foe or up from down until he trips, winding himself, eating a mouthful of dirt on that next ragged inhale; like a newbie belly-crawling to cover when he feels something wet kiss his face as his friend is shot three feet away (their gazes locked in that moment when there is nowhere to hide from the fact that there is nothing to do about it); like a boy in the morgue realizing how much his brother and father resembled each other in death; wanting only for the terror to end, Ines is out the door and down the street before she even realizes what the fuck is going on, and if you ask her

275

tomorrow what happened, she won't actually be able to tell you, the images again clouding her vision, the memory filling her body with adrenaline and her mind with confusion as surely as if it were happening again—if, and only if, he is that kind of person.

Wages did it and Bethany didn't go anywhere. But did she jump when a pot fell or a plate broke? Did she stay only because of the baby? Did she walk on a tightrope, thinking, *If I fuck up, Kyle will kill me?* Hadn't Achilles been more desperate to please his father after the night Troy first came into their house? Hadn't his mother hidden Bibles and crosses for decades? Achilles could be on Ines before she knew what had happened. Wages had said, "A woman will always forgive you," right? "Shoot her in the ass with the cat pistol." He had come for her and would leave with the prize, right? There were always the stories of guys killing their girlfriends and themselves, of preferring obliteration to isolation. He sympathized with them. They refused to concede what they had worked so hard to earn. They refused to surrender the battle of wills. They understood that you could never regain lost respect, that psychological war was not like a ground war, that you could not regain lost ground except through virtual annihilation, and *I won't let it come to that,* Wages had said. But he had. He had. Even the psychological war required occupation—wasn't that the lesson?

Ines was looking alternately at the floor then at him. She turned to look out the window when she heard children laughing. Her hair was tied hastily behind her head and tucked into her shirt, as it had been when they met, as it often was when she was working.

"I'm going home," he whispered.

She turned to face him. "I wasn't ignoring you. I just heard children laughing so hard, I had to look."

He stood beside her in the window as the wind combed water over a crest in the asphalt like a submarine rising. Achilles would have told her not to apologize for turning her back on him, that in fact he wanted to thank her for it, but for that to make sense, he felt he would have had to explain everything that had just gone through his head, and no one would understand that sudden confluence of vulnerabilities, the room of mirrors that became an emotional kaleidoscope, where for a moment everyone he knew seemed to merge into one person. She could turn her back on him as often as she pleased. He reached for her hand, and she let him take it.

Many streets were passable only by boat, except in the French Quarter and Uptown. People, mostly black and brown, remained stranded on rooftops and highways. The marooned city pumps sat surrounded by still water. Traffic signals and streetlights were inoperable, most homes uninhabitable. Wages's house and the burned-out camelback were underwater, St. Augustine half submerged. Bodies, again mostly black and brown, floated down the street, their skin stretched to bursting. Merciless heat, abandoned buildings, sporadic gunfire. In this disaster zone racked by utter confusion, this Injun Country, Achilles felt right at home.

There were people to rescue, food to distribute, and, best of all, looters to detain.

To aid in the relief, the army deployed National Guard and Reserve units, several of which were assigned local police officers or military personnel as guides. Achilles embedded with Charlie 1, which included two newbies, in immaculate uniforms, named Bryant and Wilson, and two vets, a white Mississippi farmer named Vodka and a black guy from Oakland who called himself Daddy Mention. The sole survivors of their squad's last Iraq deployment, Vodka and Daddy Mention had one month earlier loaded ten friends into a *brand-spanking-ass-new APC*. Achilles felt for them—the heat rash, Jackson's grip, Troy's skin, cold as clay—when Daddy Mention said, "That's how we learned irony. After nine months, the APCs show up just in time to be used as hearses."

Achilles enjoyed being embedded with a squad at first. It took his mind off of everything. Every morning at sunrise, Charlie 1 received orders—those divine instructions—from the temporary HQ at the Convention Center, trucked over to their makeshift dock, a former grocery store tractor-trailer loading ramp, and then spent most of the day on a boat. Vodka piloted, Achilles navigated, Bryant and Wilson acted as spotters, and Daddy Mention kept them laughing. Daddy Mention had Merriweather's sharp eyes and baritone voice, and like Merriweather, he maintained a running commentary on their progress throughout the day.

Achilles had a level of comfort that he now realized his Afghan guides had never felt. Charlie 1 swapped bullshit stories, made heroic plans, and commiserated about the food. They also shared pictures of girlfriends and wives, except Wilson, so Daddy Mention gave him one to carry in his wallet. After seeing Ines's photo, Daddy Mention teased Achilles for having a skylight, and claimed to have several of his own. As he put it, "Back home, I trade bitches like baseball cards. That's why they call me Daddy Mention."

Achilles waited for the rest of the explanation, but it never came. Daddy Mention just extended his hand, offering Achilles some dap. Bryant, though, wasn't as chipper, and said little. Whenever Achilles asked "What's up?" Vodka explained, "His pussy's bleeding."

The first day, they coasted wakeless down Claiborne Avenue through the ghost town that was the Seventh Ward. Some streets were passable; on others, houses had washed out into the middle of the road. Their priority was the stranded and infirm, aka gate bait, but they took a few pedestrians back to the Superdome that first day. According to Vodka, the senior of the two vets, watching people wade though the water just wasn't Christian, especially in this hot shit.

And there was a lot of hot shit. Alligators gnawed bodies, dogs floated at the end of their leashes like buoys, and the occasional corpse cruised by, hair fanning behind. Bryant wanted to make a skiff and bring the bodies in. After Vodka said that it wasn't their job, Bryant went back to sulking. People begged for water and food, pleaded for them to take their children. A man in a wheelchair rolled right off his roof trying to get their attention. Everyone stood at the edge of the boat and watched the murky water bubble. Finally Achilles and Daddy Mention jumped in. The old man clung to Daddy Mention's legs and they both would have drowned if Achilles hadn't managed to unbuckle the man from his wheelchair.

Henry, Henry, Henry was distraught about his wheelchair. To reassure him, they said his name constantly during the trip to the Superdome, where they chair-carried him up to the triage tent. The stadium had been converted into temporary housing and an emergency hospital. From the raised entry platform they could see for blocks. Achilles had been to the roof of the school across from Wages's house, the top of Jax Brewery, the upper levels of One Poydras Place. The view was always the same. It had to break Ines's heart. The trees at City Park: no more. The café where they went to lunch with Margaret: no more. Seaton's Diner: no more. Was this what it was like to host a war? To stand at the edge of a town and see your very memories in ruin? The city was an archipelago, and they stared in silence. Even Daddy Mention was quiet, though he was of course the first to speak, saying, "That bitch just lifted her skirt and horse-pissed on this motherfucker."

"If she were a horse, you'd put her down," said Vodka.

Everyone muttered their amens. Before they left the triage platform, Achilles and Daddy Mention were hosed down, given a change of clothing. Their old clothes were tossed in a burn bag.

Not thirty minutes later, they came across a heavyset woman seated on the edge of her porch roof, holding a shoebox on her lap and kicking her toes in the water, which was almost up to the roofline of her house. Sweat dripped from her housedress. As they drifted up beside her, Achilles grabbed the roof to steady the boat, burning his hand on the shingles.

She stared at them, narrowing her eyes but not bothering to raise her hands against the sun, as if she had long become used to it. She said, "I tell you like I told the others: I ain't going nowhere until my baby gets back home." She went back to kicking her toes in the water. "I ain't leaving without my son."

Wilson offered water. She opened her shoebox. It was filled with photos and bottled water.

"Ma'am, where is your baby?" asked Vodka. "We can take you there."

She recoiled. "He'll be right back. He went for candy. He likes Tootsie Rolls, and we was all out."

The street was empty. Rooftops peeked through stale water, some with HELP painted in large, uneven letters. One sign rose above the water: CIRCLE MARKET.

"Did your son go the Circle Market ma'am?" asked Achilles.

"Just down the street. He'll be right back." She started rocking back and forth and humming.

Bryant tied off on a porch post and held the boat steady. Something thumped against the side window of the house, startling Achilles and Bryant. The body of a child turned in the murky water and disappeared behind the floating drapes.

Vodka climbed up to the porch roof and the woman shrieked and scurried backwards toward a hole in the roof, where she must have hidden every time the rescuers came through. Achilles pointed to the hole, and Daddy Mention ran over to block her way. The body thumped the window again. The bloated facial features were indistinct, but it was clearly the corpse of a child wearing the remains of a parochial school uniform, and now momentarily entangled in the tattered, flowered curtains.

"What's your name ma'am?" asked Vodka.

"Mrs. Dennis Robicheaux."

"How about we take you to where you can find your son? O.K.?"

Bryant couldn't stop staring at the boy's body and was shaking ever so slightly, tremors in his hands, which hung at his waist as if he was an outmatched gunman waiting to draw. She started singing. Daddy Mention joined in, calming her. *"Soon now, very soon, we are going to see the King."* Once Mrs. Robicheaux was in the boat, Bryant cradled her head so she couldn't look back. Daddy Mention patted one of her arms, Wilson the other.

She said, "He's a good boy and he likes school, which is good, because I paid a lot for it. Almost all the money his daddy left."

She refused water and food, telling them, "Save it for my son." Her feet were raw and blistered from walking on the roof shingles. She and Daddy Mention starting singing again, their voices as one, loud and melodic— *"Soon now, very soon, we are going to see the King"*—and Achilles hummed along, wishing he knew the words.

At the Red Cross station, she refused to get on the gurney; she was a strong woman. The Red Cross nurses called two soldiers who were stationed there, and still it was a challenge to move her without capsizing the boat. She stiffened, and they lifted her like pallbearers, dropping her on a soldier, who collapsed under the weight. Mrs. Robicheaux resumed struggling, thinking she was still on the boat, clutching Vodka's wrist. "My son, my son. Baby, you promised me. Don't leave him here to die. He can't swim. He's afraid of the water. Even when he was baptized he cried all night."

She collapsed, her soaked body quivering with each sob. Curling into a fetal position, she kicked her shoebox into the water. Achilles managed to grab it before it sank, but several of the photos were wet. Daddy Mention was studying the sky, biting his lips. Vodka's mouth was pursed, like he had bitten something sour. Wilson kept wiping his eyes. Bryant was blinking like he had salt in his. The soldiers on the platform were breathing heavy, one with his hands on his knees. The other one pointed his weapon at Achilles. "What about him?"

"What the fuck about me?" yelled Achilles. "You couldn't even handle her."

"He's with us," explained Vodka.

"He better watch his attitude."

"You need to watch talking about me like I'm not here." Achilles thrust his chest out. The soldiers fingered their rifles.

"He's a two-timer, and he's helping us out here."

The soldiers lowered their rifles.

It was decided that they'd get Achilles a badge, a nametag, something, *anything*. As Vodka said, "Otherwise, it's like someone finds your pit bull walking the street and they just want to put it to sleep."

"I know that's right," said Daddy Mention. "A zigga can take one look at you and see you're nothing but trouble."

And it wasn't even noon.

Nola had lost the extra pounds she'd gained over the years and fit back into her prom dress: the high ground of the French Quarter, the original borders, where Charlie 1 spent their nights crawling up her skirt to hang out at Jock-Os on Bourbon Street.

Up and down the strip, the few people who were out moved in clusters and bumped into each other, though the street was nearly vacant. A street preacher, who had often stood outside St. Jude, warned them all: "Repent, repent. Fold yourself into the wings of the Lord." He had a new sandwich board. The front read, *The Lord Has Spoken, And You Have Not Listened. Don't Make Him Tell You Again.* On the back were Bible verses, mostly from Genesis and Revelations. Inside the bar, the whole company gathered and played pool and shot the shit in the back room. When gunfire went off, everyone scrambled to write their name on a dollar and toss it in a hat. The money was divided between those who correctly guessed the caliber of the weapon. Vodka played one dollar, to save face it seemed, Bryant played none, and Daddy Mention always played five and usually won. As he explained, "I'm from West Oakland." They were just like his old crew. Bryant was Wexler, Vodka was Wages, and Daddy Mention was Merriweather; he even slapped his hands on the table every time he stood, like he'd had enough.

And passing through the bar to the bathroom, the snippets of conversation were just what Achilles remembered. *Sometimes you have to backhand these heifers on the ass. Ugly girls give better head. This dude running around like he was on fire, well, he was on fire, but . . . His ass could be his mouth and you wouldn't know the difference. Jesus loves NASCAR.* The obsessions were the same as well. Charlie 3 was upset because they hadn't seen anyone except two Israeli commandos doing private security in Uptown. Charlie 2 bragged about seeing some Darkwater guys shoot a cat, though they couldn't agree on whether it was alive before that moment. Darkwater was a private security firm that employed ex-special forces. Decked out in all black, they weren't dressed to blend but to intimidate.

"Cat, zero. Darkwater, one," said Daddy Mention.

"Those guys are assholes," said Bryant. It was the first time he'd raised his voice, which was unusually deep for such a small, wiry man.

Vodka said Jesus was his commander in chief and he wouldn't soldier-of-fortune for Darkwater or any other crooked mercenary outfit that lured away good soldiers trained on the U.S. dime. Wilson said he'd work for Darkwater, or any other private security firm, because they paid more per week than he earned in a month.

"That's right, working for those dead presidents. Fuck the live one," said Daddy Mention.

"That's our commander in chief," said Wilson.

"He'll be my commander in chief when he's on a twenty-dollar bill," said Daddy Mention. "Until then, he can't do shit for me, though I'd let Laura rub lotion on my ass."

"That's sick," said Wilson. "She's like forty."

"Exactly. Think about it. When was the top last down on that convertible? It would be like a virgin."

"I don't know about the face," said Wilson.

"Lying like you care about faces, after that skank you pissed back in Columbus," said Vodka. "Put a sheet on her head and pretend you're ripping up some magic carpet. Tell him something, Achilles. You know."

Achilles said, "After your first month, any T&A is going to look good because you're never going to see them together unless you pay one to raise her shirt while you're paying another to raise her skirt. You'll fire a rocket if you see two oranges bouncing in a sack. Vodka's right. Put a paper bag on her head and call it a burka."

Vodka laughed. "Like the Ain'ts, ain't it?"

"You're all right," said Daddy Mention.

They were all "all right." They fit like keys. They were down like four flat tires. But Achilles couldn't help but wonder what Ines would say if she heard him talking like this, if she heard his soldier's humor. And the more he thought about it, it wasn't funny. The Darkwater guys they'd seen that day had offered to take Achilles off of Vodka's hands. "We're headed to the kennel," one said.

It took a moment for Charlie 1 to realize the Darkwater guys were pointing at Achilles. Vodka explained, "He's not a looter, he's with us."

He's with us, not *he's one of us*, Achilles thought. Then, *Stop reading into everything, like Ines!*

The Darkwater guys had drifted off with long faces. When they were out of sight, everyone spoke at once, except Achilles. He patted his pockets.

He didn't have his military ID with him. He wore old jeans and Hi-Teks, and wondered what would have happened if he'd been alone.

But he wasn't. Achilles felt at ease, as Ines suggested he would. *Soldiers are your tribe.* It would have been a perfect life were Ines there to greet him when he climbed the seven stories up to their condo, and lay in their bed with only the stars as company. But she refused to talk to him, so every night he slept three hours, rising at midnight, which was when Ines shut down the phone bank.

While they eventually let him go, it was always a hassle, not to mention demeaning, to be treated as a criminal by the patrolling guardsmen. He was unaccustomed to being greeted with *Let's put those goddamn hands where we can see them!* So he cut through alleys and backstreets. Moving from shadow to shadow, it was easy to stay hidden in a city lit only by stars, yet he was edgy, hoping to remain unseen, knowing it would be impossible to explain that he was acting like a criminal to avoid being treated like one.

Once at Mrs. D's, he ducked into her neighbor's stripped azaleas and spent the night keeping an eye on Ines. It was tiring, but being drunk with exhaustion only made everything easier to bear. People came and went, passing within inches of him. Ines would sit at her window and look outside, sometimes writing by candlelight. Once he thought she stared right at him, and he waved. He wasn't surprised when she didn't wave back. Of course she couldn't see him; as he'd said on their first date, invisibility wasn't a superpower. It really wasn't hard at all—people didn't look around very much.

Watching Ines hugging strangers, he thought that maybe women were brave in ways men couldn't understand. But they still needed protection, and as one who never prayed, he believed protectors were earthbound.

Mrs. Deleseppes's neighborhood didn't even look like it was in the same city as Mrs. Robicheaux's. No one was stranded, and appliances were the most common casualties. They lined the streets like fat kids awaiting the short bus, except many had been shot by angry owners.

After a few days with Charlie 1, he and Bryant were assigned night patrol to look for looters. Days were miserable because, with most of the trees gone, there wasn't any shade. But at night it was peaceful, and cool enough to enjoy the ride, if not for the stench. They each carried a flashlight, and the boat was equipped with two searchlights, but by unspoken agreement they kept the light to a minimum. After thirty minutes of silence, Bryant shared his concern about deployment, about how much he didn't want to go. "I know I'm not supposed to go."

You're right to be worried, thought Achilles. Anything could happen. Ines once explained what she had thought before she went to Afghanistan: "You hear it all about war. Bravery, depravity, insanity, terror, heroism. Lazy days followed by nights bright with artillery. Guys who charge bullets and break through doors without a scratch. Child snipers. Local police who turn on you without warning. Friendly fire. Frisbee golf on the edge of minefields. Men who run from their shadows, and men who jump on grenades. And the crazy thing was that it was all true, every last bit of it, at the same time. I was in a minefield. Three men were there. Two walked away, one saved my life."

Bryant was right to be worried. How could Achilles explain that? How could he explain why it changed you? That sometimes you looked at people you loved and pictured them dead and bleeding because you'd seen it happen so many times before. How could he explain that even if you enlisted because you thought, foolishly, that your country needed you, after arriving you realized that friends were what mattered, that man could not live by God and country alone? Achilles never wanted to go back, but if Wages and Troy and Merriweather and Wexler could all go back, he'd be there in a heartbeat, riding in an APC, blasting "Prison Sex" and "Welcome to the Jungle," wearing his battle rattle and a smile, this time sounding the drum in his chest. Bryant would feel the same way after a few weeks, especially if someone got hurt. Vodka and Wilson were focused. Daddy Mention talked a lot, like Merriweather; surely he was as reliable. He'd been through it once already. "You've got a good team," said Achilles.

Bryant grunted. "It's all wrong. It's just not the time for me. My girlfriend and I just got engaged two months ago. I know she's been with her ex. That's why I proposed, to make it real, to let her know I only want to be with her, and this hurricane fucked my shit up. I'm not even supposed to be gone for another two weeks. We were going to Vegas to get married, and now this shit. She probably only said yes because she doesn't expect me to make it back."

"Don't think about all that Jody shit. A lot of women wait. Mine did."

Someone shot off a couple of bottle rockets. Bryant ducked, dropping his weapon. He laughed when he saw the dim burst. "There is no God but MI6, and I am his messenger."

Achilles recognized the look of thin confidence. It would become real. The act would become the actor. Within weeks, Bryant would be a sheep in wolf's clothing. There was no other choice; like the saying went: *Don't bring a stick to a knife fight.*

More fireworks. Bryant said, "Now we're on the *Pirates of the Caribbean*."

Achilles considered that a fair description. He'd been trying to find something to compare the experience to but nothing came close. He'd seen photos of Venice with its proud statues and marble domes, an armada of floating castles. New Orleans looked as if it were floating—the porches were impromptu docks, the sidewalks sandbars, the roads rivers—but it wasn't. No. Nola lay facedown, suffocating under a blanket of water over which they now traveled as if it were a highway.

They drifted for blocks, sometimes brushing against cars. Residential streets felt like flood zones, but the business district was postapocalyptic. To travel by water between soaring office buildings with gaping windows—buildings so tall that even the boat's high-powered beams couldn't reach the roofs—frightened Achilles. The taller buildings all seemed to be leaning in, as if they would fall on the boat, if they weren't already touching at the top.

Passing between One Shell Square and Poydras Center, the scale of man's reach was now apparent, and they fell silent. Something plucked the water near them, then again. Another splash. They looked up but couldn't see anything. Bryant killed the engine, cutting all the lights, even the dim glow from the control panel. Achilles was tempted to tell him to turn it back on. In the last seconds as the light receded, it seemed the darkness was collapsing on them, bringing the buildings with it, crushing them. The rocking of the boat now felt exaggerated, and Achilles was aware of his knees swinging up and down as he struggled to maintain his balance. He heard the waters smacking against the boat, the cars, the skyscrapers, the entire earth in motion, nothing solid in sight. He tentatively stuck his hand out, feeling for the edge of the boat, and sat. Off his feet, rocking in the seat, he felt even less in control and reached for the rail to push himself up, but missed it and his hand grazed the water. He yanked it back to his chest, anxiously wiping it off. The boat bumped into a stationary object, nearly throwing Achilles over the side.

The darkness, his body rocking, his wet hand. The sound of the water, his heart, Bryant breathing. The moon moved out of the clouds and his eyes adjusted just enough to make out the water, the flat edges of the buildings, the cars hunched like turtles, buses like whales, and the water— a moving mirror, liquid glass that revealed only death, a great oily eye, black, inky, like a river of paint gently unrolling over itself, eating everything, one moment small crests reflecting the stars, the next moment small waves standing up and swallowing them. Brackish water slapped against a car and splashed back, and a thousand small drops arced like a bristling black cat. In the boat's wake water rose, scaling the side of a capsized bus, snaking along the windows, sketching a wet web over the door. A cloud passed above and drew a curtain across what little light there was, and it all became one: the water, the stench in the angry air, the rocking, the whole night fashioned after a noose. Tightening. He had never felt this anxious in Goddamnistan. Bryant flipped the light back on, pushing back the darkness just in time. Achilles had felt the waters would never recede, would never concede. The river would give nothing back; it would eat them all, inch by inch, winding around the city like a boa constrictor and pushing and pushing until everywhere it met only itself. Several minutes passed before he was breathing normally again.

When they passed under I-10/US-90, Bryant threw bottles of water to the people stranded above. They were met with thanks and curses, and one clear, plaintive voice asking, "Can't you give us a ride? Please?" Bryant ran his light along the bottom of I-90, trying to see where it ended. "Where does that road lead?" he asked Achilles.

"Across the river," said Achilles.

"Why don't they just cross the river? It isn't flooded over there."

"I don't know," said Achilles. He didn't know how to explain the roadblock that the Gretna police had set up to keep survivors out. Besides, those reports might not even be true. They were too senseless to be true, as was the alleged shooting on the Danzinger bridge or the vigilantes in Algiers shooting blacks. "Take me back."

"We have two hours left."

"Take me back now," said Achilles.

At Mrs. Delesseppes's, he tossed pebbles at Ines's window, pleading for her to come down or let him in, which she refused until he said, "Wexler isn't dead."

She came outside but remained a few feet from him, shaking her foot as she did when expecting bad news. He couldn't see them but knew there were two tiny indentations in her lower lip.

He showed her the photograph of the squad under the airplane wing together, headed out for R&R. "You're right. Wexler isn't dead."

"I heard that." She slapped the air.

"I didn't know how to tell you. I've wanted to say it since the day we met. My brother is in the morgue." He pointed to the photo. "My brothers," he said. "These are my brothers. All of them."

He pointed to Merriweather. "This is Merriweather."

He pointed to Wages. "This is Wages."

He pointed to Wexler. "This is Wexler."

He pointed to Troy. "This is Troy. He's in the morgue. I identified the body in Atlanta." He couldn't lie anymore, but the truth choked him. Unable to finish, his body slipped out of his control, all snot and tears, *What a fag. Don't be a sissy, Connie. How can you think under fire all pussy-lipped?* Is that all snot, that slimy skein stretching across his fingers, that salty, bitter assault on his tongue? Ines put her hand to her mouth and guided him to a seat on the porch stairs. He didn't talk Troy out of enlisting, he wasn't there when Troy needed him, he didn't do enough, he didn't even avenge Troy's death.

Ines hushed him, leading him into the house, his cries echoing in the living room and amplified by the hall. At last they were in the kitchen, where Ines gave him a paper bag to breath into, and Achilles spoke through the bag. "Dead, so many." He tried to say more, but all he could get out was that he felt like he was dying, needed to die, didn't deserve to live, why hadn't he died, why not him?

"I didn't do enough. I tried. I swear I tried."

A few bleary-eyed strangers appeared in the doorway to the kitchen. Ines waved them off. Achilles turned away and calmed himself.

"Oh, no." Ines squeezed Achilles's hand. "Achilles, baby, I know you did."

She was insistent on this point, and the more insistent she was, the worse Achilles felt, until a sob escaped him, and that look on her face, like the look on his mother's face the night Troy first came home, the look that meant she took his tears to mean something they didn't, and the tighter Ines held him the more he melted into her arms, and the more he did, the more he despised himself for crying, for failing his brother, for needing her so, for only doing his best, which his drill sergeant always said was just enough to get you killed.

"My poor Achilles. And they said there'd never be another. And Troy, poor Troy."

CHAPTER 20

O VER THE NEXT FEW WEEKS, ACHILLES INCREASINGLY REGRETTED opening up to Ines that night. The week before the funeral was especially hard. He hadn't told her much more that evening, stopping short at her reaction to learning that Troy was adopted. Now every day she shared a new tidbit about transracial adoption, prefaced always by "Poor Troy." Not in the motherly voice she used when his favorite team lost; it was a reassuring voice, the voice of heartfelt commiseration, a miracle seemingly reserved for women: the ability to care, really care, about events that affected others. At times this emotional proxy was soothing. When his frustration reached the limits of his expression—a shake of the head, a curse, a groan—she took over with a heartfelt sigh, a breathy murmur, a doleful moan, her profound empathy his release. Ines was his professional mourner, for which he was grateful until she began mourning his brother.

Poor Troy: *That's cultural genocide. It robs the black community of its most precious gift, children. Whites aren't equipped to socialize a black child. Even when raised by their own parents, black children raised in white neighborhoods have identity issues. They're never prepared for the real world. He doesn't know his heritage, or why people treat him as they do. It's like when you let a puppy sleep in your bed and lie in your lap and jump up and lick people in the face and everyone thinks it's so cute, then the puppy grows, can't fit in the bed, is too heavy for your lap, and scares people when he jumps. He's a sweet puppy inside, but everyone sees a ferocious beast.*

Achilles resented the unintentional comparison, the implication that his parents had been less than earnest in their efforts. Achilles and Troy had grown up in a mixed neighborhood, equal parts Catholic and Protestant, with some Jews mixed in. Their parents for years allowed Christmas without Mass and Easter without new suits. When Achilles entered sixth grade they even tried Kwanzaa, stopping on the third day only because of Achilles's protest. Though one had seven candles and the other nine, too many visitors mistook the kinara for a menorah, resulting in confrontations during recess when people asked questions he couldn't answer. After working hard to fit in during elementary school, he didn't want to blow it by showcasing his difference, or besting any of his friends at sports.

Everything was o.k. with his friends—until they met his mom, or asked about his real name, or met his brother. A sensation that it was only temporary hung over most relationships. Hell, one day he turns eight, the next he has a brother.

Achilles wasn't the only one put out by Troy's sudden appearance. Ken was equally distressed. Achilles and Ken would ride bikes and catch frogs and often eat at each other's houses. They were the best kickball players in the neighborhood and started a gang of two, their biceps emblazoned with magic marker tattoos—a one in a circle. Achilles preferred playing at Ken's house, because otherwise Troy would march out demanding to play and invariably didn't swing the bat fast enough or kick hard enough or run quickly enough, and someone would tease him, and Achilles would try to ignore the whole thing. This strategy worked until one afternoon when they were playing kickball and Troy missed the ball on the last play. Ken yelled "Stupid," feigning a slap. Troy flinched and ran, looking back over his shoulder at Ken while running at full speed until tripping over his own feet, scraping his knee on the hot gravel and yelping while he grabbed his right ankle like a baby. That was okay until Troy, seeing his mother in the window, started swinging, even though he only came up to Ken's chest. Even that was okay until Achilles, trying to break them up, accidentally elbowed Ken in the nose. Ken said, "He doesn't even like you. He's not even black."

As Achilles helped Troy to his feet, Troy's shirt slipped up to his shoulder revealing a crude circle with a one in the middle. Troy shot him a hateful look and placed his hand over the tattoo like it was a wound. While Achilles watched, Troy stormed into the house rubbing dirt into his tattoo and Ken slipped into the woods rubbing spit onto his. Troy told his mother that Ken had called Achilles *Black!* She gathered them to her lap and said they were his parents, *always!* When their father came home, he said, "We're your parents and love you both like you're our own children."

Troy persisted. "But Ken said Achilles is black and he's not my brother."

Their father placed Achilles and Troy on the corduroy couch, their legs grazing the carpet, and sat on the ottoman facing them.

"Your skin color doesn't matter, and never let anyone tell you otherwise. You could just as well be purple. In fact, here we're all purple from now on. Purple people eaters." Troy laughed. That was his favorite story. Their father rubbed their heads and explained that anyone who said race mattered was ignorant. But words weren't enough, and, soon after, their father started what Achilles and Troy would later jokingly refer to as the diversity action plan. As they liked to say, their father invented DAP.

Every Friday night for a month, following the airing of *Roots*, they ate at Happy Garden, wolfing down fried rice and egg rolls under the protection of red lacquer dragons. The owners' son, Sam, was in the same grade as Achilles and worked in the restaurant on weekends, busing tables and refilling glasses, when he wasn't watching ice skating on the TV behind the bar. Friday nights, Achilles's father escorted Sam, Troy, and Achilles to the skating rink. Troy found his wings. He flew across the ice but couldn't stop, always bearing down on his brother or father like an unavoidable accident. Achilles spent most of his time on his back. And Sam, for all his enthusiasm about watching, didn't actually like to skate, and moped around the ring like he was incarcerated, tiptoeing on his blades with an exaggerated T-rex gait. This playdate lasted three weekends before Sam, sensing that his imprisonment was terminal, decided to get to know his two cellmates by sharing his Chinese name and inquiring about their real names, their African names.

Their father sighed when Troy repeated the question. They had just dropped Sam at Happy Garden and now sat in the cab of their father's truck, Troy in the middle, his head barely at Achilles's shoulder. When Achilles met his father's gaze, he knew he'd intercepted a look meant for adults, the kind his parents gave each other when it snowed on a school day.

"Boys, your names are your names, your real names. And this isn't going to make sense now, but don't let other people's problems become your problems. You are better. Be the ones to beat."

Achilles knew his father hadn't meant that they were better than other people, only that they had to live by a higher standard: walk away from fights if you can, flatten the bastard if you can't, and remember that sticks-and-stones stuff. He understood that everyone was equal. But his father didn't understand that Achilles didn't start the fights, though he was always blamed for them, though even that made sense when he overheard a counselor explain, "Some kids are just more violent."

The more Ines spoke, the more he sympathized with his parents. He'd never considered how hard they worked to protect him from the world. Ines thought it hard for kids. It wasn't. How difficult, though, it must have been for his father, who knew he wasn't a purple people eater. Was it like a commander sending troops to an uncertain fate?

The Conroys hadn't made the world. Ines couldn't understand that, couldn't understand that his parents weren't to blame for how he felt when she uttered those two words, *Poor Troy.* She couldn't understand that Achilles was that puppy, nay, beast. Miles from home, he was just another black man, as he learned with Charlie 1. He loathed his birth parents intensely, more than he'd ever imagined it possible to detest people he'd never met and wasn't paid to kill. This animosity was invoked whenever she uttered those two words, as she did that morning of the funeral.

Achilles was in the bathroom wrestling his tie when Ines came in, stood behind him reflected in the mirror, and said, "Your friends had it so hard, especially poor Troy." She said it as she always did, like she'd realized only at that moment how bad Troy had it.

She wore panties and a bra, the high nylon waist and sheer legs giving her the look of a mannequin. When she fixed her bra, readjusting the straps with a snap, rolling her shoulders like a wrestler and drawing one fingertip and then the other under the underwire, the familiar, warm glow oozed through his stomach, and the hairs on the back of his neck danced as he imagined biting one gaping hole in the crotch of her pantyhose and her wearing them all day. His mouth watered until she added, "White parents who adopted black kids back then didn't have support groups."

Enraged, he couldn't complete the full Windsor he'd practiced all week, the knot Wages had tied in the wee hours, and that Achilles was therefore determined to wear that day. Ines tied it for him—a perfect plump triangle—and snapped at him when he took it off in the car because it felt too tight. She snapped again when she had to retie it in the cemetery lot. A few cars away, a little boy underwent the same ordeal, his mother straightening his tie and collar and lapels, every so often yanking his ears. Their eyes met. The boy looked scornfully at Achilles, as if to say, *Haven't you figured it out yet?* They ended up being only feet from each other in the procession to the grave. When the kid gave him another contemptuous look, Achilles stopped short of scratching his chin with his middle finger.

As the preacher spoke about the word of God becoming flesh, ashes becoming ashes, and Wages returning home, Achilles wondered who was left to bury. In every direction, swarms of black umbrellas huddled like compound eyes. Unlike at their father's funeral, where Troy and Achilles had silently flanked their mother, knowing it was their job to be strong, Achilles found it hard to hold back the tears. It was the first time he had cried since Lamont Jackson died. This felt like a service for all of them: Jackson, Wages, Troy. Though Ines often claimed he'd been emotional at the movie screening—*That's how I knew you were special*—he didn't recall feeling anything. Today, he couldn't look anyone in the eye. It had been like that for the past few weeks. Whenever he met a stranger's gaze, he wondered whom they'd lost, and if they'd find them. It was like traveling through a war zone, the faces of the survivors hungry, desperately searching, scanning passersby. People stopped him in the street, yelling or tapping his shoulder to get his attention, their smiles fading when he turned and they saw that Achilles wasn't their son, or father, or friend, or brother, or neighbor, or even the postman (he had been thrilled to bump into his postman at Lee Circle, even though he was a short, stocky, ill-tempered Episode 1 vet to whom he had never before spoken).

As the preacher droned on, Ines leaned on Achilles to adjust her shoes. She regularly shifted her weight from foot to foot. Her mother's feet were a half size smaller, as was her dress size. Ines wore a simple black sleeveless dress with a black shawl draped over her shoulders, camouflaging the zipper that wouldn't close. The dress fit like candy coating, threatening to crack every time she bent from the waist. Under other circumstances, he would have thought she wore it only to remind him of what he was missing, but he knew they were her mother's clothes. She adjusted her other shoe, leaning on him again, and he put his arm around her, pulling her close to warm the chill in his bones. They were trapped in the shade under an overhang, next to crypts stacked like the drawers of an oversized apothecary. Like most New Orleans cemeteries, all the tombs at Mt. Olivet were aboveground, walled in to prevent floods from washing the coffins away, and arranged like a grid with the graves geometrically aligned along parallel roads wide enough for cars to pass, and with a few alleys limited to foot traffic. It was arranged like a city, except everyone was dead, as were most of the people he knew.

The service was small. Achilles, Ines, Mrs. Wages, and Bethany's family were the sole attendees. Wexler hadn't come, as expected. They'd long ago agreed there was no need to attend each other's funerals.

He'd wanted Wexler to come, and maybe even Naomi. They could both meet Ines. They would see that he was different now, and Naomi would feel, well, he didn't know what she would feel, but she would see that he wasn't all bad. That would have meant telling Ines everything, but what did he have to lose? Never mind that Ines admitted coming back to the condo only because she felt sorry for him, couldn't bear another night at her mother's house, and was horny *that* night, *that one* night, *that one* night *only*. He brought that on himself, he knew, trying to laugh off his teary breakdown, blaming it first on the full moon, then on alcohol, then on hormones, meaning he needed sex. Never mind that they lived like roommates of necessity, like relocated refugees, she in the bed and he on the couch, knocking before entering the bathroom, eating only the food they individually bought, carefully refolding the newspaper like considerate travelers. He could live with that as long as he could live with her.

After Wages's service, they held no jazz procession because these now required a permit. The permit office had reopened the day before, but there was no jazz procession permit division. No one knew if it would be a new department, or considered a parade, or a protest. The last jazz procession Achilles had seen was blockaded by nearly twenty blazing police cars, the trombonist arrested for disturbing the peace. Ines, who was in the car with Achilles, called it an outrage and heartbreaking. Watching the pallbearers struggle to remain poised, the coachman soothing the horse—frightened by the sirens—with sugar cubes, and the mourners' expressions of disbelief, Achilles had agreed with her. At least she didn't say *I told you so.* Though he hated to admit it, Ines was right about transplants taking over. What else could you call it when people called the police to complain that a funeral march was disturbing the peace and squad cars arrived within five minutes? BK—*before Katrina*—you wouldn't see a cop in the Tremé until the day after a homicide. The coroner often arrived before the cops.

The memorial repast was held across the street in the vestry. He excused himself and slipped into the church next door, a small one, just a nave and an altar. The brick walls were intact, but the cupola and the cross that once stood high above it were no more. In their stead, one perfectly round hole opened to the sky, through which the waters had rushed in, fading the pulpit and rotting the dais. The stained glass hadn't yet been replaced, nor the clerestory windows, nor the side door, nor the pews, so there was no place to sit. It was dark, but he knew the church well. He and Ines attended every Sunday, because the diocese had decided that her church, St. Augustine, wouldn't be reopened because it wasn't *profitable*.

Twelve of Ines's friends, including Margaret, were staging a sit-in, but the future looked bleak for the congregation. Achilles felt sorry for them. He'd never considered that people might actually need their church, but recently worship was the center of everyone's life. Since returning to New Orleans, he and Ines had been to the same tiny, pewless church six times, gathered sometimes around a coffin, sometimes an urn, sometimes an article of clothing. He now understood that church helped people through tough times. It didn't matter whether he thought the stories ridiculous, or preachers ostentatious, or the diocese despicable for declaring a church unprofitable. He likened this revelation to the experience of someone who had never known they needed glasses, and once fitted with a pair realized that the clouds of green above the trees were comprised of individual leaves. The storefront churches weren't ridiculous. It never was about the building.

A whispering teenage couple dressed in a tux and formal gown ducked into one of the corners of the church. Seeing no one about, they started making out. Achilles knelt at the altar and thought about his father and mother, Troy, Merriweather, O'Ree, Dixon, Price, Wexler, Wages, everybody. He didn't know if that counted as prayer, but he thought, visualized them, concentrating until he saw Wages, felt Wages's hand on his head, heard Wages say, as he used to, *Let's get oscar-mike, Connie.*

The teens were still tucked into the corner, kissing in the shadow of a stack of coffins. He pretended not to see them. Achilles wanted to say good-bye to Mrs. Wages before he and Ines left. He found her at the grave. She was tall like Wages, her hair even redder. She had stood with her back rigid and stared straight ahead while the preacher spoke, her hands clasped to her chest as if in prayer, remaining a few feet from the coffin even as everyone filed by to touch it one last time. Shoulders rounded, head down, she was relaxed, as if all she wanted was privacy. The vault had been sealed, the flowers and drapery removed, and she stood with one hand on the cool cement wall, her other tracing the names carved into the stone.

Achilles softly whispered his good-bye. He wouldn't have recognized her from the pictures in which her hollow cheeks, combined with her broad forehead and large, piercing eyes, gave her an air of regency befitting an elder queen. Now, those cheeks red and puffy, the large brow furrowed, the eyes dull, called to mind his mother at his father's funeral and at the funeral yet to be, the inevitability of his own duty, and his failing as a son. Forced to look away, he was surprised to see two tombs with Kyle Wages etched into them. He had thought the infant was buried with Bethany's family. As if reading his mind, Mrs. Wages said, "His father. The first Gulf War."

They hugged, Mrs. Wages squeezing tightly, as a mother would.

"Thank you," she said. "I know how you all are about funerals."

Achilles nodded. How could he not have come? "Have you been to the house?"

"I know you stayed there, that you know it. I was hoping . . . I know it's terrible. I wanted his medals, but I couldn't go . . . up there."

Achilles held up his hands, halting her. "Of course. Where are you staying?"

She gave him the name of the hotel. "Thank you, Achilles. He said you were like a brother."

"Yes, ma'am. He was too," said Achilles. "I'll bring whatever I can find." Even as the tears welled up in Mrs. Wages's eyes, Achilles regretted the promise. He had no intention of entering Wages's house ever again. He saw Ines in the vestry entry and waved her toward the parking lot.

As soon as they were in the car, Achilles jammed the program into the glove box and Ines kicked her shoes off and rubbed her arches. "Here." He extended his hands, offering his lap, and they drove like that, he rubbing her foot with his free hand, her sighing. They went home to change and then on to the phone bank, which had been relocated to a donated office in the Quarter.

He wanted to be with Ines all day, every day, like it used to be, but she forbade it. She didn't want him volunteering because it was too *spooky*. "You spook me. I look over and see you all scarred up, like you were when I first met you, and it's like we're in a play with one act that keeps repeating itself. Besides, Charlie 1 needs you."

Ines didn't know that he hadn't patrolled with them for three weeks. During the day, he wandered around, or sometimes went back to the condo and slept. That day, he went to Wages's house as promised.

Wages's neighborhood had always been the opposite of Uptown, but never was that more evident than after the flood. Achilles hadn't even seen a rat, and no military checkpoints regulated traffic. There were a few Humvees parked on the median at major intersections, but they were empty, only reminders or warnings, which one he was never sure. He'd gone the first day that the city cleared enough debris. The little red duplex was tagged with the spray paint circle and cross and the number three, indicating that three bodies were found. He'd assumed it was for the neighbor. It had to be. He'd pushed at the swollen door and it fell over, twisting on one hinge. The smell was awful, the kind of stench that carved dread in your heart and set the pulse racing before you entered a building. From the porch he could see the furniture piled against the back wall of the living room, as if swept there by a giant broom. Each visit thereafter, he had remained on that porch like a man mesmerized by an abyss, remembering the last time he saw Wages, and all the questions he wished he had asked him. On each trip, he planned to go to the attic and salvage anything that Wages's mother might want because he knew it would eventually come to that, but he kept picturing Margaret and her book.

Margaret volunteered for the Eulogy Archive, a project dedicated to memorializing Katrina victims. Achilles had assumed Wages was okay and hadn't worried about not hearing from him. Many people were out of communication. But after he didn't hear from Wages for a couple weeks, he went to the archive. He found the ledger for the Wageses: Kyle, Bethany, and Kyle Jr. Trapped in the attic, Bethany tried to fit Kyle Jr. through the vent pipe. He got stuck and drowned shortly after she did. When Wages reached the house and found the bodies, he lay down beside his wife and shot himself. Achilles, knowing that, swore he'd never enter that house again, blue envelope or not.

This time he sat outside for almost two hours before going in. Stepping through the door he remembered his first night—the view from the rooftop across the street, the way he had been overwhelmed by the photos on the wall. Now, the walls were as bare as the ceiling, and both were scarred by a brown watermark. The plaster had fallen off in chunks larger than dinner plates. The stuffing was bursting out of the high-heeled shoe chair, and the sparkling strawberry settee was overturned. *I know, dude. Somewhere a seventies van is missing a bench seat. Don't come a-knockin'.*

When he finally worked up the nerve—he had promised, Mrs. Wages was depending on him—he dragged the dresser to the wall under the scuttle hole and climbed up to the attic. George, Wages's neighbor, had set up camp in the attic. He had a propane stove, flashlight, candles, sheets, a water bucket set up in the corner, and a row of empty two-liter bottles. He sat cross-legged with all his possessions arranged in a semicircle around him like acolytes. "What are you doing up here?"

"The ceiling's out in my half," said George.

"I mean why?"

"I couldn't stay in Houston. This here's my home. I mean the city. I mean Nola."

"I know what you mean," said Achilles. Indeed, New Orleans natives loved their city like nothing he had ever before seen.

"You going to put me out?"

No, Achilles shook his head. He'd never spoken at length to George, but knew he was in his fifties, had three adult daughters that each had at least one kid, and they all lived with him. Achilles took a seat on the overturned bucket, brushing aside the ants on his pants. A trail of them ran across the trusses at chest height.

"Where are your daughters?"

George looked down. "I don't know. You gonna put me out?"

"Stop asking that. No!"

Piled in the corner: winter clothes, photo albums, Bethany's jewelry box, and Wages's guns, all of which Bethany must have had the foresight to carry up to the attic.

"I didn't touch Mr. Kyle's stuff."

"I'm sure he appreciates that."

George was as good as his word. Wages's trunk was unopened, though it easily could have been. A few tools were scattered about: a small hammer, a few pipes, a pair of pliers, but no axe. He could see where Bethany had dug at the walls, pulled down the insulation, and clawed at the boards to get out. The vent was knocked out, the hole open to the sky, barely eight inches in diameter. No one could have fit through there. What did it take for Bethany to do that, to believe that the only chance to save little Wages was to send him up the air vent? She couldn't have known it would turn, he would get stuck, he would hear her drown, and he would soon after drown himself.

He beat the lock off Wages's footlocker. The cedar lining had separated from the tops and sides, and wood chips were mixed in with Wages's BDUS.

Achilles pocketed the Bronze Star for Wages's mom. The photos looked like watercolors. There was Wages's laminated birth certificate.

With a wife, child, and real job, Wages had always seemed so much older than twenty-six. The label had soaked off a bottle of Maker's Mark. Achilles's blue envelope was a cake of damp paper. He picked it up and it lay limp in his hand, unsalvageable. He didn't see anything Wages would want him to save, so he shut the locker back up. He sat on the floor, dropping his legs down the scuttle hole.

"Leaving already?"

He tossed the Maker's to George. George tossed it back. "Don't drink."

"Me neither, these days." Achilles tucked it in his belt anyway.

"I'll watch this stuff," said George.

He considered inviting George to stay in one of the empty condos, but that was probably a bad idea. Achilles nodded his thanks. As he lowered himself to the first floor, he saw a fingernail stuck in the wood between a rafter and the sheathing, and choked. The ant trail ended at the fleshy tip.

On the ground floor, he nudged one of the little cushions—though it was already dirty, he couldn't bring himself to kick it—revealing one of Bethany's épées. He decided to take that too. When he reached for it, he saw the starfish, with three legs missing. Soon his arms were full: the starfish, the épée, a pair of her Crocs, a somewhat salvageable photo of them at Disney, a cushion from the white couch, Wages's hunting hat, and the Maker's Mark. Though it smelled terribly, he put the hat on. If he had had a crazy straw, he would have downed the entire bottle of whiskey.

Achilles and Ines were at Harrah's Casino trying their luck at the quarter slots when Achilles felt someone watching him and looked up to see Wages tromping over. Without thinking, he scratched his right ear and looked skyward, meaning *stay away*. In Goddamnistan, it meant keep a safe distance and keep your eyes open, but it started in a bar outside of Fort Benning, where it meant stay the fuck away, *I'm on the prowl*. Wages didn't change his stride. He kept on walking without saying a word, passing close enough that Achilles felt the air move. That was the last he saw of his friend.

The last time they spoke at any length was the afternoon Wages tried to explain the Zulu warrior ritual to him. Achilles hadn't understood it at the time, but he thought he did now, after watching all the people wander through the streets of New Orleans like zombies, forever changed by what they had seen: the man in the checkout line sniffling as if he had a cold;

the guy at the corner of Canal and Camp Street, whose eyes watered when he was mistaken for someone else; the vet in the bar with Charlie 1 who suddenly teared up and didn't hide it, as if he didn't really know he was crying, sobbing, shoulders shuddering as if he were being electrocuted. How had Achilles become those men, not even realizing what was happening unless Ines was there to wipe his cheeks?

That was Wages's point. *Even if you don't remember, you never forget.* They were in the attic for that final conversation, Achilles standing and Wages stooping, putting his last bottle of liquor into his trunk, Achilles denying it when Wages said he understood that the Bethany incident made Achilles uncomfortable.

"No way," said Achilles. *Who am I to judge?* he wanted to say. I impersonated my brother, and spent time stalking ass when I should have shown Ines Troy's photos and asked for help. "I don't ever think about it."

"I do every day. That's the only time that shit ever happened. Ask Bethany."

Achilles shrugged off the suggestion.

"I'm seeing somebody to make sure it doesn't happen again. The guy's pretty good. He's a real old cat, a vet himself. Korea at fifteen, then Vietnam. He's seen it all." Wages closed the trunk and sat on the lid, patting the space beside him.

"I'm fine, dude."

"Whatever."

"That shit ends up on your record. What if you get the chance to go back? You'll be flagged as . . ." Achilles hesitated, trying to find the right word.

"I don't say I drink," said Wages. "If I did that, they'd blame the booze."

"You're still flagged."

"I've thought about that," said Wages. "I don't want to go back."

At the time, Achilles still wanted to go back, to be with his friends and brother. "We were kings."

"Don't look at me like I'm making bitch eyes." That hung in the air a moment before Wages continued. "I have so many fucking dreams it's a wonder I sleep. It's because we don't have any rituals. That's how the doctor explains it. That's why I have the dreams. I never had them over there. Know anything about the Zulus?"

"No."

"After a battle, the witch doctor takes you through the ritual so you can reenter society. The doctor says that because I didn't go through any ritual, my addiction to risk keeps me at the casino where my job is the perfect cover for my propensity to gamble." He said this last part through his nose.

"Are you going to quit?"

Wages lit a cigarette for emphasis, jabbing the evening air with the angry red eye. "I don't quit shit. I'm just telling you what he said. It explains my dreams and shit." As Wages explained it, the ritual involved a shaman helping warriors readjust to domestic life. "Even the Greeks had this problem. You have to get back into the community."

"Like redemption?" asked Achilles.

"Impossible," said Wages. "Redemption is out. Besides, it would mean we did something wrong."

Chaplain Weidman was known for his practical penance. Merriweather had admitted to once helping some friends steal a truckload of computers destined for an elementary school. His penance: do something nice for some children. Ramirez had admitted to cheating on his girlfriend, just to stay "free." His penance: If he loved her, tell her. If not, let her go. Jackson, a onetime cab driver, often claimed that his meter was broken on Friday nights. His penance: give the occasional free ride when he returned. "Is it like practical penance?"

"It's not a religious thing. It's more spiritual-like."

"Like confession?" asked Achilles. "Or therapy?"

"No and no," said Wages. "It's none of that, nothing like that at all. It's just a ritual, letting go."

"Forgetting?" asked Achilles.

"No!"

"Being forgiven?" asked Achilles.

"We didn't do anything to be forgiven for," groaned Wages. "We were hired to do a job. If there's a hell below, you know."

You're exasperated? Achilles wanted to grab Wages and shake him. "What the fuck is it then? Is it like Merriweather?"

"He just had bad luck."

"The kid," whispered Achilles. "The knife?"

"What are you talking about?" Wages stared at him. "You mean trying to dig that shrapnel out?"

Achilles listened quietly after that.

"Another person helps you let go of what you hold. Some tribes believe that the warrior is haunted by his knowledge. We call it memory, but really it's knowledge. We know how motherfuckers really are. The things we know, the things we've seen, the things we carry are a burden but also a gift, our gift to everyone else. We carry the terror so they don't have to. It's about getting back on even footing." Wages handed Achilles a sheet of paper. "It's my combat exam. Everyone should get one." He said this in an offhanded manner, as if he were referring to a platinum card with mileage rewards.

A single sheet of blue paper with two columns, it detailed his experiences on active duty. The left column listed questions: Number of times under fire? Number of times seen people hit? Number of times seen people killed? Number of times in direct danger of being killed? Number of times involved in ambushes or house-clearing missions? Number of times killed people? The right side held the answers. Under fire over 37 times. Seen people hit 40 times. Seen people killed at close range 76 times. In direct danger of being killed 32 times. Participated in 112 ambushes or house-clearing missions. Killed 12 people.

"I can't believe you don't dream about this shit."

Achilles couldn't believe it either, because he had been there for almost all of it.

CHAPTER 21

BEING HOME AFTER ACTIVE DUTY HAD BEEN A SUDDEN AND VIOLENT deceleration, like hitting the ground without a chute. He felt that way again now. Achilles had extensively researched suicide, looking for the clues he must have missed. *Talking about death, changes in sleep and behavior, heavy drinking, anxiety about losing control, and recent loss are all warning signs.* But that was how everyone he knew had lived for the past two years. *Loss of freedom, moving, death of a friend are all possible causes.* But that described how he'd felt that night in the church tower when he didn't shoot Pepper, and again in the morgue in the closet of ashes, and holding Jackson's hand. And he wasn't suicidal. The symptoms described everyone he knew, it seemed, so it was hard to guess what he should have noticed about Wages on the rare occasions when they had talked.

He wanted to believe there had to be an answer, be it prayer or the oneness of the universe, as the patchouli-scented museum lecturer said, but that worried him because if his soul was a universe, it was probably full of black holes. He even considered reenlisting, but had to admit he was no longer sure he was built for it. His body was slowing down. Mornings, he woke sore and stiff, like he had fought all night.

Some evenings he and Ines ate outside, talking constantly to beat back the silence. There were no birds, no cats, and little traffic, so every gap in conversation was deathly still. She told him about the people who came into the phone room to check the bulletin board for pictures of friends and family, the joys and disappointments, the near misses and the occasional happy connection. He nodded. Then he told her about his day. He hadn't been with Charlie 1 for a few weeks but kept in touch with them, and so knew that they were on house-clearing duty, going from door to door to alert the coroners. It wasn't hard to make up the details. He took a story from Goddamnistan, changed the complexions and the locations, and it sounded as if it happened blocks away, not in another country, in another time. The days and nights were long and restless, with Achilles facing the real fact that for the first time he had no purpose in his life and saw little to look forward to.

So he was especially heartened when about a week after Wages's funeral, Ines requested that he accompany her to Uptown. She obviously needed him to run interference, the presence of a guest ensuring that Mrs. D would be on the best of her worst behavior. Or maybe she wanted company, knowing that it wasn't safe to travel alone. Or, he thought, maybe Ines needed to show that she was maintaining this relationship, that she was stable.

Referring to her daughter as a "present-day Earl of Cardigan," Mrs. Delesseppes had once admitted that her concern for Ines's quixotic nature had abated only after meeting Achilles. "While a single enthusiast is a zealot, two, if loyal, committed, and pure of heart, could indeed a movement make." He took that as a compliment, even if Mrs. D remained reserved in his presence.

Whatever the reason, it was reassuring to be needed. When they arrived, the house was quiet. The shutters hadn't yet been replaced, but there had been a few feeble attempts to restore the property. Rocks lined the walkway to the house, potted plants either side of the porch. Though ruined by the rain and all the foot traffic to and from the phone bank, the yard was no longer a bog. It had dried out, and someone had raked it, combing the dirt in neat swirls. The sidewalk had been swept of the layer of silt that had coated it immediately after the storm, but it hadn't yet been pressure-washed and so it still looked dingy, as did the foundation, the whole house skirted in a ring of gray mud that would probably have to be painted over. During his first visit he had been so awed, he'd expected to have to pay to enter the house, or use a separate entrance, or take off his shoes. Before it had felt more like a museum than a home. In the place of the majestic home now stood this relic of a bygone era, broken down, chimney crumbling, shades drawn, falling in on itself, the house appearing to wait for the last occupant to leave so it could collapse on itself or break in two.

Inside was another world, but a different world from what he remembered. Taking in refugees had given the house life and purpose. Gone were the aprons, housekeeping dresses, and smocks. Gone were the tuxedoes and propeller ties and chef toques. Gone was the livery dressed as if to grieve. The staff wore casual clothes, which ironically only heightened the sense that the house was in mourning.

Margaret sat at the expansive dining room table, working on her archive binders, which she referred to sometimes as the Book of the Dead and other times as the Betrayed. Headphones on, bobbing her head, she hunched over the book, printing in long, fancy letters and attaching photographs. The lined journals were indexes, the binders memorials. Blank scrapbooks were stacked up like toast at one end of the table and completed scrapbooks lined up at the other end, their spines heavily creased, the covers bulging. She appeared to be on volume twelve. Each victim was allotted a two-page spread, with a bio, a photo, if available, and a memorial object. The table around her was piled with letters from relatives, obituaries, photographs, and trinkets: scraps of cloth, bandless watches, single earrings, lucky pencils, each one attached to a tiny tag upon which she had written the owner's name. He decided to bring the starfish. It was a hard job, and Achilles was glad to see her smile when Ines hugged her. They hovered in that room for a minute, and Achilles thought maybe it was just a routine trip.

"What are you listening to?" asked Ines.

"Juvenile."

Ines put on the headphones, tapping her foot for a few seconds, but not smiling. She gently replaced the headphones, smoothing Margaret's hair into place.

"It's one of those songs makes you glad your booty's hella big," said Margaret.

Ines put her hand on her knees and shook her butt, shimmying side to side, chanting a cheer. Margaret joined in the chanting.

"You look more like a sixties surfer chick than a stripper," laughed Margaret. "Doesn't she, Achilles? Doesn't she dance like a white girl? Doesn't she?"

Caught off guard by the unexpected laughter, Achilles smiled reluctantly, an expression that felt out of place with the gray in Margaret's hair, the lines around Ines's eyes, the table piled high with photos. Their sudden joy reminded Achilles that humans could adapt to anything. Morgue workers, the guys who moved the port-o-lets, spotters, soldiers, people could get used to anything, and if you couldn't adjust to it, you laughed about it, around it, or in it.

The change in mood was most palpable in the living room—*parlor, dear*—where Mrs. Delesseppes sat, the shelves bare, the lace doilies removed from the side tables, the genealogies no longer on the wall. Heavy curtains lined the windows and the light from the hallway sconces barely lit the room. As Ines had explained it, her mother suffered from a sudden morbid acuity of the senses, a ghastly sensitivity to sound, touch, and light that made it impossible for her to leave the house, except on nights hushed and solemn. She sat now with the latest edition of *The Delesseppes in the New World* open on the round antique table, which she had arranged before her chair, in easy reach, like a TV dinner table. It was the same armchair from which she had taken so many gleeful potshots at Ines in the past. Her hair was perfect, and she was dressed impeccably, her black skirt and red crepe jacket set off by wine-colored pumps and a matching scarf knotted around her neck in a big butterfly bow, all topped off with bright red nail polish and lively lipstick, none of which could camouflage her cheeks so gaunt and eyes so hollow. When had she last eaten? For the first time, Mrs. Delesseppes looked like a mother, an old and frail woman left with a house she no longer needed, no male heir to assume the mantle, and none in sight.

She merely nodded as Ines explained to Achilles why they needed to see him. It was a month after the flood, and Grandfather Paul still hadn't returned. Ines and Boudreaux had looked around, to no avail.

"In fact, Boudreaux is at this very minute returning from Shreveport, where he went to view unidentified elderly patients at LSU hospital," said Ines. "St. Bernard Parish was washed away. In some areas it looks like it never existed."

Ines sat on the love seat next to Achilles. It was the closest they had been in weeks, and he swore he felt static electricity arc between their legs, hers tinged orange and purple by the light filtering through the heavy curtains.

Ines said, "His house was completely gone. We've been to all the shelters and called every Red Cross tent, and now . . . we need to . . . we have to . . . go to the morgues."

"Go to the morgues," said Mrs. Delesseppes, hacking as if to clear her throat.

"Drink your water, Mama," Ines said gently before turning back to Achilles. "I know you're busy with Charlie 1, but could you take a few days off to come with me?"

"Of course," said Achilles. He wanted to add that it was no problem, but Ines cut him off, which was probably for the best. It shouldn't sound easy.

"And I'm asking you here at the house because it's a family concern, and we all had to agree before I asked you. Boudreaux isn't up for any more trips."

"That doesn't say anything about him. He's busy," said Mrs. Delesseppes. "I didn't mean to cut you off, dear."

Ines nodded and waited until certain that her mother was finished. "Harriet is in Atlanta and may never come back. That leaves me, and I don't want to go alone. Everyone—Mother, Boudreaux, and Harriet—agrees that it's okay for you to come with me, if you promise to never tell anyone we meet that we are related to Paul. Mother insists that no matter what, Paul be allowed his dignity and privacy."

Achilles nodded, adding, "That's easy enough."

"That's the difficulty. We can't go in and ask for him by name. We can't even claim the body." Her voice dropped to a whisper. "Mother has to know. She has to. So we have to go and look at everyone individually and . . ." At that point Ines choked up.

Achilles hugged her close, assuring her it was okay, that he understood better than she knew, and he would be glad to go as far and as often as she needed to.

"Achilles," said Mrs. Delesseppes.

"Yes ma'am?"

She had pronounced his name correctly for the first time, and now she stared as if seeing him anew. It was hard to believe he had once fantasized about her. Seeing Mrs. D now, gazing so intently, scrutinizing, he knew even given the opportunity, he could never have realized those visions. It would have been merely lust. He was ashamed that he'd thought of her as a MILF. He was no match for Ines, let alone someone of her mother's caliber. She'd opened her house to strangers in need after the flood, feeding and clothing them. Now she sought the truth, even if it was unbearable. Was this what his mother was thinking? Again it occurred to him that women were braver than men in ways he'd never considered.

Ines ran her thumbs under his eyes and hugged him close.

"Achilles," Mrs. Delesseppes said again. "I thank you for your time. I trust you will never betray the confidence this family reposes in you."

Once they were in the car, Ines took his hand and said, "Thank you. I know how much the time with Charlie 1 means to you."

That much she was right about. Charlie 1 *had* meant a lot to him.

As Troy put it, "Whiskey is for sissies, unless you drink it straight." As Merriweather always said, "The liver is a muscle, and you've got to exercise it." As Wexler said, "They have wine in church." As Dixon put it, "Agave is the nectar of the gods."

Charlie 1 was no different. As Vodka put it, "I'm aptly named." As Bryant put it, "Ain't nothing wrong a beer can't put right." As Wilson said, "If it weren't for rum, I'd have no fun." Daddy Mention's pride: a liver the size of Texas and a heart the size of Delaware, wink wink. With Charlie 1, Achilles's liver got plenty of exercise, and he was out of practice.

Mornings felt as if he'd fallen asleep with a kiwi fruit in his mouth. On his last morning with Charlie 1, when he had a terrible headache, pulsing and throbbing like a dick in the ear, they were patrolling Uptown, which meant driving and talking shit and looking for looters, which meant stopping anyone who wasn't white or accompanied by someone white, like the three black teens wading through the park across from Tulane. They had heavy New Orleans accents and wore mismatched clothing, everything two sizes too big. The kids claimed they were going to the aviary at the zoo to feed the birds, but no one believed them, even though they carried a large trash bag with a few cups of birdseed in the bottom. So they all went to the zoo and scaled the fence. Amazingly, there were three parrots in the aviary, singing as if they recognized the kids. One hundred yards upriver, volunteers hauled bodies out of the water. Gently looping adults to avoid losing limbs, carefully turning an infant like a log before scooping it up in an oversized fishing net.

Daddy Mention looked in the trash bag again and sniffed. "Crushed crackers, peanuts, breakfast cereal. Birds don't eat party mix. Where's the beer? You gonna watch the Saints' game?"

Everyone laughed except the kids.

Jokingly, Daddy Mention accused the kids of fattening up the birds in order to eat them. Their ages ranged from fifteen to eighteen, and they looked like tough kids, but immediately upon being accused of planning to eat the birds, the youngest one started running. Daddy Mention caught him before he'd gone even fifteen yards and marched him back. It's hard to run with your pants binding your legs like a geisha's kimono.

"Why you run?" asked Daddy Mention.

The youngest one shrugged. The oldest one started crying.

"Don't let 'em punk you. Come on now," said the youngest one, cutting his eyes. His skin was copper, almost reddish, and heavily freckled. His insolent attitude reminded Achilles of Pepper.

The oldest one continued to cry, sobbing in earnest. When he wiped his eyes, his pants fell down. The squad members looked at each other and stepped back. If he'd pulled a grenade out, Vodka or Daddy Mention might have jumped on him and it, but when he started crying, they backpedaled like he had AIDS. Dark skinned, with large, round eyes like a bird and hunched, heavy boxer's shoulders, he was too big to cry.

"Don't go bitch-eyed on me," said Daddy Mention.

His friends patted the older one on the back and hugged him, and told him to ignore it. The older one shook his friends off and said, "We're not animals." He picked up a rock and threw it, hitting Daddy Mention squarely on the forehead.

Wilson, Vodka, Bryant, and Daddy Mention raised their weapons and yelled at everyone to get on the ground. The kids dropped to their knees, hands up, except the crying one, who remained standing and threw another rock. Achilles had to hand it to him: he was brave. Stupid, but brave.

Daddy Mention said, "Put it down."

"We're not animals."

"Put it down, son." Daddy Mention stepped closer. His finger was outside the trigger guard, but Wilson and Bryant had their fingers on their triggers. Daddy Mention yelled, "Zigga, put it down."

Wilson and Bryant glanced anxiously at each other as they stepped back. Vodka echoed Daddy Mention, his voice steady. "Put the rock down, man. It's going to be okay. What's your name, son?"

From where they now stood, Wilson and Bryant would shoot each other. Achilles, who stood between them, backed out of their line of fire.

Vodka echoed his question. "What's your name?"

"Terius," said the older one, snot dripping from his nose. He identified his younger friend, the one who had tried to run, as Dooley. The third kid was named Jonas. "We're not animals."

"You're acting like it," said Daddy Mention. "Look at you."

"You need to get that gun out of my face," said Terius.

"You don't make the rules here, kid, this ain't *The Corner*," said Daddy Mention.

"You need to get that gun out of my face," said Terius.

"What's wrong?" asked Bryant. "You want lipstick on it?"

Terius threw the rock at Bryant and missed.

Daddy Mention struck Terius in the temple with the butt of his M16, dropping the kid like spilled water. When Dooley, the young one who resembled Pepper, tried to run again, Achilles hit him between the shoulder blades with the butt of his rifle, in the temple after he fell down, and once in the face to shut him up.

Achilles would have struck him again had he not seen movement on the other side of the park near St. Charles. It was a man pushing a stroller. Achilles scanned 360 degrees—the woods, the parking lot, the windows—catching them all in the rifle's crosshairs, finger at the ready. At the riverside end of Audubon Park, known as the Fly, they were still fishing someone out of the water. Farther away, a woman on a second-floor porch beat a rug. On a side street, two men were stacking ruined furniture on the sidewalk. He scanned again, to be on the safe side, breathing steady. Kids were often a diversion to distract soldiers from the real threat, like a sniper. By the time he'd scanned the rooftops a third time, the kids were handcuffed with plastic ties.

Watching them struggle to walk and hold their pants up with their hands cuffed, Achilles wondered if they normally wore such oversized clothes or if they were wearing what they could find.

"I think you broke his jaw," Wilson whispered to Achilles. "Collateral damage. We have to explain that."

Vodka shot Wilson a stare that shut him up.

"Is it collateral damage when someone attacks you? I don't think so," whispered Bryant.

Daddy Mention griped, suddenly pissed. Speaking under his breath to Achilles, he said, "I'm in this swamp tagging kids when I'm supposed to be on furlough. Instead, here I am busier than a beaver at midnight on payday with this shit."

"Where's Darkwater when you need them?" mused Bryant.

Because the Humvee couldn't hold everyone, Achilles offered to catch a ride with someone else. Bryant wanted to stay with Achilles, but Achilles wouldn't have it. He wanted all of them gone.

Bryant looked around nervously. "You sure? I don't know if it's safe out here on your own, double-solo."

Bryant was referring to the fact that if Charlie 1 left, they took their weapons. "I'll be cool," said Achilles.

Vodka, riding shotgun, slapped the door. "Let's go." Scanning the horizon, he added, "He's survived worse."

"He could always ride on top," said Bryant.

Vodka, Daddy Mention, and Achilles shook their heads.

"No one rides on top," said Vodka. "Let's get oscar-mike, B."

"Hoo-ah!" they yelled.

Achilles waved until they were gone, already knowing it was farewell. The birds called him back to the aviary, their caws sounding like someone frantically crying *Come! Come!* He spent a few hours there, feeding the birds and listening to the river, trying to forget the tension that had swept through his body when he found himself looking at people through a scope again, automatically arresting his breath as he rested the crosshairs over their hearts.

A patrol boat coasted by, the crew of three soldiers unconvinced of Achilles's status even after seeing his badge and military ID. The driver, a blond kid, radioed Charlie 1 for confirmation. Achilles imagined all three of them facedown in the river, turning lazily with the tide, the water crimson and hazy. He'd been mistaken for a looter six times that week alone. He sought out their eyes, but none could hold his gaze. The driver and navigator were preoccupied with the radio knobs. The gunner stood at the edge of the boat, his glances darting from Achilles, to his mates at the radio, and back to Achilles's hands, as if Achilles might produce a weapon they'd overlooked when they frisked him, like he had an SAW snookered up his ass. By the time the boat left, he was taking shallow breaths, the exhalations longer than the inhalations. He didn't see them leave. He knew they waved. He knew that he had waved in response automatically, which pissed him off. He knew they'd apologized halfheartedly—*Can't be too careful. You know that. There are some real animals here.* He was still rigid with anger. He'd never been frisked before Katrina. For a moment, he'd wanted to jump on the gunner and bite his nose off, swing the M60 on the other two, spice them up. Had Vodka left him a gun, he might have.

On the walk home, he saw the postman again at Lee Circle, and they hugged like old friends. He learned that the postman was named Chester, had two children who were both safe, and that his parents had been lucky enough to evacuate early. Though it was only the second time they'd exchanged more than a nod, Achilles and Chester chatted at the base of Robert E. Lee's statue until its shadow passed them, and for hours after, leaving only when the curfew approached. Even then, Achilles was sad to see him go.

CHAPTER 22

NO DILBERT CARTOONS HERE. THE MOST COMMON SIGN READ MORTUI Vivis Praecipant: Let the dead teach the living. The slogan was found in mobile refrigerated trucks, tents, walk-in coolers, and airplane hangers throughout the Gulf region, as well as over doors throughout the entire town of St. Gabriel—once a leper colony, and again a destination to be avoided at all costs. Often, there were more people attending the dead than helping the living. At each location a hodgepodge staff was assembled: coroners, pathologists, forensic pathologists, medical records technicians, forensic anthropologists, fingerprint specialists, funeral directors, medical examiners, crime scene investigators, forensic dental experts, dental assistants, x-ray technicians, mental health specialists, computer professionals, administrative support staff and security, all wearing badges reading Morgue Ops.

They worked out of warehouses, hangars, gymnasiums, schools, tents, and refrigerated vans. Webs of orange and yellow extension cords connected humming diesel and solar-powered generators, and one lot even had three kids running a hand crank. At some remote locations, autopsies were conducted outside, the sun being the only available light. Achilles had never been anywhere where there were so few families available to claim their dead loved ones. It was a massive effort to identify people whose bodies were often damaged beyond recognition, and often far from home. How had Mabel found Dudley? Achilles found himself wondering about Levreau, Detective Morse, Bud, Lex, Blow, and the Harpers. No one deserved this.

Ines and Achilles's first stop was a temporary morgue in an old basketball court. Ines was reserved, her eyes darting at the tables for quick peeks and then back to the floor. After each table she shook her head slightly and breathed *No*, the surgical mask bellowing. Remains were arranged in descending order of completeness. The first few rows had entire bodies, then torsos. The last two rows held hands, feet, a head in a Styrofoam cooler. There were binders with photos of personal possessions. Ines flipped through them quickly, not knowing how Paul usually dressed or if he always wore a pocket watch or what his wedding band looked like. Achilles expected to make quick work of this, planning to cover one side of the room while she covered the other, but Ines held him back, squeezing his fingers numb. Other people, individually and in groups, moved about the room with the same slow shuffle, as if they had to will themselves to take each step.

The next two morgues were the same. People were slow to enter and quick to leave. Afterwards, clustering around their cars, some huddled in prayer. Others whispered and smoked, sighing between puffs, guiltily relishing the temporary reprieve. At the end of each stop, Ines bummed a cigarette. Achilles offered to buy a pack.

"I don't even like the taste. I'm just doing it because . . . it makes me cough."

Their fourth stop was a former convenience store, the large glass refrigerator doors suited for this new role. Of the overhead signage, only the billboard frame remained, but the name was clearly stenciled on the gray stucco: Victor's Bait, Booze, and Beer. A few feet from the door, Ines vomited into her hand, retching loudly. People passed as if nothing was happening.

Rubbing her back, he suggested they stop. He was hungry anyway.

Ines shook her head. "I promised Mother." She repeated it several times as he led her back to the car, bearing her weight. He bummed a cigarette and they sat on the hood, sharing it. They were only a few blocks from the point where the industrial canal levee had failed. In some places the land was flat, as if nothing had ever been there. On one block, two rows of houses remained facing each other, the fronts of the homes intact but the backs gone, like false fronts on movie sets. Bulldozers pushed houses out of the street, in the process sometimes damaging houses still on their foundations.

"If Katrina didn't get you, Nagin will," said Ines, referring to the mayor. "I don't want to do this. I wouldn't want anyone to see me like that. Just an arm. A leg. Your head in a fucking Styrofoam cooler, the cheap kind, not that you need a Coleman if only your head is left. Listen to me. I sound like you, don't I?"

Achilles didn't see any way to answer that safely.

"Afghanistan was different," said Ines. "I once walked into a house to meet a group of women about to start a school. They were all there, all five, but dead, shot where they sat, except the leader. She was raped and strangled. I cried over that for a long time. But this is even worse, to enter each room hoping not to find what I've been sent to look for." She ground out the cigarette. "Oops, littering," she chuckled morbidly. "Let's get this over with."

"I'll run in."

"You don't mind?" she asked.

He walked off. She looked surprised when he returned so quickly, and he made sure to shake his head as soon as she saw him.

"It's not a big place," he said.

"Are you sure? I should have gone with you. I want this to be done."

"There's only so much you can do in one day. Just because he's not here today doesn't mean he won't be here tomorrow." He searched for the word to describe it. It wasn't a mission, or recon, or a task. It was a process. "It's not like a job. It's a promise, but not one you make or break in one day."

She leaned against the car, glum and listless, tracing the air around the hood ornament with her fingers.

"If I were in there or there," she said, pointing at the morgue and then at the river, "all I'd want is another cigarette, a beignet, a bad joke, another five minutes with you."

"I'd want to be with you too. Cold dead fingers, remember, cold dead fingers. That's what I want now, and I'm not there or there," he said, pointing as she had. "I'm here, and I'll go to every morgue in the Southeast for you."

He reached for her hands, and she pulled away the dirty one. He held out his palm and waited.

"That's gross."

He waited until she offered her other hand, then pressed them both to his face and kissed every fingertip, watching her eyes. He recalled the movie screening, when he had first noticed how beautiful her eyes were. His stomach flittered, then grumbled.

"Was that?"

He nodded.

"Are you hungry?" she asked, looking baffled.

He took a chance. "Very!"

"Oh my god, Achilles," said Ines, collapsing in laughter. "Actually, me too."

As he was nodding off that night, she led him to the bed, where they slept together, too tired to do anything else. But to be in her arms, to hear her breathe . . .

He awoke the next morning as he had the past few weeks, tired. The dreams were vivid, bigger than memories. He could deny memories, ignore them, like running with a sprained ankle, or how you sometimes shit yourself but kept shooting, or held your breath while searching a dead guy's pockets. He tuned memories out as he had tuned out the pleading.

Almost everyone they had dropped off for interrogations pled for release. Merri said the more they pled the guiltier they were. Wages said the opposite. Either way, you didn't need to be fluent in Pashto or Persian or Arabic or what-fucking-ever to know what they were saying: Allah, love, please, kids, wife, daughter, mother, father, son, brother, cousin, please, please, please. *Cousin, no! Brother, no!* They would say when they saw Achilles or Merriweather. *No, Cousin! No, Brother!* Sincere, imploring, beseeching. Sheepishly acknowledging the wet crotch, sweat, red eyes, pointing to the sky, especially the dark ones, as if their common skin was a badge of kinship.

He had heard none of it, not a word.

The dreams, though, were alive, like a switch from black and white to straight in your face 3D, from the peep show to the harem. He remembered the IED, holding Jackson's hand. But in his dreams he sees every wound and gash on Jackson's face—the abrasion under his eye, the cut on his chin, the missing right ear—and that his left hand has only two fingers on it, like the little girl with the burned arm. He sees Merriweather on the gurney, his foot attached by a thin white tendon. He sees Merri's kid, looking back to make sure he isn't being chased, running almost fifty yards before bleeding out, mouthing "Papa." And that look of confusion. He probably hadn't even understood why he was suddenly so tired. He remembers Troy saying, more than once, "I could have come alone."

Achilles, arms sore as if he'd been doing pull-ups all night, made his usual breakfast times two: protein powder and bottled water, three energy bars, and a spotted apple he scored from Charlie 1. He arranged the disaster zone special on a tray, fanning the energy bars out like an asterisk, and tiptoed back to the bedroom, but Ines was not in the bed, nor the bathroom, nor any place in the apartment. He found her on the roof, wearing a pair of blue fuzzy slippers with horns.

"My old favorites. The rest were in my mom's basement. All ruined. That little skirt you liked, my spiked heels." She listed a few other items, such as her velour tracksuit, his personal favorite. Under it, her tits felt so soft and furry.

"The list keeps adding up."

"Speaking of that, you're counting at night. Slow and deliberate. You go to the forties and start over. Repeatedly. You went to 112 once, but only once."

He asked her to write the numbers down.

"Who says I'll be sleeping with you again?"

"No one. I expect you to be awake. If not, your findings will be unreliable," he said in his best military voice.

She laughed. "I'm sorry about yesterday."

"I understand. I mean, I can go alone."

"I don't want to make you go through this."

"Ines, I'm used to it. I saw it every day for two years." *And I've done it for the last year.*

"This isn't your battle." She stared as if considering for the first time the full depth of his experiences. "Listen to me."

He hoped she would allow him to go alone, to be useful, to do what she couldn't do for herself. He also wanted to use an overnight trip to a distant morgue as an excuse to be gone long enough to make one last trip to Atlanta to take care of Pepper. But Ines insisted on accompanying Achilles to the morgues, even if she didn't go in. Achilles argued this point, claiming she would be more useful at the phone bank.

"So you're saying that because I can't go all the way, I shouldn't go at all?" asked Ines, her face red. "This is man's work, is that what it is?"

They finally agreed they would put up flyers with her grandfather's picture and return to the morgues the following day. The city was dotted with community bulletin boards where people had posted photos and notes. Their first stop, on Canal, was near the substation where Achilles had filed the MPR. Wanting to check on Morse, he felt imprisoned by his lies. For the first time he thought of them not as lies, but omissions, which were somehow worse. Lies filled space, creating a livable history, while omissions left him feeling incomplete, like phantom limbs.

That was certainly how everyone who posted these flyers must have felt, incomplete without these dogs, cats, a ferret, relatives. Ines touched each face, reading the names. Yearbook pictures, six mug shots, vacation photos, two boudoir shots, photo booth strips, prom pictures, wedding pictures, Xeroxes, color copies, group photos with one head circled, a mother with two children in her lap and both kids' heads circled, a Santa photo, a Halloween scene, a bar mitzvah. The lettering was typed, printed, block print, cursive, English, Spanish, French, German, Russian, and, at the very bottom, labeled in crayon, an old man in a wheelchair holding a teddy bear, each wearing a birthday hat. Like most in this morbid collage, they are smiling. Written in crayon underneath: *Lester Newman. Last seen at St. Louis Cathedral. Answers to Papi.*

"You told me they have a funny sense of humor, but this is cruel. I'm telling them what I think." She had her phone out before Achilles saw the flyer: a picture of him and Troy taken three years before at the Baltimore water park, before basic and infantry training, before jump school, before their tour of duty. Troy smiles, the gap in his front teeth prominent, his green eyes razors in the sunlight. He wears flip-flops and shorts, no shirt. It was hot that day, or so they'd thought. Against Troy's broad shoulders, the swim towel around his neck is a mere cravat. He has hair. Achilles wears a DC United soccer jersey. His hair is shorn close to his head, but it's clear he has a widow's peak. His right hand is on Troy's shoulder. His flip-flops are in his left hand because as soon as his father says, "Got it," Achilles and Troy will hit the water slide. Achilles's eyes are hidden behind Ray-Ban aviators, the glasses they thought all military men wore, and they smile as if they've won the lottery. At the bottom of the flyer there is a website, a toll-free number, and a local number.

"It's okay," he croaked, the paper trembling in his hand. "That's what they want, for you to call."

But there was no consoling Ines. "I don't get this soldier's humor! I just don't! Who is this anyway?" she asked, jabbing Troy's face. "It's got to be his idea. He'd be the only one with the photo, wouldn't he?"

Achilles nodded.

They put up a few more flyers, the mood growing heavier at each stop. The Circle Food Store, Jackson Square, the French Market; every bulletin board held at least one flyer with Achilles and Troy. Each time, Ines jabbed Troy's face, complaining. "Who is he? The one who tells the jokes? I know there's always a so-called joker. Who is he?"

"Troy."

"Oh baby. I'm sorry. I thought he looked familiar. That's poor taste." She cradled his face. "Doesn't Charlie 1 know?" She sighed heavily. "Didn't you tell them?"

Achilles shook his head.

"Okay, baby, I understand. I would be polite, of course. I wouldn't even tell them you saw it. But Troy is dead, and to keep bringing it up is painful. Okay?"

"I'll take care of it." Achilles dropped Ines off at home and spent the afternoon removing all the flyers he could find. He counted forty-three at the end of the day, forty-three copies of the photo he originally brought to New Orleans, enlarged so that Troy's face was about the exact same size it had been on Levreau's flyer, not life-sized, but close enough. He went to the website and saw the same picture there, and a few more. The website was hosted by a company that charged a fee to create and post these flyers. Must have been a good business, but never one he'd want to own.

The next morning while dressing, he asked Ines, "Did your grandfather, I mean Paul, have any distinguishing marks?"

"I'm going with you."

"I'm only asking."

Ines looked doubtful. "I'm going with you. But no. And you can call him my grandfather now. I guess you forgive people, or get closer to them, when they die. Did you feel that way about Wages and Troy?"

Achilles nodded.

Ines said, "I shouldn't have brought that up."

She was right. He was closer to them all in death, recalling things he had forgotten. When Ines went to the bathroom, Achilles left. It would be easier to move through the morgues without her.

He carried his mother's flyer in his pocket, obsessed with Wages's ritual theory, with his certainty that until you let the shit go, it ate your life. Wages was on his mind because Ines had stayed up late enough to write down his numbers: 37, 40, 112, 76, 32. *That's a hell of a combination,* she had joked. But it was no mystery. It was the list from Wages's combat report. He was counting in his sleep, confirming Wages's numbers.

Morgue Ops personnel were like spies. Prohibited from discussing work, they even removed their badges upon leaving the facilities, the logic being that the general public should never identify them as morgue workers. Alone, flashing his military ID, Achilles was one of their tribe. Faced with someone who didn't eye them like lepers, they gladly explained the process to him. The body, or what's left of it, is moved through stations.

A forensic pathologist looks for deformities, scars, tattoos, unique dental features like crooked teeth. They are fingerprinted, x-rayed, dental x-rayed, and DNA samples are taken. Then an autopsy, then they are embalmed and shipped if already identified. If not, they are warehoused for people like Achilles and Ines to identify. When only bones remained, they are shipped to the forensic anthropologist. A DNA test is usually reliable, but if the body's been underwater too long, bacteria start breaking down the proteins, making them harder to identify. A full body x-ray is helpful because it reveals shrapnel, broken bones, pacemakers, and the like. When you have only limbs, it's tough.

"The reality," said Sergeant William Bose, "is that most of these parts won't be identified." Bose had just returned from a tour in Iraq. He had been off only a month when they assigned him to the mobile morgue. He was a bear of a man with a friendly smile, and when Achilles told him what he was doing, and that he was military, Bose led him to the back room so he could take a look at a few of the recently delivered corpses. Achilles was astounded at the number of loose limbs. Apparently drowning hadn't accounted for a majority of the deaths. People had died when weakened buildings collapsed on them, from falls, and many of exposure.

"No one to sue," said Bose.

That was true. The death toll on the Gulf Coast since Katrina was higher than the U.S. casualty rate during the first two years in Afghanistan.

"What's the difference between killing people and letting them die, except one's cheaper?" Bose said, looking pissed, "Man, it's the most heartbreaking thing I've ever fucking seen, and I've seen shit. And I'm not saying this just because you're here, but you know damn well if this were Malibu or Key West or Galveston, they would have evacuated these people in a heartbeat. It's some dark shit when your country lets you sit out on a highway in hundred-degree weather and die just because you're black and poor. It's some fucked-up shit, man. It ain't a natural disaster when a manmade object fails." Bose was red in the face, stuttering, trying to explain the feeling of witnessing destruction on a scale usually reserved for wartime. "Sorry. I have to vent twice a day."

Achilles understood what he meant, and wished Ines were there to hear. "No problem." They were alone in a smaller room where bodies and limbs were held until transferred to the main room.

"So today's your lucky day. Savor it, brother," said Bose.

"Tomorrow it only gets worse," they said in unison.

Achilles stopped at the sight of a gnarled hand across the palm of which ran a scar similar enough to the one he had given Troy on that birthday.

"Oh shit, man," whispered Bose. "I'm sorry. Sit down." He picked up his phone. "I need some paperwork back here."

Achilles was finished within fifteen minutes. The call was the hard part. Holding the flyer in his hand, he dialed his mom using Bose's phone, wondering if she was at her green desk, her glasses on. But she was in town, at the market buying portabello mushrooms, treating herself to her favorite meal. She liked that market because the farmers who came in from over the hill were real farmers, she said, "Straw in their teeth and cow patties on their boots." His mother shopped at the farmer's market less frequently now that the beltway bimbos had discovered it, driving the prices up.

He heard her occasionally offer a cheery hello to one person or another, sometimes followed by sucking her teeth. "That was Geraldine, the one who dropped that dog off in a cornfield in Shippensburg and told her kid it ran away. That was Maxine, the one who thinks she's special because her car parks itself. She has a basket full of carrots, lettuce, and tomatoes. She shops here for salad. Isn't that cute?" He couldn't tell her now, alone in public, surrounded by people she despised. Yet he knew that if he didn't tell her now, he never would. "Mom, I have bad news."

Hearing "Mom," she fell silent. "I knew. I felt it for a long time."

When the call ended, Achilles was sickened by the sense of relief he felt. They had last spoken a month ago, the day before Achilles lost his cell phone pulling the wheelchair-bound man out of the water. He'd made a promise to call her at least once a week. It seemed to be enough. Over the past few months, her mood had been resigned, and somber. It was as if she was at last mourning. She had apologized. *I shouldn't have given you those papers. It was your father's idea, and I went along with too many of his ideas when he was alive. I didn't need to do it when he was dead. Last wishes aren't always best wishes.*

From the morgue straight to the condo. When Ines found him packing, he said, "A guy from my unit, a funeral."

CHAPTER 23

WAGES HAD WANTED HIS POSSESSIONS RETURNED TO BETHANY, especially his cross. He'd said, "If I get fucked, take it to my wife when it's all over. I don't want some sergeant in a lizard suit wheeling up to the door in a blue LTD, followed by a box a week later. Promise me, *Conroy*."

Achilles was Connie, Troy was Conner. At times like that, they were *Conroy*, and Wages had spoken to them as if they were one person, as if he assumed they would both survive. Achilles had always expected that both he and Troy would make the trip to New Orleans if anything happened to Wages, but he knew it would be Troy who actually placed the cross in Bethany's hands, Troy who comforted her, wrapping her in his long arms, resting his cheek against her hair and murmuring consolations in a voice so deep she felt it more than heard it. Later, when Achilles found himself on that white couch because it was Wages delivering Troy to him, Achilles had repaid that kindness by wondering more than once if delivering the cross would have been his ticket out of the living room. He had not wanted it, or wished it, only wondered. Still, the thought nagged him. How he wished he had stayed home. Wages, Merriweather, Wexler—how he loved them, but how he wished he had stayed home. It would have been better had he not gone at all.

He would be supervisor by now, or at least night shift manager of the ripping room, spending his nights among buzzing saws and idle chatter, the sweet smell of sawdust underfoot. He and Janice would have come back to town, with little Keelies in the backseat, and helped his mom decorate the house for Troy's return. Otherwise they'd only come home for the holidays, like Turkey Day. It had been almost a year since he left home, and again Thanksgiving was right around the bend. He could have been driving these same roads but with Janice in the passenger seat instead of Ines, who'd insisted on accompanying him this time.

Achilles assented, suspecting he'd be dropping her off as near as Mississippi and no farther than North Carolina, the exact location depending on when he worked up the nerve to tell her the truth. He had to tell her now, she who insisted on being there for him because he had been there for her, there for Troy, there for Grandpa Paul, there for Wages's mother.

He couldn't tell her in Louisiana, amid the wreckage. By traveling north and avoiding the Gulf Coast, Achilles hoped to avoid much of the destruction, but the damage was as extensive far inland, as upsetting as it had been when he was driving down from Atlanta, when he had wished someone was with him. Now he wished he was alone. Ines sat in silence, sometimes pressing her hand to the glass, shaking her head dreamily, other times looking straight ahead. She kept her sunglasses on at all times. Eden Isle, Slidell, Picayune, Hattiesburg—all wrecked, traces of damage vanishing only when they reached Meridian, almost two hundred miles away.

He couldn't tell her in Mississippi, she slept through it. He wanted to tell her at the rest station north of Atlanta, but she looked so peaceful feeding the ducks. He couldn't tell her in South Carolina; she was upset by the sudden ubiquity of the Confederate flag.

They'd hit snow north of Charlottesville, and he had to concentrate on driving. Meanwhile, Ines was enthralled by the scenery, the snowbanks, white fields, and bejeweled trees, cooing at a setting that took her back to her college years. It was the first time she'd smiled during the entire trip. He couldn't tell her then. The weather reduced their pace to a crawl at times, putting them behind schedule so that it was sunrise by the time they reached Maryland, where she noticed the plates and, having never been to the DC region, called it a real metropolitan area, as she could tell by the variety of license plates.

As they neared his house, Ines looked out over the carpet of subdivisions and remarked that she'd never taken him for a literal suburbanite. He assured her he wasn't, even as they passed the Kmart and Wal-Mart and Target, the outlet malls and strip malls. He disowned it all, explaining how it spread around them like fungus. But she oohed at a couple of the houses, couldn't get over how clean it all looked, imagined it to be the safest place on earth. They reached the zenith of the highway overlooking his town, and he could see the streets, black ribbons in the white snow. He admitted once taking that as evidence of a grand design.

"It does look kind of like a section of a brain."

"I thought so too. Once."

"Once?"

"A long time ago. When I was a kid."

"That wasn't so long ago."

It wasn't, but as they approached the house, it felt like part of another lifetime. "Here we are. It's not much," he said, pulling up the drive.

Trees, seclusion, red shutters; she loved it all. "It's like Santa's workshop."

Unlike Santa's workshop, the house was quiet. He hoped his aunts would be around to act as a buffer. But when he knocked and let himself in, it was clear they weren't there. The first thing he noticed was the smell of Pine-Sol, bleach, and ammonia. Ines used only natural cleaning products; by comparison, his house smelled strongly of chemicals. The odor that once signified clean was as alien as the scent that assaulted him in the back of taxicabs. His mother was in the recliner, where she'd been sleeping for quite some time judging by the cushion lines imprinted on her cheek. At least she wasn't wearing her backpack.

"Ines, this is my mother, Anna Conroy."

His mother smiled sleepily. "She's so beautiful."

Ines would see that he was poor, but that was the least of it. Whenever Ines described people spending their entire life wrapped up in their own little world, never leaving home, never getting an education, Achilles thought of his mother. He imagined every possible reaction except what he received. *At last we meet. I've been waiting for this moment. Finally. I've heard so much about you.* They exchanged lines as if they'd rehearsed for weeks, and it was at last opening night. His mother put on the kettle. Achilles wanted to tell her that Ines bought her teas from a special shop run by some Asians—*Chinese people*—but Ines graciously accepted the bagged tea, and the Ritz crackers with squares of American cheese melted over them.

Under the pretext of showing him Troy's uniform, his mother marched him off to the back bedroom, stepping over the flowers lining the hallway. The uniform was in good order, all the medals properly aligned. The recruiter had helped with that.

Achilles was ready to get chewed out. His mother closed the door and counted on her fingers as she rattled off a list of questions: *What's her last name? Where's she from? Where's her family from? What kind of work does she do?*

Then back to the living room, where his mother excused herself, giving him a wink and a thumbs-up over Ines's shoulder, leaving him with Ines, who glared at him, and asked *Is she retired? Where did she work before? Where is she from? Is her family still around here?*

His mom returned with fruit and fishsticks. "I don't eat much meat either," she said, settling into the couch. "Achilles told me about your charity, but you know how vague men are, tell me more." And Ines did, at one point relating it to accounting. Meanwhile, Achilles pondered the significance of his mother referring to him, for the first time, as a man in that way, as if he was now in his father's camp.

Achilles watched in amazement as, over the course of the next hour, they each maintained their front, privately asking Achilles questions on the sly: *Does Ines sew? Does Anna garden? Does Ines go to church? What's Anna's favorite flower?* Gospel played on the radio.

"Do you mind gospel, Ines?"

"No ma'am. I enjoy spiritual music."

"Ines is a beautiful name. Does it mean anything?"

"It's short for Esmeralda."

His mother gasped. "That's gorgeous, regal."

She was right. Ines sat there, quietly scanning photo albums, chatting pleasantly with his mother, taking it on the chin without complaint. She was regal. A real lady.

"You should see the programs, Achilles. They're on the counter," his mother said. "The paper too."

Thankful for an excuse to leave, Achilles went to the kitchen. The counter, tables, and top of the refrigerator were covered with flowers, even more than there had been for his father, who'd lived in the area his entire life. The refrigerator was again stuffed with food. The programs were piled on the table. The photo on the cover was from the third week of basic training. Wearing PT outfits, they'd lined up outside a white Quonset hut. Inside, they passed through an assembly line: one station fitted them with a jacket, the next with a shirt and clip-on tie, the next with a hat. The last station snapped the photo that everyone sent home as evidence of transformation.

Their sergeant said, "Don't slurp your own shit. This photo's what you could be, not what you are." But Troy looked like he halfway believed it, the mouth is set in firm determination, but his eyes give it away. That day Troy was happy, joking, amused by the fact that in every one of these photos they'd seen over the years, every last recruit was dressed up in a fancy jacket with only jogging shorts on underneath. All those photos and no one was wearing pants. The edge of a newspaper was barely visible under the box of programs. It was a copy of the *Washington County Reporter,* with Troy's picture on the front cover, two pictures to be exact: one from the high school soccer team and one from the military. The byline was Janice Keel *Williams;* she had taken Dale's name.

Troy Henry Conroy,
Our First Fallen Hero Buried Today
Washington County, Janice Keel Williams

There was a new hero among us, and many us of missed the chance to thank him the last time he was in town. The first hometown hero to die since this war began, Troy always answered the call of duty. He had a smile for everyone, flashing that great soldier's jaw. A sports sensation, Troy lettered in football, soccer, and lacrosse by the tenth grade. That was the kind of young man who entered 11-Bravo and came out with a Bronze Star—with a V for valor, one of the highest honors a solder can receive. He earned it carrying a wounded comrade across a minefield, risking his life and limb. He joined the army shortly after September 11 to fight the War on Terror, and after he was done there, he helped on the home front, traveling to New Orleans in the wake of Katrina. Troy was always ready to help the less fortunate. Says his brother, Achilles, "Troy was the bravest man I knew. He was always there for me, and for anyone who needed him. Selfless, brave, always extending a helping hand. He will be deeply missed." His mother, Anna, described him as "Just a good person. The kind of son you always want to have, but never believe you'll actually get." Everyone here in Washington County will miss Troy, but no one more so than his family. Troy is survived by his mother, Anna Holt Conroy, and his brother, Achilles Holden Conroy. His father, William Conroy, died last fall in a car accident.

It was hard to believe it had only been a year. Achilles heard a chuckle, but when he returned to the living room, the mood had changed. Ines sat in rapt attention while his mother told the story in bits and pieces. It's the same story Achilles had told Ines, down to the part about referring to Troy as his brother. The photos give away the end. Ines stood and paced along the mantel while his mother pointed out who was who, stopping at the photo of Achilles and Troy and their parents at Hershey Park.

They spent the night in his old bedroom. Achilles had refused his mother's offer to make room elsewhere. It reminded him too much of how little space they had. On the drive in, he wanted to impress Ines with the view from the main road, not considering that she would assume he lived in one of those McMansions. Now, back in the old bedroom, he wished he had taken the other highway in, the one that cut through the woods and small towns, the four-way intersections policed only by stop signs.

He and Ines sat on Achilles's bed. Troy's uniform lay on the bed across from them. Ines glanced around the room at the posters, their dressers, the single closet. She stretched her legs, banging her shins on Troy's bed.

He reached for her legs and she jerked away.

"Like I said, it ain't much," offered Achilles.

"Really? Achilles?"

"Do you want me to take you to the airport?"

Ines glared. "Is that going to be your answer to everything today?"

"It's the first time I've said it."

"It sounds like something you would repeat. You should have told me."

"Would you have come?"

"That's not your choice. I would have brought her something." She said this matter-of-factly.

"I'm sorry. Do you want me to take you to the airport?" asked Achilles. "Damn!"

"I knew it."

"I guess I could have said, 'Come and meet my mom, she'll take you for a ride on her bus.'"

"That's all the more reason. If you felt like I really *hated* white people, you should have told me."

Her breath was slow and steady, her eyes cool, but she seemed more hurt than angry. He reached for her hand, and she drew away.

"I wanted to, but at first it didn't matter. Then it was too late."

She pursed her lips and shook her head as if she didn't believe him. "It's just not fair, Achilles. It's not fair. There isn't enough time to tell you how much of an asshole you are. Yesterday, when you told me the news, a small part of me felt relieved that it wasn't anyone new. And I felt so guilty about that, so ashamed. And now, I feel even worse. I'll stay for the funeral, but I want to go to the airport after." The wind rattled the glass. "Regardless of the weather." She scooted a few feet over on the bed.

When he moved near, she moved farther away. This implosion was worse than the explosion he'd expected. He'd counted on anger and accusations, yelling and screaming, hoped for an argument, some of her self-righteous indignation. A fight. Instead, as Achilles made a pallet on the floor, Ines lay on Achilles's bed, clutching her suitcase, crying as if she had lost her own brother.

CHAPTER 24

U NABLE TO SLEEP, ACHILLES WANTED TO CRUISE THROUGH TOWN BUT halfway expected to be stopped at each intersection, so he sat on the cinderblock stoop all night. The Reserves were full of sheriffs and deputies, troopers and constables, and on the drive to New Orleans he'd nodded at them all. On the drive home though, he found himself gripping the wheel and hovering over the brakes whenever Smokey passed. He was still on the stoop when the morning fog burned off, the trees wavering like the shadows of people who weren't there. He was on the stoop when, unexpectedly, a donated limousine arrived at seven a.m.

Ines, Achilles, his mom, and his two aunts rode to the funeral home in the limousine. They traveled through the center of town—past the people lining the streets waving American flags as if it was a parade, past the school and courthouse with their flags at half-mast, past the signs that read, *We miss you, Troy*—picking up cars en route, until a procession of vehicles trailed behind them, all of which had to park on the street because the funeral home lot was full.

His father's funeral had started fifteen minutes late, but today Mr. Eckhart, the funeral director, was outside scowling at his pocket watch when the limousine pulled up. There was an hour before the actual service, but he hustled Achilles into a side room where five privates in dress blues sat around a folding table sipping coffee.

"It's going to be a real hero's service, Achilles. You better believe it. These gentleman from Shippensburg CC ROTC volunteered to serve as pall-bearers." To the five soldiers, Eckhart said, "Gentlemen, this is Achilles Conroy, Troy Conroy's brother."

They jumped to their feet and snapped to attention, introducing themselves and offering condolences. *It's an honor,* they all said. When the funeral director excused himself, they remained standing. With a wave of his hand he directed them back to their coffee. "Thank you sir."

"I earned my rank," Achilles said softly. He vaguely recognized the tallest one, Hausman. Achilles knew a Dennis Hausman, a lanky geek with a deadly jump shot who wore glasses so thick he could start fires with them on a cloudy day. He'd soon be armed, so hopefully the younger one had better eyes than his brother. Same thin frame and too-long arms, same prominent Adam's apple. Achilles imagined this younger Hausman squirreled into the shadow of a shredded Humvee, momentarily deafened by the explosion, squinting as it rained dirt, trying to make out a target. Or maybe nothing would happen at all. He would play Xbox when he wasn't on patrol, throw lollipops at kids when he was, and return in nine months with a tan. If they did ROTC, then college, then entered with a commission, at least they wouldn't be cannon fodder.

The funeral director returned to explain the protocol. After the viewing, which he insisted on calling it even though the casket was closed, they would carry the casket to the hearse, which would take one tour through town before returning to the cemetery for the burial. "Remember," he told them twice, carefully including Achilles in his roaming gaze as he looked at each of them in turn, "the casket is light, very light. Lift it slowly, don't jerk it, and don't look surprised at the weight." He closed his fist around his pocket watch, lifting it slowly, almost as if it weighed too much for him to hold in one hand. "No one watching you should know it's empty."

Eckhart ran the event with military precision. They had loaded the casket, driven through town, and returned by nine thirty. Five minutes later, they were gathered at the same gravesite where everything began a year ago. Achilles sat between his mom and Ines. Janice, Dale, and their new baby were seated nearby and, behind them, throngs of people stretching back nearly to the street. Kids too young to have ever known Troy fidgeted and whined while their parents jerked their arms and hushed them. Four large-breasted blondes in their late teens stood shoulder to shoulder, sniffing and wiping their eyes. Their football coach stood next to a line of beefy kids who must have been the current varsity squad.

The preacher spoke about hope, rebirth, faith, and the sacrifice each required. Eternal life was promised to all who believed in the Lord, and Troy, *We all know, was a believer, for rarely did a man make better use of his talents. Rarely did a man make so selfless a sacrifice with heart and head.* With a grand gesture, the minister pointed to the military photo mounted on an easel next to the coffin, describing Troy as a veteran who selflessly served abroad and at home, who fought to bring freedom to Afghanistan and safety to Louisiana, who exemplified Christian ideals *in life and in death*. When it was Achilles's turn, he said a few words about his bother's love and courage.

But what he was really thinking about was his brother the prankster. Troy had once mixed red Kool-Aid in the tub and lain there for hours waiting for someone to find him. Their mother flipped. The stain didn't come out for weeks. Achilles had always wanted to be the hero, to be lauded, to be idolized, until now. The more everyone spoke about Troy as a hero, the less real he became.

The preacher talked about "the Word," as had the preacher at Wages's funeral, and just as suddenly as he had started, he stopped talking and nodded at the three soldiers standing at attention fifty yards away. There were too few buglers and too many funerals, even this close to Washington, so the soldier at the far end solemnly leaned over and turned on a boombox. "Taps" played. His mother and Ines hissed gently at him for squeezing their hands too tightly. When the song was over, the same soldier leaned over and turned off the boombox. Achilles braced himself for the coming twenty-one gun salute, the seven volleys that would echo across town. At his father's funeral, he had flinched six times. This time he breathed purposefully, and his heart didn't miss a beat, not when they folded the flag and presented it to his mother, not when they lowered the coffin.

But when his mother held his hand for support as she bent for her own handful of dirt, and she said, "Thank you for bringing your brother home," he was seized by a momentary desire to take it back. His mother had asked one time, "Are you sure? How do you know? Are you absolutely sure?" He threw his handful of dirt on the coffin, and his aunts and Ines followed suit, each handful rattling less until soon you couldn't even hear it fall, the line so long it seemed there wasn't enough dirt in the world.

The entire town converged on the VFW after the service, including those who hadn't been at the funeral, resulting in a crowd thicker than the Fourth of July cookouts. Even with every window as well as both doors open, the bar was hot and sticky. He saw friends from high school he scarcely recognized. It had only been three years since he enlisted, but it felt as if he'd aged a lifetime. They patted him on the back and expressed condolences, averting their eyes as they segued into the next question or an innocent congratulation: *Man, you did it. You went and did it, and came back.*

That could have been Achilles telling the same jokes and making the same faces, huddled up with the football players who positioned themselves fifty yards from the girls, while sneaking sidelong glances and talking loudly enough to be heard across the parking lot. The girls, in their own cluster, stood with their backs to the boys, taking turns glancing over their shoulders and blushing whenever they made eye contact. All they were missing was corsages. If he had stayed, he would be hiding out behind the dumpster smoking cigarettes and then sucking up to Troy, asking him, as a Randall, Jarrell, and Howie asked Achilles, "Did you get to kill anybody?"

He might have responded differently to "have to," but as much as he appreciated the attention, he could only shrug in response to "get to."

He saw Ken and Ken's mom, who still looked sexy, wearing her hair like Farah Fawcett had on *Charlie's Angels,* a look that was back in style. Sam, the Chinese kid he used to play with, was home for the holidays. They spoke briefly, and Achilles learned that Sam had spent a few years in Korea, which was where he was actually from. The recruiter was there, which surprised his mother because, *Three of them killed themselves you know. The guilt.* Achilles wanted to explain that the recruiters had only said what they'd wanted to hear.

"She's like a hostess," she said, pointing to Ines.

She was right. Ines moved through the crowd with ease, talking to all who listened, listening to all who talked, so comfortable you would have thought she had lived there her entire life. And when she wasn't talking, she was tending to his mother. Achilles said, "She likes to tell people what to do."

"That's exactly what you need," said his mother.

"How do you mean?"

"You know what I mean," she said.

When people offered their condolences, his mother managed to reassure them, to make them feel better, as if they were the grievers, except for the recruiter, whom she refused to directly acknowledge.

"I am deeply sorry, ma'am," the recruiter said.

"I know." Quoting the officer who had given her the flag, she said, "'This flag was offered by a grateful nation in memory of faithful service performed by your loved one.'"

"I'm real sorry," the recruiter repeated himself. "That was moving, what you said, Achilles."

"I know. My son is smart. That's why I wanted him to go to college."

When the recruiter left, his mother said, "You know four of them killed themselves."

"I thought you said three."

"Did I? Wishful thinking." She pointed. "Look, it's that woman."

Three teachers were clustered at the end of the bar, among them Troy's tenth-grade math teacher, who looked devastated. As Mrs. Delesseppes once said, grief ages a person.

His mother cradled the flag like a child, her expression reminiscent of Mrs. Robicheaux, whom they'd found on that roof. He reached out and touched her face. "I love you, Mom."

She turned to him. "I know you do. I love you too, sweetie." She put the flag back on the table, arranging it so that it pointed away from her. "It fits there, with all the stains and burns, doesn't it?

"Yes."

"I never liked this bar. The last thing a bunch of old veterans need to do is get drunk. But I guess this is a celebration of his life? Is this like New Orleans?"

"Exactly," said Achilles.

"I hoped it would be. They wanted to have a parade when you got back, but it just wasn't the right time. I understand your reluctance to take that envelope now. You think you want to know, but you don't. You don't. You don't want them to be in a better place, you want them to be with you."

A better place. Everyone had said that, even at his father's funeral. He hadn't noticed as much, being only twenty-four hours out of combat. Besides it was easy enough to ignore because no one said it to his face, as if they knew Achilles wasn't buying. Once you were shot at, there was no *better place* to be than alive. A bead of sweat dripped from his nose and he decided to go outside for air. He looked back as he passed through the doorway. Ines was already at his mother's side, like all that time she had just been waiting for him to leave.

The kids behind the dumpster stopped laughing and tossed their cigarettes upon Achilles's approach. Hausman, the tall ROTC pallbearer, was among them. "I hope those weren't your last ones," said Achilles.

The kids relaxed and picked up their cigarettes, offering one to Achilles. They smoked in silence, Hausman watching Achilles out of the corner of his eye.

"What's up?" asked Achilles.

"Nothing, just telling a joke," said the young one; Bridges, according to his nameplate. Achilles recalled the shock on his face when they lifted the coffin, so light it seemed to float on air.

"Let's hear it," said Achilles. He had to prompt him a few more times, but Bridges finally resumed his story, catching Achilles up first. "There were these two scientists, see, a Russian and a Czech, and they both wanted to study grizzly bears. They'd loved bears all their lives, but there weren't any bears where they lived. So they got permission to go to Alaska. The park ranger in Alaska told them that they could go to the national park, but they'd be on their own."

Hausman was staring at the ground, his face red. "There aren't any grizzly bears in Alaska. They live primarily in the Pacific Northwest."

Bridges shrugged. "It's a joke. A horse never really walked into a bar and ordered a drink."

"Yeah, but we know that's not real. Get your facts straight."

"Let him finish," said Achilles.

Hausman huffed. Achilles nodded at Bridges. "Go ahead."

"So anyway," Bridges continued, "the scientists are in the park studying the bears, the *Alaskan* bears, and no one hears from them for a long time, so the park ranger goes looking and finds their campsite destroyed and bloody and a trail of bear prints, *Alaskan* bear prints, leading from the tents to the forest. He follows them and finds the female gnawing on a bloody boot. So he has to shoot the *Alaskan* bear and cut it open and see if it ate the scientists. When they look inside, they find the Russian scientist in her stomach. So the park ranger turns to the other ranger, and you know what he says?"

"When did another ranger show up?" asked Hausman.

"He was there all the time. They travel in pairs. Anyway, know what he says?"

Everyone shrugs.

"You know what this means. The Czech is in the male."

When Achilles laughed, the other guys joined him, except Hausman.

"Go ahead, ask me," said Achilles. Hausman was ROTC. He deserved to ask a question.

Hausman turned to face him, took a deep breath. "What's it like?"

Achilles took him by the arm and led him away. "What have you heard?"

"All sorts of weird stuff. Like it's the Wild Wild West, but it's great. There's no women. It's like being God. It's a dog's life."

"It's all true."

Hausman bit his lip, seeming to consider this an even greater dilemma. "All of it?"

"Every last bit." He wanted to tell him that's life, the fuck of it, the good, bad, and mixed in everywhere, you just choose a side when you can. "You hear about the big shit making heroes and cowards, selfish and selfless." Katrina had been no different. There were the heroic and the craven. Those who nearly died helping others and those who looted. There were white vigilantes in Algiers shooting unarmed black survivors, and there was the river of volunteers. That was the hardest part to accept. You had to choose a side. The young white couple who opened a flower shop in the Seventh Ward did; so did the street preacher, even if no one wanted to hear it. He understood why the old-timers said, *You have to live it to know it.*

Hausman looked even more uncertain than he had before.

"Don't go."

Whistles and cheers erupted behind them and Achilles went back inside to find the lights dimmed and the DJ playing. Achilles stood at the end of the bar—where as a kid he had always imagined sitting—taking it all in, and noticing for the first time the picture of Troy behind the bar and the pile of newspapers. The local press had printed extra copies. Near the photo sat a bucket and a sign made of spiral-bound paper and printed in marker: *Like Many Who Lost Loved Ones In Rescue Efforts The Family Asks That Any Donations Be Made To Charitable Organization* (no *s*). Posted behind the bar was a picture of his father that he didn't recognize, an old photo of his dad and three friends wearing fatigues and green army wifebeaters. Earl, the bartender, handed it to Achilles. "That's me and your old man one week before we came home." He tapped the third head. "Nally didn't make it. Bad luck." He handed it to Achilles.

When Achilles opened his wallet to tuck the photo away, Earl saw the small photo of Achilles and his squad.

"You bring me a copy, you can put that one up."

Achilles handed him the photo, his only one. "This is a copy."

Earl slipped the photo into the same spot where his father's had been. "You need to have a beer and some quiet, you come up here anytime. Every man needs a Batcave, and this is it. You're one of us now."

That struck him as oddly familiar. Recalling that night he spent pinned down in that cave in Afghanistan, he held Earl's gaze for an uncomfortable moment during which the feeling that he was being insolent settled into a current of affection so strong he had to restrain himself from hugging the man. He'd never really thought about Earl before, or any of the cranky old men that gathered at the VFW. He'd thought they'd been up here because their wives wouldn't let them watch the Redskins on the big TV when it conflicted with *Golden Girls.*

Achilles imagined his father after returning from Vietnam. His dad, Earl, and Nally had only been seventeen when they were shipped off. Maybe the VFW was where they could feel as if Nally was still with them. Achilles felt as if he knew Nally. They'd talked about him like a kid who moved off to college, and then even farther away, his new life soon too busy for him to visit home often. Gone, but not dead. They must have met here every Friday because it was the only place where they didn't need to talk about what happened because everyone had been there, whether in Desert Storm, Bosnia, Vietnam, Korea, or the Big One. Was lining up at these taps their version of Wages's ritual? If he stayed here, was this the only place he could go? He would have to come here when he felt that burn, his spine stiff as rebar and his muscles trembling, when he wanted to choke the fucking pizza delivery boy for wearing a POW shirt, when he wanted to put a brick through the head of the TV news reporter because she was spewing some crap about the war, when he imagined replacing Dale, or reenlisting, when he thought too hard about going back for Pepper. He'd have to come back here, sit with these men and watch hockey and football and basketball, and complain about the alderman shutting down the only strip club within a hundred miles.

"You ought to go grab the little lady for this one," said Earl when "Stand by Your Man" came on. The song was over by the time he found Ines, but they went out on the dance floor anyway, shuffling in the sawdust to "That's Easy for You to Say" by Junior Brown, her ear pressed to his chest and her hand on his face. She'd been doing that all day, in lieu of speaking.

"Baby, your heart beats so slow. You're always so calm."

The DJ dimmed the lights.

She told him about all the people she had met: high school friends, teachers, neighbors. "They all loved Troy so much. I wish I could have met him. He sounds like he was great. You already knew that. He came to New

Orleans to look for you." She kissed him and frowned. "You smell like smoke."

"I smoked a cigarette," snapped Achilles. "The truth is out."

Ines stepped back, her hand still on his face. "Maybe you should dance with your mom."

"What's that mean?"

Ines waved to his mom, who waved back.

"Mom doesn't dance, but I'll ask her."

His mother's smile grew as he neared. "You're finally getting your hero's welcome."

"You don't want to dance, do you?"

"Always."

While they were on the floor, the record skipped as the DJ cut the song short to play "Mammas Don't Let Your Babies Grow Up to Be Cowboys."

"Achilles, thank you."

Her voice was barely audible above the sound of the entire bar singing along to the song—"*Cowboys like smoky old poolrooms.*" Her hair was now nearly all white, and she moved slowly, shuffling more than dancing. "*Ain't easy to love and they're harder to hold.*"

"Did you hear me?"

"Yes ma'am."

"Achilles, you know you couldn't have done any more than you did."

"Yes, Mom." He stopped dancing and backed away from his mother, leveling his eyes to meet hers.

"He chose his own path, you have to choose yours."

"Mom, come on."

"I don't expect you to stay home. I'm serious, Achilles. She's a keeper." She gripped him tighter when he tried to pull back. "I'm telling you this right now, while everyone is looking and you can't walk away."

"Yes ma'am."

"He wrote me often. He said he was glad you were there. He said he wouldn't have made it without you." She hummed a few bars. "What was his tattoo?"

"Mom inside a heart."

The mood lightened when someone fired up Hank Williams Jr.'s "Family Tradition" on the jukebox. The bar erupted in song. Voices washed in from the parking lot, passing drivers honked their horns, and even kids yawned the chorus, sucking on pencils and straws as if they were cigarettes, acting out the song as if it was a dress rehearsal, and he remembered those kids dressed as superheroes yelling, "Fly school shit!"

They arrived home long after midnight. As the limousine climbed the driveway, his mother said, "I wish we had done this for your father."

"Had a limousine?" asked Achilles.

Ines shook her head knowingly.

"Had everyone together like this." His mother burped, grinning shyly. "Excuse me."

She had been rocking back and forth with the motions of the car, but only now did he realize that his mother was drunk, a first. Tipsy as she was, she refused his help up the porch stairs, extending her arm to Ines instead. "Men think we can't do anything without them, but we have to let them think that. They have such frail egos, it would be cruel to tell them otherwise."

Achilles stepped aside to let them pass, and as his mom went by, she pinched his cheeks. "That doesn't apply to you of course. You're a good boy. I always knew that. You were always different. Always sensitive."

The cars that had followed them from the VFW parked. Janice and Dale were there, and his aunt on his father's side. Achilles held the door for them all, delaying his entry, hoping his mom's mood would pass, a wish he knew was hopeless when he heard, "Who's cooking breakfast? Not me!" followed by the crash of pots and pans and the banging of drawers. A shiver went up his spine when he heard what sounded like the silverware drawer being dumped into the sink.

"She's a keeper, that Ines," whispered his aunt as she nudged Achilles with her elbow.

At the VFW, he saw Janice talking to Ines. It seemed like a friendly conversation, which surprised him. No cursing from Janice and no sneering from Ines. Janice was chunkier these days, but in all the right places. He had expected her to look pale and insignificant next to Ines, to appear mumbly and shy, but there in the kitchen she was bright and cheery and whatever she was whispering had Ines in stitches. For a moment they both looked at him, and he turned away. Someone clapped him on the shoulder. Dale. They shook hands.

"I'm so-so-sorry a-a-a-about your brother," said Dale. "He was a good guy." He rushed the last part out without a stutter.

"Thank you, Dale," said Achilles. "And congratulations."

Dale turned to where Ines and Janice were talking. Achilles hadn't noticed the papoose Janice wore. "That's the best thing that ever happened to me," said Dale with a wink, patting his stomach. "Little D got me off the g-g-g beer. But fuck, he cries."

Even at that late hour the crowd continued to grow, more people stopping by to eat or bring food, including Janice's brothers. They were bigger than Achilles remembered. Burly, bearded men with full-sleeve tattoos and chain wallets. Although only a few years older than him, they looked ancient. They brought a braided dog collar with them as a gift. Achilles placed it on the mantel next to the urns. When they learned that Ines was from New Orleans, they expressed their condolences. "It's a tore-up business they're doing you."

There hadn't been that many people in the house since his eighth birthday party. People were spread across the kitchen and the living room. Someone turned on the news, and the first story was about New Orleans. *In fits and spurts they return, from Houston and DC and Atlanta, by car and boat and taxi and on foot, the native New Orleanians are coming home, but many say not fast enough.* A hush fell over the living room.

Achilles's mom apologized and offered to turn it off, but Ines was glad to see it, to know that it was news, and even more, "I'm glad they're evacuees now, not refugees." The screen door banging behind her, Janice went out front to smoke a cigarette. At the VFW, she and Dale had looked so content, so happy. She had slipped out her breast to feed the baby like it was the most natural thing in the world. (It was enormous, and he wished Merri or Wages or someone else was there to gawk for him.) And when Dale whispered in her ear, she smiled that big smile of hers and looked so beautiful, as she did right then in the front yard smoking that cigarette in the moonlight, her dress just short enough that if the light were right he could have seen her little hearts. Achilles followed her outside. They smoked one in silence. She offered him another and he accepted.

"Ines seems nice," said Janice.

"I guess you want those letters back?"

"Those are yours," she said.

"Good. I wasn't going to give them to you."

"She seems real nice," said Janice.

"She's smart too."

"All that matters is that she treats you well after all you've been through. And that you treat her well too."

Achilles felt as if he was seeing her for the first time tonight, as if he'd been happy with her but hadn't known it. "You like being a mother?"

"Best thing ever happened to me."

He thought for a minute that he loved her. "I 'preciate them letters."

She coughed and glanced around to see if anyone was listening. "Don't start that now."

He handed her his locket, but she refused it. "I want to give you something to remember me by."

"A thank-you would be enough."

"Thank you," said Achilles.

"Finally! You're welcome," she said, blushing. "I'm going back inside."

"You sure about the locket?" asked Achilles.

Janice gently kissed him on the cheek. "You never forget the ones who break your heart," she said, and slipped back into the house.

Dawn was breaking as everyone left. Ines and his mother sat on the back porch, their chairs so close their knees touched. Janice and his aunt had cleaned up before they left. The only thing that remained on the table was the funeral program. Troy's funeral program said "The Word Is Your Salvation." Wages's program said "Trust in the Word." His father's program said "The Word is Life." Everyone had their party line, the manner of speaking in which they invested themselves, became real, and set themselves apart. He'd witnessed it with Bryant who, within a few days, went from moaning to saying stuff like, "Where's Darkwater when you need them?" Ines was the same, professing what she couldn't actually live because she didn't look it, saying at every turn, *I'm black, no really, listen. I am.* That's all it was, words spoken like an incantation, the power in not caring, or trying not to care. *There is no God but M16, and I am his messenger.* Had Hausman asked about Goddamnistan six months ago, Achilles would have quoted Merri, saying, "Suit up and put some fucker on the maggot diet."

He went outside to see what his mom and Ines were talking about. From the looks on their faces, it was something private. His mom asked, "Is it okay if Ines hears this?" She studied his face. "You opened it, didn't you?"

Achilles nodded his agreement. "I already opened it and everything."

He excused himself and went back inside. If they knew what was in the envelope and he didn't, wouldn't that make them even, restore balance? Wages said the warrior suffered for what he had seen, what he knew. Achilles's burden was also his gift to them: Troy's other life, emaciated and drugged, in exchange for their knowledge of his adoption. But by the time he was inside, he discarded this idea, crouching beneath the window to listen.

"I always wanted him. I was his godmother, and I was there the day he was born. Cecile, his mom, was my best friend. Her family had disowned her for marrying a white man before she married Achilles's father. I knew them. They were good people, just from a different time. I babysat him all the time. He was with me the night they died. I already knew him like my own. I had him over here all the time. Still took almost a year to work the paperwork out. We couldn't have kids, you know. We tried, but it never worked. Then he was there, like a gift. It was just a matter of making it legal. Troy was different. One day Bill comes home, says, 'We have to take this kid. We have to.' The way he says it. Well, I sign the paperwork, but I never ask to see the original birth certificate. I don't want to. I exchange that for one condition: he can never tell Troy what's in there either. Because Achilles was already here, and I didn't want him to feel displaced."

She went on to say more about his birth parents. By the time she was finished, Achilles was dizzy, his face hot. His parents were Cecile Octavia and Charles Richard Drew. He was born on March 2, 1983, not May 3, as he'd always thought. He wasn't a Taurus. His parents died in an automobile accident less than three miles from where he grew up. Killed by a drunk driver. They weren't street people. His real name was David Drew. He wasn't Achilles.

These revelations so stunned him that he didn't hear their chair legs scraping the deck, or the door, or his mother and Ines enter the kitchen to find him hunched over beside the window.

"Oh no," said his mother, as Achilles slipped by her and out the door. He walked into the woods and through the culvert under the highway, officially entering Pennsylvania, and into the wooded hollow his father called Winter's Last Bowl, a shady grove, the snow's last refuge, sometimes glowing until late May. To make room for new houses, the trees had been cleared over the years, so what snow remained turned to mush and by spring was a mosquito nest. Had his father felt as if he was being gentrified?

He sat at the edge of the culvert to watch the sun finish rising. He had planned to take Wages's hat, and Troy's boots, and Teddy Ruxpin, and bury them all at the old asylum near the water tower, but he had left empty-handed. He looked back at the house, and it seemed so far away, everything felt as if it was all so far behind him, as if it had happened to another person.

His mom had mailed notices to Wexler, Merriweather, Dixon, and the others. God, how he'd wanted to see them, but he knew they wouldn't show. The night they'd pledged revenge, they'd made another promise, spurred by Wages saying, "Remember me like this!" He clambered atop the Bradley to scan the ridge below, scaly as a reptilian spine. He stood there, binocs in one hand, M4 in the other, goggles off, red-faced and raccoon eyes smiling. Achilles preferred to remember him at City Park, feeding ducks and pigeons alike; Wexler hanging his head out of the chopper, mouth open, eating the sky, grinning to beat the band; Merriweather, teary-eyed, bouncing a little girl on his knee; Dixon wearing that balaclava with face holes in the back so you never knew if he was coming or going; Ramirez sweating over those mixtapes—should John Legend be followed by Marvin Gaye or that old Jeffrey Osborne joint?—his father snipping that fence; Troy at the kitchen table that night, thinking he was in a foster home, one moment asking how long they'd be there, the next yelling, *Daddy, stop!* If he had loved them any more, they would have held hands.

He found Ines in his room wearing jeans and a T-shirt, and packing. "Reagan?" he asked, attempting a joke. The nearest major airport was named after a president of whom Ines was not fond.

"I don't know." She shook her bag over the bed, dumping her belongings out, then starting repacking.

He took a deep breath. "I want you to stay. Or take me with you."

"I don't know, Achilles. I feel like I've been up for a month straight. I can't decide anything right now. I'm happy to meet your family. Dreadfully sad, too. Your mother must think I'm crazy. Sometimes I was talking to her and just found myself staring, seeing so many of the little things you do. No matter what, children are like their parents. No matter what."

He reached for her hand, and she let him take it. What if he and Ines had a boy? Would it be dark like him or light like Ines, playful or sullen, reserved, cool, and withdrawn, or, like his brother, damned near tireless?

"I'm confused about one thing: didn't you say you identified Troy's body in Atlanta?"

"I did. I did."

She shivered. "Oh, Jesus. Achilles . . . the morgues."

"I went back for the body, and it was gone. They'd cremated it already." He told her the entire story, crying through half of it, his words unintelligible even to him. It was as if something twisted in him, something tightly knotted finally broke, and wave after wave of deafening, roaring grief washed over him.

After wiping his face, he smiled weakly. "I'm probably dehydrated."

"Poor Troy. Poor Achilles."

"I love you, Ines." Maybe it was all like stepping into the void and hoping the night catches you. He didn't know how he expected her to react to these magic words, but it wasn't what she did next: dropping down to Troy's bed as if she was exhausted, and groaning. "I know, but it's not that easy."

"What are you going to do?"

"I don't know, Keelies. I don't know," said Ines. "Read it to me again, please?"

"What?"

"Your eulogy."

She pulled the blanket high around her neck. Achilles unfolded the square paper he had been carrying in his wallet since the morgue.

> I wet the bed until I was ten, if I had soda with dinner. So every night I drank Coke, I slept on the floor and washed my underwear out in the bathtub the next morning. But I kept asking for soda. Mrs. Tolson, I'm the one who broke your mailbox. I was deathly afraid of guns until twelve. These are things only my brother knew about me. When he died, I felt like most of me died too. Because we did everything together. But I realize that works both ways, that I have to let you know things about Troy, things that only I know. He was brave, you know that. He stood up to everyone. He never surrendered. He walked right into a minefield and carried one of our buddies out like it was nothing. Like it was a fly ball in the backfield. But here's the crazy part: he never mentioned it again. Ever. Even that night, when Wexler was being medivaced. We'd walked him to the medivac copter and he's teary-eyed. Troy had just saved his life hours before, that's not an exaggeration. Our buddy says, "Thank you, man." He's full of thanks, but Troy says, "Never mention it again. Ever." Later that night, I punched him. I'm sorry. I did. I was so mad. I'm the older one. I was supposed to be protecting him. He could have died. "Are you crazy?" I

asked. "No," he said. "Then why'd you do it?" He said,
"Because you are who you make yourself, who you will
yourself to be, against the odds. Because if we'd left him
there, a part of ourselves would have stayed there forever,
we would have died with him. We would have been
haunted by it." Then he kissed me on the forehead. I didn't
want to believe him at the time. In fact, I forgot all about
this conversation until recently. But, he was right. The
sign in the morgue where I found him reads Mortui Vivis
Praecipant—Let the dead teach the living. That's Troy's
lesson for us all.

If Achilles hadn't enlisted, would it have been easier to deliver that
eulogy? But if he hadn't gone, Achilles would have forever followed behind
his younger brother, maybe even driven the float that carried him through
town for his hero's welcome, making an extra loop around the roundabout
in the center of downtown. Troy with his picture up at the VFW. Troy with
his Bronze Star, his secrets, his memories, his stories, and no matter how
often Achilles said, *I know, I understand, I get you, I see it,* he would have really
been wondering, *Did you get to kill anybody?* Troy would have worn that look
he always had, the smug grin that said, *Achilles, you don't get it at all.* Troy
would have been a man, and Achilles forever a child. Troy would have had
a hero's welcome, and Achilles would have been among the groupies, the
hero worshippers, bearing his younger brother on a litter. It would have
driven him mad, yet strangely enough, it was exactly what happened, and
seemed somehow fair.

Ines coughed softly and it echoed in the small room. Had she ever
slept in such a tiny house, in such a tiny bedroom, on such a tiny bed? In
such a tiny town? Even her mother's maid's quarters were larger than this
room. Even that damned cave he had been stuck in had been bigger. It had
the same view, a low valley dotted with houses and shrouded in fog. He
had thought that Earl referring to the VFW as the Batcave struck the flint
of that memory. Instead it was the last thing Earl yelled as Achilles's father
steered him out of the bar that night before he shipped off to basic training: "You're one of us now."

Was he really, he wondered, rereading the obit and then the news article where he was mentioned as a survivor. Was he? He felt more like a ghost.

Ines was already snoring, her feet tangled in a sweater, her bag overturned, and her socks and underwear scattered on the bed. Achilles pushed the beds together. She was hot under the blanket—he loved that sensation, like mornings, when she was so warm. *Survivor.* But what else? And who else, he wondered as he slipped in next to her, into Troy's bed, one arm around Ines, the other around Teddy Ruxpin, feeling the pounding in her chest, a drum that beat so much faster and stronger than his, and willed and prayed for his own heart to catch up. God, to be alive.

ACKNOWLEDGMENTS

Though it often felt like it, this novel was by no means written alone.

HiTiH would not exist without the support and sangha provided by the Hurston-Wright Foundation, Arizona State University, Stanford's Stegner Fellowship, the Iowa Writers' Workshop, the Michener-Copernicus Society of America, and Western Michigan University.

As important were the many individuals who provided time, advice, and encouragement. Many thanks to: Lan Samantha Chang, who saw a novel where I saw a novella; my agent Jon Sternfeld, who advocated tirelessly; and Anitra Budd, who is truly a dream of an editor. Without you three, I might not be writing these acknowledgments. Thanks also to Erika Stevens. Anthony Swofford, Jabari Mahiri, Jane Stanley, Caroline Cole, and Terry Crisp, you have been more help than you know.

I have been fortunate to have exceptional teachers: Elizabeth Tallent, Tobias Wolff, and John L'Heurieux at Stanford; Lan Samantha Chang, Elizabeth McCracken, James Alan MacPherson, Ethan Canin, Robin Hemley, and Chris Offut at Iowa; T. M. McNally and Jewell Parker Rhodes at ASU; and, at Wilde Lake High, Mrs. Chertok, my ninth-grade English teacher, who never, ever, ever awarded me a grade higher than 99 percent with a smile. Thank you.

Never have I known kinder souls than my mentors and guides: Connie Brothers, Stuart Dybek, Richard Katrovas, and Jaimy Gordon—who reintroduced me to my own novel.

A big thanks to my early readers: Russ Franklin, Krista Landers, Jeff O'Keefe, Nora Pierce, Rusty Dolleman, Rita Mae Reese, Shimon Tanaka, Roman Skaskiw, Chris Leslie Hynan, Marjorie Celona, Kate Klein, Stuart Nadler, Marion Bright, Vivian Shotwell, Jason England, Nancy Carlynne Houghton, and Elinathon Ohiomobo.

A special thanks to Benjamin Hale, James Mattson, Kate Sachs, Will Smith (for all that extra reading), Abdel Shakur, and Shane Book.

I'm especially grateful for those whom I now so seldom see: Byron, Dave, Dave, Dave, Hari, KCA, Kevin, Lisa, Lita, the Manager, Mia, Michael, Paul, Scott, Sugar; the years have taken me far from home, but I couldn't write better friends. You have been here since the beginning. If you see yourselves in this book—the good parts: your verve, your duende, your soul—it's because you are always with me.

About my family there is too much to say here. My parents, Irene English-Johnson and Tyrone Geronimo Johnson, my sister Ingrid, and my brother-in-law Pierre all believe in me so much it's just plain silly. And special thanks to Elizabeth Cowan, who may know Achilles better than I do.

That should sufficiently spread the blame.

That we authors should thank the writing communities that sustain us is obvious. But, in truth, *HiTiH* would not exist were we not living in the wake of Hurricane Katrina and the constant shadow of war, and my heart goes out to all who have been displaced, literally and figuratively, directly and indirectly, by the upheaval that marks our last decade.

Acknowledgments are generally reserved for those we know, but there are many people I have only read about, people whose families and friends have been deeply affected by recent events, people whom I thought of daily while writing this novel. My only wish is that I have done you justice, and that where talent has failed, empathy has bridged the gap, and where empathy has failed, passion has stepped in, and if that has failed, hope sparked enough to see you through.

MISSION

The mission of Coffee House Press is to publish exciting, vital, and enduring authors of our time; to delight and inspire readers; to contribute to the cultural life of our community; and to enrich our literary heritage. By building on the best traditions of publishing and the book arts, we produce books that celebrate imagination, innovation in the craft of writing, and the many authentic voices of the American experience.

VISION

LITERATURE. We will promote literature as a vital art form, helping to redefine its role in contemporary life. We will publish authors whose groundbreaking work helps shape the direction of 21st-century literature.

WRITERS. We will foster the careers of our writers by making long-term commitments to their work, allowing them to take risks in form and content.

READERS. Readers of books we publish will experience new perspectives and an expanding intellectual landscape.

PUBLISHING. We will be leaders in developing a sustainable 21st-century model of independent literary publishing, pushing the boundaries of content, form, editing, audience development, and book technologies.

VALUES

Innovation and excellence in all activities

Diversity of people, ideas, and products

Advancing literary knowledge

Community through embracing many cultures

Ethical and highly professional management
and governance practices

Join us in our mission at coffeehousepress.org

COLOPHON

Hold It 'Til It Hurts was designed at Coffee House Press,
in the historic Grain Belt Brewery's Bottling House
near downtown Minneapolis. The text is set in Centaur.

FUNDER ACKNOWLEDGMENT

Coffee House Press is an independent nonprofit literary publisher. Our books are made possible through the generous support of grants and gifts from many foundations, corporate giving programs, state and federal support, and through donations from individuals who believe in the transformational power of literature. Coffee House Press receives major operating support from the Bush Foundation, the Jerome Foundation, the McKnight Foundation, the National Endowment for the Arts, a federal agency, from Target, and in part by a grant provided by the Minnesota State Arts Board through an appropriation by the Minnesota State Legislature from the State's general fund and its arts and cultural heritage fund with money from the vote of the people of Minnesota on November 4, 2008. Coffee House also receives support from: several anonymous donors; Suzanne Allen; Elmer L. and Eleanor J. Andersen Foundation; Around Town Agency; Patricia Beithon; Bill Berkson; the E. Thomas Binger and Rebecca Rand Fund of the Minneapolis Foundation; the Patrick and Aimee Butler Family Foundation; Ruth Dayton; Dorsey & Whitney, LLP; Mary Ebert and Paul Stembler; Chris Fischbach and Katie Dublinski; Fredrikson & Byron, P.A.; Sally French; Anselm Hollo and Jane Dalrymple-Hollo; Jeffrey Hom; Carl and Heidi Horsch; Alex and Ada Katz; Stephen and Isabel Keating; the Kenneth Koch Literary Estate; Kathy and Dean Koutsky; the Lenfestey Family Foundation; Carol and Aaron Mack; Mary McDermid; Sjur Midness and Briar Andresen; the Rehael Fund of the Minneapolis Foundation; Schwegman, Lundberg & Woessner, P.A.; Kiki Smith; Jeffrey Sugerman; Patricia Tilton; the Archie D. & Bertha H. Walker Foundation; Stu Wilson and Mel Barker; the Woessner Freeman Family Foundation; Margaret and Angus Wurtele; and many other generous individual donors.

To you and our many readers across the country,
we send our thanks for your continuing support.